THE BLACK JACK CONSPIRACY

DAVID KENT

Pocket Books
New York   London   Toronto   Sydney

This book is a work of fiction. Names, characters, places and
incidents are products of the author's imagination or are used
fictitiously. Any resemblance to actual events or locales or per-
sons, living or dead, is entirely coincidental.

An *Original* Publication of POCKET BOOKS

 POCKET BOOKS, a division of Simon & Schuster, Inc.
1230 Avenue of the Americas, New York, NY 10020

ISBN-13: 978-0-7434-9751-0
ISBN-10:   0-7434-9751-1

This Pocket Books paperback edition December 2005

10 9 8 7 6 5 4 3 2 1

POCKET and colophon are registered trademarks of Simon &
Schuster, Inc.

Cover art by Jae Song

Manufactured in the United States of America

For information regarding special discounts for bulk
purchases, please contact Simon & Schuster Special Sales at
1-800-456-6798 or business@simonandschuster.com.

For the generations of an American family:
    Tabananika
    Po-Kin
    Luisa Roche Trevino
    Marie Luisa Trevino Watson
    Martha Claire Watson Anderson
    Benjamin Joseph Anderson, William Patrick Anderson,
      Samuel Leon Anderson

ACKNOWLEDGMENTS

I AM GRATEFUL FOR THE OPPORTUNITY I HAVE BEEN granted to live a lifelong dream, that of being a published author. Two people in the publishing world have made this happen: John Talbot and Kevin Smith. As agent and editor, respectively, they have believed in my work, challenged me to make it the very best work I could do, and worked tirelessly to help me build a career as a writer.

There are so many others that do things, large and small, that allow me to continue doing what I do. Two of those who are long overdue for acknowledgment are Susan James, for a great website, and Shaman Hennigh, for the bookmarks.

This book began with my in-laws, Harold and Mary Watson, who told me twenty years ago of Tabananika's strange death.

I am also grateful to Jimmy Arterberry of the Comanche Nation Office of Environmental Programs, who took time to give me some historical perspective and directed me to Tabananika's grave.

M. C. Smothermon gave legal advice once again, concerning the Supreme Court and the nature of the appeals process.

I was delighted during the writing of this book to reconnect with my cousin, Carl Anderson, PhD, who showed me around his adopted hometown of Pittsburgh and helped cement the decision as to where certain parts of this story would be set.

And my squadron of science teachers: Joe Atwood, Kim Ross, Louis Watson, and Lane Whitesell, who helped me out of a dilemma concerning plant-based poisons. Lane also offered an early critique of the manuscript.

I would be lost without my critique group of Mike Miller, Sami Nepa, Dave Stanton, and Judy Tillinghast. They tell me when it's good and they tell me when it's bad and they are always, always supportive. Mike even made house calls to fix my computer and helped with the computer forensics aspects of this book.

Extra-special thanks go to my friend JoLynda Hennigh. Not only did she lend me her name for a character in this book, she offered valuable feedback and a sympathetic ear during times of great personal crisis. We should all have such good friends.

The staff of the Neonatal Intensive Care Unit at Integris Baptist Medical Center of Oklahoma not only saved the lives of my children, they gave me a glimpse into a world few people ever see: the care of critically ill newborn babies. Other medical information was provided by Michael Bloomfield, MD, and Laura Mitchell, RN.

Family has many meanings to me, and I am grateful to Martha, Will, Sam, and Ben for being so supportive of my writing. My professional family at KCSC and my spiritual family at NWCC remain constant and faithful and help to keep me anchored.

Finally, thanks to Full Circle and Best of Books, and thank you, Reader, for spending your dollars on these words of mine.

David Kent
Oklahoma City, Oklahoma

People are trapped in history, and history is trapped in them.

—James A. Warren

"If I said I'd marry you, it was only for to try you.
So bring your witness, love, and I'll not deny you."
"Oh, witness have I none, save God Almighty.
And may He reward you well, for the slighting of me."
Her lips grew pale and wan, it made her poor heart tremble,
To think she'd loved a one, and he'd proved deceitful.

—"The Blacksmith," English folk song

PROLOGUE

April 28, 1893
Anadarko, Oklahoma Territory

THEY HAD BEEN TRYING TO KILL HIM FOR HIS ENTIRE life, and they had finally succeeded.

They'd tried at Palo Duro Canyon and Adobe Walls. The white soldiers and the Texas Rangers and the Mexicans had chased him across the plains, from the Rio Grande to the Canadian, and had tried to destroy the People. Then the buffalo grew scarce, the People had nearly starved, and he was finally forced to "surrender."

So they'd put the People on a piece of land and said they could not freely roam the plains any longer, but must stay within certain boundaries, and that they should raise cattle and plant corn. Their commissions and councils then decided that the big pieces of land should go to the white cattlemen, and the People were each given small plots of land. For fifteen years now he'd been considered a "prisoner of war." But there was no more war. He was really a prisoner of the tiny little plot of land.

He was an old man now, with pains in his legs, and he walked with a cane. And now, after all that came before, they had killed him.

He felt the fire inside himself, the pain growing and spreading, the same way the stalks of corn now spread across the plains, the corn the People had been forced to plant. Somehow, some way, they'd found a way to put the pain and the fire into his belly, and it was starting to spread up through his chest, toward his heart.

He felt a rough hand in his back and looked around. Cleaton, the interpreter, a little man with crooked teeth and a tobacco-stained beard, was motioning to him.

"Go," Cleaton said in the language of the People. "Run if you have to, but don't be late." There was a taunt to his voice, as if he were talking to a small child.

The man nodded to him without speaking. He already had his ticket, and he walked into the Rock Island station, a beautiful gabled building, the color of sweet cream, with ANADARKO in huge black letters above the door. He walked through the foyer, leaning on his cane, blinking against the fire.

He looked back once at Cleaton. The little man smiled and spat a stream of juice onto the floor. Behind him, the two soldiers just looked bored. As far as they were concerned, he was just an old man. Just another Indian.

No, he thought. *I cannot die now. There is too much to do. Too much to tell.* He had ridden trains before, of course, and had even taken one of the noisy beasts all the way to Washington, to the seat of the white councils. He had shaken his fist and talked to them about the land and the People, and they had nodded and muttered and put him back on the train.

But now . . . this was different.

Many were dead. Not just men, but women and children as well. Even women who were with child.

He knew the truth. He knew why. He knew what had really happened, and he would ride to Washington again, would go to the councils, and would tell them. He would not die here. Not until he told the truth.

He almost smiled. This time, he was not alone. Another man knew the truth, the strange little white man named Doag. He had left already, had been gone six days. They would meet in Washington and they would go together to the councils.

The man willed the fire within him to die. He blinked against the pain, fighting as he had fought at Adobe Walls. It was becoming difficult to see and hear now, but his head jerked when he heard the whistle.

"What a shame, Chief," Cleaton taunted. "Too late."

He whipped around, stared at the man so long and so hard that the interpreter finally dropped his eyes. He began to move more quickly. The train was making smoke, the steam rolling up into the pale sky, a cloudless blue spring sky over the plains. A sky that would make men in the great cities go blind, he thought.

Now he was running, tossing his cane away. He ran onto the platform, then jumped off it to the soft ground below. The train's wheels started to turn.

For a great moment he was a free Comanche again, running on the plains under the pale sky, smelling the sweetness of the grass, high from the early spring rains. There was no pain in his legs, and he'd quenched the fire they'd lit inside him. By the force of his will, he'd conquered it. They thought they'd killed him, put something inside him that would silence him. But he had overcome, and he would be on the train to Washington.

The train was moving, but for a moment he could almost reach out and catch the railing of the caboose. He would close his fingers over it. . . .

He stumbled.

The fire and the pain roared back, a predator demanding to be fed. It crackled within him. It was in his belly, his heart, his throat, a thousand times worse than before.

He raised his hands toward the sky, that expanse of blue that went on forever. He implored the Spirits to give him strength, to propel him forward, to not take him yet, to let him—

He fell.

He toppled to the side of the railroad track, and he lifted his head just in time to see the train leaving the station, pulling around a bend. In a moment, it was out of sight.

He screamed an ancient war cry, one of the cries he'd used so many times in his life. They had killed him, after all. Now everything depended on the white man. Everything depended on Doag. *He* would tell them. He would tell them the truth and they would have to listen.

He raised his arms again. He turned his face toward the sun and listened. His name meant "Voice of the Sunrise," and now, with a thousand suns lit inside his body, consuming him from the inside out, he heard the sun itself speak to him.

People at the train station were shouting, running, pointing toward the old man. One of the soldiers was first off the platform, Cleaton close behind him. The soldier reached him first, grabbed the old man's body, and rolled him over.

"Chief?" the young soldier said. "Hey, Chief!" He looked helplessly around him.

Cleaton knelt down beside him, noticed how pale the man's coppery skin had become. His face was frozen in a knot of anguish. Cleaton spat into the grass. "Someone go to the agency," he finally said. "Tell them Tabananika is dead."

The Same Day
Washington, D.C.

Jonathan Doag was not normally the kind of man who slept until noon, but it had been a long, long train ride from the Territory, and he'd been beset by bad dreams on the trip. In the dreams he experienced it all again: the blood, the smoke, the screams. The screams of the children.

He bolted upright in his feather bed, bathed in sweat, eyes darting to every corner of the room. *His* room. He blinked, feeling his heart race.

His room, in Washington. In Georgetown, a short walk from the White House. He wasn't in the little room at the back of the Kiowa/Comanche/Apache agency in Anadarko, where he'd lived for two years. He wasn't in his cramped berth on the train. He was *home*, in the beautiful town house he'd leased when he first came to Washington.

His heartbeat began to slow. Doag put a hand over his chest.

He was safe here.

He breathed out slowly.

Tabananika was scheduled to leave today. He would be in Washington four days from now. It was going to be all right, all of it. They couldn't touch him here.

Doag lay back on the feather bed. It was a fine spring morning, Washington's azaleas in bloom outside his window. He pulled up the quilt his mother had made. It had been a gift on his graduation from Harvard. He nestled himself against the pillow.

No more dreams.

What had happened was over. He couldn't change the horror, couldn't erase the blood, but he could help bring justice to the Territory. He and Tabananika would do it together, a historic cooperation between the white man and the Comanche. Doag began to drift off again.

He was fast asleep when the downstairs door opened and a man quietly entered the town house. He walked to the staircase and ascended slowly, holding the rail. He turned to Jonathan Doag's bedroom and opened the door, silent as a cat in a dark house. He positioned himself in the chair at the foot of Doag's bed and watched the small young man sleeping. All he could see was the top of Doag's head, the blond hair sticking out. The man smiled.

He sat that way for over an hour, until Doag began to stir. "That's it," the man said. "Time to wake up, Mr. Doag."

Doag jerked as if he'd been poked with something sharp. Still not fully awake, he remembered the dream. The voice . . . *that* voice. He'd heard it before.

I don't care if she's with child. Line her up with the rest of them.

Doag opened his eyes.

No one leaves alive, understand?

The voice had haunted him, the voice behind the smoke and the blood and the screams of the babies.

Burn them down! Every last one of them!

Doag screamed.

"Come, now, Mr. Doag," the man said. "You wail like a woman. That's not befitting someone who's been out on the wild frontier, who's dealt with the Comanche like you have. You're stronger than that, aren't you, Mr. Doag?"

"How did you—?"

The man crossed his legs at the ankle and propped them on the edge of Doag's bed. He clucked his tongue. "Don't ask questions. Questions got you into this mess."

Doag started to edge toward the other side of the bed, away from the man, away from the voice.

"Don't run away," the man said, then the voice turned harder. "We had an agreement, and you broke it."

Doag gathered his nightshirt around him. "I don't know what you're talking about."

"Don't insult me. Why the sudden need to come back to Washington? Your tour's not up for nearly a year."

"Family emergency," Doag mumbled, his eyes growing wide.

"You don't have any family in Washington. You're lying to me, and I hate being lied to almost as much as I hate being betrayed."

"No, no, I—"

The man thundered up out of the chair and kicked it away. "I told you to keep quiet and you would live. That's pretty simple, isn't it? What's difficult to understand about that?"

Doag began to cry, tears streaking down his thin face. "I don't—"

"But you weren't going to keep quiet, and now you don't get to live. You and the old Indian."

Doag jerked. "Leave him alone," he said, finding his voice. "His people have been through enough, especially after—"

The man took out a pocket watch and snapped it open. "Too late," he said. He closed the watch and looked at Doag. "Too late."

Doag screamed again and clambered out of the bed. The

man was big but quick, and he followed Doag's every move. "We had an agreement," the man whispered, closing on him.

Doag backed away. His arms flailed. He knocked a lamp off his bedside table. "Don't kill me," he murmured. "My family has money."

"Too late," the man said. "What your family could pay is nothing compared to what I'm going to make in the Territory and Texas. I'm a hero, you know, and heroes are rewarded."

Doag dodged to his left and stumbled against his old rocking chair. Then the man was on him. He picked up the smaller man, like a groom taking a bride across the threshold, and carried him back to the bed. Then he straddled him, powerful legs on either side of Jonathan Doag.

"Guns and knives are so messy," the man said. "This is really more close-up work, don't you think?"

Doag whipped his head from side to side. "No—"

The pillow came down on Doag's face. The little man struggled, but he was frail and his attacker strong. The struggle lasted only a few minutes, then Jonathan Doag stopped moving. The killer removed the pillow and put it under Doag's head. The little man looked much the same as he had when his killer entered the room. The man arranged the covers around him, then went through Doag's desk, taking money and Doag's watch so it would appear to be a robbery.

The killer walked to the edge of the bedroom and looked back at Doag's body. "See what your little attack of conscience got you?" he said, then left the room and closed the door. He left the town house as silently as he had come.

On the street, he turned left and walked in the general direction of the White House. It was a fine spring morning, and he whistled as he walked.

Part One

1

ALEX RARELY SLEPT WELL THESE DAYS, AND WHEN THE phone rang she was only dozing, halfway between asleep and awake. Her mind floated in a thin mist, thinking of the soft sands beside the Gulf of Mexico, a few hundred yards away; of the rolling Oklahoma prairie she'd left behind; and thinking that if she'd really embezzled all those hundreds of thousands of dollars, she wouldn't have stayed in this budget motel, but in one of the big beachside condominiums.

The first thing she did when the phone rang was to reach beside her in the bed, instinctively feeling for what wasn't there. When her hand touched only the cool sheets, she slowly balled it into a fist. Gary was gone. Her husband wasn't coming back. It was almost as if he'd left her twice—the first time, the day after she found out about the baby, waking up to his note taped to her guitar case, filled with phrases like *too needful and dependent* and *can't envision having a child with you.* The second time, a month later, it was the strange voice on the telephone: *"Detective Ford from the St. Louis Police Department . . . shooting in the Central West End . . . he was dead at the scene . . . involved in drugs . . . very sorry . . ."*

She was alone. Of course, she'd felt alone for most of her life, but somehow her brief time with Gary had churned up her expectations, like a handful of pebbles tossed into a pond. She'd had to reacquaint herself with the aloneness.

She unclenched her fist and rolled toward the phone beside the bed. "Alex Bridge?" said a man's voice. "Don't answer me. Don't speak at all. This is Wells."

"I—"

"I said don't speak! After I hang up, stay where you are for fifteen minutes, then come and meet me. I'm on the beach across the street, just off Thirty-ninth. I'll be under the last beach umbrella before the rock jetty at Thirty-ninth. I've found something that will help you clear your name."

Alex sat perfectly still.

"I'm hanging up now. Fifteen minutes, Ms. Bridge."

She lay back in bed, breathing quietly. She ran a hand down across her stomach, felt the swelling. She did it these days without even noticing that she was doing it.

She let herself think of Gary's note, scribbled on a piece of yellow legal paper, and then the other note, this one on official company stationery from Cross Current Media:

> TO: Alex Bridge, Traffic and Billing Dept.
> FR: Edward Mullaney, Vice President for Administration & Human Resources
>
> You are being placed on immediate administrative leave from your position, pending the outcome of the investigation into the $498,207.33 missing from corporate accounts as of today's date. Officers of the Federal Bureau of Investigation will be contacting you. You are to cooperate fully. In keeping with company policy, this leave will be without pay.

She thought of the first call from Wells, three days ago. "Galveston, Texas. Find a hotel along the Seawall. That's where the final truth is. Meet me there. . . ."

"I've found something that will help you clear your name," Wells had said just now.

She watched the clock, the red digital numbers floating

beside the hotel bed. Ten minutes slipped by. She got out of bed and stood beside it, barefoot, her long maternity night-shirt falling past her knees.

This is crazy, she thought. FBI agents don't ask for late-night meetings on secluded beaches.

"I've found something that will help you clear your name."

She stumbled into the bathroom and squinted at herself in the harsh light above the mirror. Twenty-nine weeks along, people liked to tell her about the pregnancy "glow" she had. It was absurdly true: she often had high color in her cheeks these days, contrasting deeply with her dark skin. She fussed a little with her hair, dark brown with blond streaks, in a short, simple shag. She raised her arms, frowned at the stretch marks, ran a hand across the tattoo on her upper arm, a crown of thorns intertwined with roses and crosses. Just above her ankle was another tattoo, an intricate Celtic knot. She pulled on a plain white T-shirt and blue denim mater-nity shorts, then found her sandals. *This is crazy,* she thought again.

Alex ran a washcloth over her face, feeling the four holes in her left earlobe, three in the right. She felt naked without at least two pairs of earrings, but this was no time to acces-sorize. She ran her thumb across her ring finger. She'd barely gotten used to wearing the simple silver wedding band be-fore Gary left, and now she hadn't been able to bring herself to take it off.

She silently moved toward the door, catching the outline of two of her instrument cases—just the flute and violin this trip. Sometimes the music was all that could center her. Be-fore Gary had come into her life, it was all she had.

She left her room, turned into the hall, walked through the hotel lobby, and emerged silently into the night. She in-haled the thick air, so different from that of the plains. Across Seawall Boulevard was Galveston's famous seawall it-self, the wall that gave way in the famous flood of 1900. Alex hummed a few bars of "Wasn't That a Mighty Storm" and started across the road.

The street was deserted. Unlike some resort towns, and unlike its own notorious past, Galveston actually slept sometimes. A single car sat across the street, at the row of parking meters by the sidewalk that ran along the top of the seawall. *Wells's car?* she wondered. She looked at it as she passed. Texas plates, a rental sticker on the window. Her pulse quickened.

She crossed to the stairway that led to the beach, held the rail, and started down. The steps themselves were fairly steep, and she didn't much like going either up or down steps lately. She could hear the surf, the waves rolling into the shore. They never stopped: that had been her biggest surprise, when she stood beside the Gulf for the first time a few hours ago. The waves were never silent. They continued their assault on the shore, relentless in their pursuit.

The only good light here came from the street above, casting the beach into deep shadow against the surf. She stepped onto the sand and started down toward the row of nicely spaced beach umbrellas and folding wooden chairs that stayed on the beach year-round.

Alex began to sweat: nerves and pregnancy, she thought. She was warm-natured anyway but, being pregnant, she always seemed to be sweating. What had Wells found? she wondered. Clerical errors, computer problems, or something darker? Someone else embezzling money and trying to blame Alex? A setup?

She shook her head, squeezing a droplet of perspiration away from her eye. She came to the end of the beach and turned right at the edge of the Gulf. She left the soft, fine sand to wade through a few inches of water, letting its coolness wash through the hot summer night.

Everything was still. No horns honked. She heard no birds. The only sound was the surf. It was *too* still, Alex realized as she approached the last beach umbrella. Beyond it was the rock jetty, one of many that jutted out from the beach at regular intervals.

Alex cleared her throat. "Agent Wells?" she said, ten feet from the umbrella.

Only the surf answered her.

"Hello?"

Even as water dripped from her ankles, covering her Celtic tattoo with bits of foamy surf, Alex's heartbeat began racing again. *Careful,* she thought. *Think of the baby.*

"It's me," she said. "Alex Bridge." She took a few steps.

A beach chair sat on either side of the spot where the umbrella was staked into the sand. The one nearest Alex was empty.

She ducked under the umbrella.

"Agent Wells, I'm here. Are you—"

The man was sitting in the other chair, opposite where she stood.

"Hello!" Alex shouted. Anger started to grab her: this was his idea, the least he could do was stay awake. She thumped the beach umbrella stand with her fist.

Wells didn't move.

Alarm bells started to go off behind Alex's eyes. She hunched down and circled behind the two chairs until she was directly behind Wells.

"Hey!" she yelled at the top of her lungs.

She reached over the back of the chair and shook the man's shoulder. His head lolled to one side.

Alex drew back her hand, feeling the warm stickiness on it. She brought it close to her face and sniffed.

She swallowed hard, fighting the urge to scream.

Oh my God, oh my God, oh my God . . . now what?

She took a tentative step around the chair.

From what she could tell, Special Agent Paul Wells of the FBI had been in his midthirties, with a slim build, blond hair cut short and a well-groomed mustache. She put a hand against his arm and felt more stickiness.

The blood was everywhere. His light-colored polo shirt was soaked through, the stain spreading out from his chest. Alex realized with dawning horror that some of the blood was dripping onto her foot in its open-toed sandal.

"No," she whispered.

She started to back away.

Thoughts began to tumble out of control: Wells had been killed, Wells had information that could clear her of the embezzlement, Wells had told her to come to Galveston, someone wanted Wells dead, *Wells was dead!*

Alex stumbled and fell to the ground, bracing with her wrist, automatically angling her body so she wouldn't fall on her stomach. Her breath started to jerk in short gasps. Her fingers clawed the sand.

Her mind churned. She had to get away, away from the blood, away from this beach. She stood unsteadily, backing farther away from Wells, toward the jetty. The waves crashed the shore. The lights of an offshore oil rig blinked. Above and behind her, she heard a car.

Light exploded onto the beach. An amplified voice screamed down at her: "Police! Don't move!"

Alex threw her hands over her face, shielding her eyes from the light, and instinctively spun away, back toward the Gulf.

"Stay where you are!" the voice thundered. "Keep your hands up front! If you still have the gun on you, put it on the beach in front of you!"

Gun?

Alex gazed toward the light. More cars sounded. A siren. Running feet.

"No, you don't understand," she called.

"Be quiet! Don't move!"

She saw vague shapes moving on the staircase coming down from the street.

"No," she said.

Alex ran.

Somehow, she kept her mind focused while she fled across the sand, kicking off her sandals as she splashed through the edge of the surf. Wells had been investigating her for fraud and embezzlement. Wells was dead. She was caught standing over the body, his blood literally on her hands.

Gun? she wondered. They could see she wasn't armed. And how did the police happen to get there at just that moment?

Alex stumbled against an incoming wave. She'd been set up. The whole thing—the embezzlement investigation, the meeting on the beach, all of it.

But I'm a nobody, she screamed inwardly. *Why me? I'm just a data-entry clerk who took the job to pay the bills so I can play music on the weekends! I'm nothing!*

The steps quickened behind her, more of them, thundering against the surf. The voices started to lose their shape, melting into one another, screaming at her to stop. They were growing louder.

Alex veered toward the water, and a wave crashed into her. She kept her feet for a moment, struggling against the current, inertia pulling her down. Another wave was hard on the heels of the first one, white foam at its crest. It washed over her and Alex was soaked. She fell, pain exploding in her head.

She coughed water out her nose and mouth, rolling to her side, clutching at her abdomen. *They set me up . . . but why?*

For a moment she caught a faint glimmer of memory, a voice speaking quietly, hastily on her cell phone while she sat in a park and ate her lunch. Then more words, weeks later: a message on her computer screen at work. Words she couldn't understand.

Footsteps stopped over her, and she heard a male voice. "Ah, shit, it's a woman—and, ah, Jesus, she's pregnant." The voice faded slightly, as if the cop had turned away. "Better call a second ambulance!"

Gary . . . the baby . . . Wells . . . They all started to run together. Just as another wave broke behind her, Alex Bridge began to lose consciousness. In a moment of startling clarity, she tried to reach the words, to wonder what they meant and why someone wanted to destroy her. But she couldn't think.

It all slid away from her, like a child's ball rolling unchecked into a busy street.

For a moment Alex's entire body felt hot, electrically charged, the world blazing around her. Then she surrendered to the darkness.

2

July 13, 10:00 A.M.
Oklahoma City, Oklahoma

THE FACT THAT FAITH Kelly was about to have a private meeting with the president of the United States wasn't the problem. The problem was *why* she was having the meeting.

A couple of years ago, Faith had been fresh out of the Federal Law Enforcement Training Center in Glencoe, Georgia, a newly minted deputy United States marshal assigned to the Oklahoma City office. Then she'd met a man named Art Dorian, who became a mentor and father figure to her. It turned out that Dorian worked for Department Thirty, one of the Justice Department's most secretive units. It was similar to the Marshals Service's Witness Security program, but instead of granting immunity and new identities to those who were witnesses to crimes, Department Thirty dealt with those who had committed crimes, in some cases serious ones.

After Art Dorian was murdered, Faith had found herself inadvertently immersed in Department Thirty, and last year had accepted a full-time job with the unit. In the space of a few months, she went from a life of conventional law enforcement—the life she'd been working toward since she was nine years old and had ridden in her father's patrol car for the first time—to a life of protecting secrets.

Shortly after she joined the department, one of the cases under her management erupted into crisis. A man under Department Thirty's longtime protection had linked the president to violent political extremists who targeted law enforcement officers. It had been a political nightmare for the administration and had in fact been designed so that the Department Thirty "protectee," Nathan Grant, would weaken the president to the point where Grant's puppet candidate would be elected with ease. Faith's efforts had exonerated the president and crumbled a conspiracy that had been unfolding for nearly half a century.

Now the president wanted to meet her.

He was coming to Oklahoma City as part of a fund-raising tour through the Midwest and Southwest. The e-mail from his chief of staff had said that Faith and Department Thirty helped to "save the administration."

The problem was, Faith didn't like the president or his policies. In the course of doing her job, she may have in fact kept the man in office. But she didn't have a clue what to say to him.

She smoothed out her blazer, catching her reflection in the window of her stark second-floor office in Oklahoma City's federal courthouse. She fussed with her red hair, which fell past her shoulders, and stretched her long legs under the desk. She didn't want to do this. She hadn't voted for the man the first time he ran for president, wouldn't vote for him next time, and didn't want to have to admit that to his face.

At exactly ten o'clock, the knock came on the door. She cleared her throat, said, "Come in," and two Secret Service men, in their dark suits with their curling wires from flesh-colored earpieces, entered the room.

One of them nodded to her. "Officer Kelly," he said. "You've been briefed?"

"Yes."

"Good. We'll just need to do a personal sweep."

Faith stood up. The advance team had already swept the office itself twice since eight o'clock. Presumably they thought she might have a weapon secreted in her bra, she who had "saved" the president's administration. She let a small smile escape, and the Secret Service agent frowned.

"Something funny, Officer Kelly?"

She looked down. At five ten, Faith had a good three inches on him. "No, Agent. Nothing's funny. Let's just get on with it."

"You have something better to do than meet with the president?"

Yes, my job, she considered saying, but didn't. "Not at all, Agent," she finally said.

The agent remained still, then leaned into the hallway. "Send Delp in." A moment later a female Secret Service agent came in and ran an electronic wand over Faith's body. It didn't beep, and the woman withdrew without a word.

Ten seconds later, the president of the United States walked into her office. He was smaller than he looked on television, standing eye to eye with Faith. He was an average-sized man with an "everyman" face.

"Officer Kelly," the president said, and smiled his on-camera campaign smile.

"Mr. President," Faith said. The butterflies in her stomach bumped into each other. "It's an honor, sir."

The president nodded once, then turned to the two Secret Service men. "Outside, gentlemen. This meeting is private."

The door closed behind the two bodyguards. Faith shifted from one foot to the other. "It's your office," the president said. "You can sit down, you know."

Faith sat and offered him the only other chair in the room. His eyes traveled over it. One desk, one filing cabinet, a long folding table, a stuffed catfish mounted on one wall. He lingered on the catfish.

"You fish?" he said.

"No, sir," Faith said. "That belonged to Art Dorian. He was my—this was his office before I took this job. I decided to keep it."

"You need some plants," the president said, as if he hadn't heard her. "Plants are good for a room." He spread his hands apart. "So here we are. On my official agenda, I'm in a meeting with the U.S. attorney now. No one except my chief of staff, your director, and my Secret Service detail know I'm here."

Faith nodded.

The president crossed his legs at the knee. "You know, I wanted to do away with Department Thirty."

Faith looked at him and nodded. "Yes, sir."

"You don't seem too surprised."

"No, sir. I—" She closed her mouth.

"Oh, come on. 'Permission to speak freely,' as they say in the military. Go ahead and say it."

Faith swallowed. "I sometimes wonder about our mission, if we should be in the business we're in."

The president nodded, a jerky motion, just like when he was being grilled at press conferences. "Holding hands with criminals. Murderers, terrorists, thieves, embezzlers, even traitors in a few cases. As soon as I came into office, and I learned of the department's existence, I wanted to chop it right out of the Justice Department budget. Then, after that fiasco last year, when one of . . ." The president stopped, a muscle in his jaw working.

"One of our people," Faith offered.

"One of your people. That's as good a description as any. One of your people targeted me personally, tried to tie me up with that Sons of Madison group that wants to eliminate all police as unconstitutional. I was ready to pull the plug."

The man waited, ran a hand over one ear, smoothing down his graying hair. It was a gesture the media loved and often exploited.

The silence drew out, then Faith realized the president was waiting for her to ask the obvious question. "Why didn't you, sir?" she finally said.

"You don't have to call me sir. With the corruption of your former director, all the attacks on me, I was ready. But your new director convinced me that under new and honest leadership, the department's mission could continue to bring in new information. Information that can help all of us in government work better, work more efficiently, and serve the American people."

Was that a campaign speech? Faith wondered. She nodded.

The president leaned forward, touching Faith's desk. His elbow landed on a pile of her papers. "By the way . . . " he said.

Faith's eyebrows went up.

"Thank you," he said. "Your work at getting to the truth helped save my presidency."

Under the desk, Faith twisted her fingers around one another.

The president smiled and leaned back. "And now you're wondering if you did the right thing. You're a member of the other party, you didn't vote for me, you don't like what my administration stands for. How am I doing so far?"

Faith unclasped her hands. Her shoulders sagged a little, some of the tension draining away. "That's pretty accurate."

The man laughed out loud. "Relax, Officer. I do understand that not everyone I meet voted for me, even those who work for me. You did your job. You exposed high-level and long-standing corruption. You got to the truth. I understand it was at some cost."

Faith nodded. She had shot and killed Nathan Grant, the man she had originally been paid to protect, standing in a driving rain outside the Oklahoma state capitol, a year ago in May.

She shrugged and cleared her throat. The president was still waiting. *Dammit, he wants me to talk about it.*

No. I won't rehash it, not even for the president of the United States. It's over, it happened, Grant is dead, his wife and the others are alive, and I'm still here. Case closed.

She met the president's gray eyes head-on, her gaze unflinching. She wouldn't have looked at most men—much less the president of the United States—that way two years ago. But then, her life had been twisted into a completely new shape in the last two years. She didn't drop her eyes.

"I don't need the details," the president finally said. "It's actually better if I don't know." But he couldn't hide the disappointment in his voice. "Keep up the good work, Officer Kelly. May I call you Faith?"

"If you like."

They looked at each other across the desk. Finally the president stood, and Faith followed him. "Faith, I just wanted to thank you for the work you did. We politicians come and go, but people like you, and entities like Department Thirty, have a role to play for all of us. Remember that."

"I don't know if it's quite that simple," Faith said. For a moment she glanced out the window. Below and across the street, the Oklahoma City National Memorial stood. It was there, next to the Survivor Tree, that she'd been recruited into Department Thirty. "I can't see things as so black and white anymore."

The president's expression changed, softening into something almost natural. For a moment she caught a glimpse of a man under the veneer of the politician. "That's just what I mean. We need the people who deal in gray areas, Faith. I'm a politician. I have to deal in black and white. Whoever said politics is the art of compromise was dead wrong, at least in this country. That's one thing this office has taught me. Politics is about absolutes. The courage of your convictions, don't back down, don't give in to the other side of the aisle. People seem to have this need to see that in their political leaders. But see, while I'm pounding my fist on the table and refusing to concede anything to the other side, there needs to be someone else who tries to understand the truth that falls in between. Someone like you, Faith. You and your five other Department Thirty case officers around the country." He glanced at the fish on the wall again. "You and your fish stories."

Faith blinked. Art Dorian had always said that Department Thirty was about making up fish stories, hence the stuffed fish in his office.

"I knew Arthur Dorian too," the president said. "He was a fine man, a great scholar, and a very capable public servant for a long time." He extended his hand. Faith shook it. "Good-bye, Faith." He took a card from his pocket, scribbled a number on it, and handed it to her. "If you ever need anything, let me know. That number will get you past all the gatekeepers and right to my chief of staff."

"Thank you. Good-bye, Mr. President."

The president went to the door, put his hand on the knob, and turned back around. The candidate smile was back. "Think about voting for me next time, will you?" He took a step into the hallway, then turned as if he'd forgotten something. "Oh, there's someone else here who'd like to talk to you. Director Conway said he wanted to pay you a visit."

"Who?" Faith said, but the president was already gone.

A moment later a heavyset man in late middle age, with wisps of gray hair around a mostly bald head, strolled into the room, carrying a manila envelope in one hand.

"Why, Officer Kelly," he said.

Faith sat down. "Conway? *Director Conway?* What's that about?"

The man she knew as Dean Yorkton chuckled lightly, thumping his fingers against his leg. "I have a real name, just like everyone else. Since I'm the director of Department Thirty now, I use my birth name. Richard Matthias Conway."

"Matthias?"

He waved a dismissive hand. "It isn't important. What did you think of the president?"

Faith steepled her fingers. "Interesting man."

"Come, now. That's very vague."

"We're in the vague business, aren't we?"

Yorkton—Faith still couldn't help thinking of him that way—sat down and began drumming his fingers on the edge of the desk, irritating her the same way as the first time she'd met him, over two years ago. "Not getting cynical, are you?"

"I was already cynical. What did you do, just hitch a ride on *Air Force One*?"

"A perk of directorship."

"And how do you like being director?"

"It's different, I grant you. After being in the field for nearly twenty-five years, it's strange to sit on the other end—strange to just be Dick Conway after all this time." He moved around in the chair. "But I'm cleaning up the mess Daniel Winter made of our department, repairing the black eye his corruption gave us on the Hill."

"Where is Winter these days?"

Yorkton stared at her without speaking.

Faith leaned back in her chair. "I had to ask. So why the visit now?"

"I wanted to see you."

Faith sighed. "Why?"

Yorkton shook his head. "*Still* cynical. I'm fond of you. I think you're a good officer, whether you think so or not. I think you can go far. And—"

"Here it comes," Faith said.

Yorkton plopped the envelope on her desk.

Faith picked it up. "What's this?"

"A new experience for you. I think you're ready for it, and it's in your region."

Faith still had little patience for Yorkton's failure to ever answer a direct question. She shook out a few papers, then looked up at him. "Background?" she said.

"It's all there. You're going out to recruit a new case into Department Thirty. Your first case to build from scratch. The first contact, the interview, the testimony, the construction of the identity. The first case to be truly yours."

Faith breathed out slowly. *Oh, shit,* she thought. She'd known this would come. It was part of her job. It was what Department Thirty was all about, but somehow she'd been able to push it out of her mind while working the existing cases.

Yorkton drummed his fingers a little more, then swept his arm across the desk in a grand gesture. "Everything you need is in there," he said. "Faith Kelly, meet Alex Bridge."

3

FAITH SHOOK THE ENVELOPE OUT ONTO THE DESK. THE first thing out was a photograph, roughly an eight-by-ten. She held it up and scrutinized the young woman. Alex Bridge was sitting in a wooden straight-backed chair, playing a teardrop-shaped stringed instrument. It took Faith a few moments to figure out what the instrument was, then she remembered a friend from college who'd been into bluegrass music: it was a mandolin.

The woman in the photo had a dark skin tone, though she still looked Anglo. Her hair was short, straight, and dark, with lighter streaks. She was wearing jeans and a T-shirt advertising the North Texas Irish Festival. Her eyes were closed, her feet bare. She looked to be deeply into whatever music she was playing. Faith spied the two tattoos, one encircling her upper arm, the Celtic knot just above her ankle, half hidden under the leg of Alex Bridge's jeans.

"Alex Antonia Bridge," Yorkton said. "Not Alexandra, not Alexis, just Alex."

Faith rattled the photo. "What . . ." She cleared her throat. "What did she do?"

Yorkton made a clucking sound. "No, no, no. See, you're still thinking like law enforcement. 'What did she do?' is not the first question we ask in Department Thirty cases. We ask, 'Why do we want her?'"

Faith dropped the picture to the desktop. It seemed hard to believe that this young musician would satisfy any of the requirements of Department Thirty. She pulled out a thick file, bound up with a rubber band.

"It's all there," Yorkton said. "Everything you need is there. Since this will be your first recruit, I've taken the liberty of getting things started."

Faith started to sift through the papers.

"Alex Bridge is thirty years old," Yorkton said. "Her mother was full-blood Comanche. Her father is white."

Faith looked at the photo again and nodded. "You say her mother *was* Comanche. Past tense. She's deceased?"

"She left the family when Alex was three years old. Alex was born in Lawton, Oklahoma, and after the mother left, the father moved around to various towns in Oklahoma and Texas. He worked odd jobs, as a sort of traveling handyman. Took up with several other women but never remarried. Alex has four half-brothers from these liaisons but only sees one of them with any regularity. She graduated high school here in Oklahoma City."

Faith flipped a few pages. "Went to four different colleges. Music major, then sociology major, then humanities major, finally settled on broadcasting major."

Yorkton nodded. "Always searching for something. A common trait among those who eventually find their way to us."

Faith looked up. "No one 'finds their way' to Department Thirty."

"A figure of speech, nothing more. Young Alex worked in retail stores, had a couple of short-term jobs as a late-night announcer in small-town radio stations, then was hired by Cross Currents Media as a traffic and billing clerk."

"Cross Currents Media? That's a good-sized corporation."

"Indeed. Headquartered in San Francisco, they have a large data and accounting center here in Oklahoma City. They own small and medium market radio stations nationwide."

"What does a traffic and billing clerk do for a media conglomerate?"

Yorkton began drumming his fingers again. "The way I understand it, they enter advertising orders for business clients into a software program. Ms. Bridge's job was to track orders for national clients that advertised on Cross Currents stations across the country."

"How exciting."

Yorkton gave one of his thin, mirthless smiles. "Yes. Her main interest is music. She seems to be able to play any instrument she wants—guitar, violin, mandolin, flute. She plays with a couple of ensembles: one that specializes in Celtic folk music, one a bit more contemporary. Coffeehouses, college bars, that sort of venue. Her politics are rather leftish. She's interested in peace and so-called social justice causes."

Faith caught the slight tone of disdain in Yorkton's voice. It was the first time he'd ever betrayed any kind of personal feeling one way or the other. *File that away,* Faith thought.

"She was married briefly, a man named Gary St. James. She did not take his name. He left her when she informed him she was pregnant. He turned up dead in a drug-related shoot-out in St. Louis a few weeks later."

Faith winced.

"So you're beginning to see the psychological profile emerging," Yorkton said. His tone had taken on the quality of a professor delivering a lecture.

"Have I ever told you how much I hate jargon?" Faith said. "What I see is a woman whose loved ones keep leaving her in one way or another."

Yorkton shrugged. "Semantics."

Faith leaned back in her chair. "Okay, you've given me the bio. Now the two big questions: what did she do and why are we interested in her?"

"Ah." Yorkton stopped drumming and steepled his fingers. Faith resisted the urge to throw something at him. "She embezzled nearly half a million dollars from Cross Currents over the last year. It was quite an ingenious scheme, actually, having to do with changing the codes for advertising accounts and rerouting money to an account of her own. Very arcane rules about advertising agency commissions. It's in the file. When the corporation started to notice the missing funds, they did an internal audit, and then turned it over to the FBI. An agent named Paul Wells was assigned to the case. He had our Ms. Bridge dead to rights.

"Two nights ago, on a deserted beach in Galveston, Texas, she shot and killed Special Agent Wells. The evidence is overwhelming, both for the embezzlement and the murder. A trial would be a mere formality."

Faith was flipping through pages in the file. Her eyes zeroed in on a police incident report. "Two thirty in the morning? It says here the murder took place at two thirty A.M."

"Correct."

She looked up at him. "What was an FBI agent doing meeting a suspect on a beach in the middle of the night without backup? And for that matter, why the hell were either of them in Galveston? That's a long way from Oklahoma City."

Yorkton folded his hands together as if praying. "I don't know, Officer. Perhaps Ms. Bridge lured Agent Wells onto that beach by saying she was going to give herself up. Perhaps she was planning to leave the country, catching a boat from Galveston. Perhaps she wanted a last vacation, a little time alone, before her child is born."

"That's a lot of perhapses."

"So it is. But the evidence is there, and the evidence says Alex Bridge took the money and then killed the FBI agent who was investigating her."

Faith drummed her fingers in unconscious imitation of the big man. "She's pregnant."

"Seven months."

Faith shook her head. "So now the payoff. Why does Department Thirty want this woman?"

"The SEC has been investigating Cross Currents for some time now. More than two years, as a matter of fact. Suffice it to say that they have engaged in some, shall we say, 'accounting irregularities' that will make Enron and WorldCom look like mischievous college pranks. Officer Kelly, we are talking about amounts in *billions* of dollars. Cross Currents Media has a finger in every aspect of American society. Broadcast outlets, cable franchises, recording companies, concert promotions, even book and magazine publishing. What Alex Bridge did—half a million dollars—is nothing compared to what the financial officers of Cross Currents have been doing for years. They formed shadow companies to hide their shadow companies. They have poured money into the campaigns of politicians whose names you know. They are everywhere, and they are completely rotten."

"And you think Alex Bridge can point to who was doing what to whom, and why and how much."

"She had access every day to information on how much the company was making in advertising revenues. She wrote reports and sent them to the executives. This obscure young woman can point the investigation right where it needs to go." Yorkton shrugged. "And she shouldn't be too difficult to reassign to a new identity. With her diverse background, you should be able to find a good job for her without too much trouble. She has no close family ties. Your first recruit, my dear Officer Kelly, will be a good one."

Faith put all the papers back into the envelope except the photo. She glanced at it again. "A seven-months-pregnant folk musician is the key to a multibillion-dollar corporate scandal." She shook her head. "Only in Department Thirty. Where is she now?"

Yorkton's head bobbed. "I had her removed from the Galveston jail a few hours after her arrest. She was transported here and is being held in the new safe house."

"Who's secured her?"

"Deputy marshals. Some of your former colleagues, as a matter of fact. At this point they don't know Ms. Bridge is a Department Thirty candidate. They have been led to believe she'll be processed into the standard Witness Security Program. The rest is up to you."

Yorkton stood up abruptly. "I'm sure the president's meeting with the U.S. attorney is nearly over. I'll fall back in with his entourage."

Faith had almost forgotten that the president of the United States was in this room just a short while ago. The morning had taken on a surreal, glassy quality. For an insane moment Faith thought that if she put out a hand and tried to touch Yorkton, that her hand would simply go right through him.

"Just like that?" she said.

Yorkton looked down at her. "Just like that." He pointed at the envelope. "This is why we're here. This is why we do what we do."

"What if she doesn't want to work with us?"

"Do you think she'd rather face a federal trial for murdering an FBI agent?"

"People aren't always so cut-and-dried, you know." Faith remembered the president's words about needing people who could see the gray areas. "She may want to take her chances."

Yorkton's voice hardened. "Well, then, you'll just have to convince her." He put his hands in his pockets, turned, and shuffled out of the office.

4

July 13, 4:30 P.M.
Harpers Ferry, West Virginia

THE MAN WHO CALLED HIMSELF ISAAC SMITH SAUN-
tered through the well-kept grounds of Harpers Ferry National Historical Park. He walked with hands clasped behind
his back, a mildly curious look on his face. He blended with
the tourists and their cameras and guidebooks, though he
had been here many times before and knew the grounds almost as well as the park employees did.

It was really quite picturesque, Smith thought. Pastoral.
Peaceful. The carefully tended sidewalks, manicured lawns,
and strategically placed historical markers gave no sense
of the powder keg that was October of 1859, when John
Brown had come here and taken control of the United
States military's arsenal. Now Harpers Ferry was a tiny town
built up the side of a hill, with brick streets and thousands
of tourists.

Smith stood slightly apart from a group of a dozen or so
of those sightseers as they came to the building known as
"John Brown's Fort." It was here that Brown and his men had
barricaded themselves during the last day of the raid as they
stood against Colonel Robert E. Lee and the U.S. Army.

Smith shook his head as he looked at the little building.
Even it—the very structure where the Civil War had truly
begun, he would argue—stood not in its original location
but some 150 feet away. At one point, after the Civil War, the
building had actually been disassembled and moved to

Chicago to be an exhibit in the World's Fair, only to later be shipped back to Harpers Ferry, again in pieces.

It was an unassuming, weathered brick structure with off-white paint over its series of wooden doors and curving windows. The old lookout tower sat atop it, also painted white. There was no hint at all of what happened here. This was history, but *clean* history. And the history of this land was anything but clean.

The other tourists moved off, but Smith lingered, staring up at the lookout tower. He circled the building, his back to a grove of trees, where he could watch the parking lot across the way. At exactly four thirty, a black Cadillac Escalade SUV pulled into a parking slot. Smith smiled. The man was nothing if not precise.

Unseen from the other side of the building, Smith watched as the driver got out of the car, a slim yet muscular young man in a dark suit, even in the July heat. The bodyguard, Smith thought. He knew that a large-caliber automatic pistol would be somewhere under the young man's suit jacket.

The SUV's back door opened and Smith breathed out slowly. He had doubted that the man would actually come, up until this moment. All their business thus far had been by phone. The man who had come to Harpers Ferry to meet Smith wielded awe-inspiring power, yet went virtually unrecognized. Hence only a single bodyguard/driver. Most Americans might recognize him in a vague sort of way, but very few would make the connection as to who he was and what he did. Most Americans, Smith knew, were woefully ignorant.

The man was in his midfifties, tall and fit. He had the requisite distinguished-looking gray in his brown hair, and his face was a study in prominent angles. The face of a man accustomed to making important decisions. But Smith first looked at his feet, to see if what he had been told was true. And it was: it was said that the powerful man always wore the same old, scuffed pair of gray cowboy boots, no matter the rest of his wardrobe. Today he wore khaki pants and a light blue polo shirt, but it was said that he even wore the boots when dressed more formally.

The man in the scuffed boots approached John Brown's Fort, leaving his bodyguard by the Cadillac. Smith circled the rest of the way around the building and stepped up to the man from behind.

"It's interesting," Smith said. "John Brown was a radical, an extremist. By our definition today he'd be called a terrorist. And yet, his act of terrorism ultimately led to the destruction of slavery in this country. There's the age-old question: does the end truly justify the means?"

"I know the history," the other man said in a soft drawl. He turned to look at Smith. "This is an elaborate little production you've put together here. Having me come all the way up here, using the name of Isaac Smith, asking rhetorical questions. Is there a point to all this, or do you just think I like to play games?"

Smith smiled. "Congratulations, sir. Very few people know that John Brown used the alias of Isaac Smith when he first came to this area and started scouting his raid."

"Well, I'm not most people."

"Indeed you are not. And I *know*, sir, that you like to play games. Otherwise you wouldn't have hired me." Smith looked the man in the eye for the first time. "Would you?"

The man looked at him for a moment, then made a show of pulling a handkerchief from his pocket and mopping his forehead. "Too hot to be out on a day like this. And I don't want to be out here too long."

"Afraid of being seen with me, are you?"

"No, that's not it. I could walk naked down the middle of Pennsylvania Avenue and most people would think I was just another nutcase. I just want this business over and done with." He lowered his voice a notch. "You had the FBI agent killed."

Smith nodded and ambled a few steps around the fort, stopping to look at a historical marker. The booted man followed. Two tourists, taking in a slice of American history on a summer afternoon.

The booted man cleared his throat. "You told me there wouldn't be any bloodshed."

"No," Smith said. "Actually I told you the primary target would not be killed or physically hurt in any way. That's the guarantee I make to all my clients. But sometimes in the course of doing the job, I have to use other people. Those other people may have to resort to violence." He shrugged.

"God Almighty, man! He was an FBI agent, a federal law enforcement officer. What the hell were you thinking?"

Smith kept his voice even. He'd never worked with a client who had the clout of this one, but really, they were all the same. There came a point when they questioned his methods, even if the methods achieved their objectives. "I was thinking," Smith said, "that Special Agent Wells had to die in order to fully implement the plan."

The other man slapped a hand against his leg. "I don't like it. For the record, Mr. *Smith*, I don't think that was necessary."

"For the record?" Smith smiled again. "There is no record. I don't exist and you're not here. So let's not waste time with objections for the record. I have run into a problem and it has to be fixed."

"A problem? I was told you don't have problems. That's why I hired you."

"There are always risks. If you don't think so, then you're a fool, and I know that you aren't a fool. The woman has disappeared."

They had been walking around the side of the fort as they talked, keeping a casual gait. Now the other man stopped short, almost stepping on Smith's foot. "What do you mean, she's disappeared?" His voice was a stage whisper.

Smith stuffed both hands into his pockets and moved a step away. "She was in the Galveston jail. Everything had worked perfectly up to that point. But sometime, around twelve hours after she was arrested, she was gone. My subcontractor in Galveston says a group of federal marshals came in and took control of the prisoner. Since Wells was a federal agent, this was not unexpected. But then . . ."

"Tell me."

"That was the last anyone's seen or heard of her. She hasn't shown up in any federal holding facility. My sources are solid, and there's no trace of her."

"A girl can't just disappear out of the justice system," the other man said. "If anything, federal agents are going to watch her even closer, since she's supposed to have killed one of their own."

"I talked to one of my inside sources at DOJ this morning. I asked her—hypothetically, of course—what this could mean. She mentioned WITSEC, the Witness Security Program. That makes no sense. WITSEC doesn't protect murderers, especially not murderers of FBI agents."

The other man nodded, wiping his face with the handkerchief again. "You're right. There's no way in hell they'd offer a deal to someone they thought had murdered another federal officer."

"There is one thing," Smith said.

The man's eyebrows went up.

"My DOJ contact said something else, and I have no idea what it means. She said, 'Maybe Department Thirty's got her.' She laughed like it was quite funny, then got very serious and hung up quickly."

"Department Thirty."

"Department Thirty," Smith repeated. "Is it a federal agency? Is it part of DOJ?"

Smith waited.

"I've only heard talk," the booted man said.

"What talk?"

The booted man shook his head.

"Can you find out? Hard facts, details. I need them quickly."

The man looked down at the shorter Smith. "Yes," he said finally.

Smith nodded. "You have your ways, I'm sure, just as I have mine."

"I do. This has to stay under control, you understand? You

have to find her. *Find her.* You have no idea what's at stake here."

"Of course I do," Smith said, looking up at John Brown's Fort again. "I've understood from the very beginning." *Even if you haven't,* he thought but didn't say.

They'd reached the other side of the little building, the side facing the parking lot. "I'll see if anyone's heard of this Department Thirty."

"I'll be in touch, then," Smith said, watching the man's booted feet scuff away from him. The heels made a hollow thump against the concrete sidewalk.

The man who called himself Isaac Smith stayed in front of John Brown's Fort for another half hour, watching groups of tourists come and go. He was surprised that the man with the boots didn't know what this Department Thirty was. This was both troubling and exciting to Smith. Troubling because it presented an unforeseen challenge in an otherwise painstakingly planned and implemented series of events. Exciting for the same reason.

Whatever Department Thirty was, it was simply an obstacle to be overcome. He would find Alex Antonia Bridge, and he would make sure that she was utterly destroyed.

5

THERE WERE SOME HABITS THAT COULD NOT BE BRO-ken, Faith thought. Getting up early seemed to be hers.

Even though she no longer had a supervisor to report to on a daily basis, even though she could work either from home or her office, she simply could not stay in bed later than six o'clock on a weekday morning. Too many years of listening to her father, Detective Captain Joe Kelly, bellow at her brother and her that only the lazy, the slothful, the scum of the earth, would waste time sleeping late. Too many years of needing extra time in college and graduate school and the academy, of wanting to get ahead of everyone else.

And what did it get me? she wondered. *I'm neither ahead nor behind. I'm Department Thirty. I'm like those people on e-mail lists that never post anything. I'm a lurker.*

She put on her running shorts and soft gray U.S. Marshals Service T-shirt, tied her green bandanna around her head, and took her run through The Village. It was a generally middle-class suburban area of Oklahoma City, with homes from the 1950s and green lawns and lots of families with children. She was the odd one—again—the only single woman on her block.

She took her run, feeling the impurities sweat their way out. She wasn't in the condition she'd been in when she'd run the New York and Boston marathons, but she could still do five miles and feel great afterward. She watched the city wake up, letting her mind be blissfully blank.

Back at the house, she showered and dressed, made black coffee, and read the newspaper. A death row inmate in Texas had just had a firm execution date set, for the murder of two men in a Houston bar in 1998. Eduardo Rojas allegedly had some low-level ties to the Houston underworld, and now his attorneys had filed an unusual appeal, saying Rojas had offered to cut a deal with prosecutors at the time, presumably to offer up some of Houston's big fish in return for not seeking the death penalty. The prosecutors had evidently not even entertained the notion, and the DA was quoted as saying that "Mr. Rojas did not have a constitutional right to make deals."

Faith shook her head. There was no way in hell such a silly appeal would work at the U.S. Supreme Court. She kept reading. Democrats and Republicans in the Oklahoma legislature were wrangling over teacher pay and the administration of the new state lottery. The new Iraqi government was in gridlock. Israel and the Palestinian Authority had traded shots in Gaza. The president had just unveiled his new tax plan at a speech in Albuquerque.

Nowhere in the paper was there any mention of an Oklahoma City FBI agent named Paul Wells, found murdered on a beach in south Texas.

The Department Thirty secrecy machine was up and running. Faith put the paper aside, opened her briefcase, and took out the file on Alex Bridge. It was all there: the account on Grand Cayman where she'd hidden the money she embezzled from Cross Currents, the records showing electronic funds transfers, transaction confirmation numbers. Wells had her dead to rights on the embezzlement.

Faith turned pages. The gun that killed Wells was found in a Dumpster along Seawall Boulevard, not far from where the FBI agent was found. Alex Bridge's fingerprints were on it.

If it had been me, Faith thought, *I would have thrown it in the ocean. That way, even if it washed back to shore, the fingerprints would be gone.*

She shrugged. Alex Bridge may have been creative in her

embezzling technique, but she'd also been a sloppy criminal. Faith wasn't sure if she should feel sorrow or contempt for the woman. In the end, she decided on neither. Her job was to get information from Alex Bridge, information that would further the investigation of Cross Currents Media. Then she would create a new life for her and send her on her way.

At nine o'clock, she left the house and started her gold Mazda Miata. She drove west, mentally preparing herself to meet her first Department Thirty recruit.

In front of the last house on the block, before it intersected the busy thoroughfare of May Avenue, a muscular man with a brownish-gray goatee sat in the front seat of a black Ford Taurus. As Faith's Miata passed him, he bent his head and appeared to be writing in a spiral notebook.

When the Miata turned left onto May, the man dropped his pen and picked up a camera with a telephoto lens. He focused on the driver's-side window of the Miata and got two good shots of Faith Kelly behind the wheel, before the car was out of his view.

The earlier writing he'd done in the notebook had been only a diversion, a series of nonsense scribbles. He turned to a fresh page, noted the time, and wrote: *Surveillance begun.*

He closed the notebook and started the car. He placed the book and camera on the seat beside him, right next to his SIG Sauer nine-millimeter automatic pistol.

6

ALEX WAS ALLOWED TO GO INTO THE BACKYARD OF THE "safe house," which was a new three-bedroom home west of Oklahoma City, in a semirural area between the suburbs of Yukon and Mustang. A wooden privacy fence enclosed the backyard, and there was a small patio with white wrought-iron lawn furniture.

She liked to sit on the patio in the morning, before the heat became too stifling. But the heat usually chased her inside before ten o'clock, with the temperatures already into the nineties. She'd never had much patience with hot weather, and had even less since she'd been pregnant.

Her babysitters—that's how she thought of them—worked two twelve-hour shifts, changing at seven A.M. and seven P.M. She understood that they were deputy U.S. marshals, very polite and very firm. They asked her what kind of food she liked, and she'd once sent one of them all the way into the city for a burger from Johnnie's, just to see if they'd really do it. There was a man and a woman on each shift, and one of them—usually the woman—was never more than ten or twenty feet away from her.

The house was comfortable if a bit sterile, but all in all, it was a lot better than the twelve terrifying hours she'd spent in the Galveston jail. All the deputies would tell her was that she was now in federal custody and would be talking to someone soon.

"Can't I have a lawyer?" she'd asked.

They didn't answer her.

At least they'd let her bring her flute and fiddle. Mainly she played slow Irish airs on flute. Their plaintive, haunting melodies echoed how she felt.

Absolutely, utterly alone.

She assembled the wooden flute and moved around in the wrought-iron chair, looking for a comfortable position. There wasn't one, of course: the baby saw to that. She raised the flute, did a few scales, and closed her eyes. The tune she found was the air *"For Ireland I'll Not Tell Her Name."* For a while she was gone, absorbed into the ancient melody. Her mother and her husband, her late nights in small-town radio stations, Cross Currents Media and Special Agent Paul Wells . . . all were gone, receding into a blurry nothingness.

When she finished the tune, she opened her eyes and saw a very tall woman, a few years younger than she, with red hair, standing beside the sliding door that led into the house.

"That's beautiful," the redhead said.

"Thanks," Alex said, annoyed that she had to come back to reality.

"Do you know *'Sheebeg, Sheemore'*?"

Alex raised her eyes in surprise, meeting the redhead's deep emerald eyes. She nodded, raised the flute, and played the lilting melody of the bard Turlough O'Carolan's most famous composition. When it was done, the redhead was nodding with a hint of a smile.

"I've never heard it on the flute before," the redhead said. "I guess that's a flute?"

"Irish flute," Alex said. "It's made of wood. Not like your concert flutes in the band or orchestra."

"May I sit?"

Alex shrugged.

"My grandfather plays that tune on the fiddle," the redhead said, settling in across from Alex and slapping a thick file folder down on the table. "I never knew what the title meant, though, and I don't speak Gaelic."

"It means 'The Big Fairy Hill and the Little Fairy Hill,'"

Alex said. "There was a battle between two queens, and each claimed dominion over the other's country. Their armies fought and fought, but the battle was a stalemate. Then they saw the fairies who lived in their two hills approaching each other, and they declared a truce so the fairies wouldn't get involved." Alex looked away, toward the privacy fence that encircled the yard. "I suppose you don't want to get fairies started fighting. So the mythology goes."

The redhead was silent a moment. "It's a good story."

"You're Irish?"

She extended a hand. "Faith Siobhan Kelly. My grandparents came from county Donegal and county Wicklow."

Alex shook her hand briefly. "Alex Bridge. But then, I guess you already know that. I'm not Irish at all. My dad's people were all English, and my mother's . . . well, I'm not Irish. I just love the music. Are you going to tell me why I'm here?"

Faith blinked at the abrupt change in topic. "As a matter of fact, I am." She seemed to hesitate. Her eyes strayed almost involuntarily to Alex's belly. "How do you feel? Have you been comfortable here?"

Alex shrugged again. Her hands, never still, ran over the contours of the flute in her lap.

"Okay, that was a silly question," Faith said. "Alex . . . Ms. Bridge . . ."

"Alex is fine."

Faith nodded. "Alex . . . you're in a difficult position."

Alex waited.

"There's a mountain of evidence against you, both for the embezzlement and for the murder of Agent Wells."

"I didn't do it."

Faith looked at her sharply, then the look softened. She flipped open the file. "Agent Wells discovered how you transferred the funds from Cross Currents to the accounts on Grand Cayman."

"I don't have any accounts on Grand Cayman."

"The funds transfers from your computer at work have

been verified. They came from advertising accounts you were responsible for tracking. The FBI searched your apartment the morning after you were arrested and they found the bank documentation. The numbered account at the bank in Grand Cayman matches the documents in your apartment."

"I don't have any—"

Faith silenced her with a wave, the hard look returning to her face. She leaned forward. "Your gun was found near the spot where Wells was shot. It was the murder weapon. That gun . . . *your* gun, Alex . . . killed Paul Wells."

Alex blinked. She felt tears welling, and she willed them not to come. "I don't have a gun."

Faith flipped a few more pages. "You bought it last March at a pawnshop on Northwest Twenty-third in Oklahoma City. We have the receipt."

"I don't like guns," Alex whispered.

"It's a Smith & Wesson thirty-eight caliber revolver. It was used to shoot Paul Wells on that beach. You ran from the scene of the crime."

"I want a lawyer." Alex's fingers tightened around the flute.

"Alex, listen to me. Look, I think you just got in over your head. But you have to consider what you're facing here. With the murder of a federal agent, you could be facing the death penalty."

The words hung between them like polluted air. Alex blinked over and over again.

"I can help you," Faith said very softly.

"I didn't do it!" Alex screamed.

There was movement inside the house behind them. The female deputy marshal appeared at the kitchen door. Faith waved her away.

"Alex," Faith said, "the evidence says you did. The U.S. attorney will eat this up for political gain." She thumped the files in front of her. "It's the kind of evidence juries love, a paper trail. The gun, as physical evidence. You will be convicted."

Alex was silent a moment. "Joan," she finally said.

"Excuse me?"

"Joan. It's the English translation of Siobhan. You probably didn't know that, did you?" Alex rubbed the flat of her hand across her belly, then looked across the table. "Who *are* you?"

"My parents never told me the translation of the name. I'm just as glad they didn't. I work for a special unit of the U.S. government. We erase criminal records. We erase identities, in exchange for information. We believe you can help us, and we can help you."

"Oh God," Alex said, and started to cry.

Faith signaled the deputy in the house, and pantomimed the act of drinking. A moment later, the deputy opened the sliding door and handed her a glass of ice water. Faith put it in front of Alex and waited.

Alex took the glass and rolled it against her forehead, her neck, her arms. Little droplets streaked across the tattoo of the crown of thorns intertwined with the roses and crosses. It looked as if the tattoo were weeping along with Alex.

Alex tried to recapture the thought she'd had on the beach, just before she'd fallen and passed out in the surf. She'd almost been able to grab onto something, a half-formed memory. But then all she'd been able to think of was her baby—protecting her unborn son. The thoughts, the memories, had vanished like mist in sunlight.

She looked up at the woman with the Irish name and the intense green eyes. "Heat," she finally said, and she wiped her tears. "I can't stand the hot weather. I must have been from Siberia or someplace in an earlier life. Witness protection. You're talking about a witness protection program."

Faith blinked, still slightly off balance from the other woman's ability to shift topics so quickly and so radically. "It's sort of like that," she said. "Except we don't work with people who've witnessed crimes."

"You work with people who commit crimes."

"Yes."

Alex shook her head. "I didn't do anything." Her voice dropped to a whisper. "Why can't I remember . . ."

Faith leaned forward. "Remember what?"

Alex kept shaking her head. "I don't know. But I didn't take any money, and I didn't kill that man. He . . . he ruined my life. He . . ." She stopped, thinking of the implications of what she was saying.

"Alex," Faith said, nodding, "here's why we've come to you. Cross Currents Media is under investigation for all kinds of financial misdealings. Huge amounts of money, funneled in illegal ways. You were right in the thick of it. You had financial records of their revenues. We want to know who was doing what, and where, and how much. You give us the higher-ups at Cross Currents, and you'll get a new identity. You'll be relocated to a new city, with a job, where you can start over. There will be no prosecution for the embezzlement or Agent Wells's death. The amount of money you took is nickels and dimes compared to what the Cross Currents executives are doing. You'll be free to live your life, to raise your child."

Alex studied the other woman's face. Faith Kelly looked flushed, the line scar beside her nose a deep red. Alex wondered where the scar had come from. She swallowed some water from the glass. She gently placed her flute on the table and folded both hands over her belly. "I didn't do these things," Alex finally said.

"But you know what's going on at Cross Currents," Faith said.

"You still believe I did it, that I killed Wells."

Faith waited a moment. "Yes, I do. The evidence—"

"Yeah, I know, I know. The evidence is overwhelming." A tone of bitterness had crept into her voice.

"Cross Currents."

"Cross Currents. Do you know how much they pay me?"

"Around twenty thousand a year."

Alex nodded and blew out a breath. "You probably know

what I like to eat for breakfast and what I'm going to name the baby too. Right?"

Faith smiled. "No and no."

"Well, that's comforting, at least. They pay me that lousy salary, and I sit there for nine hours a day and watch money come and go from all over the country. Now you're thinking that I figured I'd help myself to some of it, that they'd never miss it, right? Don't answer that. No, I didn't embezzle that money. Yes, I made notes. I crawled around in the company database to see if I could figure out what they were doing."

"And did you?"

Alex shrugged. "I'm not a financial analyst, and I'm not a computer whiz. I'm a musician and a data-entry clerk who knew where to look. Every quarter, when a new earnings report would come out, I would laugh out loud because it didn't match up with the numbers I saw."

"You documented all this?"

"Sort of."

"What do you mean, sort of?"

"I downloaded files into my computer at work."

"Yes!" Faith said.

"Don't get too excited, Faith Joan. I deleted them all."

"You deleted them? Why?"

"When this so-called investigation started and I was suspended from my job, I deleted everything from the computer. I could see they were already looking for ways to hang me, so I decided I better not help them. Viewed the wrong way, someone could think that anyone who had that kind of information in their computer—"

"—Could have embezzled half a million dollars," Faith finished for her.

Alex shrugged wearily. "What happens now?"

Faith Kelly sounded as though she was struggling to keep her voice even. "You decide. You cooperate with us, help us reconstruct that data, give us names, give us every scrap of information you know about Cross Currents' financial dealings. We give you the new life I told you about. Or . . . you go back to the Galveston jail. You'll face the charges. In a federal court, charged with murdering an FBI agent, there won't be any mercy."

"They'll really prosecute a pregnant data-entry clerk for all this stuff?"

"It won't matter. The prosecutor will even turn your pregnancy around and make it work against you, somehow, some way." Faith leaned forward, placing both hands flat on the table. "It's a pretty clear choice, Alex. You have a chance to do the right thing now. I suggest you do it."

Faith stood up. "I'll give you some time to think about it." She pulled out a dozen or so stapled pages from the file and dropped them on the table. "Here's our entry questionnaire. It lets us get to know you even better, so that we can try to create a good situation for you in your new life."

Alex felt nothing but an overpowering weariness, a deep aloneness. She couldn't think straight, couldn't feel anything. She didn't look at the questionnaire.

Faith paused with her hand on the sliding door. "Tell me this. If you didn't do this, Alex . . . who did?"

Alex had no answer.

Faith nodded. "You have to trust me, Alex. Right now I'm the only chance you have for a life. If not for you, then for your baby." She slid open the door, then turned, almost as an afterthought. "One thing has been bothering me, though."

Alex looked up at her, eyes red but dry now.

"Why Galveston?" Faith said. "Why were you there?"

"Wells," Alex said. "He said to meet him there." She gave a slow, sad smile. "He said he'd cleared my name. And he said the truth was in Galveston."

7

FAITH WALKED BACK THROUGH THE HOUSE, THE FILE clutched under her arm. The male deputy on duty was Leneski, a friend of hers from when she'd worked in the Oklahoma City office. She exchanged a few distracted words with him and told him to call her if anything unusual happened with Alex Bridge.

On the street, she started the Miata and sat in it for a few minutes, letting the hot steering wheel burn her hands. She'd tried for a combination of tough guy and compassionate concern with Alex. She didn't know if she'd balanced it right or not. The other woman had denied everything, of course. But that, in and of itself, didn't surprise Faith. They all denied everything, all of them. No one in America was ever guilty of anything.

But something was wrong about all this.

She couldn't tell what—not yet. She had her instinct, and she had facts. Faith knew that instinct could often lead to uncovering facts, which was how cases were built. But right here, right now, she had facts in black and white, and they all indicated that Alex Bridge embezzled half a million dollars and then murdered the FBI agent who was investigating her.

But her instinct tingled. The only decent piece of advice her father had ever given her was that all a good cop has going for him is instinct. It had been a slow process, but over the last couple of years she'd come to understand and even to trust her own instincts. And they all said that something was wrong about Alex Bridge.

"Pregnant women don't kill," Faith said aloud, to the interior of the car. A droplet of sweat trickled down her forehead and off her nose. She switched on the air conditioner.

"Now *that* is really logical and scientific," she said as the air began to hum.

But the conclusion was inescapable. Faith had read reams of case studies, from college to the academy and beyond. As long as crime statistics had been kept, there were very few murders committed by pregnant women. The few that had were generally crimes of passion, not premeditated, cold-blooded executions.

Faith shook her head. Maybe this was just first-recruit jitters. The evidence was compelling, from the computer records of funds transfers to Grand Cayman, to the gun on the beach and the receipt from the pawnshop. Faith dropped the Miata into gear and pulled onto the suburban street, which had the all-too-suburban name of Hyacinth Hollow Road. She put Joe Sample's *Ashes to Ashes* CD in the car stereo, and as Sample's funky piano filled the speakers, she headed toward Interstate 40, which would take her eastward back into the city.

Half an hour later she was at home, changing from "business casual" into her best black suit, with a white silk blouse and medium-heel black pumps. She brushed out her hair—as usual, she couldn't do much with it—and touched up her makeup. She was on her way out of the bedroom when she caught sight of her computer on its little desk by the window.

She checked her watch. There was still plenty of time, and she hadn't checked her mail in several days. She sat down, taking care not to rumple her suit jacket, and booted up the machine. She logged onto the mail program and watched as the messages came in—eighty-one of them.

She smiled, then methodically deleted the ones for Canadian pharmacies, porn websites, penis enlargement—she always had to laugh at that one—and credit card offers. That left a smattering from the listservs she belonged to: one for women in law enforcement, one for unsolved crimes, one for jazz, one for marathon runners. There was one from a college friend who had just made sergeant in the St. Louis Police Department. And one from her brother.

"Well, Sean Michael Kelly," she said to the screen, giving the middle name the Gaelic pronunciation of *MEE-hall*.

> Hey F,
> The Chinese say, "May you live in interesting times." It's a curse, not a blessing. My times are way too interesting lately. I should've gone to Ireland and raised turnips. Hang in there,
> S

Faith frowned. Sean's e-mails had been growing more and more cryptic lately. He was a U.S. Customs Service agent, currently assigned to Tucson. His messages were fewer and further between than ever, and now he rarely asked anything about how she was doing, or about the family. He was eighteen months older, and they'd grown up with the intense rivalry and close relationship of siblings who were close in age and temperament. Now, she thought, he needed a kick in the pants from his "little" sister. Her fingers went to the keyboard, and almost out of habit, hit the Delete key.

"Oh, shit," she muttered. She'd meant to hit Reply so she could write back to him. Now Sean's message was gone.

She stared at the screen. Her heart almost stopped.

On the left side of the e-mail screen was the list of her local folders: Inbox, Outbox, Sent Items, Deleted Items, Drafts.

Deleted Items was in bold, and beside it the number of messages she'd deleted. She moved the mouse and clicked on it. The messages appeared, and there at the bottom was Sean's note, completely intact.

She'd deleted it, but it wasn't gone.

"That's *it*," she said. Part of the mystery of Alex Bridge, right in front of her, in an e-mail message from her brother that was gone, but not gone.

Faith checked her watch, grabbed her purse and the Bridge case file, and ran out of the house.

First Presbyterian Church of Oklahoma City was one of the oldest churches in a young city. Gothic in architecture, constructed of gray stone, it sat at the corner of Northwest Twenty-fifth and Western Avenue, at the edge of two paradoxical cultures: Little Saigon, home of the city's thriving Asian community, and the Paseo, the quirky, bohemian arts district. Faith's friend Scott Hendler, who'd grown up in Oklahoma City, had once told her that the church itself boasted four working pipe organs.

She left the Miata in a corner of the nearly full parking lot and hurried to the main sanctuary entrance. It was huge inside, with cathedral ceilings, ornate fixtures, and exquisite stained glass.

The front half of the church was filled with dark suits and somber dresses. She recognized many faces. A good bit of the federal law enforcement community in the area was here. She saw Leo Dorsett and Cal Riggs, the Special Agent in Charge and Assistant SAC of the Oklahoma City FBI office. Several people from the Marshals Service were there as well: she saw her friend Derek Mayfield, and Chief Deputy Mark Raines. Down at the front was the U.S. attorney himself, Owen Springs, who was in the midst of his campaign for the U.S. Senate. She looked for Scott Hendler but didn't see him anywhere.

Faith sat in the back of the church. While many of these people could be considered friends, her entry into Department Thirty had been awkward and of necessity put a psychological distance between her and conventional law enforcement officers. Given her direct involvement in the case of Paul Wells and Alex Bridge, that distance had expanded to roughly the size of the Grand Canyon.

The crowd hushed and a tall, attractive blond woman in a

black dress and pearls walked slowly into the aisle. Following her, hand in hand, were two little blond girls, about ten and seven years old. The younger one's tears were flowing freely, while her sister held her head up in an almost defiant manner. Faith could imagine her thinking: *I won't cry in front of all these people. I won't cry. I won't . . .*

Next came the silver casket, wheeled by two men wearing white gloves. Faith assumed they were the funeral directors. Behind the casket walked six men, three groups of two. The pallbearers. Scott Hendler was one of them.

Faith swallowed. She'd only met Paul Wells once, at the annual federal law enforcement barbecue last summer. Hendler had introduced them. Wells had transferred to Oklahoma City about a year before that, one of the new breed of FBI agent, a CPA with extensive computer skills. His specialty, of course, was financial crimes. Wells had been pleasant, but Faith was distracted. At the time she was only a month or so past having killed a man, having run the case that earned her the gratitude of the president.

The service began. Faith missed most of the Bible readings and listened to the eulogies from Cal Riggs and U.S. Attorney Springs. Springs praised the fallen agent's community work, from volunteering at a summer day camp for special-needs children to coaching youth soccer. He vowed justice for the Wells family. Faith flinched as if he'd thrown something at her.

A young woman got up and sang a capella in a clear, earthy alto: *"Tempted and tried, we're oft made to wonder, why it should be thus all the day long. While there are others, living so wicked, never molested, though in the wrong."*

Having grown up Catholic, Faith hadn't heard many of these kinds of spirituals. Her mind strayed, and she wondered if Alex Bridge knew this song.

"Farther along, we'll know all about it, farther along we'll understand why. Cheer up, my brother, live in the sunshine. We'll understand it all, by and by."

Faith had to get out. She slipped out of the church and

down the front steps. Outside, in the midday heat, she started to breathe again. Owen Springs had stood in a pulpit and promised "justice" to Special Agent Wells's family. Faith was prepared to give sanctuary to his killer. And for what? Information on financial misdeeds by some faceless corporation. Was that a fair trade? Somehow she didn't think Paul Wells's wife and daughters would buy it.

In ten more minutes people started to come out the door. A few people spoke to her. Mayfield gave her a hug, Chief Deputy Raines talked to her for a few minutes. She said hello to Cara Dunaway, one of the female FBI agents from the local office, whom Faith had come to know over the last year. U.S. Attorney Springs nodded to her, then looked quickly away.

The casket came, with the funeral directors positioning the pallbearers. They each grabbed a handle and slid the remains of Paul Wells into the back of the hearse. The funeral directors thanked them and slammed the door closed.

Faith caught Hendler's eye. "Hey," she said.

"Hey yourself." Hendler was three inches shorter than Faith, so he had to lean up to kiss her on the cheek. "I didn't know you were coming," he said. "If I'd known, we could've ridden together."

Faith shrugged. "I was out and about this morning, and barely had time to go home and change."

"Oh."

They were silent for a while, watching as Mrs. Wells and the girls were escorted into the limousine. The widow had kept her composure, but Faith saw the wetness around her eyes. The younger daughter was still crying—great keening sobs that wracked her little body. Every now and then she would murmur, "Daddy, Daddy, Daddy."

"What do you say let's get out of here?" Hendler said.

"You're not going to the house?"

"No. Funerals give me the creeps anyway, much less going to the house and eating casseroles while people sit around and make small talk."

Faith nodded.

"Buy you a cup of coffee?" Hendler said.

"Okay. I'll drive if you buy."

"It's a date."

Faith smiled in spite of the circumstances. Scott Hendler was understated in almost every way, with the exception of his tendency to shout "Holy shit!" whenever anything unexpected happened. Otherwise he was soft-spoken and calm, so calm that he'd earned the nickname of "Sleepy Scott." He was about three years older than Faith, with a growing, premature bald spot. They'd been seeing each other for over a year now, and had been friends longer than that. Hendler generally didn't complain about Faith's need to go slowly, and he was a terrific listener. Still, she wasn't sure she loved him, and neither of them had brought up the l-word, although she suspected he wanted to. She was comfortable with him, and in her complex life, comfort was enough for now.

She drove the Miata to Java Dave's on Tenth, where she ordered a cup of dark roast and Hendler got a double latte. They sat in a booth and drank in silence for a couple of minutes.

"How's she doing?" Faith finally asked.

Hendler shrugged. "Okay, I guess. She's a strong lady, but she and Paul were really close. And he adored those girls."

Faith nodded.

"And such a strange case," Hendler said. "It's not some big organized crime, money-laundering operation or fraud or anything like that. This woman, this *nobody*, wants to set up a trust fund for her own kid and embezzles half a million. Paul gets too close to her, she lures him down to the Gulf and kills him."

"She lured him down there?"

"Yeah. A lot of people in the office were wondering why the hell he went to Galveston. Well, he told me before he left. This Bridge woman called him. She was ready to come in, but said she'd only surrender to him in Galveston. Said the truth was down there."

Faith jumped and spilled coffee.

Hendler jumped back instinctively. "Holy shit, Faith! Watch it!" He grabbed napkins and mopped up the mess.

"Sorry," Faith said.

He said he'd cleared my name, Alex Bridge had told her. *And he said the truth was in Galveston.*

"At least we've got her in federal custody now," Hendler said. "Evidently the marshals took her to a transfer center. No one's sure which one, though."

Faith's heart was pounding wildly. "Scott," she said— *careful, careful!*—"how did Wells know she was going to set up a trust fund for her kid?"

"I don't think that's hard evidence. That was just Paul's gut instinct. He didn't really think the woman was a criminal at heart, but just got tired of being poor and used her brains and the company computer to move some money around."

Faith exhaled very slowly. She thought about the e-mail message from her brother, how it was gone but not gone. "Was her computer impounded? Is that how he got the evidence of the money transfers?"

"Yep, Paul executed the warrant the day after the company put Bridge on suspension." Hendler finished his latte and pushed the cup away. "What's up?"

Faith shook her head. *Deleted but not deleted. Gone but not gone.*

"Faith? Hello?"

"Were the transfers deleted?"

"What?"

"The electronic transactions, the money transfers to Grand Cayman. Had they been deleted from the computer?"

"Whoa, Faith. This is all still ongoing, and technically you're not—"

"Goddammit, Scott! Tell me!"

Hendler leaned forward, his bland face clouded. "What's going on?"

Faith was silent.

"Faith, what's going on? Why are you so interested in all this?"

"Scott . . ."

"Oh, shit," Hendler whispered. "Holy shit. Bridge isn't at some transfer center. You've got her. Don't you? *Don't you, Faith?*"

Faith raised both her hands in a "Calm down" gesture.

"You're going to protect her. Thirty's going to protect Paul's murderer!"

"Scott . . ."

Hendler pushed himself away from the booth and was out the door of the coffee shop before Faith knew what was happening. She left her own coffee half-finished and followed him out into the sun. He was wandering the parking lot, hands jammed in his pockets.

"Scott, listen to me," she said.

"No! I won't listen to you!" He circled the edge of the building, dodging a car coming to the drive-through window.

"It's not that black-and-white, Scott."

"Yes it is!" He turned on her. "Jesus, Faith! She murdered a federal agent in cold blood. Now those two little girls don't have a father. That's pretty damn black and white to me!"

Faith grabbed the sleeve of his suit jacket and spun him around. "I can't explain it to you, and I won't pretend to try. That's insulting to both of us. But I have a job to do. This is my job now, Scott, and whether you like it or not—hell, whether *I* even like it or not—there's always more to it than you think."

Hendler stood there, clenching and unclenching his fists. Some of the anger seemed to drain away after a moment. He kicked a stray pebble in the parking lot. "Dammit," he said.

"Scott, please," Faith said, "just tell me. Did Wells have to recover the data, or was it still there in the computer?"

Hendler's shoulders sagged. "It was all still there. That's

part of why Paul said she wasn't much of a criminal. She didn't even bother to cover her tracks."

Faith let go of his arm.

"He was an accountant, Faith," Hendler said. "The guy was an accountant, for Christ's sake."

"I know," Faith said. "Scott . . . where's the computer now?"

"The box is in the evidence room. Paul was the best computer forensics guy in our office. He made a copy of the hard drive that he'd been working on. After he was shot, the hard drive was sent over to Nina Reeves on contract. She'll finish what Paul started." He met Faith's eyes. "Does it matter now if she does?"

"It might," Faith said.

Hendler nodded. "You're going to have a hard time explaining this to any law enforcement in this town."

"I can't explain it. You know that."

"Yeah, I know, but . . . you've still got some friends in law enforcement now. But people won't understand this. The murder of an FBI agent, especially one like Paul . . ." He shuffled his feet. "Faith, you're my . . ."

Faith raised her eyebrows.

"I mean, I care about you," Hendler said. "But I don't understand this, either. And look . . . I don't know who you've got securing her or where she is, but if this gets around, those people may not understand."

Faith stared at him.

"Do you see what I'm saying to you?" Hendler said. His voice was very quiet.

Faith nodded.

"Okay, then. I've got to go."

"I'll take you back to your car."

They drove back to First Presbyterian in silence. Faith put her hand on Hendler's arm before he got out of the Miata. "I'll call you later," she said.

Hendler didn't reply.

Faith watched him drive away, her heart thundering, rivulets of sweat running down the back of the silk blouse. After Hendler's car turned the corner at Twenty-third, she took out her legal pad and scribbled some notes. Alex Bridge had told her that Wells called her to go to Galveston. Wells told his colleagues just the opposite.

The data showing that Alex transferred nearly half a million dollars of Cross Currents' money to Grand Cayman was still on the hard drive of her computer, easily reachable by anyone who went looking for it. Yet, Alex said she'd deleted the information she'd downloaded about Cross Currents.

Faith thumped her pen against the pad.

Alex deleted information that would have incriminated Cross Currents, yet saved the data that would incriminate herself. She thought again of her brother's e-mail, how she'd deleted it but it wasn't really gone.

"So who's lying?" she asked the interior of her car.

She needed to talk to Nina Reeves. She had to know what was really in Alex Bridge's computer.

The man with the brown-gray goatee, sitting in his Taurus, snapped a couple of more pictures from the parking lot of the huge Asian market on the other side of Western Avenue.

He noted the time, then made a call on his cell phone. "She went from the safe house to her home, then to the funeral. Hendler took her for coffee, and they had a bit of a blowup in the parking lot."

"Blowup?" said the man on the other end of the line.

"Lovers' quarrel, professional jealousy, who knows? I don't have audio."

"Maybe you should."

"Too risky."

"True. Stay with her. We need to know where she goes, what she does, who she meets. Too bad we can't tell what she's thinking."

The man with the goatee exhaled noisily. "That's a little beyond what I can do."

The other man sounded amused. "So it is. Do what you can, then."

The goateed man grunted and ended the call. This was a strange surveillance. Faith Kelly was an unusual target, not at all the kind he was accustomed to stalking. But then, he rarely concerned himself with why he did what he did.

He put the car in gear and moved to catch up with his target.

8

SMITH SAT ON A RUSTIC WOODEN BENCH ACROSS THE concrete walkway from John Brown's Fort. A short summer rain squall had passed through the mid–Appalachian region a couple of hours ago, and the sidewalks were still slick. Most of the tourists had hibernated during the rain, but they'd begun to come out again, cameras clicking.

He held one newspaper, today's *Washington Post.* Another was folded neatly on the bench beside him, the *Houston Chronicle.* More unrest and ambushes were unfolding in Iraq. The *Post* carried an excellent piece on Bosnia, a dozen years after the war there ended. A group of American clergy had visited the country recently and the story was written from their point of view. Congress was haggling over the budget.

The *Chronicle* carried many of the same stories. And of course, in that part of the country the Eduardo Rojas death-row story continued to have large play. Rojas's unique appeal was about to be filed with the U.S. Supreme Court, and there was evidently some bickering amongst the court's factions as to whether it should hear the case. The story—regionally, at least—had captivated the public's imagination.

America was truly a great country, Smith mused. But his smile quickly faded, looking at John Brown's Fort. He remembered the words from Brown's last letter, written the day the man was hanged: *I, John Brown, am now quite certain that the crimes of this guilty land will never be purged away, but with Blood.*

This guilty land, indeed, Smith thought.

Nowhere in either newspaper was there any mention of the murder of an FBI agent on a beach at Galveston. Nowhere was there a reference to a young clerk named Alex Bridge being arrested for the murder and for embezzling half a million dollars from Cross Currents Media.

It was as if all his meticulous planning, all his careful, painstaking designs, had vanished into the night air over the Gulf of Mexico.

He heard run-down boot heels *thock-thock*ing on the concrete, folded the *Post*, and placed it beside him.

"What, no cryptic comments today?" said the man with the boots. Today he was in black slacks, a white dress shirt, and red club tie loosened at the throat. Smith checked his feet: the boots, which didn't match the rest of his clothing, were there. "No philosophical statements?"

"You seem distraught," Smith said without moving.

The other man smiled hollowly and tossed an envelope onto Smith's lap. "Department Thirty," he said. Smith looked up at him. "It seems to be a bit of an open secret inside the Justice Department. Outside DOJ, it's almost totally anonymous. Even at Justice, people don't talk about it. It took quite a bit of doing for me to get this information."

Smith crossed his legs at the knee. "From the attorney general himself?"

"Never mind that. The person who gave me this called Department Thirty the 'dark twin' of Witness Security. They do what WITSEC does, except with the people who commit the actual crimes." The man wrinkled his nose as if he'd caught a whiff of garbage. "They wipe out criminal identities in return for information. It's not a large program. They only have a handful of people in the program nationwide. I couldn't find out exactly how many."

Smith began to tap a finger against his kneecap. "What could they possibly want with Alex Bridge?"

The other man propped one of his scuffed boots on the bench. He pulled out his handkerchief and mopped his forehead. "The rain doesn't even bring any relief, it just gives us higher humidity." He folded the handkerchief carefully and returned it to his pants pocket. "All I can conclude is that it must be something to do with her employer. There have been a lot of rumblings about Cross Currents Media. The SEC and FBI are on a crusade now to deal with these 'corporate crimes.' Ever since Enron, it's become open season on every corporation's books. The president's even jumped on that bandwagon."

"Yes," Smith said, nodding. "I may have outsmarted myself this time."

"What do you mean?"

"Setting her up for embezzling from a corporation that was engaged in illegal financial dealings. So this Department Thirty comes along and believes the disappearance of $498,000 and the murder of one FBI agent can be traded for the big corporate fish. It makes a sort of sense."

The other man picked up the two newspapers, plopped them onto the wet sidewalk, and sat heavily beside Smith. "This sort of thing is just what I didn't want to happen. She's not supposed to talk to the government. She's not supposed to have any credence at all. Her credibility was to be totally destroyed, so that no one would believe anything she said." His voice dropped. "Do you understand?"

Smith looked at him, irritated. The man was making a habit of dropping his voice melodramatically and asking Smith if he understood. It was cheap theatrics, and while it may have intimidated those who dealt with the man in his daily life, Smith only found it annoying. "But the only information the government wants from her is financial, all about her employer. They're not going to be asking any questions about . . ."

The booted man leaned away from Smith, his mouth set in a grim line.

". . . other issues," Smith finished. "It shouldn't come up."

"What if she brings it up?" said the other. "They want dirt. What if she tells them *everything*? Now they'll be listening to her, whether it's about Cross Currents, or about me."

Smith waited a few moments. A small knot of tourists walked by, a man and a woman with a little boy toddling between them. The man wore a Boston Red Sox jersey, the woman a T-shirt with HARVARD LAW on it. The man glanced at the two men on the bench, looked away, then looked back toward them again. He said something to the woman, who also cast a furtive glance.

"Some of your admirers," Smith said.

The family was out of earshot by now. "I don't have admirers," the other man said. He *thock*ed a boot heel on the sidewalk. "When you're in my position, there's no such thing as admirers. Most people don't even know I exist, much less have a clue as to what I do."

"Do I detect a note of bitterness?"

"You detect a note of dislike for stupidity."

Smith smiled. "We have something in common after all, then, sir." The smile faded. "Alex Bridge is accused of murdering an FBI agent. The trail of evidence leads right to her. If she brings up anything outside what Department Thirty wants to know, it'll sound crazy. They shouldn't put any stock in it."

"*Shouldn't*, you said."

"It all depends on who's talking to our Ms. Bridge. They might believe her. They might not."

"I can't stake everything on *shouldn't* and *might*!"

"True. I can't be certain. The human factor means there's no certainty." Smith slapped the envelope against his leg. "Do we know anything of Department Thirty's people?"

The other man pointed at the envelope.

Smith opened it and took out a single paper-clipped page. "They have a national office, somewhere around D.C., then six regional offices around the country with one case officer each. The regional offices are Hartford, Charlotte, Indianapolis, Salt Lake City, Sacramento . . ."

"And Oklahoma City," Smith said. "Smaller cities. Interesting idea."

"I have the names of the six case officers on there. I had to make threats to get these. But in the end, I got what I wanted. I usually do."

Smith looked the man in the eye. "But not always."

They held each other's gaze for a moment. Smith knew the other man was beginning to wonder just who held the power in their relationship. It wasn't a position the man with the boots was accustomed to, and it frightened him. Smith saw it in the way his eyes finally moved, in the tilt of his head, in the way his boot heel moved back and forth on the pavement.

Smith smiled.

"I don't want to see you again," the man with the boots said.

"Of course not," Smith said. "I'll deal with Department Thirty, and I'll find Alex Bridge. But you should know, now that things have changed, that it might not be enough just to ruin her. There's always a chance they *might* believe her."

The other man stood up. "So be it, then," he said after a moment, and thumped away.

Smith watched until the Escalade had pulled out of the parking lot, then went back to the list of Department Thirty office locations and case officers.

He took out his pen and drew a large circle around the one that read, *OKLAHOMA CITY, OKLAHOMA—FAITH KELLY.* Then he put the envelope in his pocket and started toward the parking lot. He looked once back at John Brown's Fort. It would be a while before he would be able to come here again.

9

FAITH TRIED TO CALL HENDLER'S HOME NUMBER AND his cell, but got voice mail both times. Was he really unavailable, or just watching his caller ID and avoiding her? That didn't sound like the Scott Hendler she knew, but then, she'd never seen him as agitated as he'd been this morning.

She puttered around the house, ate a sandwich without really tasting it, and did some halfhearted straightening of the living room. Her mind was still in overdrive, her body tense and tight. She contemplated driving to Edmond to the Jazz Lab, but she didn't know who was playing tonight and didn't really want to go alone to a bar. She could have called a friend, but then, almost all her friends were in law enforcement, and she didn't think many of them would feel like going out after this day.

She'd already called Nina Reeves and was going to see her first thing tomorrow morning to talk about Alex Bridge's computer. Reeves was an independent contractor, a technical consultant who did work for many of the area law enforcement agencies, including the Bureau. She'd turned her small apartment into a digital wonderland of computers, sound equipment, and video. If it was digital, Reeves was a wizard with it. She and Faith had become close a couple of years ago, right after Faith's mentor Art Dorian was murdered and she found herself starting to make the descent into Department Thirty's world.

"To hell with it," Faith said aloud. She'd just decided to go for an evening run when the phone rang.

"My dear Officer Kelly," said the man she knew as Yorkton.

Faith grunted. The man couldn't just say hello. "Well, Mr. Director," she said back to him.

"How goes the case?"

"I met Bridge this morning. She says she's innocent."

"Of course. What's your sense of her access to Cross Currents information?"

Faith hesitated. "I'm not sure yet. I'm still working on it." She decided against telling him about the paradox of the computer. For now, at least. "Tell me something. How do we identify people for recruitment?"

There was a long pause from Yorkton. "We identify our national objectives, be they political, military, economic, or otherwise. We study backgrounds of large pools of people. We wait and see if some of them make choices that get them into trouble. Then we assign a case officer and they begin the recruitment process."

Faith sat down heavily and kicked off her shoes. "That's about as vague as everything else you've told me since the day I met you."

Yorkton chuckled. "Look at it this way. In the Cold War era, our objectives had to do with containing Communism. Since Oklahoma City and September 11, it's been terrorist cells of any kind, domestic or foreign. Occasionally a new topic creeps into the national consciousness and we have to keep up with it."

"Corporate scandals."

"Indeed."

"So after the SEC started its inquiry into Cross Currents, you decided there might be possibilities there."

Yorkton didn't pick up the sarcasm. "Exactly. We began a surveillance of around two hundred of their employees. Our Ms. Bridge was in the top ten from the beginning. Her psychological makeup, family history of abandonment, her tendency to drift from one thing to another, low income . . ."

"I get the picture, though after meeting her I'm not sure it's the same picture you have. You're really pushing this. Are you getting pressure from somewhere above?"

Yorkton was silent.

"What, don't case officers get to know such things?" Faith said.

"It could taint your management of the case."

The man was utterly maddening, she thought. "So who's putting on the pressure? The attorney general? Who?"

Yorkton exhaled into the phone. "You are a very frustrating young woman, Officer Kelly. Brilliant, but frustrating. Let's just say that our mutual friend at sixteen hundred Pennsylvania Avenue has an interest in this issue."

Faith tapped her foot. "The president is *not* my friend."

"Oh, on the contrary. He thinks very highly of you."

"Okay, fine." She tapped some more. "I do remember that he's been talking a lot about these corporate scandals and getting tough on them. He's thinking ahead to reelection, and he's trying to make sure the average voter doesn't see him as just another tool of big business."

"And so it goes," Yorkton said. "Which brings us back to Ms. Bridge."

"Working on it. It's too early for me to tell much. But I have to say this after meeting her: She doesn't strike me as a murderer. Maybe an embezzler, I don't know. That's just an impression, and I may be way off base. The evidence all points the other way."

"You'll keep me posted, then?"

"I will."

"You're doing well, Kelly. Arthur Dorian would be proud of you."

Faith hung up and stared at the phone for a few moments. Her life had turned into a Salvador Dalí painting, too surreal to be understood. People like the director of Department Thirty were living proof of it. The fact that the president of the United States considered her a friend was definitely proof of it.

She took out all the information she had on Alex Bridge and spread it on the wooden dining room table. In a few minutes she had papers fanning out in a half-moon shape. She placed her legal pad in front of her and thought about Alex.

Even though she didn't have the questionnaire back yet, and Alex hadn't yet even consented to enter Department Thirty protection, Faith could start working on an identity for her, at least on the basics. Like a name.

She sat completely still. How do you give someone a whole new life? How do you erase everything they've been and create a new human being? A living, breathing adult with a past, a present, and hopefully, a future.

She doodled on her pad, drawing a square with a circle inside it.

A name. She needed a name.

She doodled a car, then a cat, then more squares and circles.

Alex. Alex. Alex was an androgynous name. Okay, we'll stick with that.

She remembered the *Saturday Night Live* bit of a few years ago, with the androgynous character named Pat. Faith smiled a little and wrote Pat on the legal pad. That was followed by Chris, with the alternate spelling of Kris.

"This is crazy," she said aloud. She was sitting at her dining room table, creating a new person and thinking of old late-night comedy sketches.

In another minute she added the name Lynn to her list. That was followed by Taylor and Tyler, then Robin. She smiled again. Robin Stricker had been her first boyfriend, in fourth grade. By the time they reached junior high, he'd been known as "Rob." She'd also known a female Robyn at the academy.

She circled the name Robyn, and then laughed at the absolute absurdity of it all. She was contemplating giving this name to Alex Bridge, simply because she'd known both a male and a female with that name.

Faith sobered quickly and began thinking about a last name. Alex Bridge did not have Irish heritage, but was very interested in Irish culture and music.

"I'll make her Irish," she said.

She thought about her own family, the Kellys and her mother's people, the O'Connors. She closed her eyes and thought of the trip to Ireland when she was in college, and the walk she'd taken in a cemetery in western Donegal, where many of her ancestors were buried. She pictured the grave markers, gray and weathered.

She began writing names. Moloney. Miller. Cooley. Egan. O'Brian. McMartin. McNulty. Connolly.

Alex Bridge. A short name.

She looked back at her list. Robin Cooley. No, that didn't sound right. What about Robin Egan?

"Hmm," she said.

Robin Egan. She scratched out the *i* and made it a *y*.

Robyn Egan.

"What's in a name?" she said. She thought of her other five cases, scattered through her region of Oklahoma, Texas, New Mexico, Kansas, and Missouri. All had been given new names by Art Dorian. They'd all had to make the same adjustment. They'd all had to tell what they knew to Department Thirty to escape prosecution for whatever crime they'd committed.

Then, for no reason, she thought of what she considered the "other" side of Department Thirty, the unintended consequences, the people who believed they were one person, only to be told at some point in their lives that they were someone else. Ryan Elder, whose parents had once been the world's top assassins-for-hire. Eric Anthony, whose parents participated in an infertility experiment and wound up in the middle of a forty-year conspiracy that nearly brought down a president.

She pushed the papers away from her. She would work on it in the morning, and then she would visit Alex Bridge again. For now, it had been one hell of a day, between her initial visit to Alex, Paul Wells's funeral, and the bad scene with Hendler.

Alex Bridge. Robyn Egan.

Faith stopped cold. Ever since she'd officially joined Department Thirty, Faith had felt somewhat ambivalent, even cynical, about its mission. But now, sitting at her dining room table and beginning the process that would lead to a new identity for Alex Bridge, she felt something else, a creative jolt, a rush of adrenaline.

She felt power.

She could go into databases that held details of surveillance on thousands of people. She could even order such surveillance herself. With a few strokes on a computer keyboard and maybe a couple of phone calls, she could probably find out almost anything about anyone. Sometime in the next few days, she would make a phone call to an office that Department Thirty called "The Basement," where she would request official documents to bring Robyn Egan into existence—a birth certificate, Social Security number, driver's license, voter registration. And it would all be done, simply because she asked for it.

Faith squeezed her eyes closed, opened them, tapped a fingernail on the wooden table. She had to be very, very careful. That kind of power brought corruption. The former director of Department Thirty, Daniel Winter, had given in to it. It would be so easy for anyone else to do the same. She called up a mental picture of Art Dorian, who had stayed above the fray for thirty years, wallowing around in all of this but without dirtying himself.

Of course, Dorian paid with his life too.

It had been an emotional day, and Faith's mind was still in overdrive. She decided she needed to go for that run after all. She changed clothes and pushed herself through the dark residential streets of The Village, doing nearly four miles altogether.

When she finished, the impurities were gone, washed away. Or at least they'd receded to a far corner of her mind.

She had too much to do to muddy her thoughts this way.

But then, perhaps those muddy thoughts would be what kept her balanced in the crazy gray world of Department Thirty.

She showered and went to bed. She fell asleep instantly, and she dreamed of someone playing a flute.

It was just past one A.M. when the phone jarred her awake. She knocked a few things off her nightstand before locating the phone and mumbling her name into it.

"Sorry to wake you, Kelly," said a too-alert female voice. "This is Deputy Marshal Hagy. I'm on duty with your . . . suspect."

Faith sat up. She didn't know Hagy well. The woman had recently transferred to Oklahoma City. "It's all right, Hagy. What's up?"

"She's insisting that she has to see you," Hagy said.

"What, now?"

"You got it. She was asleep and everything was nice and quiet. Griffin was napping and I was just sitting here reading. Then she comes running out of the bedroom screaming to call you, that she has to talk to you. We got her calmed down, but she says it can't wait until morning."

"I'm on my way."

With very little traffic, it only took Faith twenty minutes to reach the safe house on Hyacinth Hollow Road. Both Hagy and Griffin were awake now, looking nervous. Alex Bridge sat on the floral-print sofa in the living room, wearing a long blue maternity nightshirt. Her feet were bare, and Faith saw the Celtic tattoo on her ankle for the first time.

"I remembered," Alex said, before Faith was even fully through the front door.

Faith looked at Hagy and Griffin "Would you excuse us, please, Deputies? Take a break."

They both looked doubtful, but walked outside into the night. Faith looked back to Alex. "Remembered what?"

Alex's hands were never still, the index and middle fingers of her right hand alternating in an unusual rhythm. *The curse of the musician,* Faith thought.

Alex got up from the sofa, pushing herself with both hands. "Hard to get up these days," she said. She folded one hand over her belly. "You came. You actually came in the middle of the night."

"That's what I do," Faith said. "It's part of my job. What did you remember?"

"On the beach that night, the night that Wells . . ." She blinked hard. Instantly the tears were running down her face. She wiped them angrily. "I hate these mood swings. Raging hormones, my body all confused. I cry all the time. I never used to cry this much. Now I'm a faucet. I can't help it."

Faith gave her a tissue from a box on the end table. "Here you go."

Alex wiped her eyes again. She rubbed a hand over her belly. "You're not judgmental. That's good." She dropped her hand, the fingers still dancing. "But you still think I'm guilty."

Faith shrugged.

"On the beach," Alex said. "I was running. They were chasing me, screaming at me to drop my gun. A gun I never had. I was running, and you just can't run when you're this pregnant. You can kind of do a fast trot, and that's it. I tripped and I fell right at the edge of the water, into the surf. And I had this thought. No, not really a thought, a memory."

"Tell me," Faith said.

"A year ago, maybe more than that, because it was winter, I got a phone call. I was on my lunch break. There's a little courtyard in the Cross Currents building and I was out there having my sandwich. I was the only one out there, because it was cold. But I don't mind: cold doesn't bother me. I'm eating and my cell phone rings, and it's a man and he says . . ." Alex wrapped both arms around herself.

She waited a moment, hugging herself. "He says Tabananika was murdered because he knew the truth about the

Blackjack Comanches. And he says *he* knows the truth, and that I should know it." The tears welled again. "He said the truth was in Galveston."

Faith felt a muscle in her jaw twitch, an involuntary reaction. She thought for a moment before speaking. She had to tread carefully. "Alex," she said. "I don't know what—"

"I'm not crazy!" Alex shouted, then her voice softened. "To tell the truth, that's what I thought about whoever this was on the phone. I thought it was insane. Tabananika was some ancestor of my mother's, but I don't know anything about him. And I never heard of the Blackjack Comanches. I've never really been into all the Indian stuff, and I don't know any of my mother's family. And I'd never even been to Galveston. So I just hung up and forgot about it."

"Alex—"

"Please," Alex said. "Please listen to me. Please believe me. You're keeping me here, you think I committed all those crimes, you want to make me another person. At least let me speak."

"I'm listening; it's just that—"

"You don't see how this ties in to the embezzlement and to Paul Wells. A couple of months or so after that phone call, I got an e-mail at work. I don't know who it was from. You know the little line where it says who the sender is? There wasn't a name there, just an e-mail address. I didn't pay much attention until I opened the message. But there it was again, all about Tabananika and Blackjack Comanches and learning my own history. There was another name in there, not an Indian name, but I don't remember it. And there it was again, saying I would have to go to Galveston for the 'final truth.'"

"'The final truth.'"

"That's what it said. But I just deleted it, I didn't have time for this stuff. Gary and I were about to get married, and I was playing a lot of musical gigs, and I wasn't interested in some Comanche weirdness. But look"—she started to circle the room—"it wasn't long after that, everything came crashing down. That money disappeared and Wells starting calling me and Cross Currents suspended me."

Faith took a deep breath. "How does this explain what's happened?"

"Someone's trying to ruin me, destroy my life. It has to have something to do with that call, that e-mail. Nothing else makes sense."

The two women stood facing each other. Alex was breathing hard, high color in her cheeks. Her short, streaked hair was tangled, her dark eyes lined in red and still moist. A worry line slashed her forehead.

She looks like she's been through hell, Faith thought. She waited a moment. *But then, so did Paul Wells's wife and daughters.*

"This doesn't make sense either, does it?" Alex said. "It sounds like a crazy conspiracy theory. That's what you think. Isn't it? Be honest with me."

Faith waited, then nodded. "Yes."

"Don't you see?" Alex whispered. "They were telling me these things and trying to get me to do something. I don't know what, but *something*. When I didn't do anything, they ruined me. Set me up for the embezzlement, the whole thing. Then Wells must have found something that would clear me: that's why he wanted to meet me in Galveston. But they found out about that, killed him, and set me up for it."

"Alex, Wells told his colleagues that you called him, that you lured him to Galveston."

Alex's eyes widened. "That's not true! Why would I—"

"To surrender. That you were ready to come in and admit everything."

Alex stamped her foot. "No! I don't have anything to surrender for. He called me! Why don't you people understand?" The tears were coursing unchecked down her face again. She balled her fists at her side. "You have to believe me! Someone is trying to destroy me!"

"Why?"

"I don't know!" Alex shouted. She made a sudden lunge

at Faith, but the movement was awkward with her swollen belly. Faith sidestepped her and grabbed both her arms firmly. "Let me go!"

"Alex." Faith's voice was quiet. "You're getting hysterical, and it's not good for you or your baby. You need to settle down."

Alex squirmed in Faith's grip. "I didn't do it. I didn't do any of it."

Faith very slowly let go of Alex's arms, and the shorter woman backed away.

"I think you should fill out that questionnaire," Faith said. "I think you should take steps toward a new life for you and your baby. You've been through a lot, and you're getting a chance here. I don't know what to think about this stuff you just told me. Yes, it sounds crazy"—she smiled slightly—"but I'll tell you this, Alex: in my world crazy is perfectly normal a lot of the time. I'm meeting in the morning with the person who has the records from your computer. We're going to see what kind of data can be recovered from it. Then we'll see where the case goes from there."

"I'm not a 'case,'" Alex said. "I'm a person. At least I was, until all this started. Things were starting to go right. My music was really taking shape. I'd finally met an incredible man that I wanted to be with. But Gary and I . . ." She closed her eyes, a soft pain in her face. "And then it all came apart. We were going to have a baby, but then Gary was gone, and then he was dead, and then I was a criminal, and now I'm nobody. You're telling me I don't even exist anymore."

Faith remembered something Art Dorian had told her a long time ago: *It's about the people.* How had Art been able to keep all this straight? How could he tell what was real and what wasn't?

"I'm sorry, Alex," Faith said. "You do exist, and you're not just a case. But right now you need to rest. For you, for the baby, just rest. I'll think about all this, I'll talk to the computer specialist, and I'll get back in touch with you." She pointed at the questionnaire, which sat on the end table. "Go ahead and fill that out. It'll help me understand you better. It'll help me come up with some answers."

"You think that little questionnaire will tell you why someone would want to totally ruin my life?"

"No," Faith said.

"Then I don't see a reason to fill it out."

Alex turned and walked down the hall toward the bedroom, leaving Faith standing alone in the living room. Faith waited a couple of minutes, then turned and walked out into the night.

10

NINA REEVES LIVED AND WORKED IN AN UPSCALE apartment complex along Northwest 122nd Street in far north Oklahoma City. She was still something of an enigma to Faith: a gorgeous blue-eyed black woman, even in her midforties she looked more like a runway model than a technical wizard. She'd dropped tantalizing hints about her past without giving many details: childhood in Bermuda, ten years in Britain, and living all over the United States, including stints in both New York and Los Angeles. Faith had no idea how she'd come to be in Oklahoma.

Reeves opened the door almost before Faith took her finger off the bell, as if she'd been waiting just inside. "Faith, my dear," Reeves said in her beautiful Caribbean/British accent. "What a delight to see you."

The two women embraced, and it occurred to Faith that Reeves had many of the same speech mannerisms as Yorkton. But with Reeves, the language sounded perfectly natural, while Yorkton only seemed pretentious.

"Hello yourself," Faith said, breaking the embrace. "Keeping busy?"

Reeves stepped aside to let Faith into the apartment, then closed the door behind them. "The world is a busy place, so I'm a busy woman. Come in, come in. Want some tea? Have you had breakfast?"

"No, no. I've already eaten."

"I was just getting myself some tea. Have a seat."

The living room of Nina Reeves's apartment was unlike any living space Faith had ever seen. Instead of sofas and coffee tables and TV sets, Reeves's space consisted of a horseshoe-shaped desk that was loaded with carefully arranged computers and audio and video equipment. She had all the latest digital editing systems and video monitors mounted on stands at either end of the room. Stereo speakers the size of large file cabinets anchored the desk. There were at least six separate computers.

Faith sat in the only "guest chair" in the place, an orange folding director's chair. "I think you have even more stuff in here than the last time I was here."

"Quite sure that I do," Reeves said from the kitchen. "I've taken on a bit of consulting work for Homeland Security now, in addition to all the FBI and state police projects."

Faith shook her head. "I don't see how you—" A loud thump sounded from the rear of the apartment. "What was that?"

"Oh, dear," Reeves said, coming back into the living room with a cup of tea. "I had an overnight guest who's rather in a fog in the mornings."

Faith knew this apartment only had one bed, and after getting to know Reeves these last two years, she understood that Reeves's frequent "overnight guests" had neither name nor gender. It was a topic of endless fascination for other federal law enforcement officers in the area, but Faith never asked. She had a hunch this was part of the reason Reeves had come to respect her.

"Ah," Faith said sagely.

Reeves smiled. "Ah, indeed. How is Scott these days? I haven't seen him in a while."

Faith shrugged. "Okay."

Reeves settled into her chair inside the horseshoe, looking over her teacup. "Really, Faith."

"Okay. Okay, okay, okay. We had a big blowup yesterday. It was about this case, the Bridge thing."

Reeves blew on the tea and set the cup down very gently. "I admit that I didn't believe you called me just to chat about my new equipment. So you have an interest in the strange case of young Ms. Bridge."

"So what do *you* think is strange about this case?"

Reeves smiled again. "As you know, I'm just a techie and not too well versed in human nature."

Faith smiled back. Reeves had some of the best people instincts of anyone Faith knew. "Uh-huh."

"So any impressions I might have should be taken with the proverbial grain of salt."

"Proverbially."

"Yes." Reeves took another sip of tea, then put the cup down again and leaned back in the chair, folding her hands in her lap. "Paul Wells was a fine FBI agent. He knew money, he knew accounting procedures, and he was quite good with computers. He was perfect for the assignment he had, investigating financial crimes."

"You're about to say *but*," Faith said.

"But . . . he didn't seem to have much judgment about people."

"How so?"

"All I know of this case is from Wells's reports and the little bit of work I've done with the hard drive, after it was sent over here. If I didn't know better, I'd say that young Ms. Bridge had been set up."

Faith's heart hammered. She leaned forward.

"But," Reeves said, "there's the business of the evidence. It's all there, the t's crossed and the i's dotted. Everything tied up nicely with ribbon. The funds transfers, where the money came from and where it went . . . all still on the hard drive of her computer."

"But it doesn't feel right."

Reeves nodded. "Exactly! You've learned to look beyond the so-called hard facts and see what's under them. And underneath the perfect trail, this most certainly does not feel right." She leaned back again. "When I first met you, you would have argued this point with me. You would have insisted that the evidence alone was enough."

Faith tapped her foot, thumping out a little bit of Joe Sample rhythm. "What I do now has changed a lot of things about me."

"So it has. I'm not going to ask about your connection to the case. I have a hunch I already know, and it's not my affair. But I will ask you this: What do you think I can do for you?"

"You have her computer here, right?"

Reeves's hand fluttered down to the top of a computer CPU that sat on the floor next to her. "I have the hard drive."

"What have you gotten from it?"

"I told you about the documents relating to the embezzlement. Account numbers, amounts, the advertising accounts from which the funds came. There were six different documents with that range of information. The rest is fairly ordinary."

Faith thought of Sean's e-mail, deleted but not gone. "And all of that was easily accessible, right on the hard drive?"

"It came right up." Reeves steepled her fingers. "Ask me what you really want to ask, Faith."

"Did you go further than that? I mean, *can* you go further? There's a way to recover deleted material, right?"

"Certainly. You've had some computer forensics training, then."

"An overview in grad school, and the basic course at the academy. But then"—Faith smiled widely—"I'm not a techie, either."

"And so it goes. What are you looking for?"

"Financial documents, mainly dealing with the earnings reports of Cross Currents."

Reeves's eyebrows went up.

"Now we're getting into the territory where I have to stop telling you why I want what I want," Faith said. "I'm edging into Department Thirty shadow lands now."

"What a pleasure to see that you're so philosophical

about it." Reeves pressed a button on the front of the CPU and watched as the computer booted up. "I'll need Quick View," she muttered.

"What's Quick View?"

"It's a little utility program that lets you do a quick view of any file without opening it with an application. Say it's a Word file. You don't have to actually open the Word program to get to the file. Marvelous little creation." She entered a few keystrokes and clicked the mouse a few times.

"If I remember my academy course, when you have a Windows-based computer, it doesn't really delete something, even if you hit the Delete key. Just like an e-mail I got from my brother yesterday. I accidentally deleted it, but found it in the Deleted Items folder."

Reeves nodded without taking her eyes from the computer monitor. "Exactly. The image is still there. The system just marks the space as free, or slack, space. The problem— or, if you're like me, the challenge—is that if that slack space is used again, then the files would be overwritten and gone for good. And that's something we don't know until we get into the system and dig around a bit."

"Wait a minute." Faith dug into her little soft-sided brief-case and came out with her rapidly expanding Alex Bridge case file, which included copies of Wells's original notes and reports, as well as Yorkton's Department Thirty case profile and her own notes. She'd begun keeping it with her at all times, never leaving it at the office or at home. She turned pages back to the beginning, until she found a copy of the internal Cross Currents memo that placed Alex Bridge on ad-ministrative leave. She noted the date, then turned a few more pages. She found the subpoena for impounding the computer, and Wells's report and chain-of-custody forms showing when it had been impounded.

"Here," Faith said, waving the forms. "The computer was im-pounded the morning after Alex was placed on suspension."

Reeves saw it immediately. "So maybe that slack space wasn't reused after all."

"Maybe not."

Reeves began moving the mouse again. "Then let's get to work."

Reeves settled into the meticulous, painstaking work for which she was renowned, and after the initial bout of excitement, Faith began to feel the fatigue creeping in on her. She replayed the late-night excursion to the safe house, the strange encounter with Alex Bridge, her near hysteria when recounting the phone call and e-mail she said she'd received.

Of course she's hysterical. Her world doesn't exist anymore. She's seven months pregnant, alone, charged with horrible crimes, and then there's me. She can't figure out if I'm friend or foe.

Now I'm nobody, Alex had said last night. *You're telling me I don't even exist anymore.*

Faith dozed a little in the director's chair while Reeves worked on the computer. Periodically she heard more thumps and the sound of someone shuffling around in the back of the apartment. Shortly after noon Faith stood up and stretched. She pulled out her cell phone and called the safe house. Leneski reported that Alex was fine, playing fiddle in the kitchen. She was more subdued, less talkative today. Faith thought she detected a note of satisfaction in Leneski's voice when he told her that.

Faith waited a moment, then called Hendler's office. She left another message on his voice mail, then gave up.

"Earnings reports," Reeves said.

Faith swiveled around to face her. "Found them?"

Reeves tapped the computer monitor with one manicured nail. Faith came around the horseshoe and leaned over her shoulder. "These are spreadsheet files," Reeves said. She traced them down the screen, tapping headings like "_Spring," "_Winter," "_Public Files," and "_Internal Only." Then there were other, more enigmatic headings of document files: "_Catbird Memo" and "_Barbara Allen Cruelty."

"What's with all the underscores in the file names?" Faith asked.

"Deleted files," Reeves said. "When they're recovered, the system puts an underscore there to note that it had been deleted earlier."

"Can you view them from here?"

Reeves clicked on "_Spring." Faith leaned in farther. Columns of numbers appeared.

"Oh, yes," Faith whispered. Now she needed Alex Bridge to explain what each column meant, to authenticate the data.

They went through several more documents, including several of the ones with strange titles. There were copies of many memos between individuals, but Faith began to see a common thread: no names were mentioned. There was still no clue as to the meaning of some of the enigmatic titles of the files.

Faith upped her estimation of Alex Bridge's intellect. She'd made sure there were no names in the documents she'd scavenged. Whether to protect herself or someone else, Faith didn't know. Now she'd have to go back to Alex to fill in the blanks.

But the nagging question came roaring back: Why had the self-incriminating material not been deleted, when the material that implicated Cross Currents was?

Faith put a hand on Reeves's shoulder. "You're a miracle worker, Nina. Can you put all this on disc for me?"

"Technically, no."

Faith looked at her.

"Chain of evidence. This came from the Bureau."

"Well, I'm certainly not the Bureau," Faith said.

Reeves shrugged.

"This is Thirty's case now," Faith said. "I'll call my boss, he'll call the director, and the director will call Dorsett in the local office. Dorsett will call you."

"All of which could take a while."

"It could. You know how we government bureaucrats are."

"Whatever you are, Faith, I think a bureaucrat is most assuredly what you're *not*." Reeves did a few mouse clicks and a different screen came up on the monitor. "I'll make your disc, to save a little time. I'll wait for SAC Dorsett to call me and act surprised when he does."

Faith patted the other woman's shoulder. "Thanks."

"I'll also put together a full autopsy report on this machine."

"Autopsy report?"

"It's computer forensics. Just extending the metaphor."

"Uh-huh."

"Anyway, I'll write a full report with appropriate legal jargon and chain-of-custody confirmation, all the usual things that could stand in court." More mouse clicks, a few keystrokes. "Oh, here's her e-mail. Do you need anything from here?"

Faith remembered the wild conversation last night, Alex's near hysteria. Cryptic phone calls and e-mail messages. *What the hell?* she thought. "See if there's one in there with a subject of something like 'Your History.' "

"And this has to do with . . ."

"Shadow lands," Faith reminded her.

"An interesting place to live," Reeves said, scrolling down. "It appears she didn't use e-mail all that much."

Faith wasn't listening, eyes riveted to the screen.

"Stop!" she said.

In the center of the screen was an e-mail with the subject line: History Lessons.

The sender was listed as johnbrownsbody@hubopag.com.

"Oh my God," Faith said. "She was telling the truth." She pointed at the screen. "Open that."

Reeves clicked on the message.

> *To Alex Antonia Bridge.*
>
> *Tabananika was murdered because he knew the truth about the Blackjack Comanches. It is time for you to learn the same truth. Learn your own history. Learn of the Blackjack Comanches. Jonathan Doag's family can help you—he, too, paid the ultimate price. He came from Pittsburgh, PA. But the final truth is in Galveston, TX.*

There was no signature.

"Intriguing," Reeves said.

Faith's heart was beating wildly again. Alex was telling the truth about this. And if this was true, what else was?

She read the message again, then a third time. She glanced back up at the sender: johnbrownsbody@hubopag.com.

"What's Hubopag?" she asked.

"It's a free Web-based e-mail service, like Yahoo or Hotmail. Even more intriguing is the screen name, though. John Brown's Body?"

Faith wasn't listening. "Can you trace this? Can you find out where it originated?"

"You know better than that. I can locate the Internet service provider and maybe narrow it down to a region of the country, but I can't go much further than that."

"Dammit," Faith said, "I need to know who this is."

"You knew about this, then."

Faith nodded. "Alex told me about it, last night. She was spinning out some grand conspiracy theory about people setting her up for the embezzlement, the murder, everything. I thought it was nonsense. Even in Department Thirty, there's such a thing as being too far out in left field. Why would someone want to frame a person like Alex Bridge?"

"Maybe you should ask John Brown's Body."

"Maybe I should. Can you print me a couple of copies of that?"

"Of course." Reeves clicked and one of her six printers whirred. "Does this change your view of the case?"

"It has to."

"Do you still think she did all of it?"

Faith waited a moment. The questions still nagged, but the evidence was still overpowering. The money did go to Alex's offshore account. Wells did find the bank transactions. Wells was still dead, killed with Alex's gun, which was found near the scene of the crime.

The crime scene.

In addition to the computer discrepancies, something still bothered Faith about the crime scene, the Galveston beach. She'd seen the photographs taken by the officers on the scene, and the detective's sketch of the area. But there was still something not quite right. The problem was, Faith couldn't reach it. It stayed carefully hidden from her, lurking somewhere in those shadows she'd come to know so well.

Reeves handed her two printouts of the e-mail message from John Brown's Body. "What now?" she asked.

Faith stuffed the printouts into her case file and zipped up her briefcase. "I'm going to see Alex Bridge, and I'm going to try to sort out what's fact and what's fiction."

"Not easy in your world, Faith."

"Not even a little."

Faith sat in the Miata in front of Reeves's apartment and called Yorkton. She asked him to begin the chain of phone calls that would officially place the evidence into Department Thirty's jurisdiction. He sounded pleased with her progress.

Then she called the safe house. The female deputy marshal on daytime duty, Paige Carson, answered.

"This is Kelly," Faith said. "I need to speak to Alex."

"I think she's in the bathroom."

"I'll wait."

Five minutes later, Alex Bridge's soft, husky voice came on the line. "Hello?"

"The e-mail. The one you said you got after the phone call. I have it."

"What?"

Faith rattled the printout and read the message aloud. "Is that it? Is that what you're talking about?"

Alex's voice dropped. *"Yes!* Yes, that's it! How did you . . . ? That's it! So now you believe me?"

"I don't believe anything right now. But I see you were telling the truth about this."

"Read it to me again."

Faith read it again.

"Oh God, that's *it!*" Alex said after a long pause. "I'm not crazy. You see that I'm not crazy."

"No, Alex, I definitely don't think you're crazy. I also have your data from the computer, all the Cross Currents material, with all your cute little file names."

Alex's voice became guarded. "I deleted all that."

"Remember my friend the computer specialist? She recovered the data. I'm coming out there. Just sit tight."

"I'm not going anywhere, am I?"

"Just hang on. We'll figure this out."

She clicked off the phone and closed her file. As always, Faith found many questions and precious few answers everywhere she looked. Political pressure from far up the ladder, high-tech evidence, a dead FBI agent, a corporate scandal in the making, a young pregnant woman's life in limbo . . . It was a Department Thirty case, all right.

"Just another day at the office," Faith muttered, put the Miata in gear, and roared out of the parking lot.

Smith watched her pull out. He'd been rereading the slim dossier he'd built on Faith Kelly in the last twenty hours or so. There hadn't been time for him to properly research her, so he only had the basics. Twenty-seven, single, from a law enforcement family near Chicago, master's degree, Federal Law Enforcement Training Center, former deputy U.S. marshal before joining Department Thirty last year. He had her home and office addresses and telephone numbers from the Department of Justice's personnel database.

But he had no *feel* for her. He knew only cold facts. He felt ill prepared for the job. Smith's successes came from exhaustive preparation, knowing his subjects inside and out. Once he *knew* them, he could manipulate them so easily, without them even knowing they were being manipulated.

He'd arrived in Oklahoma City just before midnight, the first time he'd been back to the city in several months. He admitted that he missed the night summer air of the prairie.

It felt different—more open, more free—than the East. Truly a land of opportunity for him.

He'd begun watching Faith Kelly's house at just past five o'clock in the morning. He'd made an approving note in his dossier when he saw her go for her predawn run. Now she'd been at this apartment complex for more than three hours, and left in a fit of nervous energy.

Time to draw her out.

Time to plant some seeds.

Smith smiled. It was really more than a job. It was a calling. Even though he kept up the façade of being a detached professional for the clients' sake, he enjoyed it. He loved the meticulous nature of it, the planning that went into it, the different personas he assumed at various times. He liked to watch the fruits of his labor as people's lives tumbled out of control around them. People thought they controlled their own lives and destinies, but the reality was different. Lives were managed externally, outside the realm of any individual's control. And Smith had learned how to manipulate those external factors.

Time to plant some seeds, Faith Kelly.

He put the rental car in gear and followed her out of the parking lot.

11

FAITH PICKED UP THE TAIL JUST AS SHE TURNED SOUTH on May Avenue from 122nd Street. It was a dark blue four-door economy model, something like a Cavalier or a Neon. Traffic was in its heavy lunchtime mode, but the blue car stayed with her, two cars back in the outside lane.

She'd become much more adept at spotting tails. She'd learned some of how to read traffic at the academy, but she'd only really put it into practice since she joined Department Thirty. Things—and people—tended to jump out of those shadows from time to time.

So who the hell is it?

In theory, no one outside the Department of Justice knew what Department Thirty was. Its existence was one of DOJ's most closely guarded secrets. In reality, Faith knew that people talk and that there were indeed some "civilians" who knew what Thirty was and what it did.

It could be related to any of her five active cases, or her pending case . . . Alex Bridge. Another, darker thought crept in as she remembered what Hendler had told her. It could be the FBI. They knew that she was involved in the Bridge/Wells case now, and they didn't take the murder of one of their own lightly.

But we're all supposed to be on the same side.

She snorted a little at that. There were oo many sides now that no one could keep up with them all. She checked the mirror: still there. A single man was driving, though she couldn't make out features. He wore sunglasses, and looked to have light-colored hair.

She crossed Hefner Road, now not far from her own home in The Village. Faith had no patience with foolishness like this. She also had no time. She had to talk to Alex Bridge. The whole thing was about to break open, one way or another. She felt a rush of adrenaline.

"You want to play?" Faith said to the rearview mirror. "Okay, I'll play."

She spun the Miata's wheel to the left and went quickly around a slow-moving minivan. A horn honked somewhere.

"Sorry," she said, and Faith floored the accelerator.

Smith was humming along with Grieg's *Peer Gynt Suite No.1* on the car radio, remembering that one of the things he liked about Oklahoma City was that it had an excellent classical music station, better than those in many larger cities. "In the Hall of the Mountain King" was reaching a crescendo when the gold Miata suddenly darted out in traffic and sped away.

Smith smiled. He'd wondered how long it would take her to see him. He'd used the classic techniques of staying a couple of car lengths behind, matching the Miata move for move. Anyone with half a brain could pick up a tail like that. Of course, Kelly hadn't known he followed her from her home this morning. He'd been both more and less subtle then, staying right behind her in the rush-hour traffic.

The rental car wasn't made for performance as the Miata was, but he knew Faith Kelly wouldn't get too far ahead of him. She wouldn't be too reckless. She came from a law enforcement background, and she wouldn't want to endanger the proverbial "innocent bystanders."

He hummed a few more bars of Grieg, then he, too, jerked to the left in traffic and began to close in on the gold car.

The blue car was still with her, and Faith could tell the driver wasn't worried now if she spotted him. She caught the green light at Britton Road but had to swerve quickly around a furniture delivery truck in the middle of the intersection. Tires squealed, leaving rubber marks in the street.

She mentally went through the route in her mind, considering options. The blue car hung with her, staying close but never trying to overtake her. Her pursuer seemed to want to follow her, rather than take his first opportunity to run her off the road.

Another mile brought her to the light at Wilshire Boulevard, then to Grand Boulevard, a strange, meandering thoroughfare that circled Oklahoma City and had once marked the city's outer limits. Faith almost sped through the light at Grand, then she remembered what lay a little to the west.

Halfway through the intersection, she spun the wheel back to the right and jumped a median onto Grand, grimacing at the sound of the car's suspension.

Her pursuer was surprised but wasn't as far along, so he made the turn more smoothly. This was a quieter, more residential area of brick homes, right on the edge of Nichols Hills, the city's wealthiest old-money enclave. But Faith knew that the street opened up in short order. It widened and climbed onto an overpass over Lake Hefner Parkway. There, ahead and to the right, was the lake, one of the jewels of the city's north side.

When she came down from the overpass, Grand had become South Lake Hefner Drive. Jogging and biking trails lined the park area to the right. Thick trees momentarily hid the lake from view.

Faith knew instantly where she was going. She and Hendler had come here on a picnic last Memorial Day. She still didn't know the city as well as a native, but she was beginning to learn its quirks, its nooks and crannies.

She glanced in the mirror. The blue car was just coming off the overpass. Faith stepped on the gas. Now it was critical that she get far enough ahead of him so that he would lose sight of her for just a few seconds. Half a minute at the most.

She cut the corner where Portland Avenue dead-ended at

the entrance to Stars & Stripes Park. The Miata raced across the bike trail and bounded into the park, the lake straight ahead and now to her left as well.

At noon on a weekday, there were few people around the park. Hefner itself wasn't a swimming lake, left mainly to sailors and fishermen. An old man sat in a folding chair on the bank to the left, turning and shouting something toward her. No doubt she was scaring the fish.

Ahead, the narrow strip of road branched off into a one-way circle with a picnic pavilion and playground area at its center. She veered to the right and into the circle.

"Confused yet?" she said to the blue car behind her, glancing into the mirror again.

What was she doing?

Smith downgraded his opinion of Faith Kelly. She wasn't thinking clearly, and was now literally driving herself into a corner.

He'd only been to this park once, but he remembered the layout. On the other side of the circle was a brick and concrete plaza, and a low concrete wall. Beyond that was the lake. In the center of the plaza was a huge raised flagpole, presumably giving the park its name.

There was no way out.

Then again, he hadn't had time to study Faith Kelly. He didn't know the way her mind worked.

He decided she was either very clever or very foolish.

Smith followed her into the circle.

Faith knew she would only have seconds out of the blue car's sight to make her move. She scanned the area: An old woman was walking a dog. A young mother was swinging a toddler on the playground. She saw no one around the plaza.

As soon as she made the curve and was shielded by the picnic pavilion, she swung the car onto the grass. In one smooth motion, she had her nine-millimeter Glock out of the glove compartment and tucked into the waistband of her jeans.

Faith sprinted out of the car and onto Eisenhower Plaza. With only seconds to go, she didn't glance back this time.

Brick walls enclosed the entryway of the plaza with the bronze bust of Eisenhower. Faith pounded around the wall, where the plaza opened toward the lake. It was a strange layout, with at least a dozen brick alcoves, each open on one end, and each holding two plaques engraved with quotes from Eisenhower.

She veered away from the alcoves, skirting the concrete steps that led up to the flagpole. She was steps away from the wall and the lake now. It had rained for three days last week, brilliant summer thunderstorms that dropped several inches of rain on the area. The lake level was up, and water sloshed right around the top of the wall. Hendler had told her that during the flash floods of a few years ago, the entire plaza was underwater.

She heard the other car behind her, tires screeching, the door opening and closing.

The man would be on her in seconds.

She ran flat-out to the far left end of the curving stone wall, grabbed the edge of it, and vaulted over it into Lake Hefner.

Smith didn't like not knowing what was going on. He knew that most operations failed in the planning, not in the execution. Planning was his forte, it was his life. If a plan was good enough, the execution could not fail. It was that simple.

This was a "secondary" operation, not part of the overall plan, hence not something he had plotted out. He hadn't had time to properly deal with Department Thirty and Faith Kelly, so it was more of a challenge than he'd anticipated.

Still, Kelly had driven herself straight into a place from which she had no escape. He knew she'd graduated from the Federal Law Enforcement Academy, and that was one of the first and most basic lessons: never get into a place if you can't get out.

He'd heard her footsteps quickening, and then they abruptly stopped. Smith slowed, not liking that at all.

He had a fleeting thought: *What if I, not her, am the one who's in a place from which I can't get out?*

Then: *Don't be ridiculous.*

He slowed almost to a walk, coming around the corner of the plaza's entryway. The plaza was empty.

The last time Faith and Hendler had come to this park, the lake level had been way down, and Hendler showed her that just on the other side of the wall was a line of large rocks. They'd been most of the way out of the water that day, arranged as stepping-stones, and the two of them had run laughing from rock to rock, each daring the other not to fall in the lake.

Today the rock she was standing on was underwater, and she was waist-deep herself. She had to crouch just a bit to make sure the top of her head wasn't showing above the wall. She clung to the edge of the wall with one hand, resisting the pull of the water, gripping the Glock in her other hand.

She heard the footsteps enter the plaza, then slow, then stop altogether.

Come on, she silently urged him. *Come closer. I have a big surprise for you.*

Somewhere far away, she heard a dog bark. Behind her, on the lake, was the sound of an outboard motor.

Steps scrabbled across the plaza. She remembered there was loose concrete by the brick alcoves with the Eisenhower plaques. It sounded like the man was scuffing through it.

Over here. I'm waiting for you.

The steps stopped again, then turned.

That's right. Keep coming.

The water pulled at her, and she had to tighten her grip on the wall to keep from being pulled backward off the rock.

Likewise she tightened her other hand on the butt of the Glock. Surprise was essential.

The man above her cleared his throat. He was close, very close.

The steps started up again. He was moving along the wall. If he reached the point where it curved and he looked over it, he would see her.

A few more steps. Timing was everything.

Just a few more . . .

Faith let go of the wall, wrapped her other hand around the Glock in a solid firing stance, and stood up to her full height.

She turned to her left. The man was six steps away.

She swiveled her head, long hair trailing her. While she was crouching, the ends of her hair had been in the water, and now they flung droplets onto the wall.

Faith leveled the gun.

"You are one lousy driver," she said to the man.

The look on his face said it all: unmitigated shock from a man who wasn't used to being surprised. At first his bland face froze, then a muscle in his jaw began to grind.

"First turn around," Faith said, keeping her voice very level. "Face away from me. Then get on the ground, face-down."

Much to her surprise, he cooperated without hesitation. She pulled herself over the wall, regained the firing stance with the Glock, and placed a soaking-wet Reebok in the middle of the man's back.

"I'm not armed," Smith said.

"Uh-huh," Faith said. She straddled his back, using her legs to pin his arms, and searched him. He was telling the truth. No weapon. "I'm going to get off you and walk around in front of you. You're going to be absolutely still until I say move."

"This really isn't necessary. I assure you, Ms. Kelly, if I wanted to hurt you, you would be dead right now, and you would have no clue who or why."

"Oh, really? We'll get to who and why in a minute." Instead of moving off him, Faith put the Glock against his left ear.

"I'll grant you this. I didn't expect this move. You have the upper hand. Will you get off me now, please?"

"Thanks for the compliment. Who are you?"

"Isaac Smith. Sometimes I'm known as John Brown's Body."

Faith climbed off him and moved warily in front of the man. "Get up," she said. "Slowly."

He did, shaking his arms about. "Thank you. That wasn't necessary."

Faith gestured with the Glock. "Walk over there. Back to the bust of Ike, inside the brick wall."

Faith covered him from behind, and they walked back to the plaza entryway. The area around the bust was much less open, offering some amount of protection.

Faith kept the gun on him. "You sent the e-mail to Alex Bridge."

Smith nodded. "Yes."

"Did you make the phone call?"

"Yes."

"What does it mean?"

Smith shifted from one foot to the other. "Is that really what you want to ask me, Ms. Kelly?"

"See, you're not getting what's going on here. I ask you the questions. You give me the answers. How do you know me?"

Smith gave a modest shrug. "Faith Kelly, case officer for Department Thirty, U.S. Department of Justice."

Faith was silent, not moving a muscle.

"That's all right," Smith said. "Don't confirm or deny the existence of your department. You don't have to."

"What's your interest in Alex Bridge?"

"Now, *that* is an intriguing question. Lower your weapon, please. I've already told you—"

"Yeah, I know. It's not necessary. But it's such a comfort to me. What's your interest here?"

"My interest," Smith said, "is justice."

Faith waited, barely breathing. For a moment she heard nothing, all sensory input seemingly muted. Then it came back, a little at a time: the water lapping at the wall on the plaza; the dog barking; a sailboat just coming into view; the heavy smell of the midday heat.

"Perhaps I should ask you the same question," Smith said.

"Meaning?"

"What is *your* interest in Alex Bridge?"

"I'm not answering that. If you know what Department Thirty is, then you know what we do."

Smith looked off toward the lake, catching a glimpse of the brilliant white sailboat gliding by. "You're in the business of information, and I'm sure Alex has some that you, or someone, thinks is important."

"Why did you call her? Why did you send that e-mail with all the vague stuff in it?"

"It's like this: I know things, but I can't prove them. And it really doesn't mean anything to me whether they're proven or not. But it means something to Alex, whether she knows it now or not. And since you've inserted yourself into all this, now it means something to you. All I did was try to point Alex in the right direction."

"Why?"

"Because I don't think that justice delayed is justice denied. I think that no matter how long it takes, justice should be pursued." His hazel eyes bore in on Faith. "Don't you?"

"What's all this business about Galveston? Everything keeps coming back to that. Even before Alex went there, you were telling her the truth was in Galveston."

"It is. But it's useless for her to go there now, if she—and you—don't understand what came before." Smith shuffled his feet again. "Then again, maybe it would be useful for *you* to go there. Have you been to the crime scene?"

"No."

"Maybe it would be a good idea, then. Have you made a timeline of everything that's happened to Alex Bridge? No, probably not. That would also help you."

"I'll run my own investigation, thank you. I'm going to lower my weapon now. If you make a move I don't like, I'll shoot you. That's pretty simple to understand, yes?"

Smith smiled. "You are a surprise, Ms. Kelly. May I call you Faith?"

"I don't care what you call me. Why are you doing all this? And don't give me any more crap about believing in justice. Justice is a concept, and a pretty good one, but it's also pretty rare, so let's leave it to the Supreme Court."

Smith's smile faded. "The answer's in the question. You'll find out why I'm doing this, once Alex does what she was supposed to have done a long time ago." He cocked his head toward the lake. "Tell me something. Do you believe Alex Bridge stole $498,000 from Cross Currents Media? And do you believe she shot that FBI agent?"

Faith blinked. The water from the lower half of her body was pooling on the concrete under her, some of it running in little streams toward the wall, as if it were trying to get back to the lake. "I don't know," she finally said. "Do you?"

Smith smiled. "If you want answers, first ask the right questions." He spread his hands apart. "May I go? You don't have any authority to arrest me, if I understand Department Thirty correctly. You could shoot me, but you can't hold me. And who knows? We may be able to help each other."

Faith backed up a couple of steps, until she was behind the Eisenhower bust. "Go on. You're right, I can't arrest you." She tucked the Glock back into her waistband.

"Follow up on those things I mentioned to Alex. The proof is there. I know it's there for the finding."

"How can I find you?"

"You'll find me."

The man was as vague as Yorkton, she thought. "Go," she said.

Smith folded his hands together as if praying, then gave a short deferential bow in Faith's direction. He turned and walked out of the plaza.

She waited until she heard his car leave the park before running to the Miata, parked at its odd angle on the grass. An elderly black man on a bicycle rode by and glared at her. She shrugged at him.

In the car, she stowed the pistol and reached for her cell phone. After Leneski brought Alex to the phone, she said, "I have to check something out. I'm going to catch a flight to Galveston. I'll be back late tonight, maybe tomorrow morning."

"What are you—"

"Later," Faith said. "Just hang on."

She pressed END, then made another call. When Yorkton's voice came on the line, she said, "We have a problem."

Smith waited until he was back in his hotel in downtown Oklahoma City before he made his calls. The encounter with Faith Kelly had left him feeling oddly exhilarated, the way he felt when he overcame a challenge. It remained to be seen exactly what kind of challenge the woman was, but he was intrigued by her, and was beginning to get a glimmer of understanding as to how her mind worked. Contrary to what he had first thought, Department Thirty's entry into the equation might prove to make the whole experience all the more enjoyable.

The man with the scuffed boots answered on the fourth ring. "I'm in Oklahoma City," Smith said. "I've met with the Department Thirty woman. She's curious now, wondering how I fit into what she already knows."

"Dammit, you talk in circles! Make some sense, if you can."

"It's perfectly sensible. You paid me to make plans, to create a design that would ruin Alex Bridge. The design just looks slightly different now, and it involves Faith Kelly and Department Thirty."

"You're sure the Kelly woman will lead you to Bridge?"

"Oh, yes. I have no doubt of it."

Smith clicked off without waiting for a response. He ordered a chicken Caesar salad and mineral water from room service, then took off his shoes and sat on the bed. He flicked on the television and surfed through bad daytime programming until he found *CNN Headline News*. Baghdad, Belfast, Los Angeles, Washington, Jakarta, Houston. Tragedy, corruption, death, and stupidity. He turned off the TV.

At exactly three o'clock, Smith made another call. A craggy, drawling voice answered. "Yes?" the man said.

"Give him a message," Smith said.

"Oh, hell," said the other man. "It's you. All right, go ahead. I'm seeing him in the morning."

"You're such a busy man. How do you have time to fit everything in?"

The other man coughed, deep rattling phlegm-laden coughs, into the phone. "Don't screw around with me, son. I don't have time for it, and neither does he. What's the message?"

"Tell him Mary Surratt will have to be hanged."

There was a long pause. "Jesus Christ, boy," the other man finally said. "Do you always talk in these goddamn historical riddles?"

Smith closed his eyes, willing patience. "He'll know what it means."

"Tell me what it means, then."

"You don't want to know. You don't *need* to know. For all of our sakes."

"Tell me."

Smith shook his head. "Mary Surratt was alleged to have been one of the conspirators in the Abraham Lincoln assassination conspiracy. She was the first woman ever hanged in the United States of America."

"The point, dammit!"

"He'll understand," Smith said. "There are certain . . . parallels to our situation. A powerful man will be brought down. Perhaps not in the same way as President Lincoln, but the similarities exist. A woman, who may or may not have been guilty of anything at all, will probably die."

The craggy voice took on an air of disbelief. "What the hell is this all about?"

"Give him the message," Smith said.

12

July 15, 6:30 P.M.
Houston, Texas

THE IDEA OF PALM TREES IN TEXAS SEEMED SOMEHOW
wrong to Faith.

She'd spent a fair amount of time in Texas in the last year
or so. Two of her cases lived in the state, one in a Dallas suburb and the other in the small town of Brownfield, in the far
west. The Texas Faith knew was rolling prairie land, much
like her home in Oklahoma City, or flat, desertlike tableland.

But here she was in south Texas, and here were the palm
trees. She'd caught a Southwest flight into Houston, then
rented a car and was headed south on Interstate 45. She
drove through the seemingly endless suburbs, rapidly approaching land's end. In half an hour she drove over the
causeway, left the mainland, and came down on Galveston
Island.

The palms were more pronounced here, towering in the
road's center median. It was an odd mix: pickup trucks and
palm trees, Texas drawls and shrimp boats, cowboy boots
and beach flip-flops. An unusual city with a notorious red-
light past, now marketing itself as a family vacation spot.

It was also 494 miles from Oklahoma City, and yet the
"final truth" to Alex Bridge and Paul Wells and Cross Currents Media—and the enigmatic man known as John
Brown's Body—was supposed to be here, on the Gulf coast.

Faith pulled off at a convenience store, bought a bottle of

water, and studied her case file. She read the crime scene reports from Wells's murder, and the notes made by Detective Perry Covington, the first investigator on the scene. The clerk in the store gave her directions to Seawall Boulevard, and she was there in ten minutes.

Even in the early evening, there were still families on the beach, though it wasn't as crowded as Faith had expected in the middle of tourist season. She had no trouble finding a parking spot right along the Seawall. As soon as she stepped out of the rental car, she felt the humidity descend on her like a thick curtain.

For a moment she stood, transfixed by the Gulf of Mexico. She'd seen the ocean twice before, once on a family vacation to Maine when she was a teenager, and in college when she'd taken the trip to Ireland. But still, like so many others raised in landlocked areas, the ocean was mesmerizing. The idea that this was the place, this very spot, *right here*, where the land ended, where the United States stopped, and she was standing a few yards away from it, gave her a sense of perspective that she'd sensed in no other place. She listened to the waves for a couple of minutes, inhaling the air, thick, wet, redolent with the Gulf. Then she took her case file and cell phone and walked along the top of the Seawall until she came to the staircase that led down to the beach. At the bottom of the steps, she consulted the sketch that Detective Covington had made of the area, and then walked toward Thirty-ninth Street along the beach.

A couple of families with children were in the area. A toddler filled a bucket with sand, then poured it all over himself. A young couple, presumably the toddler's parents, both sat under a beach umbrella reading. A bearded man was standing on the beach, shading his eyes from the sun, calling to three boys who were playing in the surf. The boys, each with a different color hair, didn't seem to hear him. Faith smiled.

She came to the last beach umbrella before the rock jetty

at Thirty-ninth Street. She didn't know what she'd expected, but there was nothing there. The crime scene tape had already been taken down.

But this was the spot, the place Paul Wells had been murdered.

Faith ducked under the striped umbrella and touched the back of the wooden folding beach chair. Paul Wells had sat right here, had bled right here. Faith saw a small rust-colored stain on the back of the chair.

A gangly young man wearing only a bathing suit rushed up to her, holding a clipboard. "Do you want to rent this umbrella and chairs?"

Faith looked up at him. "What?"

"I'm with the rental company. Want to rent these?"

Faith shook her head slowly. "No."

The kid looked sour. "You'll have to get out from under the umbrella, then."

Faith considered giving him her *I'm a federal agent* routine but decided against it. This place wasn't what bothered her about the crime scene. It was straightforward. At two thirty A.M., Paul Wells had been sitting in this chair, under this umbrella, and presumably Alex Bridge approached him from behind, called his name, and, when he turned to look, she shot him twice in the chest.

The rental kid was still looking at her, no doubt wondering why she was just staring down at the chair.

"Sorry," Faith muttered, and ducked out from under the umbrella.

The father with the three boys was calling out to them again, telling them to get out of the water because they were going to go have dinner. His tone was beginning to sound strained, Faith thought.

She looked up and down the beach. She'd already checked the location of the hotel where Alex had stayed. It was on Seawall, half a block back to the east.

So Alex had called Wells, told him where to meet her, then climbed down those steps, the same steps Faith came down a few minutes ago. She shot him. Faith closed her eyes. She could almost hear the two shots.

Then what? What had Alex done then?

Faith went back to the crime scene reports. The local cops had arrived on the scene at two thirty-eight A.M., after a 911 call from a driver who said he'd heard what sounded like gunshots on the beach. The cops found Alex standing beside Wells's body, and when they yelled down to her, she ran. She was arrested farther down the beach, a hundred yards or so away.

But she didn't have the gun when she was caught.

Faith slipped off her sandals and dug her toes into the hot sand. She walked a little ways, scuffing the sand, letting it cover her feet. Alex Bridge hadn't had the murder weapon on her at the time of her arrest. It was found a few hours later in a nearby Dumpster.

Faith looked around. There was nothing on this stretch of beach that could be called a Dumpster.

She slipped her sandals back on and started up the beach, toward the stairs that would take her to the street. At street level, she stood on the Seawall and glanced up and down. She found the Dumpster a block away. It was the only one in view on the street.

"Oh my God," Faith whispered.

Alex's hotel was half a block east. The Dumpster was a full block west.

Faith grew very still.

Droplets of sweat began to dribble down the back of her neck. She opened the case file, found Detective Covington's report again, and turned pages furiously. She slapped the pages against her free hand.

"I'll be damned," she said. Faith started moving at a fast walk, then a jog, and finally a run toward Alex Bridge's hotel.

The man with the goatee looked perfectly normal in Galveston. In a T-shirt, denim shorts, and rubber thongs on his feet, camera around his neck, he was just another tourist on the

Seawall. He took it as a point of pride that Kelly hadn't spotted him, not even when he'd boarded the Southwest flight just behind her. She'd spotted the tail this morning, though, the one that led to the lake. Strange business, that. But the man following her—the *other* man following her, he thought—seemed like he'd wanted to be spotted.

The man with the goatee was a professional, and he'd been at this a long time. He could tell an amateur tail from a pro, and he could tell when someone wanted to be seen. No matter. They would know soon enough who the other man was. He'd already sent the pictures up the chain of command.

He focused his camera on the Gulf, turning away from Faith Kelly as she ran past him, not ten feet away. "Interesting," he whispered to himself.

10:05 P.M.
Oklahoma City

Faith was almost running again as soon as she stepped off the plane in Oklahoma City's Will Rogers World Airport. She retrieved the Miata from short-term parking, paid her ticket, and roared north. She had to see Alex, but she needed to change clothes and get her thoughts organized.

She headed for home. As she always did, she scanned her entire block after turning onto the quiet street from May Avenue. A car sat in front of her house, a dark Toyota Camry four-door that she'd seen many times before. She pulled into her driveway. Scott Hendler got out of the Toyota.

"How long have you been here?" Faith said.

"Awhile," Hendler said.

"I was out of town." She started up her steps, pulling keys from her purse. "Come on in."

"Out of town?"

"A whirlwind to Galveston and back."

"Galveston, as in Galveston Island, as in the Gulf of Mexico?"

"As in all of that." She unlocked the door and they went in.

"Faith—" Hendler said.

Faith winced. She couldn't have a heart-to-heart with Hendler right now. She was in investigative overdrive, and her love life—if indeed that's what she had with Hendler—had no business here.

She dropped her purse and briefcase on the floor, turned, and took both Hendler's hands. "Scott, let's not talk about it now. I know you were upset and so was I. I even understand *why* you're so bothered by all this." She dropped his hands. "But you may not have reason to be bothered after all."

"Am I that transparent?" Hendler almost smiled, though it looked weary on him.

"You, Sleepy Scott, are the most transparent man on this earth. You'd never make it in Department Thirty."

"I'm a lousy poker player too. What do you mean, I may have no reason to be bothered after all?"

Faith was heading into the kitchen. "I'm starving. You want something to eat? Or a beer?"

"I could use a beer, if you have any."

She came out with two bottles of Harp and gave one to Hendler. "I have leftover pizza," she said.

Hendler made a face. "No, thanks."

"Suit yourself." She put two pieces of pizza in the microwave and pushed the button, then came to the dining room table. "I'm not so sure anymore that Alex Bridge killed Paul Wells."

Hendler cocked an eyebrow, a gesture that often made Faith laugh. But not tonight. Faith held up a finger and retrieved the case file from her briefcase. "I knew something bothered me about the crime scene," she said, sitting back down and pulling from her own bottle of Harp. "The reports, the sketches—something wasn't right, but I couldn't figure out what it was. That's why I had to go down there." She decided against mentioning the encounter with Isaac Smith, "John Brown's Body."

"And?"

"The timeline. It's all in the timeline."

Hendler nodded. "Okay, I'm listening."

"The desk clerk at the hotel says that Alex went through the lobby at exactly 2:31 A.M. He noted it in his desk log. After eleven P.M. they note all comings and goings through the front door. It's hard evidence, in black and white. At 2:34 the Galveston police receive the 911 call of shots fired. Their response time is four minutes. They're on the beach at 2:38, where they find Alex Bridge standing right beside Wells's body."

"Seven minutes, start to finish," Hendler said. "She could easily have shot him in seven minutes."

"Sure she could have." Excitement crept into Faith's voice. "But could she have left the hotel, shot him, gone all the way back up to the street, walked a full block, thrown the gun in the Dumpster, and walked back to the body? All in seven minutes? And why would she go back to the body after dumping the gun anyway? It doesn't make sense."

Hendler was silent a moment. "It sounds quick, but come on, Faith. You've seen crimes committed on a timeline like that before. And remember, criminals do lots of things that don't make sense."

Faith nodded. "But none of the crimes on this kind of timeline were committed by a woman who was seven months pregnant."

"I don't see what—" Hendler broke off, then his eyes locked onto hers. "Holy shit, Faith."

"I tested it four times. I walked the exact same route she would have to take, from the hotel lobby to the spot on the beach where Wells was found. One time I allowed thirty seconds, a couple of times a minute, and once ninety seconds, to actually shoot Wells. I went back up to the street, to the Dumpster, back down to the beach."

"How long?"

"Minimum of eight and a half minutes every time. Nearly eleven minutes once, with me going at a fast walk. There's no way Alex could move that fast. The woman's seven months along, and she moves like it. Plus, she's only five three, with short legs. I'm five ten, not pregnant, and look how long it took me."

They were both silent, letting the implications sink in. A beeping filled the silence between them. Faith got her slices of pizza and brought them back to the table. She took another long drink from the beer.

"What does it mean?" Hendler finally said. "I mean, to you."

Faith poked at a slice of pizza but didn't pick it up. "It's officially a Department Thirty case until and unless I 'remand' it to a different jurisdiction. But I can't just give it up, either."

"Why not? If she's not guilty, you can't do anything with her, right? Isn't that the whole mandate of Thirty?"

Faith remembered Yorkton's words. *Your friend, the president.* Political pressure from on high. Whether Alex Bridge was guilty or not, she still had information the powers-that-be wanted.

"It's complicated," Faith said.

Hendler made an exasperated sound. "What's not complicated about you these days?"

Faith smiled, still flushed with the excitement of discovery. "You know what?"

"What?"

"I'm glad you're here. I'm glad you came over. I know that what I do with Thirty is confusing. It's even confusing to *me.*"

Hendler reached across the table. He took her hand, then reached up and traced her scar.

"I deal with all these people," Faith said. "All these people with shattered, fractured lives. Victims of crimes. People who commit crimes. Look at Alex Bridge. Her mother abandoned her when she was three. As an adult, she thinks she's finally found the life she wants with a man she's crazy about. She gets pregnant and the husband can't handle that. He takes off and then gets himself killed in a drug deal. Jesus Christ, Scott. This is the kind of stuff I deal with all the time." She looked at him, eyes clear and direct. "In the middle of all that, it's nice to have a little bit of sanity."

"Is that me? Am I your little bit of sanity?"

"You, my friend, are the most sane person I know." She leaned over and kissed him. "I'm sorry for the scene in the coffee shop. When I'm working, I just have to *know* things. That's what my job is all about."

Hendler shrugged. "You know, I guess I was kind of emotional. The funeral and all that."

"Ah, a man in touch with his feelings. How thoroughly modern."

Hendler smiled.

"Scott," she said. "Why don't you stay here tonight? I don't have to go see Alex until morning."

She kissed him again, this time with growing urgency. He ran his hand down her back, and her body suddenly felt like it was one big bundle of nerve endings.

Hendler cupped her breast. Faith closed her eyes and leaned into him. She inhaled him, a wonderful mixture of musk and sweat and Harp ale.

"Come on," she said, and led him to her bedroom.

It occurred to her that it had been more than two years since she'd been with a man. And she wasn't even sure if that counted: she'd been a different person before Department Thirty. She blinked at the memory.

"Faith, are you—" Hendler said.

"Yes, I am," she said.

She pulled him by the hand and leaned down to kiss him. She opened her mouth hungrily, as if a sudden fever had gripped her. Faith's tongue sought Hendler's, and the feelings exploded in her mind. Once upon a time, she remembered that she'd enjoyed sex. Despite a vague Catholic sense of guilt, she'd always thought of it as the ultimate expression of humanity. But now, for these two long years, she'd held so much of herself inside. She'd dealt with so much grief and death, and so many lies—always the lies—that she hadn't had much of herself to give.

She felt the fever even more, and she felt it radiating from Hendler as well. His hands were on her breasts again, and then they were fumbling at the buttons of her shirt.

"Forget that," she whispered, pulling the shirt over her head.

Hendler smiled and reached behind her, unsnapping her bra with a deft movement. He gently pushed her back onto the bed and his lips touched her nipples. Faith almost screamed. His touch was just the right combination of gentleness and heated sexuality.

"You're good," she murmured. "In more ways than one."

She arched her back, and he suckled her nipples for what seemed like forever. He slowly worked his way up—kissing her throat, her jawline—and finally their mouths were on each other again as they twisted limbs, pulling at each other's clothes.

Hendler rolled onto his back and held the headboard. Faith lowered herself onto him and he moaned his pleasure. She rode him with ferocious intensity, feeling connected—literally and figuratively—as she never had before. When he climaxed, he screamed her name.

Later, when Faith reached her own orgasm, it felt so intense for a moment that she thought she would pass out. This was *life*, and Department Thirty couldn't take these moments, these feelings, away from her.

When they were finished, they lay together for a long time, Hendler's leg draped over Faith's. He traced lazy circles across her breasts.

"Wild woman," Hendler said, smiling.

"Damn right," Faith said. "And that's a couple of years of seriously pent-up emotions and frustrations and you-name-it."

Hendler put mock disappointment in his voice. "Oh, so the next time won't be as good. Oh, well."

Faith raised herself up on one elbow. "Why, you—" Then she leaned over and kissed him. It quickly grew urgent, and her hand snaked between his legs. "Here, what's this?"

"You tell me."

"We may find out about the 'next time' sooner than we thought."

"Good, I hate waiting."

They came together again, more relaxed, exploring each other, taking their time after the initial heat. They made love until well after midnight, and Faith never thought once of Alex Bridge or Galveston or John Brown's Body.

13

ALEX HAD BEEN WIDE-AWAKE FOR AT LEAST TWO HOURS. She lay in the unfamiliar bed and stared at the ceiling and the bare, sterile walls, with various melodies floating through her head. A couple of times since they'd brought her here, she'd actually gotten up in the middle of the night to play, just to work the melody out of her system.

Now she lay there watching the dawn steal through the blinds of this suburban house-prison, and thinking of all of it. She couldn't reach any of her friends, and most of her coworkers at Cross Currents believed she'd stolen the money from the company. She had a pretty good relationship with her father and her current "stepmother," but there was no way to contact them.

Her only link to the world was Faith Kelly.

Did Kelly believe her now? She'd actually gone to Galveston, Alex supposed to check out part of the story. But who was Faith Kelly, really? Someone who wanted to give her a new identity, to get information out of her. Alex thought the woman was sincere, but she was also doing a job Alex couldn't understand.

All of which brought Alex back to one undeniable conclusion: she had to get away.

Her body ached, and the baby had been moving a lot lately. It was still hard for Alex to process at times that there was a life inside her, a life that belonged to her . . . and to Gary.

She blinked fiercely, not wanting to cry. For the briefest of times—not even a full year—she'd felt complete. Gary had been everything she wanted. They knew each other. From the moment they met, one night when she was playing a solo gig at Full Circle Books, they'd known each other. She thought Gary had a very old soul, and they had absorbed themselves into each other. It was simple: Before Gary, she hadn't been a complete person. With him, she was.

She'd never felt anything like the joy when the doctor confirmed that she was pregnant. Then it had all shattered, like a house built of matchsticks. Twelve hours after Alex left the doctor's office, Gary was gone. In six weeks he was dead.

And still the baby boy inside her lived and breathed and kicked.

Alex chewed on one of her knuckles. She wanted to ask Gary why. Why was he so afraid of being a father? Alex certainly knew nothing about being a mother. She'd never had much of an example. How had he gotten mixed up in drugs in St. Louis?

Why?

She balled her fist and pounded the bed. No one was going to help her. No one.

She made herself quiet and still and practiced her breathing. In a moment her mind was clear, and there was nothing but her own breath. The entire world revolved around her breathing. She closed her eyes.

Sixty seconds later, she opened them. She let go one final cleansing breath.

A plan began to form.

She swung her legs out of the bed, then propelled herself up with her arms. Her sling bag was in the corner. It was all they'd let her bring when the federal marshals had taken her out of the jail in Galveston. She threw in her basic toiletries, then broke down her flute and put it in the bag. Then she grabbed the piece of paper on the bedside table—the paper on which she'd written the words Faith Kelly said. The words from the e-mail, the one that started everything.

She read the words again. She knew where she had to go.

It may have taken a year and a half and a living nightmare, but they'd wanted her to do something with this information, whoever they were. Now . . . now she was going to do it.

Faith had gone for her run, showered, and dressed before seven o'clock, when Hendler stumbled out of the bedroom. One part of her couldn't believe what they'd done, but cherished the connection they'd made. Another part of her—the cold Department Thirty professional that she'd become—wondered if she'd lost her mind.

"Hey," Hendler said.

"Hey yourself," she said.

"Did I ever ask you if you get up this early all the time?"

"No, you didn't. And yes, I do. There's coffee in the kitchen, but not much else. I don't usually eat in the mornings."

"Coffee's fine."

On his way to the kitchen, he turned. "Thanks, Faith."

"It's just coffee."

"Not the coffee. For the night. For not running away."

Faith stood up. "Spoke too soon. I'm getting ready to run away."

"Don't joke your way out of this."

"No, seriously. I need to get down to the office and then to see Alex. I need to put together a few more things before I talk to her. I think . . . I think I also need to talk to my boss."

Hendler nodded, his face impassive. "Duty calls. I have a lot of paperwork to catch up on. Everything kind of slid the last few days, after Paul . . . well, you know."

"I know."

Half an hour later Faith was at her desk in the downtown office, staring at the catfish on the wall. She tapped a nail on the desk, remembering the encounter with Isaac Smith. John Brown's Body.

The timeline.

She started to go back through the case file. A complete timeline of the Alex Bridge case hadn't been constructed yet. She started looking up dates, typing them into her computer and moving them around as she went.

First she entered the dates Wells had assembled: the date in January of this year when Cross Currents first reported the $498,000 missing. Alex Bridge was interviewed for the first time a month later, one of dozens of employees questioned. Wells identified Alex as a suspect late in February. Alex was suspended from Cross Currents in mid-March. In May and June Wells began to find the tracks that led to the account on Grand Cayman. Faith went back and inserted the funds transfers into January.

That was where Wells's trail stopped. Faith tapped a nail on the desk.

Now she began working on the thread of Wells's murder. She entered the date earlier this week when Alex and Wells both wound up in Galveston and Wells was killed on the beach. Alex had bought the gun on March 15. She inserted that date into the timeline.

What else, what else?

She crossed over from the realm of hard fact into the shadows. At the top of the timeline she typed in the date Alex received the cryptic phone call from John Brown's Body. It was a year ago January, a full year before the Cross Currents situation began. The follow-up e-mail came that March, a year before Alex was listed as a suspect and bought the gun that eventually killed Wells.

According to Alex, there was nothing else until the Cross Currents money disappeared.

Faith closed her eyes. In any investigation, the ordinary leads to the extraordinary. Art Dorian had told her that many times. Minutiae were vital. Things that were irrelevant to the situation at hand were often very relevant to the people involved.

In the months between the time Alex Bridge received the phone call and e-mail, and Paul Wells's criminal investigation of her began, she got married and conceived a child.

Faith paged back through the file to the initial briefing paper Yorkton had given her. Alex married Gary St. James on May 2 of last year. St. James left her two days after Christmas, upon finding out she was pregnant. St. James was killed in a shoot-out in St. Louis on February 10 of this year, a little more than a month before Alex bought the gun.

"What a life," Faith muttered.

It was an incredibly intense eighteen-month period in the life of one young woman.

In the midst of all this, she'd found information on the dirty deals at Cross Currents. Information that was important to some very powerful people.

Your friend the president, Yorkton had said.

And yet Alex had been smart enough to give vague code names to the files in which she stored the explosive information, and to remove any name references. Then she deleted the whole thing. But she left incriminating information on the hard drive, documents that would hang her.

Very smart in one way, very foolish in another.

Inconsistent.

She tapped the desk some more. She looked away from the computer to the fish on the wall. "She didn't do it, did she?" Faith said.

But why? Who would go to this much trouble, plant this many details, to set up Alex Bridge? Alex was a self-admitted "nobody," just a clerk who liked to play music.

Faith looked back at the printout of the e-mail. Tabananika. Blackjack Comanches. Jonathan Doag. None of the names meant anything to her.

John Brown's Body.

I don't believe justice delayed is justice denied, he had said.

What justice? Faith wondered. And how did he fit into this mess?

A few months ago Faith had spent an evening at Hendler's house when Hendler was babysitting his niece and nephew, who were eight and six years old, respectively. They'd watched movies, and every time a new character would come into a scene, the little boy would ask, "Is he a good guy or a bad guy?" Hendler had finally gotten exasperated with the question and said, "Maybe neither. Maybe both."

That was Faith's question about John Brown's Body. Good guy or bad guy?

Maybe neither. Maybe both.

In the midst of all this tumult was Alex's marriage to Gary St. James. The husband was an intangible. There hadn't been a bio in Yorkton's original briefing paper. Since he was dead, nothing more was said about him. He was a footnote to Alex Bridge.

Faith shook her head. Some footnote. She remembered the pain in Alex's eyes when she talked about her husband.

Faith decided to connect the dots, to see if there was anything else to be added to her timeline. She opened her personal address book and found the number for the detective division of the St. Louis Police Department. Her college friend Jennifer Ghezzi had applied to the SLPD at the same time Faith applied to the Federal Law Enforcement Training Center. Ghezzi made detective in two years and had been promoted to sergeant in less than five.

"Jennifer Ghezzi," said the familiar voice in her ear.

"Hey, Luigi," Faith said.

"Mick!"

Faith laughed. All through college they'd called each other Luigi and Mick, based on their ethnic background. "Hey, girl. Or I guess I should call you Sergeant. Got your e-mail."

"Thank you, thank you, thank you," Ghezzi said. "I got the stripes in the shortest time of anyone in the SLPD in the last fifty years."

"Impressive."

"Damn right I'm impressive. How's the marshal?"

As far as Ghezzi knew, Faith was still a deputy U.S. marshal. "More interesting than I ever thought. In fact, that's why I'm calling. I'm working a fugitive case that may be related to a homicide in your neck of the woods."

"Well, you know that we local cops always cooperate when the federal government comes calling."

"Of course you do."

"Got a case number?"

"No, but I have the date and the name of the victim."

"Okay, that's good." Faith heard her friend tapping computer keys. "I'll see if I can pull anything up. Give me the info."

"February 10 of this year. Victim's name: Gary St. James. I don't have a middle name. The shooting was reportedly drug-related and took place in the Central West End. You know where that is?"

"Oh, yeah. Nice little area, actually. Trendy shops and restaurants, cobbled streets." More keystrokes followed. "Hmm."

"What? What hmm?"

"You're sure on the date?"

"February 10," Faith said. "I have that on pretty good authority."

"Hmm."

A few more seconds went by, with no sound but computer keystrokes on the phone.

"Mick," Ghezzi finally said, "I think someone's messing with you."

Faith's stomach began to churn. "Tell me."

"No homicides at all in the city that day, drug or otherwise. In fact, that was a clean week. We didn't have a single homicide for the entire seven-day period. And there's no Gary St. James in the database anywhere. I even fooled around with the spelling. Nothing even close."

"Shit," Faith whispered.

"Mick? Faith? What's the deal with this?"

Faith turned a page in her file. "The investigating detective in your department called the widow personally."

"What officer?"

"Detective Ford."

More tapping. "Faith—" Ghezzi said.

"Oh, shit," Faith said.

"We don't have a Detective Ford. Not then and not now. I don't know what—"

"Jen, I have to go."

"Wait, I—"

"I'll e-mail you. Thanks for your help."

Faith hung up. Lies, lies, and more lies. It seemed she ate, drank, slept, bathed in lies.

The file Yorkton had given her included the note about Gary St. James leaving Alex, then being shot to death six weeks later. So either Yorkton had been lied to, or was doing the lying himself. Faith didn't want to believe it. Yorkton could be infuriating, but she didn't believe he would lie to his own people, as the last director of Department Thirty had done.

But what were Yorkton's sources? If he hadn't obtained the information from official sources, then there was only one other place from which it could have come.

Alex.

Much of Department Thirty's anecdotal information in building a dossier on an individual came from the individual's own daily actions, the way they interacted with others, the things they talked about, the places they went, the life they lived. Art Dorian had told her that the only way to construct a new identity that would be true to the individual was to take lessons from the old identity.

So she came back to Alex.

Faith dashed off a quick e-mail to Yorkton, asking for whatever he could find on Gary St. James, and asking if he'd had any luck finding out anything about Isaac Smith, John Brown's Body.

She hit SEND, then picked up the phone. Paige Carson was still on duty with Alex this morning. Hagy had called in sick and Carson pulled a double shift along with Hunnicutt, a male deputy with a reputation for quiet efficiency.

Carson answered her cell phone, sounding rushed. "Carson."

"This is Kelly. I'm on my way out there. I should be there in half an hour. Tell Alex to sit tight."

"We're not at the house, Kelly."

"What?"

"We're in the car, on the way to Memorial Community Hospital."

"What the hell are you talking about?"

"It's Bridge," Carson said. "Her water broke. She's going into premature labor."

14

July 16, 7:27 A.M.

ALEX TWISTED SIDEWAYS IN THE CAR SEAT AND PULLED her knees up toward her belly. Periodically she let out a grunt or a moan. They were on Northwest Expressway now, heading east into the city. Memorial Community Hospital, known locally as MemCom, was near Council Road and served the sprawling, rapidly growing far west area of Oklahoma City.

Deputy Carson—the one Alex had come to think of as "the bitchy one"—threw down her phone, hands on the steering wheel. "Kelly's going to meet us at the hospital," she said. Hunnicutt was a little older, in his forties, and rarely spoke. Alex named him "the silent one." He sat in the backseat, warily watching both women.

Alex grunted again. "Thought she was out of town," she said, a little out of breath.

"Well, she's back," Carson said.

Dammit! Alex thought. It could still work, but the plan was better without Faith Kelly being around.

As it was, Alex had banked heavily on Carson not having children. The deputy didn't wear a wedding ring, and though many married women didn't wear rings and God only knew how many unmarried women had kids these days, Carson just didn't seem right for motherhood.

And I do? Alex wondered.

If only Gary had stayed.

If only Gary hadn't gotten killed.

If only . . .

THE BLACKJACK CONSPIRACY 123

Alex blinked herself back from fantasyland. Gary left, Gary was dead. Gary would never see their son. Gary would never know that Alex now had to fight for her very identity, and that of their child.

She blinked again. The ruse had been easy enough. Alex had slipped out of the bedroom, nodded to the bitchy one, and went into the bathroom of the safe house, just as she did every morning.

She counted off two and a half minutes—150 seconds— then turned on the faucet, filling the cup that stood on the sink. Then she arranged herself on the floor, in a sprawled position beside the toilet. She poured some of the water on her panties and the rest on the floor between her legs. Then it had just been a matter of screaming for Deputy Carson.

I think my water just broke.

I thought you weren't due until the end of September.

I'm not.

Carson's eyes had widened in panic, but she'd stayed relatively calm. Now they were five minutes away from Mem-Com. Alex was grateful that the safe house had been west of the city. If it had been in another part of town and they'd tried to take her to Mercy or Baptist or one of the other hospitals, the plan wouldn't work. As it was, the plan might not work anyway.

Even as she kept up the pretense of being in labor, Alex's anger grew. Someone was using her, and had been for a long time. Now she was finally ready to find out who, and why.

Easier said than done, Alex. You've got no money, no ID, nothing. All you have is an e-mail from a phantom.

Alex moaned.

The car screeched through the morning traffic and turned into the MemCom emergency parking lot. Alex sat up, scanning the area. Just beyond MemCom's property, across a low wall, was a huge car dealership, acres of gleaming new vehicles that stretched almost to Council Road. With a little luck, that dealership would be Alex's saving grace. She had a momentary flash of panic. It wasn't quite eight o'clock yet, and she had no idea what time the service department at the dealership opened.

Please, she prayed silently. *Please let him be there, and let me get to him.*

Carson stopped the car in the pull-through in front of the emergency doors, then raced to the passenger side and helped Alex out. Alex clasped her sling bag and let Carson help her. Hunnicutt stood silently by, his eyes darting all around the area.

The emergency doors slid open with a hiss. A large waiting room opened in front of them, with check-in and triage areas to the right. Straight back, the waiting room narrowed into a hallway that led into the main body of the hospital. Alex started toward the corridor.

"Here, what are you doing?" Carson said.

Heads turned in the waiting room.

Alex, holding her belly with one hand, stopped and half-turned. "We don't want the ER. We need to go straight to the third floor." Carson looked blank, and Alex knew instantly that she was right: Carson did not have children. "Labor and delivery."

Carson nodded. "Where the hell's Kelly?" she said over her shoulder to her partner.

Hunnicutt shrugged. "On her way."

They rode the elevator to the third floor and stepped out into a brightly decorated hallway, with a brilliant mural depicting babies of different ethnicities: white, black, Latino, and Asian. Alex bristled a little: even though she'd never been particularly interested in the Native American half of her heritage, it bothered her that Indians were the forgotten minority, even here in the state with the largest Native population in America.

Alex led the way to the nurses' station, Carson and Hunnicutt trailing by a couple of steps. A black nurse in pink and blue pastel scrubs looked up at her. "May I help you?" The nurse wore a name tag with *M. Francis, RN, 13 years service* printed on it.

"My water broke," Alex said breathlessly.

"How many weeks are you?"

"Twenty-nine."

The nurse sharpened her gaze. "Who's your doctor?"

"Dr. Melton. Carla Melton."

"All right, honey," Francis said. "What's your name?"

"Alex Bridge."

Francis made some notes. "Are you preadmitted?"

Alex leaned against the counter and closed her eyes. "Yes."

"Okay, Alex, hold on and we'll get you into a room. We just had a couple of moms go home, so we're okay on rooms. I'll notify NICU and call Dr. Melton." She tapped a few computer keys under the counter, then looked up at Hunnicutt. "Are you the dad?"

Carson stepped forward, pulling out her identification. "I'm Deputy U.S. Marshal Carson, and this is Deputy Hunnicutt. This woman is in federal protective custody."

Francis was not impressed. "All right, then." She looked at Alex. "Is Dad in the picture?"

Alex shook her head. "He's dead."

"Oh, honey. What about a childbirth partner?"

"I had a friend who did the childbirth classes with me, but . . ." She glanced at Carson and Hunnicutt.

"Uh-huh," Francis said, looking at the deputies, her eyes turning glacial.

"Wish Kelly would get here," Hunnicutt muttered, looking at the ceiling.

In less than five minutes, Alex's room was ready. Francis stopped Carson and Hunnicutt at the door. "You can wait out here," she told them.

"But she's—" Carson said.

"In protective custody," Francis said. "I heard you the first time. She's safe in here."

"But—"

"You're not a family member, you're not her childbirth partner. You can wait outside."

In the room, Francis helped Alex onto the bed. "We'll get you hooked up to the fetal monitor—"

Alex looked at her. "I'm not in labor."

Francis went absolutely still.

"My water didn't break," Alex said. "I told them it did so I'd get out of that house."

Francis started to back away.

"Please," Alex said. "Please listen to me. I haven't done anything. I'm not a criminal."

"They said 'protective custody,'" Francis said.

Alex nodded. She decided not to mention Cross Currents and the murder of Paul Wells. "They want to put me into some sort of program where they give me a new name in exchange for me telling them things."

"Witness protection program."

Not quite, Alex thought, but she nodded again. "I don't want to do it. They shouldn't be able to force me. I don't want my whole identity wiped out. When my baby's born, I want him to know who he is." *At least that's the truth.*

Francis stared at her.

"Please," Alex said. "I need your help."

Francis kept staring.

"How do I know you're telling me the truth?" the nurse finally said.

"You don't. But I am."

"Your baby's dad being dead? Is that's true?"

Alex blinked. *Oh, Gary,* she thought. "That's the truth. He left me the day I told him I was expecting. A few weeks later he was killed in a shoot-out. He was somehow involved with drugs." A tear spilled over. "I didn't know—"

Francis edged back toward Alex. "Oh, honey," she said. "My first husband died a month before my oldest daughter was born."

Alex looked up at her.

"He was a drunk. He got all liquored up one night and was driving down Twenty-third Street at about eighty miles an hour. He crossed the centerline and ran head-on into a car with a mom and two little boys in it, just coming home from a football game. Ernest—that was my husband—died when he went through the windshield. The mom and one of the little boys died. The other little boy never walked again. I was so mad at Ernest that I went to the cemetery and kicked his gravestone, over and over again. He tore up not only our family but another family at the same time."

"I'm sorry," Alex said, then felt ridiculous for saying it.

"No need," Francis said. "But I think I understand what you're going through. I don't know anything about witness protection, but I know about going through a labor and delivery by yourself."

"Help me," Alex said.

"How?"

"I just need to get away from them, to get away. I don't want to give up who I am, who my baby is. I haven't done anything wrong, and they can't make me become someone else."

"No, honey, they can't." Francis smiled. "I believe in God and the law, Alex, but I've gotten mad at God a time or three, and I've gotten mad at the law too." She touched Alex's hand. "I can get you out of the hospital, but that's all. I can't leave the floor for very long."

Alex nodded. "That's all I need."

The Miata roared into the MemCom parking lot, tires screeching. Faith found a space in the ER lot and took off at a full run. Carson's car was still sitting in the pull-through. She ran through the doors and was headed for the ER check-in desk when she saw Hunnicutt coming down the hall.

"Where's Alex?"

"Third floor," Hunnicutt said. "Carson's with her."

"What happened?"

"Carson already told you, her water broke. It was all over the bathroom floor."

"She's not due until the end of September," Faith said.

Hunnicutt shrugged.

"Why didn't you call me when it first happened?"

"We thought you were still out of town. If you were in another state, Kelly, you couldn't get here."

Faith shut up. She hadn't checked in last night to let them know she was back from Galveston. Alex Bridge's life was in her hands, and yet, Faith had spent the night screwing Scott Hendler's brains out and hadn't checked in with the protective detail.

"Dammit to hell," Faith said, following Hunnicutt to the elevator.

"Okay, let's go," Francis said.

"You understand that you could get in trouble," Alex said, picking up her bag.

"Sometimes, you do the right thing, you get in trouble. But not for long."

Francis hauled open the door of the birthing suite. Carson stood just outside.

"Where are you going?" Carson asked.

"I'm taking her down to NICU," Francis said.

"What's that, and why?"

"Neonatal intensive care unit. Her contractions aren't coming that close, so it'll be a while before she delivers. But once she does, that baby's going to NICU. Any child eleven weeks early is going to have some problems. I need to show her the unit. It can be a scary place, and she needs to be prepared for it."

Carson nodded and fell into step behind them.

"NICU is a closed unit," Francis said. "Deputy, you can wait outside the door."

Carson creased her brow, but nodded.

"Where's your partner?" Alex said.

"He went downstairs to wait for Kelly."

NICU was around the corner, past the elevators and the bright mural. A set of double doors, recessed into a short hallway, led into the unit. "Wait here," Francis said to Carson. She entered a series of numbers on a keypad and the doors swung outward.

When the doors closed behind Francis and Alex, the nurse led Alex around a corner. The unit desk was in front of them. Behind, a narrow corridor led to the unit itself, where premature and critically ill newborns were treated. Another corridor led off to the right.

Francis pointed to the right. "There's another door to the unit. It opens out to the NICU waiting room. When you go out that door, she won't be able to see you. It's out of sight of the one we just came in. Don't go to the elevator: she'll see you. But there's a stairway just outside the waiting room to the left. It comes out close to the main entrance."

Alex hugged the older woman. "What will you tell them?"

"Oh, let's see. I'll tell them that we determined that you weren't in labor after all and released you. And I'll tell them that unless they have a warrant or a court order or some other piece of paper, that I don't have to turn you over to them. And if they do have the piece of paper, I'll tell them they should have shown it to me up front."

"Wow, you're good."

"I read a lot, honey. Go on, and take care of yourself."

"I will."

Clutching her bag, Alex started around the corner.

Faith and Hunnicutt stepped off the elevator and Faith jogged to the nurses' station. A young, ponytailed blond nurse looked up at her.

"Alex Bridge," Faith said. "She was just brought in."

The nurse checked her computer monitor. "Room three-twenty-three. It's just down there and to the—"

Faith ran down the hall, knocked once on the room door, and thrust it open. It was empty.

She turned to Hunnicutt. "Where is she? Where's Carson?"

"They were here," Hunnicutt said.

The dread, which had been like storm clouds circling,

erupted into a full-fledged thunderstorm. "Shit," Faith said, shouldering past Hunnicutt and running into the hall.

Alex eased through the wooden door that took her out of NICU. Only two people were in the waiting area, an old man reading a newspaper and a middle-aged woman curled up in exhaustion on one of the sofas. The old man looked up at Alex as she emerged. He gave a slight smile and a nod, then went back to his paper.

Alex spotted the stairway door that Francis had told her about and stepped into the hall. The nurses' station was at the far end. She could see the recessed area that led to the other doors to the NICU. Francis was right: Carson was nowhere to be seen.

She took a deep breath. She would be exposed for a few seconds. If Carson chose one of those seconds to step out of the alcove and into the main hallway, Alex was dead.

She exhaled. She hurried across the hall in four steps and pushed the metal bar on the stairwell door. She set one foot on the stairwell—*almost there!*—and heard a voice, one she'd heard recently.

"Then where did she go?" said the voice.

Faith Kelly.

Alex didn't stop to see where the red-haired woman was. She let the door close behind her and started down the stairs.

"I don't know," said the nurse with the ponytail. "She's admitted into three-twenty-three."

Another nurse walked by the desk. "Meg took her down to NICU. She's not in active labor and her doc's not here yet, so Meg was going to show her the unit, since the baby—"

"Where?" Faith demanded.

The ponytailed nurse pointed. Faith ran.

Meg Francis walked out of the double doors from the NICU, steeling herself for the storm that was about to hit. The woman deputy was still standing there.

"Where is she?" Carson demanded.

"Well, you see, we determined—"

A tall woman with red hair ran into the alcove, with the male deputy behind her. The redhead took in the scene, zeroed in on Francis, and said, "Do you know where Alex is?"

"I was just getting ready to tell . . ."

Francis gave them the whole spiel, though she could tell no one believed it. Much to her surprise, no one said a word about warrants or court orders.

The redhead turned on the other two. "Call your office. Get backup. Leneski and Griffin. They've been on the detail, and they know what Alex looks like. Cover the exits."

She sprinted for the elevator and jabbed at the button.

The second floor of MemCom was the surgery floor, and Faith's elevator stopped on it. A postoperative patient, IV lines running into both arms, was wheeled in on a gurney. The two young men who were transporting the patient fussed with the gurney and the sheets covering the form on it before finally pressing the button for the first floor.

Faith thumped her foot on the floor. "Shit," she said, and they stared at her.

When the elevator finally stopped on the ground floor, Faith hurried past the gurney and turned back toward the ER. She stopped in the waiting area, scanning the room. There were more people than there had been just a few minutes ago. Faith ran to the check-in desk.

"A pregnant woman, about thirty, short dark hair," Faith said. "Did she come this way?"

"Was she an ER patient?" asked the clerk.

"No! Did you see her?"

"I don't know. A lot of people come and go through those doors."

Faith ran out the doors and into the morning heat. Carson's car was still sitting there, hazard lights flashing.

Faith thought of the horrible irony. *I was going to tell her that I finally believe her story, and now she's gone.*

For a moment she was paralyzed, as if her feet had planted roots in the concrete.

A young woman in blue scrubs stepped out of the ER doors, moved a few feet away, and lit a cigarette.

Faith stood rooted to her spot.

I believe her story.

If she didn't do the crimes, she's not eligible for Department Thirty anymore.

A man and woman rushed past, holding a young boy who was bleeding from his ear. The boy wailed. Faith felt the rush of cool air as the ER doors slid open again.

I can let her go.

No, I can't. We don't know who set her up or why.

Faith's heart thundered. Sweat rolled down the back of her neck.

She couldn't just let Alex Bridge wander off into God knows what. Someone was willing to go to extraordinary lengths to destroy her. But she still had the information on Cross Currents that her superiors wanted.

Faith shook her head. There were two ways: chase Alex, get her back into custody, and force her into Department Thirty's protection; or let her go, let her face whatever was waiting for her, and Faith would face the wrath of Yorkton and those further up the line.

But maybe there was a third way.

She stepped out from under the pass-through. A thin strip of concrete opened into the main MemCom parking lot. Beyond that was the low wall, and on the other side, row after row of new cars.

Just stepping over the wall, clutching her bag, was Alex Bridge.

The ER doors whisked open again, and running feet sounded behind Faith.

"There she is!" Carson shouted. Her hand went to her hip, and Faith knew she was about to draw her weapon.

"Don't do that, Deputy," she said in a quiet voice.

Carson froze.

"Stand down, Deputy," Faith said. She felt as if she were saying the words in a trance, or hearing someone else say them.

"What? What the hell—"

"I said stand down. Let her go."

"What do you mean, let her go?" Hunnicutt said.

"I mean let her go."

"She killed Paul Wells!" Carson said.

"No," Faith said. "I don't think she did."

Carson looked as if she'd been hit in the face.

There was a long silence, then Hunnicutt took a couple of steps forward. "Dammit, Kelly," he growled, "I don't take orders from you."

"Actually, you do," Faith said. "You need to read the manual again. 'All units within DOJ are to provide technical, operational, and protective support to Department Thirty on an as-needed basis, with personnel being under the supervision of the assigned case officer.' This is an as-needed basis, and I'm the case officer."

"You can't be serious," Carson said.

"Don't I look serious?"

"What about that nurse? She obstructed—"

"Oh, leave her alone. She followed her conscience. We ought to take lessons from her."

"You're just letting Bridge go," Hunnicutt said, the disbelief still thick in his voice.

Faith nodded. "Yes." She watched as Alex worked her way through the cars, winding her way toward the dealership's buildings. "She's not free, but I'm letting her go."

"What the hell does that mean?"

Faith didn't answer. She watched Alex's form grow smaller until the pregnant woman disappeared into the car dealer's service building. Then she turned, brushed between Carson and Hunnicutt, and started toward the Miata.

15

ALEX WAS BREATHING HARD BY THE TIME SHE WALKED into the service garage. She smelled gasoline and oil and rubber and sweat. A dozen or so cars, in various states of repair, were parked in service bays. She saw no one.

She bent over, working to catch her breath, placing her hands on her knees. In a moment a door opened to the left and a man walked through it holding a cup of coffee. He wore a blue uniform shirt and pants and scuffed work boots.

"Can I help you?" he said.

"Danny," Alex said. "Danny Park. Is he here?"

"In the break room. He just got here. Are you okay?"

Alex nodded, straightening up. She adjusted her bag and looked back over her shoulder, back toward MemCom. She could see the ER entrance, but no sign of Carson or Hunnicutt or Kelly.

That doesn't mean anything, she thought. *They could be surrounding this place.*

Alex followed the way the man pointed and found the mechanics' break room. It was filled with young to middle-aged men in identical clothes, drinking coffee and smoking cigarettes. Off to one side, leaning against the wall, was Danny Park.

Danny's mother had been Alex's first unofficial stepmother. He was the only one of Alex's half-brothers that she actually saw on a fairly regular basis. He was the oldest of the bunch at twenty-four, six years younger than she. His mother was first-generation Korean-American, and Danny was a striking presence, with classic Asian skin and features and their father's cobalt-blue eyes.

When they were kids, during the time Danny and his mother had lived with them, they used to tease each other about their last names, Bridge and Park. As a young teenager, Alex had put the two names together into Bridgepark or Parkbridge, telling Danny that it sounded like the name of a suburban neighborhood. They also called themselves "the two half-breeds." She wasn't sure Danny ever got the jokes, and shortly after that his mother and Bill Bridge had broken up.

"Alex?"

He was looking at her with those intense blue eyes from across the room. All heads turned toward the doorway.

Danny started toward her. "Hey, Alex, what are you doing here?" He stopped short. "Whoa, hey, you're pregnant."

"Can't get anything past Park," one of the other mechanics said.

"My sister," Danny said, and the guys quieted.

He came to her and stood at arm's length for a moment. She took his arm, then wrapped her own arms around him and buried her head in his shoulder. "Danny," she whispered.

They held each other for a long moment, then Park stepped back. "Hey, what's going on?"

"I'm in trouble, Danny," she said. "I need your help."

"Anything, sister." He smiled.

She laced her fingers into his. "I'm sorry I've been out of touch. My life . . . my life's been too bizarre."

"I guess. How's Gary? I guess he's treating you all right." He gave a pointed look at her belly.

"Gary's dead."

Park took a step back, his eyes widening.

"It's a long, long story," Alex said, "and I don't have time to tell it right now. Can you take me somewhere?"

"Well, I'm just going on my shift. . . ."

"Danny."

The smile again. "Just tell me where."

"I need to get out of town." Alex's heart started racing again. She pulled him into the hallway, away from the other mechanics in the break room. "People are after me. I can't explain, but I have to get out of town."

"You want me to take you to the airport?" They walked a few steps down the hallway.

"The airport," Alex said. "No. I bet they'll be looking for me there. I can't go home, either. They'll have my place covered."

They walked back into the service area, and Park steered Alex along the wall toward the door farthest from MemCom. "Alex, you sound paranoid."

"I *am* paranoid." Alex clutched her bag more tightly. "But they're . . . oh God, Danny, I think I'm falling apart. I think I'm losing it."

Park stopped, taking her hands in his. Alex looked down at them. She knew that his dirt-under-the-fingernails persona and auto-mechanic machismo masked a sensitive interior, burnished by a lifetime spent trying to understand two different cultures. He would never let his buddies at the shop see it, but Alex knew that her half-brother wrote beautiful, expressive, lyrical poetry and was working on a novel.

"Hey, sister," he said in a very soft voice, "I'll do anything for you, you know that. You've gotten me out of some stuff, and I'll do the same for you."

When he was nineteen, Park had been arrested for possession of marijuana. Alex had scraped together enough money to bail him out and paid his legal fees, all without their father or his mother ever knowing. She'd extracted from him a promise never to do any kind of illegal drugs again, and as far as she knew, he'd kept it. The six hours he'd spent in the county jail had been harrowing enough.

"I have to go somewhere," Alex said. "And I have to go without anyone having a way to track me down."

"Alex," Park said gently, "what are you into?"

They emerged from the garage into bright sunlight. "I'm not *into* anything. But I'm about to be."

They looked at each other. Alex felt her heart beating, seemingly all over her body: her neck, her forehead, her wrists. She ran a hand across her belly. She imagined that she could feel the baby's heart beating as well.

Park called to his supervisor that he had a family emergency and had to leave for a while. The supervisor looked sour but nodded.

They reached Park's Chevy pickup with the toolbox in the bed and a tarp folded neatly to one side. Park had once joked to her that he was "the only blue-eyed Korean guy in Oklahoma who drives a truck, works on cars for a living, and listens to Mozart." He opened the door for her and helped her into the seat.

After he'd slid into his own seat, started the engine, and turned on the air conditioner, he said to her, "Where to?"

Alex closed her eyes. "Just drive further back into the city."

"Okay, sister."

They pulled onto the Northwest Expressway, with Alex casting looks toward the hospital next door. "How do you feel?" Park said, then laughed. "Man, that's lame. I mean, being pregnant and all. I never knew. . . ."

Alex closed her eyes again. As far as she could tell, no one was following. She saw no sign of Carson's car, or Faith Kelly. "My life . . ." she said, then stopped. She didn't really know anything about her life anymore.

"My life," she said again, "isn't really my life."

Park waited a moment, steering past the light at Council Road, dodging morning rush traffic headed into the city. "Well, that clears it right up." His tone turned serious again. "If you need to get out of town fast, I have a suggestion."

She looked at him.

"Take the bus," he said.

"What?"

"Cross-country bus. My aunt—you remember my mom's

sister, don't you?—lives in Florida now, and I rode out to see her last year. It takes forever, and it's not very comfortable, but it'll get you there, and it's cheap. You can buy a ticket right at the station, with no advance reservations."

Alex's mind began to churn, thinking of the e-mail that Faith Kelly had read to her over the phone. That and the phone call had started everything, had put her life into this strange netherworld.

"Yes," she said. "I'll do it. But, Danny . . . here I go again . . . I don't have any money, and if I use a credit card, I bet they'll be able to track it."

Park shook his head. "Who's 'they'?"

Alex shook her own head, mimicking his action. "Don't ask me any questions."

"Okay, then. Where are you going?"

"That's a question. Take me to the bus."

"Alex, if I have to buy you a bus ticket, I need to know where you're going."

"No! I don't want you to know. That way if someone comes knocking on your door, you can tell them you don't know where I went, and it's the truth."

"You're driving me nuts here. If I—"

Alex sat up straight. "If you buy a bus ticket for a certain place, can you get off at another stop before you get to that place?"

Danny shrugged. "I guess so. I suppose you can get off anywhere, as long as it's between where you bought the ticket and the destination on the ticket."

Alex nodded vigorously. "That's what I'll do. That'll throw her off, at least for a while. Maybe it'll be long enough . . ." Her voice trailed away.

"'Her'? It'll throw 'her' off? Who's 'her'?"

"That was another question."

"Shit, Alex!"

"Drive, Danny."

Park thumped the steering wheel. After a few minutes he flipped on the radio. Classical music played for a few minutes, then a news report came on. Park listened in silence. Alex stared out the window as the streets went by: Meridian Avenue, Portland Avenue, Lake Hefner Parkway, May Avenue . . . They started to blur.

"Man, what a deal," Park muttered, listening to the newscast.

"What?" Alex turned back to him. She'd almost forgotten him, as if the truck were driving itself.

"That guy Rojas, down in Texas. You keep up with all that stuff?"

"No."

"You can bet if he was rich and white, they'd be paying attention to his appeal. Or he probably wouldn't even be on death row in the first place."

"What are you talking about?"

"He knifed a couple of guys in a bar fight. I'm willing to bet that if he was pure white and had a rich daddy, they would've claimed self-defense and he'd be drinking champagne somewhere today. But no, the guy's a poor Latino, so they're gonna give him the needle and the Supreme Court won't even listen to his appeal." Park glanced at her. "Face it, sister. If you look like that guy—or like you or like me—the system doesn't work the same way."

Alex blinked. Danny had always been a lot more sensitive about racial and ethnic issues than she. As for Alex, she couldn't really remember her mother and had never been around any of her Comanche relatives, so she didn't think about it. She wondered how her other half-brothers felt. Her father had this thing for dark-skinned ethnic women: Alex's mother was Indian, Danny's mother was Korean, and of the next three "stepmothers," two were black and the current one was a Latina. As adults, Alex and Danny had teased that Bill Bridge was single-handedly working to increase the world's population of biracial children.

She thought of the e-mail, all that talk about Tabananika and Blackjack Comanches.

No.

I was never Indian before, and I'm not about to start being one now.

But I may have no choice, she thought.

"Maybe you're right," she said.

Twenty minutes later they were at the bus station, a strangely incongruous structure in downtown Oklahoma City, at the corner of Sheridan and Walker. It was directly across the street from the architecturally remarkable Stage Center theater complex, and just west of the heart of downtown with its modest cluster of high-rises. In the face of downtown Oklahoma City's renewal and redevelopment as an "arts district," the bus station was a tired, worn building, a reminder of what had gone before in the city center.

Danny had stopped at an ATM and withdrawn two hundred dollars in cash, which Alex tucked into her bag. Inside the terminal, with its combination diner/gift shop and rows of hard plastic seats—on which more than a few people sat with suitcases, pillows, and glazed looks—they walked to the ticket counter. Alex asked for a map of bus routes.

The ticket agent, a young black man with gold-rimmed glasses, handed her a thick map with an embossed cover. She began tracing lines, seeing what cities the routes went through. In two minutes she whispered, "New York."

Park's eyes widened. "What are you—"

"Questions, Danny."

"Dammit," he muttered, and bought a ticket to New York, reserving the seat in his name.

When the designated bus began boarding, nearly an hour later, the two of them split up and each went to the appropriate bathroom. The restrooms were around a corner and down a short flight of stairs from the main terminal, well out of sight of any bus station personnel. When they emerged from their respective rooms, Park handed Alex the ticket.

"Okay, now you're me," Park said. "You're a girl named Alex. I guess a girl named Danny isn't too far-fetched. I showed my ID when I bought the ticket, so you shouldn't have to show yours when you board. Just keep the ticket and the reboarding pass together."

Alex hugged him hard, conscious of her belly between them.

"Should I tell Dad anything?" Park asked her.

Alex frowned. "No. Yes." She broke the embrace. "I'm not sure. I guess . . . I guess just tell him I'm okay and not to believe anything he hears about me."

"What does that mean?"

"It means I better get out of here."

"Last chance. You want to tell me what this is all about?"

"No."

"Damn stubborn Indian," he said.

"Damn pushy Korean," Alex said.

They smiled at each other. "Go on, then," Park finally said. "I hope you find what you need."

"So do I," Alex said. But as she started back up the stairs toward the bus terminal, she couldn't help wondering exactly what it was she needed.

16

THE PHONE WAS RINGING WHEN FAITH WALKED IN THE door to her office. "That better be you, Yorkton," she said as she crossed the room. She scooped the receiver and barked her name into it.

"My dear Officer Kelly."

"Mr. Director," she said, trying not to sound sarcastic. "Do you have anything for me?"

"How is young Alex?"

Faith threw her briefcase on the floor and sat heavily into her chair. "Alex is fine. Anything on Gary St. James or Isaac Smith?"

"You sound rushed."

"I don't have time to play! Things are moving very fast and I need information."

Yorkton made a clucking sound with his tongue. "Pace yourself. Don't let yourself be caught up in the events around you. The stress will consume you if you let it."

"Goddammit, Yorkton!"

"Patience is a virtue, Faith. But, be that as it may, you seem to have a great talent for unearthing things and people that others can't find."

Faith pulled the Glock out of her shoulder holster and slid it into a desk drawer. "Meaning?"

"Isaac Smith. John Brown's Body."

"What about him?"

"He's an operator, a freelancer."

"Assassin?"

"No, no, and this is what makes him so interesting. He doesn't believe in assassination."

Faith remembered the man's words back at Lake Hefner: *I assure you, Ms. Kelly, if I wanted to hurt you, you would be dead right now, and you would have no clue who or why.*

"Really," she said, this time leaning heavily on the sarcasm.

Yorkton didn't seem to notice. "Indeed. Over the last ten years or so he's been on everyone's radar, the FBI, CIA, Treasury, and all the other children. All the sources I could assemble seem to think he's actually foreign, born somewhere in Europe, but we don't have a name. The Bureau profilers think he came here as a boy, and at some point along the way he decided to start hiring himself out. He built up an astonishing knowledge of American history, and for some reason became fixated on the Civil War."

"And John Brown."

"The profilers theorize that, based on the tidbits they've been able to glean, that he could probably be this country's preeminent John Brown biographer, and one of the top Civil War scholars in general, if he so chose. But he uses his talents in other ways."

Faith tapped a nail. "So if he's not an assassin but is a freelance operator, what does he do?"

"He ruins people."

"What?"

"Simply put, he ruins people. He hires himself out to various individuals or groups who have an interest in seeing someone destroyed. He asks for ridiculous sums of money, tells his employer they must be patient, and he very meticulously creates a plan that will ruin whoever the target is. He doesn't kill them with the assassin's bullet. He kills them by destroying their reputation, corrupting their identity, slowly manipulating them into situations from which there's no escape."

"Just like Alex Bridge," Faith said slowly.

Yorkton tongue-clucked again. "But, based on what you told me about your little encounter with Mr. Smith, he seems to be concerned about Alex's welfare. Interested in 'justice,' wasn't it?"

"That's what he said." Faith rolled the chair away from the desk, extending the phone cord as far as it would go and pulling up the window blinds. Sunlight flooded in, and Faith counted thirty-nine tourists at the National Memorial two floors below and across the street. "Where did your information come from?" she finally asked.

"Various places," Yorkton said.

"This is no time to be vague. I've seen this guy up close and personal, and he's in the middle of this Alex Bridge thing."

"But it doesn't fit his normal modus operandi. You say he's concerned about Alex's fate, that he's trying to point you in certain directions. It wouldn't seem to add up."

"Hell no, it doesn't add up, and that's the problem."

"In addition to the fact that he somehow knows of our department's existence and the fact that you are Alex Bridge's case officer."

"That too. How would he find that out?"

Yorkton cleared his throat. Faith held the receiver away from her ear for a moment. "He must be well connected," Yorkton said. "The rumblings in Washington are that he's had his finger in several political scandals over the last few years. Finding mistresses for congressmen, financial shenanigans, that sort of thing." Yorkton cleared his throat again. "This is a problem, but I don't think it should have an effect on the case itself."

Faith stared at the phone as if she hadn't heard right. "Are you kidding?"

"No, I most certainly am not kidding, Officer. Move forward with the processing of the Bridge case and we'll worry about John Brown's Body after young Alex is safely in protection and we have the information we need from her."

"This changes everything! His presence here changes the whole complexion of the case. He knows things. He—"

"I understand it's an unexpected addition," Yorkton said. "Work around it and stay focused. How close is Alex to coming in?"

Faith gripped the phone. After a moment she realized her wrist ached from how hard she was clutching the receiver. She thought of how she'd chased Alex Bridge through Memorial Community Hospital, how she'd stood in the morning heat outside the emergency-room entrance and made the decision to let her go.

God help me, she thought. "She isn't," Faith said.

"What do you mean?"

Faith closed her eyes. "I don't think she embezzled the money or murdered Wells."

Yorkton made a sound into the phone that sounded halfway between a cough and a laugh. "You don't *think*? You don't *think*, Officer? You don't have to think. The evidence is quite clear."

"No, it isn't. That's the problem. Holes have started to appear in the evidence, and I can't just ignore Smith."

"What holes in the evidence?"

Faith noted that Yorkton had ignored her reference to Smith. She explained about the hard drive to Alex's computer, and the timeline of Wells's shooting.

Yorkton sounded almost relieved when she finished. "That's it? That's all conjecture, speculation. It sounds as though she's cast a spell on you and now you want her to be innocent. That's not an uncommon—"

"Bullshit!" Faith shouted. "Don't patronize me! You forget that, unlike you or anyone else in this department, I was a real law enforcement officer before you snagged me into this. Believe me when I say there's something wrong with all this evidence."

"Kelly—"

"Think about what you've just told me about this Smith.

Manipulation, ruining people's lives—that's what's happened to Alex Bridge. This is no coincidence."

Yorkton's voice was even. "Then why is he so concerned about her? Based on what we know of him, he doesn't suddenly change his mind about ruining someone. It's a job and he does it well. That's how he continues to function underground. He has a reputation."

Faith shook her head. "I don't think the evidence is strong enough to support bringing her in. She might be able to qualify for conventional Witness Security. I could remand the case—"

Yorkton raised his voice for the first time. "You will do no such thing! This is a Department Thirty case, and it will stay one. You bring her in. Do you understand me?"

"Even if she's not guilty?"

"She's guilty, Officer. This is your first case to build and you just can't see it. That's understandable. But you *will* bring her in."

Faith waited a moment. "This isn't you talking, is it?"

"What?"

"This comes from higher up." She kicked the underside of her desk. "It's all about politics. The president wants to use this issue, and he's using us to get to Cross Currents, come hell or high water."

"Listen to me, Kelly. Listen closely. The business last year gave this department a serious set of problems. Yes, you saved the day and earned the president's undying gratitude, but you didn't have to deal with Congress. *I did.* I had to go up to the Hill and tell them that yes, our department director was corrupt for thirty years, seeking only to increase his own power and that of Nathan Grant. I had to plead for a budget for this year, to prove to them that we deserve to exist. Department Thirty will bring in this case and we will hand the proper data to the administration and the Congress. Do you understand?"

"Even if Alex Bridge didn't do these things."

"She did them. Don't look for what isn't there. There are

little inconsistencies in every single case that was ever made."

Faith kicked the desk again, harder this time. "This is hardly a little inconsistency! I won't make this woman give up her identity when we don't have conclusive evidence that she has to."

"Bring in the case, Officer."

"This isn't right. I won't do this. I will *not* do this, York-ton."

"You *will* do this."

"I'll resign first. I'll quit this fucking department and I'll go on CNN and I'll tell the whole world about Department Thirty." Faith was actually shaking with rage, something that had rarely happened in her life. "Did *you* do this? Did you set Alex Bridge up, just so you could get your precious data, to score your political brownie points? *Goddamn you!*"

"How dare you," Yorkton said, his voice low, dangerous. "How dare you imply that I am corrupt. I have fought against government corruption for my entire career. What Daniel Winter did to this agency disgusted me. He abused the system. I would never, ever abuse the system, no matter how much was at stake. But what you fail to grasp is that when the situation arises, I will use the system to get the job done. No, I did not set up Ms. Bridge. She did a fine job of that herself, and all the conjecture and speculation in the world won't change it."

"Where do you get your information about the people we're supposed to recruit?"

Yorkton paused, no doubt taken aback by the abrupt shift in topic. "Various places. Why?"

"Gary St. James. What do you know about him?"

"Alex's husband? I saw your request for information on him. That's a waste of time. The man is dead."

Faith told him what Jen Ghezzi had told her about Gary St. James's non-death in St. Louis.

"Interesting," Yorkton said, his tone neutral again. "But only mildly so. The only factor concerning him is that his disappearance and death made Alex more vulnerable."

"Exactly! Her life, ruined. Her dreams, torn apart. Doesn't that sound like our pal Smith's fingerprints?"

"You're speculating again."

"You didn't check on St. James, even after I asked for the information?"

"No. As I said, it's not pertinent."

"Jesus Christ, can anyone be this dense? I don't believe in coincidences, and I can't believe that you do, either. Your plan to grab a little political capital on behalf of the department has got you blinded."

"Do not—I repeat, do *not*—talk to me that way, Officer Kelly. Bring in this case."

"I won't. Like I said, I'll quit first."

"No one 'quits' Department Thirty."

Faith was quiet a moment. "What do you mean?"

"Do you think people just retire and go off to write their memoirs? Arthur Dorian wasn't really going to retire. He knew he couldn't. When case officers feel they can't continue, they're moved inside. Some of them do things in Virginia here for me. Some of them work in The Basement, handling the construction of the identities. You don't just quit, not with what you know."

"What are you saying? Just what the hell are you saying?"

"All I'm saying is that you need to bring Alex in. Focus on that, and only on that. It's better for everyone. We'll think about Isaac Smith after Alex is in. Perhaps we'll be able to bring *him* in. That would be interesting, wouldn't it?"

Faith hung up the phone without answering. She was shaking again, clenching and unclenching her hands. She finally got up, pacing the tiny office, and in one swift movement, grabbed the catfish mounted on its wall plaque, and threw it across the room, where it bounced off her file cabinet.

Oddly enough, she believed Yorkton when he said he hadn't been involved in setting up Alex. The department's precious reputation was everything to him, and he'd been genuinely offended by the previous director's long-standing corruption. But the man was blinded by politics. He couldn't see what was right there.

Isaac Smith, John Brown's Body, had plotted all this to ruin Alex Bridge. But why?

And what about the phone call and e-mail? They came before Alex's life started its downward spiral. Were they part of the setup? If so, why did he come to Faith now with all his talk about justice?

Faith crossed the room and picked the catfish up from the floor. She turned the plaque over.

It read: *Lake Texoma, July 4, 1981*.

Art Dorian hadn't caught the fish at Lake Texoma or anywhere else.

Fish stories, he'd told Faith. It seemed like a long time ago that he'd said that. *My whole career is about making up fish stories*.

She carefully set the fish on her desk. "But someone else made up this story," she said aloud.

She'd only gotten as far as thinking of a name for Alex Bridge's new identity. Robyn Egan, that was it.

"Stupid," Faith said.

The anger began to take hold again. Just like when she'd let Alex walk away from the hospital, there had to be more than two choices. She could choose to track Alex down and resume the case, turn the young woman into Robyn Egan. Or she could walk away from Department Thirty and look over her shoulder the rest of her life.

She sat back down, feeling the beginnings of a headache in her temples. Faith pressed her fingers to her head and massaged it a bit.

She leaned back. The office was silent.

She sat, not moving, hands on her temples, for a long time.

Then, she slowly sat forward and turned on her computer.

How can I find you? she'd asked Smith at the lake.

You'll find me.

She waited, fingers hovering above the keyboard.

Alex Bridge. Yorkton. Paul Wells. Gary St. James. Isaac Smith.

Phone calls and e-mail messages.

"You bastard," she said, thinking of Yorkton.

You'll find me.

In the e-mail program, Faith typed johnbrownsbody@-hubopag.com in the address box. She waited a moment, then she began to write a message to the man who ruined people for a living.

17

SMITH WAS WAITING.

Once a project was in as advanced a stage as this one was, much of his time was spent waiting. But Smith was a patient man. It was why he'd been so successful, making millions of dollars while enjoying his work and never coming close to being caught.

The authorities had heard of him, of course. That much he knew. But as far as he could tell, not a single government agency had a photo of him or had any clue to where he lived.

So Smith didn't mind waiting. It allowed him time to enjoy the satisfaction he felt in what he was able to create. Writers created with words, artists with paint, composers with music. He simply manipulated the forces of people's own lives to create chaos, to watch a slow disintegration of their existence.

The gradual ones were the best, when he was allowed time to really work. If he could make his clients understand that would achieve their objectives over time, he could relish every bit of it. Most of them were impatient, but he could eventually convince them that if they didn't rush him, he would fulfill their requests to perfection.

It had been especially gratifying to watch what was going on now. It was the largest canvas he had ever painted, the equivalent of Richard Wagner composing the *Ring* cycle of operas. Nothing had ever been attempted on such a scale, and he alone had done it.

The one change was Faith Kelly. Now, instead of waiting for Alex Bridge to make a move, he waited for the Kelly woman to act. It was as if she was Alex's proxy. A complication? A challenge? Yes, on both counts.

Smith smiled.

He was sitting on a wooden bench overlooking the small pond beside the Nigh University Center building on the University of Central Oklahoma campus in the suburb of Edmond. Smith loved university campuses: he always felt at home in centers of learning and tried to visit university libraries in every city to which he traveled. UCO had been a commuter university serving the Oklahoma City metro area for many years, but had recently made an effort to attract more students to live on campus. Hence the construction of new student housing, the expansion of the University Center, and this lovely little pond with its three fountains.

None of the summer-school students gave him a second look, sitting on the bench with his laptop open and running. In his khaki pants and light blue oxford shirt, with a pair of glasses added for effect, he looked like a young assistant professor taking time to sit in the sun and work on his next lecture.

The laptop's e-mail program beeped to let him know he had new messages coming in. He angled the screen away from the glare of the sun and smiled when he saw the sender.

Kelly, Faith S.

He opened the message.

I need to meet with you. Soon. No theatrics necessary.

There was no signature. The woman was completely no-nonsense. He was beginning to get a feel for her, which helped his own peace of mind greatly.

He pulled the computer to him and typed out a reply.

I knew you would find me. The pond behind the University Center, UCO campus, Edmond. I'll be waiting.

He sent the message. Her reply came back less than two minutes later.

I'll find you.

"Of course you will," Smith said. "Because that's what I want you to do."

He sat back, crossed his legs, and went back to watching the fountains. And waiting.

Forty-five minutes later, students—most in shorts, sandals, and varying styles of T-shirts and tank tops, with the ubiquitous backpacks and sling bags—were milling about. Several passed right in front of Smith's spot on the bench. A couple of them actually nodded and smiled to him.

"A scholar like yourself, going back to school?"

Smith turned. Faith towered above him, standing three steps behind the bench. With the low hum of noise from all the students around, he hadn't heard her approach.

He waited a moment before speaking, then turned his back to her, looking at the pond. "Oh, no. I'm no scholar. But I do enjoy campuses."

Faith came around the side of the bench. "Oh, don't be modest. I hear that you could be one of this country's leading Civil War experts."

"An exaggeration, but thank you for giving me the compliment of checking up on me."

"It was the least I could do."

"Sit, please." Smith moved the laptop to his other side and made room on the bench.

Faith sat down at arm's length from him.

"Thank you," Smith said. "This is much more pleasant than our first meeting."

"I said no theatrics were necessary."

"So you did. If you've done some homework, you understand that none of your colleagues in the government have put two and two together about me. You're the only one who's seen me, knowing who I am."

Faith nodded. She crossed her long legs and leaned back against the bench. She wore a white tank, jeans, and a little gray flat-brimmed "newsboy" hat. Smith thought she blended in quite well with the campus surroundings.

Faith nodded. "I'm wondering why that is."

Smith shrugged. "We need each other. I take my work seriously, as you do. I have to recognize that sometimes I need help to achieve my objectives."

"Who's your client?"

Smith shook his head and said nothing.

The silence lingered. Several students walked by. They both looked at the fountains.

"All right, I'll play the game," Faith finally said. "Neither confirm nor deny that you have a client."

Smith smiled, still looking out over the pond. "How is Alex?"

"Alex is gone."

The smile vanished, Smith's face furrowing. "Gone?"

"Gone."

"Escaped or released?"

"A little of both."

With some effort, Smith returned to his casual look and tone. "You're being very vague this morning."

"It comes with the territory. I need some information from you."

"I suspect you do."

"The e-mail you sent her . . . I got it from her computer. I read it to her. Something clicked."

"And what about you? Did anything click with you?"

"I went to Galveston, if that's what you mean. I've been to the crime scene."

"And?"

"And . . . I'm not sharing my conclusions with you."

"But you expect me to share information with you?"

Faith Kelly looked at him dead-on, green eyes unflinching. Before she even spoke again, Smith decided that under the college-student look lay pure steel. "Yes, Mr. Smith, I do."

More silence. They stared at the fountains awhile longer. The clusters of students drifted into buildings. A couple of cars wandered in and out of the parking lot. "You think she's ready to pursue it," Smith said after nearly five minutes.

"I think so. After all this, she's been motivated to act. I don't know that she ever would have if my department hadn't been thrown into the mix, but I guess that doesn't matter." Faith took off the gray hat and hung it on one knee. She pulled her hair back from her face. "You seem to know her. Where do you think she'll go?"

Smith made a show of shutting down his laptop, then snapped it closed. "This is about her history, and how it intersects with that of others."

"That sounds like the beginning of a lecture."

Smith smiled. "We are in academia, after all. But no, this is no lecture. Understand this about Alex Bridge: she's spent her entire life denying one-half of her history."

Faith twirled the gray hat on one finger. "Her mother."

"Bravo, Ms. Kelly. Since her mother left when Alex was so young, and her mother was Comanche, Alex has never been exposed to the Comanche side of her heritage."

"She never saw *any* of that side of her family?"

"Her father moved from place to place. Every time he took up with a new woman, they moved to a new town. She never had the opportunity. When she got older, she simply didn't have anything to do with Native American culture. The fact that she had Comanche bloodlines didn't interest her. To her mind, her mother wasn't interested in her, so she wasn't interested in her mother or her mother's people."

"So she's run away from being Comanche."

"You could say that. Now . . . now she's armed with information that tries to force her to pay attention to what she's always run from before. She'll fight it every step of the way. She'll try to attack from every other possible angle before delving into that part of herself."

Faith sat very still for nearly a minute. Then she turned to Smith very slowly. The green eyes blazed again. Smith felt mesmerized by them.

"The other name in the e-mail," Faith said. "Jonathan Doag. You said he came from Pittsburgh."

"Yes."

Faith jammed the gray hat back on her head and pulled her keys from her jeans pocket. "Alex is on her way to Pittsburgh."

Smith chuckled, looking away from her eyes. This was a remarkable young woman. She had the potential to be as good a manipulator as he. A bit rough at the edges, but certainly talented.

"Have a good trip," Smith said.

"Is there anything else I should know?"

"What a question!" Smith laughed again, this time more heartily. "I told you before, my interest is in seeing Alex find justice."

Faith put a hand on the back of the bench, car keys dangling over it. "That doesn't quite jibe with what I've heard about you."

"Really?"

"Really. You ruin people's lives, manipulate them into impossible situations, destroy them from the inside out. So pardon me if I still don't get what your role is in all this."

Smith shrugged modestly. "I know things, but—"

"I know, I know, you can't prove them. Only Alex can find the proof and all you can do is point her in the right direction."

"You understand perfectly. Justice will be done. In fact, I can see that you'll be the one to make sure that it *is* done. Strange, considering your job description."

"Touché. But I'm wondering . . . why would you ruin

Alex, then go to all this effort to help her 'get justice'?"

Smith cocked his head and his voice softened. "I'm just doing my job. But . . ." He thought for a long moment. *Be very, very careful. It's so very easy to slip from being the manipulator into being the one who is manipulated.* "Alex is an intriguing woman. I meet many people, and very few of them are truly interesting. Alex doesn't even know half of how intriguing she is. But she will."

Faith looked at him for another moment, then without a word turned and jogged to her car. A minute later, Smith saw the gold Miata roar out of the lot.

He turned on his cell phone and called the man with the scuffed boots.

"Where is she?" the man said when he heard Smith's voice. "Do you have her?"

Smith looked out at the fountains again. "Oh, yes, I have her," he said.

Standing at the back entrance to the Communications Building, northwest of the spot where Smith sat overlooking "Broncho Lake," the man with the goatee repositioned his camera. He took a long shot of a beautiful blond college girl, then swung the camera slightly to the right. Kelly was already in her car. But Kelly didn't interest him anymore. He zoomed in on the man who sat on the bench.

Smith was facing away from him, talking on the phone.

Turn around now, the man said silently. *Come on, turn to look at the girls, at the satellite dish, at the mural on the building . . . anything! Just let me get a clear shot of your face.*

He waited two more minutes, pretending to take pictures of various campus buildings.

When Smith turned, looking casually this way and that, he snapped off four pictures in a row.

"Yes!" the man whispered.

He put the lens cap back on his camera. Taking the long way around Thatcher Hall, to avoid any chance of Smith seeing him, he headed toward the pay lot where he'd left his car.

He needed to catch a plane. He had a feeling he needed to deliver these pictures in person.

Driving with one hand, Faith was on the phone before she was even off the UCO campus. By the time she was headed south on Broadway, back toward Oklahoma City proper, she was booked on a flight to Pittsburgh.

Faith grimaced. She'd been in a crash of a small plane last year, landing in the middle of a wheat field in west Texas. Only the skill and coolheadedness of the pilot had saved them.

"I hate flying," she said aloud to the interior of the car as Bobby McFerrin vocalized on her stereo.

She was agitated, but not about what Smith had told her. Her instinct had already told her that Alex would first try to seek out the descendants of this Jonathan Doag, whoever he was. But she'd wanted the confirmation from Smith before she tracked Alex all the way across the country.

No, it was something else from her second encounter with Smith. Something he said, a certain look, a gesture, an attitude . . . what?

She had just left the Edmond city limits, speeding past the entrance to the Kilpatrick Turnpike, when she said, "It couldn't be."

She needed quiet. She snapped off the stereo. The only sound was the engine and the air conditioner.

She replayed the conversation at the pond in her mind.

"No," she said.

Faith eased off the accelerator and coasted the Miata to the shoulder between Memorial Road and 122nd Street. Traffic blew past her in the morning heat.

She replayed the conversation again, thinking of everything she could about the way Isaac Smith looked, the way he talked, the way he moved, what he'd said.

It can't be, she thought.

But it would explain a lot.

She slammed the car back into gear. She drove nearly

eighty miles an hour all the way to the downtown exit, then blew a couple of red lights on the way to the U.S. Court-house.

In her office, she went straight to the computer, then to the telephone. After ten minutes on the phone with the Oklahoma Department of Public Safety, she raced down the hall to the Marshals Service office.

The Department Thirty office did not have a fax machine. Yorkton didn't want to "attract attention" by paying for another phone line into the office, so Faith was allowed to pick up faxes from the Marshals Service. There were actually very few, as most department business was done by telephone or computer.

Absorbed in her shadow world, Faith barely acknowledged the few deputies who spoke to her: Mayfield, Leneski, Chief Deputy Raines. She saw Paige Carson, but Carson pointedly looked the other direction, suddenly interested in the wall of her cubicle.

Faith stood at the fax machine, muttering "Come on, come on" several times. Finally it rang, then began to whir. She ripped the page out of the machine almost before it had finished feeding.

She held the paper up to her face. She drew in a breath so sharp that Derek Mayfield, at the desk closest to the fax machine, looked up at her.

"You okay, Faith?" he said.

"Oh my God," Faith said.

Then she thought: *Oh, Alex, I'm so sorry.*

Part Two
18

July 17, 3:30 P.M.
Pittsburgh, Pennsylvania

THE FIRST LESSON ALEX LEARNED WAS THAT PEOPLE who travel cross-country by bus are smokers. Smoking wasn't allowed on the bus itself, but at every stop—whether five minutes in Vinita, Oklahoma, or a two-hour layover in Columbus, Ohio—three-fourths of the people on the bus would rush immediately outside to smoke. Other needs, such as going to the restroom or getting food and drink, were all secondary to the nicotine fix.

Alex was fortunate in that the bus driver considered her "disabled" due to her pregnancy and she was able to sit in the very front row for the entire trip. Danny had been right: once she was on the bus the first time, no one asked her for identification again.

The trip was a mind- and body-numbing thirty hours. Alex had no music to listen to, nothing to read. She just sat in the front seat and watched America slide past. When others on the bus went out to smoke, Alex would find a quiet corner and play her flute for a few minutes. By the time the bus reached St. Louis, she'd begun attracting a small group of ten or so every time she played. No one spoke, but Alex knew they were listening. It was all that kept her sane during the crazy ride.

The bus station in Pittsburgh was a long building with tile

floors and bad acoustics, sound bouncing off every wall. As soon as she was off the bus, Alex found a ladies' room and washed her face. She'd had toothbrush and toothpaste in her bag, and that was the extent of the "freshening" she could do. Her hair was hopeless, but then she never paid much attention to her hair anyway.

Shouldering her bag, her lower back aching and joints complaining, she walked the length of the building and stepped out into an overcast sky. Coming into the city, she'd been surprised at Pittsburgh. She expected steel mills and smokestacks. What she saw was rolling, lush green hills, and a clean, comfortable city.

Three taxis were lined up outside the bus station. Alex climbed into the nearest one and sat motionless. The driver, a big, bald black man who was relentlessly working a toothpick in his mouth, said, "Where do you want to go?"

Then it struck Alex. She had no idea what to do next. She'd come to Pittsburgh, home of Jonathan Doag—whoever he was. How did she find his descendents? Would they even talk to her?

"Hello?" the driver said.

"I—" Alex said. *What do I do now?* "I'm sorry, I—"

Without warning, she started to cry. She felt like a fool. With hormones raging and her life hanging by a brittle thread, it seemed she wept all the time.

"I'm sorry," she said. "I feel like an idiot. I came all this way, and I don't know—"

The driver rolled his eyes. "Do you want to go someplace or not?"

"Yes, I—" Tears welled again and Alex blinked fiercely. "I have to find the descendants of this Jonathan Doag, and I knew I had to come to Pittsburgh, but I don't know—"

"Doag?" the driver said. "Did you say Doag?"

Alex glanced up. He was looking at her in the rearview mirror. She nodded. "Doag."

"Why didn't you say so?" The driver put the car in gear and pulled away from the curb.

"Wait a minute! Don't tell me . . . you've got to be kidding. In a city this size, you know these people?"

The driver smiled into the mirror as he pulled around a corner between the downtown Pittsburgh high-rises. "Tell me something, missy. You think of Pittsburgh, what do you think of?"

"Steel."

"What about names? What name pops into your head?"

Alex thought for a moment. "Carnegie. And what about . . . Isn't Heinz here? The ketchup people?"

"There you go. Carnegie and Heinz. Way back when, they helped make this town."

"I don't understand. What does that have to do with this Doag family?"

The driver smiled again, turning onto Liberty Avenue. "See, everyone has to start somewhere, right? You get an idea, you want to do something with it—like put up a steel mill or make ketchup—you gotta have a start. You need some help. Where do you go? You go to a bank and you get yourself a little loan."

"I don't—"

"Missy, Carnegie and Heinz may have built Pittsburgh, but the Doags gave 'em the money to get started."

Alex leaned forward. "They ran a bank?"

"Not ran. Run. One of the last family-owned banks anywhere. A Doag has been running Merchants Bank of Pittsburgh since way, way back. Don't know any Jonathan. The guy up there now is Russell Doag. He took over after the old man died a couple of years ago."

Alex's heart began to triple time. "Do you think he'd talk to me?"

"Can't tell you that. All I can do is get you to the building. And here we are."

He stopped before a glass-fronted high-rise. Alex estimated it at thirty or so stories, ten stories higher than anything in Oklahoma City. An ornate sign, looking out of place on such a modernistic building, stood just above the revolving door entrance. MERCHANTS BANK OF PITTSBURGH at DOAG CENTER.

"Amazing," Alex said. She dug in her bag. "How much do I owe you?"

"Missy," the driver said, "this one's on me. I didn't even start the meter."

"Oh, no," Alex said. "I can pay. I may look ragged, but I have a little money."

"I believe you do. But you look like you need something and maybe I helped you get to it."

"I don't know what to say."

"Well, just remember this: God loves you and so do I, and there's nothing you can do about it."

Alex looked up. It sounded like something the driver had said hundreds of times.

"I'll remember that," she said. "Thank you."

She stepped out of the cab and watched as it pulled away. Tall buildings surrounded her. In the space between two of them, she saw a plaza with trees and benches in the next block. Just beyond Doag Center was a traffic light, and on the other side of the street she saw the entrance to a park of some sort. She walked to the corner. The sign across the way announced: POINT STATE PARK.

Alex walked slowly back to Doag Center. A man and a woman, each in expensive business suits, brushed by her. The woman glared at her.

She caught a glimpse of herself in the mirrored glass of the building. She had "bus hair" and her clothes were rumpled. Her eyes were hooded, wary. Alex shook her head and tried to smooth down her hair in the back, to little avail. She needed a shower.

"Oh, well," she said, and entered the revolving door.

The lobby of Doag Center was all dark wood and muted tones. A young man wearing a slim headset sat behind a horseshoe-shaped desk. With a neutral expression, he looked at Alex.

"May I help you?" he said, sounding like he wanted to do anything but.

Alex walked to the desk. "This is going to sound crazy," she said.

The man's expression didn't change.

"I'd like to see Mr. Doag." She waited. "Please."

The man ducked his head slightly. "Do you have an appointment?"

"No. No, I don't. You see, I've just come a very long way, all the way from Oklahoma, and I know this sounds totally insane. I'm doing some . . . I guess you could call it family research, and the name Jonathan Doag came up, and I understand that he's an ancestor of the Doags who have this bank."

Alex stopped. The words had all come out in a rush, tumbling over each other. She tried to slow down. "I know, it's crazy. If I were you, I wouldn't let me in to see someone as important as Mr. Doag. But this is very important, and I just need a few minutes."

"Your name?"

"Bridge. Alex Bridge. I'm from—"

"Just a moment."

He turned away from her and clicked a mouse in front of him. He whispered a few words into the boom microphone by his mouth, then turned back to Alex. "You understand that Russell Doag is the president and chairman of the board of Doag Financial, and he's an extremely busy man."

"I'm sure he is. I just—"

"He's also very interested in family history. He'll give you ten minutes. Go to elevator number six. That's an express that will take you up to twenty-seven, where his office is. His assistant will meet you."

Alex rode the elevator, and was met on the twenty-seventh floor by another sharp-eyed young man in a dark suit.

"This way, please," he said, and led Alex through a maze of hallways. The final one dead-ended at a huge mahogany door. The nameplate read: *Russell Doag, President & Chairman.* "I'll be back to escort you out when you're finished."

The assistant rapped on the door, then opened it. He retreated and Alex walked into Russell Doag's office.

She hadn't been sure what to expect. She knew now that Russell Doag came from old money, and was the current leader of a family of vast wealth. Alex had always been intimidated by material success. While not exactly poor, her father never had much to spare, either. They didn't go hungry and Alex never wore rags, but as a child Alex had been utterly cowed by rich kids. In one small town where they lived for three or four years, one of the kids whose family owned both the bank and the local funeral home—*They get you coming and going,* her father had said—had bedeviled her without cease. Once, after school, for no apparent reason the girl had told Alex to stand in a certain spot and not move until she was told. Then the girl left. Alex, who was supposed to walk home, was terrified and stood rooted to the spot for over an hour, until her "stepmother" came looking for her. Later, when her father asked why she didn't just leave, she told him she thought she had to do what the other girl told her, because of who she was.

Now an adult, Alex was still innately uncomfortable with, and even somewhat resentful of, material wealth and power. She thought from time to time that was what had motivated her to quietly assemble her files on Cross Currents. And if she hadn't done that, perhaps none of this would have happened.

She shook her head. No time for foolish thoughts.

Russell Doag's office was large, but wasn't a shrine to himself. There were no photos of him with dignitaries, only a couple of college degrees on the wall. The only pictures were of a woman and four children.

Doag rose and stood behind the desk. "Come in," he said. "I'm Russ Doag."

He wasn't wearing a suit, like all his subordinates did. He had on gray Dockers and a polo shirt with the Duquesne

University logo across it. He was in his forties, blond, tall, slim, but with something of an impish air to him. Alex remembered something she'd read about old money versus new money. Old money families, while very aware of their wealth, thought it vulgar to flaunt it. It made her wonder about Russell Doag.

"I'm Alex Bridge," she said very softly, then cleared her throat and said it again.

"Sit down," Doag said. "You look tired."

"Thank you." Alex sat in a plush leather chair. "I am. I just rode a bus all the way from Oklahoma."

"And you did all that just to see me?"

"Yes, sir. I—"

"Oh, please, don't call me sir. I get enough of that from my employees, and it's really kind of silly, if you ask me."

"Okay, I . . ." Alex closed her eyes for a moment, feeling the exhaustion almost overwhelm her. "Now that I'm here, I'm not quite sure what to say."

"Family history?" Doag prompted. "That's what my bulldog downstairs said you asked about."

Alex nodded. "Bulldog?"

Doag smiled, showing straight white teeth. "They think they have to protect me from riffraff." He sat back down behind his desk and leaned back, lacing his fingers behind his head. "But, see, I'm what's commonly known as a figurehead. I'm just the current Doag, and there always has to be one in this office. I don't really run the bank or any of the other companies. I hire guys with MBAs to do that. I run the Doag Foundation and I play tennis and I travel and I go to my kids' soccer games." He spread his hands apart. "So what can I do for you, Alex?"

Alex smiled back, almost in spite of herself. "Well," she said. "I'm still not sure where to start. I . . . the name I have is Jonathan Doag. I . . . I'm not sure what to ask. I think he was somehow connected to some of my ancestors. I don't have much to go on. I'm sorry if I'm wasting your time."

Doag leaned forward. He smiled again, his eyes crinkling.

The man looked as if he'd never worried about anything in his life. "You're not, Alex. Let me set that to rest right now. Let me tell you something about my family. The Doag men don't live long."

"Excuse me?"

He nodded vigorously. "It's true. There's only been one male in the whole Doag line, for over 150 years, who lived past the age of fifty. That one was my grandfather. He died two years ago, at the age of ninety-one. My father died at thirty-eight. I'm forty-five now, and I have no illusions about anything. I live my life, and I don't think family is wasted time. Even family that's been gone for a century."

"What . . . what do they die of? The men in your family."

"You name it. Cancer, heart disease, accidents. My father drowned off the coast of Maine on a summer trip. The whole line, except for my grandfather, just seems to have been cursed. Take Uncle Jonathan, for example. He's still one of the best family stories. He was only twenty-nine."

"What happened to him?"

"You don't know? Well, of course you don't. All you have is his name. He was murdered, Alex. Smothered to death with his own pillow."

Alex heard the words but for a moment couldn't process them. Was this where it had all led? To this plush office so far from her home, with this wealthy yet easygoing man and his murdered ancestor? *But what does it have to do with me?*

"Did you get that?" Doag said gently.

Alex nodded.

"Okay. You said you're from Oklahoma, right?"

"Yes."

"That's very interesting, because Jonathan Doag—he was my great-great-uncle, by the way—spent some time there."

"What?"

Doag waved a hand. "Oh, yes. He was notorious in the family. He didn't want to be a banker, and he didn't like Pittsburgh. Sort of a black sheep, you understand. When he graduated from Harvard, instead of coming home and going into the bank like everyone expected him to, he went to Washington."

"D.C.?"

"D.C. Jonathan's older brother Hamilton was my great-great-grandfather, and his journals say that Jonathan was always fascinated by the West. He was especially interested in Indians. Or should I say Native Americans? I'm never quite sure."

Alex shrugged. "Makes no difference to me."

"Oh, good. Jonathan wanted to help the Natives, thought they'd gotten shafted in the years after the Civil War, with all the westward expansion. Of course that was true, but it took the rest of us a lot longer to come to that conclusion. So Jonathan thought he could fulfill his dream of going west and serving the people at the same time by joining the government. Hamilton, in true older-brother fashion, told him he was crazy, and he was a Doag, and how could he, and on and on and on. Hamilton's journals are full of all kinds of colorful language about what he thought of Jonathan."

"So he went west."

"He did. He signed on with the Department of the Interior and became an assistant Indian agent in Oklahoma Territory."

"And he was assigned to the Comanches."

Doag steepled his fingers. "Aha. Now we're making some connections. That's exactly right. He was there for nearly two years. Hamilton was so disgusted with the whole business that he didn't mention Jonathan in his journals again. At least, not until Jonathan died."

"You seem to have studied this a lot."

Doag shrugged. "I'm not as bright as you think I am. I told you my grandfather died two years ago, and I'm just getting around to dealing with his papers. He wanted to create a Doag archive, to be part of our charitable foundation. He seemed to think people would be interested in the papers of the Doag family. I personally think that's nonsense. Just because someone's rich, that doesn't mean that every scrap of paper from their life is suddenly more interesting, does it?"

Alex waited, then realized he actually expected her to answer. "Ah, maybe I shouldn't comment on that."

Doag laughed. "No, you probably shouldn't. And maybe you'd be a good diplomat, Alex Bridge. Seriously, though, my grandfather wanted to build this archive and I've been going through his papers. Some of these things of Hamilton's are in there, and I came across them not long ago. That's why it's still fresh on my mind. The interesting thing about Jonathan Doag is that after two years out west, he suddenly requested an emergency leave to come back to Washington. His hitch wasn't up for another year, but all of a sudden he was on a train back east.

"His train arrived and he went to his town house in Georgetown. The very next day, he was asleep in his bed when someone came into his bedroom and smothered him to death. His money was taken, and his watch, which had belonged to his own grandfather. The police called it robbery, and that was the end of it."

"No one was ever caught?"

"No. Never. The police kept it open for a while, then it was listed as 'unsolved' and passed into Doag family folklore. Hamilton just wanted it all to go away. He considered Jonathan an embarrassment and didn't want to attract even more attention by a drawn-out investigation. He was happy to let the murder case just fade away."

Alex was almost trembling. "When did all this happen?"

"Eighteen ninety-three, in the spring. Remarkable story, isn't it?"

Alex nodded, squirming on the leather chair. "It is, but . . . I don't know how it connects to me."

"I'm afraid I can't help you there," Doag said. "But there is one more interesting little puzzle piece. Come with me."

He helped her up and they left the office. Suited subordinates stood at attention as they passed in the hallways. "They're so silly," Doag said to Alex. "They know how to make money, but they don't know how to act around people."

"I have to ask," Alex said. "I saw your degrees on the wall, but you don't seem like a businessman to me. No offense."

Doag laughed. "None taken. I think that's a compliment, actually. I was a theater major as an undergraduate, then picked up a master's degree in interpersonal communication. I suspect old Hamilton Doag would have considered me an embarrassment too."

Alex laughed with him. They reached the elevator, not the express Alex had ridden before, and Doag punched the second floor. When they reached it, the doors opened onto sawdust and plaster and paint buckets.

"We're renovating the Doag Foundation offices," Doag explained. "Grandfather's archive will be here." They entered a small room filled with bookshelves and crammed with papers of every kind. A small table was jammed against the far wall.

Doag went to it, opened its only drawer, and took out a manila envelope. He opened the envelope and slid out a single sheet of white paper. Alex read it over his shoulder, a few lines written in thick black ink, in old-fashioned, flawless cursive:

22 April 1893

My dear brother Hamilton,

There have been so many times we did not concur, but you are still my only brother, and I must entrust you with the protection of these documents.

I will be returning to Washington soon, and will come to Pittsburgh as time allows. Until that time arrives, I beg you to protect the enclosed.

I have been friendly with Tabananika, a chief of the Comanche. He and I have witnessed a horrific series of events, and a conspiracy of silence threatens us. The enclosed is my affidavit of said events, as well as that of the aforementioned Comanche, translated to English. Injustices have

*been done, and many innocent lives lost. I cannot and will
not stand by and be a party to such conspiracy.*

   *Keep the affidavits safe. Perhaps you would lock them in
the bank's vault.*

   Godspeed, my dear brother.

   Yours, as ever,
   Jonathan

   Alex finished reading, then read the words again. There was the connection between Jonathan Doag and her mother's ancestor, Tabananika. But what did it mean, here and now? Why would it make someone want to destroy her, 112 years later?

   "The affidavits," Alex said.

   "Sorry," Doag said, slipping the letter back into its envelope. "I've looked through everything, and haven't seen any affidavits. This is the only thing from Jonathan that's here."

   "Would his brother have destroyed it?"

   Doag shook his head. "His brother never saw it."

   "I don't understand."

   "Remember I told you the Doag men all die young? Well, you have to also remember that the mail in those days was slow. It could take months for a piece of mail to work its way across the country, especially coming from a place like Oklahoma Territory that was still sort of wild. It took nearly three months for this package to reach Pittsburgh."

   "So? I still don't understand."

   "Jonathan was murdered on April 28, 1893. Hamilton caught a fever of some sort and died on July 15. He was only thirty-three. His wife said he was being punished for not trying harder to solve his brother's killing. That package bounced around through the family for a long time, unopened. My grandfather was the first person to open it. When he was dying two years ago, he'd already started me on going through his papers. I came across the cover letter and took it to him. I had to ask him about it."

"What did he say?"

"I asked him where the affidavits were that went with the letter. He wasn't very lucid right then, slipping in and out. But I kept after him about it. I asked him if he had the affidavits. And he said—I'll never forget this—he said, 'Not anymore.' He lost consciousness the day after that and died a week later."

Alex stood there, smelling sawdust and fresh paint, over a thousand miles from her home, and listened to her heart beating, thinking of two men, one her ancestor, one the ancestor of the man standing beside her.

Injustices have been done, and many innocent lives lost, Jonathan Doag had written.

Alex thought of her own life, of the nightmare she'd stepped into, and from which there was no waking. Someone wanted to destroy her, and was coming close to succeeding.

Just as they'd destroyed Jonathan Doag.

Had they done the same to Tabananika?

"It's time I found out," Alex said.

19

July 17, 5:06 P.M.

FAITH WALKED ALONE THROUGH POINT STATE PARK, the site of the original Fort Pitt. She had been surprised to see that downtown Pittsburgh itself was actually an island, and all accesses into the city were either by tunnel or bridge. From Doag Center, she'd walked to the end of Liberty Avenue and crossed Commonwealth Place into the park. She crossed under the I-279 and found herself staring at the spot where the Allegheny and Monongahela rivers came together to form the Ohio River.

She walked around the fountain and stood at the wall overlooking the three rivers. She'd been exhausted and her nerves frayed by the time her flight reached Pittsburgh last night, so she'd simply checked into a hotel near the airport and crashed for her first decent night's sleep in a while. Up at five, after going for a run around the hotel grounds, she'd spent some time with her laptop doing Internet research on the Doag family. At eight A.M. she'd been at Doag Center, and she met with Russell Doag when he arrived at nine.

Russell Doag was a curious man, in more ways than one. He seemed to have not the slightest interest in the company he ostensibly managed, yet he had spent over an hour telling Faith about his family history. He seemed particularly proud of the macabre fact that men in his line were so short-lived.

Faith made notes about Jonathan Doag and Tabananika—for the first time, there were both names, connected in something other than Smith's e-mail to Alex—and then told Doag about Alex. She wanted Alex to discover this on her own, to have some sense of independence. Alex Bridge had almost lost everything that she was, with Faith pulling the strings. Now she would let Alex find Jonathan Doag before she met up with her again.

When her cell phone rang, it was Russell Doag.

"Alex just left here," he said.

"How is she?" Faith asked.

"That's a good question. A little shaken, perhaps? Confused? And why wouldn't she be? It's certainly a confusing situation. But I also detect strength in her, maybe a strength she doesn't know is there."

"You're quite the observer of human nature."

"I take that as a compliment, Ms. Kelly."

"Thank you for your help."

"I get the feeling," Doag said, "that the young woman has been through a lot. Take care of her."

"That's the idea," Faith said.

She clicked off and started toward the street. She waited for the light at Commonwealth Place, as an off-ramp from I-279 fed right down to it and the afternoon rush was starting to build. She crossed to the far end of the Doag Center building and waited.

Five minutes later she saw Alex come out through the revolving door and stand on the sidewalk, unmoving. The clouds had broken somewhat, and sun was filtering through the tall buildings. Alex turned her face toward the sky, as if searching it.

I'm sorry, Alex, Faith thought, and started toward her.

Take care of her, Doag had said.

Ten steps away, Alex turned toward her.

"Oh God," Alex said, backing away.

"Alex, don't run," Faith said. "Please listen to me."

"Get away from me. I'm not giving up who I am."

"Alex, I believe you."

"Don't do this to me! You're just messing with my mind again."

Faith raised both hands. "No, I'm not. I've never meant to mess with your mind. I've just been doing my job. But Alex, listen—"

"No! Get away from me! Why are you here?"

Faith raised her voice for the first time. "Why do you think it was so easy for you to get in to see Russell Doag? Do you think a guy like him just talks to everyone who shows up at his office?"

Alex clenched her fists. "I thought he was actually pretty nice."

"Yeah, he's a good guy, but he's also a billionaire. I paved the way for you. I was here when he got here this morning. He showed me the letter, Alex. The one from Jonathan Doag to his brother. The missing affidavits . . . I know about them. We're starting to make some connections, some things that should help us figure out what's happening to you."

Alex started to back away. "Leave me alone! I want my life back. I can do this myself. I can . . ."

She turned and moved down the sidewalk at a fast trot, which wasn't very fast at all.

"Alex!" Faith shouted. "I'm not your enemy! I know you didn't do it, Alex! Wells, the money . . . I understand now. Let me help you!"

Alex kept going, oblivious. Faith ran into an executive coming out of Doag Center. She spun around him, barely keeping her feet, while the man sprawled on the ground, chasing his expensive leather briefcase.

Alex was almost to the corner at Commonwealth Place, showing no signs of stopping.

"Alex!" Faith shouted again.

"Leave me alone!"

Faith played her last card. "Alex, I think your husband is alive."

Alex had gone right into the middle of Commonwealth Place, just as the light for cars coming down from the ramp turned green.

She turned with excruciating slowness, halfway toward

Faith. Faith saw the look on her face—surprise mixed with fear, anticipation—and then all Faith could do was watch in mute horror as the car barreled down the ramp and turned onto Commonwealth.

There was no time for the driver to even sound the horn. Faith heard tires squealing, and a second later the car's grille slammed into Alex's belly, which was facing straight toward the car since she'd turned to look back at Faith. Alex was briefly airborne, then she was rolling, rolling into the grass of Point State Park. She rolled at least five times before coming to rest halfway down the gentle slope.

Faith ran, ignoring the drivers who were now erupting out of their cars like smoke from a fire. A woman with a cell phone yelled that she'd already called 911. A man told someone that *she just ran right out there in the street*. The woman who'd hit her sat behind her steering wheel, sobbing, seemingly unable to move. Sirens sounded. A child cried.

Faith reached Alex, calling her name. Alex didn't move.

She had cuts on her face and arms, though none seemed to be bleeding very much. Alex's knees were drawn up to her stomach, and her arms were wrapped around her midsection. Taking care not to move her—the EMTs might need a backboard and she didn't want to do any further damage—Faith felt along her leg.

That's when she found the blood. Hot and thick and still flowing, it coated the entire area between Alex's legs.

20

THE NATIONAL HEADQUARTERS OF DEPARTMENT THIRTY was a small gray stone building across from the main campus of James Madison University, in the small wooded college town of Harrisonburg, in the Shenandoah Valley. Yorkton had just taken a walk around the JMU campus, something he often did when he needed to think. The temperature was around eighty, a few puffy clouds sailing overhead, and he had to admit that he enjoyed the summer here. It was considerably milder than the summers he'd grown accustomed to when he lived in Oklahoma.

Thinking of Oklahoma brought him back to business. Faith Kelly. Alex Bridge. Isaac Smith.

He was still troubled by Faith's phone call. She'd been a case officer now for over a year, and he had expected that she would have settled down and accepted the department's mission a little more readily. Instead, she still seemed to question it at every turn, thinking through her old law enforcement perspective. As talented as she was, it had become an annoying habit to Yorkton.

Conway, he thought. *Plain old Dick Conway. I'm not Yorkton anymore, even if Kelly likes calling me that.*

As he finished his walk and let himself back into the department's building, for a moment he was unsure of who he was supposed to be. He'd lived Dean Yorkton's cover for over

twenty years as a field officer. But now he was an administra-
tor, the director of Department Thirty, and he was Richard
Matthias Conway again.

Or am I? he wondered. *Maybe I'm really more Yorkton than
Conway after all these years.*

With so many identities—fifty-eight protectees, their original names and those the department had given them—floating
through his head, a few flashes of uncertainty were bound to
happen. He shrugged it off, coming back to Kelly. There was
work to be done.

At a few minutes past six, he was back at his desk, alone,
catching up on some forms that needed to be sent over to
the attorney general in D.C. The doorbell buzzed and he
glanced at the TV monitor over his desk. The security camera
showed a tall man of around forty, casually dressed, with
glasses and a brownish-gray goatee. Yorkton buzzed him in.

A minute later the man entered his office and tossed a
thick folder onto Yorkton's desk. "Well, Officer Simon,"
Yorkton said. "How was the flight?"

The man shrugged. "It was a flight."

Yorkton nodded. He knew the man didn't like small talk.
He opened the folder and pulled out the photographs Simon
had taken yesterday: Faith Kelly, in tank top, jeans, running
shoes, and the gray hat, leaving her house, climbing into the
Miata. Faith Kelly getting out of the Miata in the parking lot
behind Thatcher Hall on the UCO campus. Faith Kelly sitting
beside the man Yorkton believed was Isaac Smith, John
Brown's Body.

Yorkton made a clucking sound with his tongue. "Officer
Kelly," he said softly, without looking up. "As angry as you
are at me right now, you're still helping the department,
without even knowing it."

Simon cleared his throat.

Yorkton looked at him. "Good work."

Simon shrugged. "I admit I was surprised that I was following and photographing one of our own."

"You shouldn't be."

They stared each other down.

"I'm getting too old for this shit," Simon finally said.

"I trust that's a joke," Yorkton said.

"You wish." Simon stood up. "You want me back on Kelly, or what?"

"No. This will do for now. I have what I need." Yorkton bent back to the photos. "She's courageous. I'll grant her that. Meeting with someone like Smith . . . it's dangerous, but could be very fruitful in ways Kelly can't even begin to imagine."

"Fruitful? Do you always talk like that?"

Yorkton looked up slowly. "You're dismissed, Officer Simon. I'll let you know if I need you again."

Simon shrugged and shuffled out the door.

Yorkton looked at the photos again. At the end of the sequence was an excellent one that Simon had clearly shot with a telephoto lens. Isaac Smith was looking directly at the camera and his features were quite clear.

Yorkton breathed out very slowly. For the last decade, Isaac Smith, the man known as John Brown's Body, had been a mystery in Washington and beyond. He existed—that was all anyone knew with certainty. The havoc he created was well known in Congress, on Embassy Row, on Wall Street, and of course at DOJ. But to Yorkton's knowledge, no one had ever been able to photograph him.

And now, quite by accident, while trying to make the pieces fall together in the Alex Bridge recruitment, Department Thirty's newest case officer had dropped Smith into his lap.

This case might be doubly profitable, Yorkton thought.

He took the best photo of Smith and scanned it into his computer. Then he accessed DOJ's huge photographic database and asked it to search for a match, to find a face that matched that of Isaac Smith.

The screen flashed: YOU HAVE REQUESTED A SEARCH ON THE ENTIRE DATABASE. THIS COULD TAKE SEVERAL HOURS.

"That's all right," Yorkton said. "I can wait."

21

July 17, 6:15 P.M.
Pittsburgh

FAITH HAD DANCED ALONG THE EDGES OF PANIC AS THE ambulance arrived. The first EMT to reach Alex saw her condition, the blood between her legs, and very quietly said, "Oh, no."

They were at Allegheny General Hospital within ten minutes of the time the car struck Alex. Faith had a few difficult moments explaining that she wasn't Alex's family but was the only person she knew in Pittsburgh. The EMTs eventually relented and allowed her to ride in the ambulance. Without even thinking about it, Faith took Alex's hand and held it all the way into the emergency room.

The ER doctor on duty immediately paged the ob-gyn on call, then began treating Alex. She had cuts and abrasions on her face, arms, and legs, and two cracked ribs, but otherwise there was no further direct injury to Alex. The blood flow between her legs was stemmed, and the doctors conferred in worried tones, then called Faith outside while two nurses stayed with Alex.

"Are you family?" the OB doctor asked.

Faith shook her head. "I'm a . . . I'm a friend. We're from out of town."

"What about the father?"

"The father is out of the picture."

"What do you mean, out of the picture? I'm sorry to pry, but . . ."

Faith hesitated. "It's . . . complicated." She wasn't going to share her thoughts about Gary St. James with this doctor.

The ER doc, a woman with short gray-streaked reddish hair, said, "Are you her . . . I mean, are you partners?"

It took Faith a moment to figure out what the doctor meant. "No, no," Faith said. "It's not like that." She decided to stick with the truth as Alex knew it. "The father, her husband, is dead. As I said, I'm just a friend. Just a regular friend."

"Had to ask," the ER doc said.

"Here's the situation," the OB man said. "She's gone into preterm labor. How many weeks is she? Do you know?"

"Twenty-nine," Faith said. "Wait, thirty. It's thirty by now."

The doctor shook his head. "We've had the fetal monitor on her since she was brought in, and we're seeing some signs of fetal distress, such as erratic heartbeat."

"Was it brought on by the car hitting her?" Faith looked at both doctors. "I guess that's a silly question. Of course that's what brought it on."

"It's not a silly question at all," the OB said. "She's a very fortunate young woman. Aside from some contusions and a couple of cracked ribs, she's not seriously injured. In trauma-induced labor, we don't usually see direct injury to the baby, either. The bigger concern is placental abruption, which is separation of the placenta."

"Is that dangerous?" Faith asked. Her stomach was starting to go queasy.

"It can be. It can lead to sudden fetal death and maternal hemorrhage. She's had some bleeding, but fortunately we were able to stop it. But the fact that she's gone into preterm labor tells us something by itself. That could be her body's way of telling us that there's been a partial placental abruption, and that would mean we'd need to go ahead and deliver her."

"This early?"

The doctor nodded again. "If the baby's in distress, we need to deliver and get the baby to NICU. Even though she's not bleeding now, she could start again. With fetal distress being an issue, we'll probably need to do a C-section."

Faith closed her eyes. Having Alex's baby arrive, ten weeks early and over a thousand miles from home, had not been part of the plan. Could she have handled it differently? If Alex hadn't felt that she had to get away from her, would any of this have happened?

"Will she be all right?" Faith asked. "Another silly question, I guess."

The OB doc smiled. "We'll do our best." He looked at his colleague. "Let's get a room prepped."

A nurse stuck her head out the door of Alex's room. "She's awake."

Alex was struggling into a sitting position. Her clothes had been cut away, replaced by a hospital gown. A strap leading to the fetal monitor went around her swollen stomach. There were bandages on her forehead and left cheek, another, larger one on her wrist. Just under her breasts, a beige bandage held together by a clip circled her body. Faith could see blood in her dark hair. IV drips ran into both arms.

Faith swallowed hard, standing in the doorway. The ER doc was at Alex's side. "Alex, I'm Dr. Rice." She gestured at the OB man. "And this is Dr. Kaplan. You're at Allegheny General Hospital. Do you remember what happened to you?"

Alex looked from one face to the next, then caught sight of Faith in the doorway. "I . . ." She leaned her head back against the pillow, and her face twisted in pain. "Oh God! Oh my God . . . the baby, the baby."

"You're having contractions, Alex," Kaplan said. "You've gone into preterm labor. Do you remember your breathing exercises?" He turned to Faith. "Did you go through childbirth classes with her?"

"Me?" Faith said. "No, I . . . no."

"Faith?" Alex said. Her voice, naturally low and husky anyway, was a gravelly rustle. "You're here? What are you doing here?"

Faith went to her. "Alex, listen. I'm sorry for . . ."

Alex shook her head. "You're here." She sounded more surprised by Faith's presence than by the news that she was in labor.

"I'm here."

Alex reached across the bed rail and took her hand. "Shouldn't have run. That was stupid."

"What do you remember?"

The contraction wracked Alex's tiny body and she grimaced, then shouted. "Breathing, breathing . . . I'm supposed to be breathing. Oh God, oh God . . . my baby!"

"Come on, Alex," Faith coaxed. "Show me the breathing. Show me how you do it. I'll help you through this if you want."

The contraction subsided, Alex breathing out through her mouth. "Don't leave." She lay back against the pillow, her hair matted with blood and sweat. "I remember walking away from you. That's all. I was trying to run down the sidewalk, but I couldn't go very fast. . . . Then it's all blank."

"Alex," Kaplan said, "we've had the fetal monitor on you the whole time." He went on to explain what he'd already told Faith, about the possibility of partial placental separation and the baby's irregular heartbeat.

Alex started to cry, but it was a silent weeping, large tears streaking down her dirt and bloodstained face. "I'm sorry," she muttered through the tears.

"Why are you sorry?" Faith said. "You shouldn't be. You're doing what you need to do."

Rice and Kaplan exchanged puzzled looks.

"It's a long story," Faith said, looking at the doctors.

"We're going to get a room ready for you upstairs," Kaplan said. "It should just take a few minutes."

"Take care of my baby," Alex said.

"And you," Kaplan said, "you're going to be fine. You seem to be a pretty tough young lady." He and Rice both left. The nurses fussed with Alex's IV lines, assured her they'd be right outside, and left Faith and Alex alone.

"Would you call my dad?" Alex said. "I wanted to have

him and Celia and maybe Danny around when the baby came. It'll be Dad's first grandbaby."

Faith patted her hand. "I'll go you one better than that. I'll get them here. I'll make all the arrangements. Who are Celia and Danny?"

Alex smiled wearily. "You mean you don't know already?"

Faith smiled back. "Don't have my file right here with me."

"Celia is my dad's current live-in. She's sort of like my stepmother. Danny's my brother . . . half-brother. How can you get them here? Who'll pay for it?"

"Don't worry about that. I'll take care of it." Faith pulled her hand back and looked down at Alex for a long moment. None of this seemed real. But then, that was Department Thirty. It frequently felt unreal. "Alex . . . tell me about your husband. Tell me about Gary."

Another contraction struck, and Alex doubled forward. One of the nurses came in, timed the contraction, and showed Faith how to help Alex breathe, counting to ten during the contraction, letting out the breath and starting again. Alex kept hold of Faith's hand the whole time, and the grip was surprisingly strong.

After the contraction, the nurse checked the fetal monitor, frowned, and left the room again.

"Gary," Alex said.

"Gary," Faith said.

"Why now? Why are you asking me about Gary now?"

"I need to know. I don't believe in coincidences, Alex. I think everything all ties together. Somehow, some way, everything that's happening to you is connected." Faith shrugged. "Gary's part of your life."

Alex closed her eyes. "You have to understand. I never thought I'd get married and have kids. When I was a kid I had pretty low self esteem. I never thought anyone would want me. I was a half-breed, I wasn't a long-legged blonde with big boobs, I came from a screwed-up family . . . I didn't know what I wanted. I dated a few guys in college, but none of them ever called me back after the first date. I even thought I was a lesbian for a while and dated a couple of girls. I really wasn't ever attracted to women in that way, but I tried it. After a while I just figured it wasn't going to happen. I committed myself to music and went on with my life. And I was generally pretty happy, I think."

"And then Gary came along."

Alex had lain on the pillow with her eyes closed the whole time she spoke. Now she opened her eyes and looked at Faith. "Have you ever been to Full Circle Books? It's in Fifty Penn Place."

"Yes, I have, as a matter of fact. I've bought several books there."

"It's a great place, one of the best independent bookstores on the planet. They've started having live music on weekends too. I've played there a few times. It's a great intimate atmosphere, perfect for the kind of music I play. Anyway, one night I was there playing some tunes. I was mainly playing fiddle that night, and at about nine o'clock, this guy walks through the door. He goes to the counter and gets a coffee and sits down to listen. At the break he walked up to me and started asking me about tunes. That was it."

"That was Gary."

Alex nodded. "He knew Irish music, and even American folk music, up and down, backward and forward. Said he wasn't a musician himself, but was more of a 'professional listener,' is how he put it. He knew tunes that even I hadn't heard of, and I know a lot. We went to his apartment and he showed me his CD collection. Hundreds of discs, all great stuff. It was like . . . it was like he already knew me. We thought alike. I mean, he was a peace activist like me. He even had a tattoo that was a lot like mine." She pointed to the Celtic knot on her ankle. "It was on his shoulder, and except for the colors, the design was identical. It sounds corny, especially now, but I thought, *Where has this guy been all my life?*"

"What did he do for a living?"

"He installed computer networks. He traveled quite a bit. But, see, he was a lot like me on that too. The job was just a means to an end, to make enough money to pursue music. We went to all the festivals we could, we joined the folk dance group. . . . It was incredible. We were even saving money for me to produce a CD." Alex closed her eyes again.

Faith looked at her. The depths of Alex Bridge's pain struck her like spear points.

"And then he was gone," Alex said. "Just gone. There was nothing to . . . I mean, we'd talked about having kids but hadn't really come to any decision about it. And then the decision was sort of made for us. I was on the pill, but . . ." She clasped her hands together. "You know the rest."

Do I? Faith wondered. *Or do I know more than you do?*

"This is a strange time for you to ask me about Gary," Alex said.

"Alex," Faith said. "Listen to me. I believe you now. I don't think you took that money, and I don't think you killed Paul Wells. I think you're in the middle of something, and I'm not quite sure why."

"But it has to do with Doag."

"And with your ancestor. Tabananika." She stumbled around the pronunciation of the name. "Sorry."

"That's okay. I really don't know how to pronounce it, either."

Another contraction hit, and this time they worked through it together, hands clasped, Faith counting while Alex concentrated on her breathing. When it was over, Kaplan came back in. "We're ready for you," he said.

"I'll call your folks," Faith said to Alex.

"Hey, Faith Kelly," Alex said. "You didn't have to stay here. You don't have to care about what happens to me. That's not in your job description."

"No, it's not."

Kaplan looked at both of them strangely.

"I told you," Faith said, "it's a long story."

Faith called an astonished Bill Bridge, explained to him that his daughter had been in an accident and was in preterm labor, and told him she was making arrangements for him, Celia Morales, their six-year-old son Miguel, and his older son, Danny Park, to fly to Pittsburgh. They could pick up their tickets at the airport in Oklahoma City.

"What the hell's she doing in Pittsburgh?" Bridge had asked.

"She wants you here," Faith said, evading his question. "She *needs* family here."

"Who the hell are you?"

"A friend," Faith said, and hung up before he could say more.

She made the arrangements, charging the airline tickets to her government credit card. If Yorkton didn't like the expense, he could take the funds out of her personal discretionary account. She didn't care. Alex Bridge's family would be with her, and that was that. It wasn't too much to ask, considering what she'd gone through.

Alex was taken to surgery at seven thirty, as the shadows were lengthening across downtown Pittsburgh's three rivers. Faith sat in the surgery waiting room, drinking cup after cup of vending-machine coffee before realizing she'd barely eaten anything all day. She wandered downstairs to the cafeteria and ordered a cheeseburger, which turned out to be surprisingly good. She called Hendler and left a message on his voice mail. She tried to explain where she was, then stopped and went with the vague "I had to go out of town on a case" and promised to call him later.

Back in the waiting area, she paced and drank more coffee. A little after ten o'clock, Dr. Kaplan came into the room and said, "She came through the surgery just fine. Lost a little blood, but not too much."

"What about the baby?"

"There was a partial placental abruption, but I think we got him in time. His lungs are very underdeveloped at this stage." He squeezed Faith's arm. "Our NICU is one of the best in the country. They'll take good care of him. Here they come now."

A nurse in blue scrubs, face mask flapping down around her chest, was carrying a tiny bundle. Two others came behind, wheeling Alex. Faith fell into step beside the rolling hospital bed. At the elevator, the bed turned one way and the nurse with the baby another. Faith stopped.

Kaplan saw her confusion. "Would you like to carry him to NICU?"

Faith put up her hands. "Oh, no. I can't . . ."

"When we have NICU babies," the nurse said, "a lot of times we'll let the father carry them in, or some other family member."

"But I'm not family," Faith said. "Her family's on the way here."

"You're all she has right now." The nurse thrust the baby into Faith's arms.

The baby was swaddled tightly in a white blanket. He'd evidently been cleaned up already, as there was no blood or fluid on his face. He was very tiny, a pale, dusky color, his eyes a slate blue. He had a tangled mass of thick brown hair—Alex's hair, Faith thought.

She looked at him. His eyes were open and staring up at her, but Faith had read that newborns couldn't see very far. She lowered her face close to his and said, "Hi, baby."

He seemed to respond to her voice, opened his mouth, and made a strange gasping sound.

Faith looked up in alarm. "What . . ."

"That sound he's making is called 'grunting,'" the lead nurse said. "Since his lungs aren't fully developed, he can't cry. It tells us we have to get him to NICU and get him on oxygen."

Faith looked at the baby again. His eyes were fluttering. "What's your name, baby? Did your mom give you a name yet?" It suddenly seemed very important that she know that this child had a name—a name chosen by its mother, and not by Faith or Yorkton or someone else.

"Daniel Alexander Bridge," the nurse said. "I believe she said Daniel was after her brother, and Alexander to be sort of after herself."

Faith nodded, but couldn't talk anymore. She was feeling the beginnings of a great anger, a rage at the forces that caused this boy to be born premature and to make him struggle for his life from the moment of his birth. She tried to stuff the anger down: Faith had perfected "professional detachment" to an art form. This time, though, she wasn't sure it would stay put.

They reached the neonatal intensive care unit, and the nurse led Faith and Daniel to a corner cubicle. Each baby was assigned a cubicle—which were called "pods," according to the nurse—where they could be monitored constantly. It was a small unit, and the nurses' station had a view of every pod and every child. Most of the babies were covered in wires and tubes, IV lines and monitors. The place was never quiet, it seemed: the electronic beeps and clicks of monitoring alarms went off every few seconds in one pod or another.

Faith looked around at the nurses, wondering what it took to work in a unit surrounded by premature and critically ill newborn babies. She wasn't sure she could have done it, and had a sudden and overpowering urge to get away from the NICU. She placed little Daniel in the raised, clear bassinet in his pod, then backed away.

"There are some things we have to do for him now," the nurse said gently. "You go back and stay with Alex. She might want a familiar face when she wakes up."

Faith nodded. A small, middle-aged Asian man with glasses was approaching. A name tag clipped to his shirt identified him as Dr. Nguyen, Neonatologist, NICU. The nurse spoke quietly with him. Faith heard "three pounds, two ounces" mentioned. Daniel Alexander Bridge was going to have to fight hard. Faith felt the anger begin to rise again as she left the NICU.

July 18, 9:10 A.M.

Faith had spent the night beside Alex's bed, dozing a little, watching Alex float in and out of sleep, holding her hand, talking to her in low tones during the short periods she was awake.

She was sitting on one chair, her long legs stretched onto another, when the door opened and a motley assortment of people walked in.

Alex's father, Bill Bridge, was a short, burly man in his fifties, with a thick gray beard and sharp blue eyes. Faith noticed a tiny silver stud in his left earlobe. *Aging hippie,* she thought. A tall, tired-looking Latina who Faith assumed was Celia Morales followed him. In her thirties, barely older than Alex, she was a good twenty years younger than Bridge. She held the hand of a little caramel-skinned boy. A young Asian man with Bill Bridge's startling blue eyes came last. That would be the brother—half-brother, Faith reminded herself, looking at the group.

"She's sleeping," Faith said. "Let's go out in the hall."

They did, and Bill Bridge said, "Now, who are you again?"

Faith gave a tired smile. "It's a really long story, Mr. Bridge. But I was here with Alex when everything happened. I'm glad you're all here now. It was important to her to have you here."

"Are you one of her music friends?" Danny Park asked.

Faith looked at him. "Can't play a note. I just got to know Alex not long ago."

Alex's brother watched her without speaking. She saw a shadow cross his face.

Faith cleared her throat. "Now that you're all here, I'm going to leave. I have to get back to Oklahoma." She explained about the baby and the NICU. "When Alex wakes up, tell her I'll get in touch with her as soon as I can." She wrote her cell phone number on a piece of notepaper and gave it to Alex's father. "If you need anything, you can reach me at that number any time, day or night."

Bill Bridge looked at her. "I still don't understand. . . ."

Faith shook his hand. "Don't try to, sir. Don't even try."

She started down the hall. Danny Park ran after her. "I'll walk you out."

In the elevator, Park said, "The last time I saw Alex, she was scared to death. She was running from someone."

Faith watched the floor indicator above the elevator door. She said nothing.

"Was that you? Were you the one she was running from?"

"Were you the one who gave her money and helped her get out of Oklahoma?" Faith said, still looking straight ahead.

"There's no right answer to that question, is there?"

"No. Same thing with the question you asked me."

Park nodded. "I see." He put a hand in his jeans pocket and jingled some keys and coins. "So if you're the one she wanted to get away from, I guess it didn't work. You found her. But you've stayed with her through everything that's happened here, you paid for Dad and Celia and Mickey and me to come out here, and now you're leaving." The elevator doors opened onto the first floor. "Seems a little screwy, if you ask me."

Faith stepped into the main lobby. Park held the elevator doors. "It is," Faith said. "Even though I didn't ask you."

They looked at each other for a long moment.

"I'd do anything for my sister," Park said. "She's really a special person, and she's been hurt enough in her life already."

The doors closed. "I know," Faith said.

She drove her rental car to her hotel, checked out, and returned to the airport. While waiting for her flight to be called, she pulled her case file out of her carry-on. On top of the other pages was the fax from the Oklahoma Department of Public Safety. It was a copy of the driver's license for Gary St. James, with an address on Northwest Fifty-second Street in Oklahoma City. The home he had shared for those precious few months with Alex Bridge.

Faith looked at the face on the driver's license and felt the anger again. She had no more room for professional detachment on this one. A young woman—quirky, enigmatic, talented, and deceptively intelligent—lay in a hospital bed far from her home. A tiny child, born before its time, struggled for its very life.

And this man played games.

"Miserable son of a bitch," Faith said to the photo.

The man next to Faith glared at her, got up and moved.

The airport sounds faded into dull white noise as Faith stared at the picture. "You asshole," she muttered.

She pulled her laptop out of its carrying case, and with the anger building white-hot, powered it up. She didn't think about what she wanted to say, but just started typing, as if she could channel all the rage and all of Alex Bridge's pain through her fingers and into the little computer.

When she finished, she sat back and looked at the photo of Gary St. James again.

She'd seen it back at UCO, beside the pond, the way his entire body language changed, the way his face and tone of voice softened, when she asked him about Alex. It was as if he'd become another man, a totally different person.

A person who had confused feelings about Alex Bridge.

She slipped the fax page back into the file and looked at the face again. Gary St. James's ordinary, unassuming face smiled up at her. It was also the face of Isaac Smith, John Brown's Body.

22

July 18, 12:00 noon
Oklahoma City

SMITH CLOSED THE PAPERBACK OF *THE SECRET SIX:*
The True Tale of the Men Who Conspired with John Brown by
Edward J. Renehan Jr. and leaned back on the hotel bed. He
loved the idea of The Secret Six, mostly New Yorkers and
Bostonians, men of means who opposed slavery and helped
to bankroll Brown from his Kansas days forward. In fact,
while there had been conspiracies for as long as humanity
had attempted to govern itself in organized fashion, Smith
believed the modern American conspiracy had begun with
John Brown and his six backers. A line could be drawn directly from them to the assassinations of Lincoln and
Kennedy, Teapot Dome, Watergate, Vietnam, Iran-Contra,
Timothy McVeigh, and so many others.

But some conspiracies, Smith knew, didn't die. They only
ripened with time, aging well until all that mattered was to
protect what had gone before. It was what had kept him in
business, and what had brought him to this point.

He put away the Renehan book, stacking it atop another,
United States–Comanche Relations: The Reservation Years by
William T. Hagan. Smith hadn't read all that much Native
American history before this job, but of necessity he'd had to
learn. Alex Bridge's ancestor, Tabananika, was even mentioned
a couple of times in the text. While Hagan's book was more of
a straightforward history, Smith could read between the lines.
He saw how the government had conspired with powerful

economic interests to rob the plains tribes of all they had.

Depriving the tribes of their culture, languages, and religion wasn't about "assimilation," as the Department of the Interior so often asserted in the post–Civil War era. It wasn't about bringing them into "the fabric of American society." It was about money.

The government and the economic syndicates wanted the tribes' land, which translated into fortunes won and lost.

And it was amazing what the powerful would do to protect that power. A strange twist on that very concept was what had led Smith here, to Oklahoma, to Alex Bridge.

He ordered a salad and mineral water from room service, then opened his laptop to check his mail. There was only one message.

The subject line read: GARY ST. JAMES. The sender was Kelly, Faith S.

Smith's blood ran cold.

He opened the message.

If I look on your shoulder, will I find a Celtic knot tattoo?

"Oh my God," Smith said. He reached over his shoulder and felt the bandage where he'd had the tattoo laser-removed a few weeks ago.

Alex wasn't supposed to get pregnant, was she? That was what really messed you up. It wasn't part of your plan, but I guess you used it anyway. It just destroyed her in a different way—her husband left her, then got himself killed. That would give her even more motive for the embezzlement and murder.

And now you have a son, fighting for his life in a hospital in Pittsburgh.

Bet your client didn't pay extra for that.

The message was unsigned.

Smith's hands were shaking.

He laid his hands flat on the hotel bed and closed his eyes, trying his meditation techniques. After a few moments he gave up.

In ten years of this work, no one who had seem him face to face knew that he was John Brown's Body, until Faith Kelly. And now she had connected him to Gary St. James.

He pictured her stabbing at the computer keys, angry, the green eyes blazing, shaking red hair out of her face.

She knew him.

At least, she knew his cover. She knew he'd carried out the assignment on Alex Bridge. But she couldn't know all of it. She couldn't know the identity of his client, or what was really at stake here. She'd been to Pittsburgh, so she would know about Jonathan Doag by now. That was to be expected. She would probably know about Tabananika and the Blackjack Comanches soon. Again, that was part of the plan. Admittedly, he hadn't counted on Kelly being a part of it. It was all supposed to be Alex, from the very beginning. But they'd been doing just what he wanted them to do.

She knew him.

It wasn't safe for Smith to stay in Oklahoma any longer. He had to get out now.

And now you have a son, Kelly had written.

Smith's hands began to shake again.

He'd had a vasectomy ten years ago. He'd known that he would have to use sex for some of his assignments, and he could not afford to have children emerge from the required relationships. He'd known even then that would be far too complicated. Counting Alex Bridge, he'd been married to three women, in three states, under three different names, as part of fulfilling his assignments. He'd also had a six-month homosexual affair with another target, which was the very thing that had destroyed the other man. Smith had delighted in watching the man jump off a bridge into the Potomac River, thinking about all he had done to turn the man's sense of himself inside out.

But never children.

Never.

And now you have a son, fighting for his life in a hospital in Pittsburgh.

Something had happened. Alex wasn't due until September. The child was at least ten weeks premature.

A calming feeling came across Smith. He breathed slowly, deeply. His hands stopped shaking.

Premature babies often didn't survive.

Smith nodded. He thought of his own father, of all the man had endured, of how he'd told Smith over and over again, even on his deathbed, that it had all been for *him.*

See how much I've suffered for you, my son? It was all for you. I left my life behind so you could be better, so you could be something else. All . . . for . . . you.

For a moment he wasn't Isaac Smith. He wasn't John Brown's Body or Gary St. James or any of the other dozens of people he'd been. He was himself, watching his father die, loving him, hating him, eventually pulling him off the oxygen and watching his breathing slow and finally stop, then reattaching the line when he was sure the old man was dead, so that the home health nurse would have no clue as to what had happened.

It had been his first experience with destruction, and it had been too quick. After his father was buried, he'd decided to launch his career, but he wouldn't be an assassin. He would be a "destroyer," and he would make sure he could watch and savor the deterioration of his targets.

But he would never, ever have children, would never take a chance on history repeating itself. At all costs, Smith would never father a child.

And now you have a son.

A sharp knock sounded at the door. "Room service," came the muffled voice.

"Take it back," Smith said. "I'm checking out."

He walked to the balcony of his room, where he could look out across downtown Oklahoma City's modest skyline to the Ford Center and Cox Convention Center. He pulled out his cell phone and called a local number. Smith was a contractor, but a contractor who didn't use weapons. His weapons were his mind, his creativity, his knowledge, his skill with computers and databases. But when violence was required, as it had been with Special Agent Paul Wells, he hired "subcontractors."

The phone was picked up on the fourth ring, but no words were said. Smith knew the man never spoke a greeting on the telephone.

"This is Smith," he said.

"This is Jones," said the other man.

It wasn't his real name, of course, and the subcontractor had found it amusing to think of the two of them by those names, conjuring images of the old television program *Alias Smith and Jones*, about two outlaws of the American West who were given new names and promised a pardon by the governor if they could stay out of trouble. It struck Smith now that the show's premise had an uncanny resemblance to the real modern-day mission of Department Thirty.

"I have a new job for you," Smith said.

"I'm listening."

"The target is a woman named Faith Kelly. She lives here in Oklahoma City, though she's out of town right now. But she'll be back soon, I believe. I'll e-mail you the details."

"Level of difficulty?"

The man was all business. "One to ten, I'd say seven or eight. She's had some training." Smith didn't go into further detail.

"Right up there with the FBI agent," Jones said. "The fee will be the same."

"Right. I'll e-mail you. Do it soon."

"Of course." The phone line went dead.

He would immediately wire $25,000 to the man's off-shore account, and the same amount when he knew Faith Kelly was dead.

He looked back at the laptop, where Kelly's message was still displayed.

Very slowly, Smith leaned down and pressed Delete.

Then he began to pack, and to make travel arrangements. He had to get to Pittsburgh.

Same day, 3:30 P.M.
Harrisonburg, Virginia

Yorkton had slept on the small sofa in the Department Thirty office, as he frequently did. He kept an apartment on the other side of town, but was there rarely. He had more than once considered simply moving his few possessions here and never leaving the headquarters.

The DOJ photo database was still searching for Isaac Smith when he'd awakened at six o'clock in the morning. He left the machine running, changed clothes, and drove the hundred miles to Washington. He was scheduled to testify at a closed hearing of the Senate Judiciary Committee, part of the annual congressional review of Department Thirty. Yorkton had been working hard to massage the Hill in the wake of Daniel Winter's startling legacy of corruption. So far, his congressional overseers seemed to be impressed with Richard Matthias Conway.

They and the president will be more impressed if I can deliver them Cross Currents Media and John Brown's Body all in one package, he thought as he drove back to the Shenandoah Valley in the late afternoon.

He settled in behind his computer, where a screen saver of clouds in a blue sky floated serenely. He touched the space bar.

One match found.

Yorkton's pulse quickened. Was it possible he was about to succeed where every other level of the Justice Department, as well as State, Defense, and the CIA, had failed? That he would find John Brown's Body?

He pressed Enter.

On the left side of the screen was the photo he'd scanned into the system, the one Simon had taken in Oklahoma. On the right was the same man, about ten or twelve years younger, in his early twenties, with slightly longer and darker hair. But everything else was the same. The younger photo had been taken in an outdoor courtyard-type café, and he was sitting in a wrought-iron chair, one arm resting on the table, fingers curled around the handle of a coffee cup. The posture was the same, the way the man shifted his body slightly to one side, his legs crossed ankle over knee, always the right ankle on the left knee.

"Well, hello," Yorkton said to the screen.

He clicked on the younger photo and opened the Justice Department file.

He began to read about Mikhail Gerenko, who would now be thirty-four years old. He'd been born in Kiev, in what was then the Soviet Union. His father was the eminent Soviet physicist Pyotr Gerenko, who in 1983 had defected to the United States, bringing with him a treasure trove of information about the Soviet nuclear program. Some sources within the CIA believed the senior Gerenko's defection, and the Kremlin's fear over what he could tell the Americans, had led directly to the policy shifts, glasnost and perestroika, that eventually spelled the end of the Soviet Union.

Yorkton kept reading. Gerenko had only been able to get his twelve-year-old son out of Kiev, leaving his wife and a daughter behind. The Gerenkos had been resettled in Maryland after debriefing. The physicist became a paid consultant to the U.S. Department of Energy while continuing to provide information to the CIA on a regular basis.

After the fall of the Soviet Union, the CIA apparently decided they no longer needed Gerenko, and the old man was cut loose from the Energy Department with no severance. Pyotr Gerenko, one of the leading physicists in the world, who had risked everything and left behind half his family to come to the United States, wound up teaching English to Russian emigrants in New York City. His last years were spent in an alcoholic haze, then he was consumed by liver cancer.

The old man died eleven years ago, in a tiny rented house

in Queens. His son was by his side. Even though the CIA no longer had official ties to him, the FBI had kept up a routine surveillance. It was standard procedure for former "assets" to be followed for years after their service. The elder Gerenko's cancer was slow moving, and he was being treated on an out-patient basis. He'd been quite ill but not considered imminently terminal at the time of his death. One of the FBI analysts had put a note in the file that the death was "consistent with his illness, but not timely." Apparently there was no follow-up.

Mikhail Gerenko was twenty-two when his father died. He'd been in college at New York University as a history major. Little had been known about him: he was a minor footnote in his father's file. But surveillance continued on an irregular basis for a while after Pyotr's death. Mikhail left NYU and dropped out of sight for a time. Six months after his father's death, Mikhail Gerenko—using the Americanized name of Michael Green—purchased a small farm in rural Washington County, Maryland.

Yorkton pulled out one of the many maps he kept in the office and turned pages to Maryland. Washington County was in far western Maryland, just across the state line from West Virginia. From Harpers Ferry. Yorkton looked closely at the landmarks, outlined in red, on the map. A mere four miles from Harpers Ferry was the Kennedy Farm. Yorkton remembered what he'd read a few days ago when Faith Kelly first asked him about this. The Kennedy Farm had been John Brown's staging area for the Harpers Ferry raid in 1859.

And in 1994 Mikhail Gerenko, aka Michael Green, aka Isaac Smith, aka John Brown's Body, lived very near it.

Yorkton went back to the database. The FBI had stopped its occasional surveillance of Mikhail Gerenko in 1997. He still lived in Washington County, and the file noted that he seemed to make a living as a "computer consultant," traveling often. No evidence was found of illegal activities, nor were any such activities suspected.

Of course, there had never been any reason to think that

the son of a Soviet defector who had come to America as a child would be the same man who made a living destroying the lives of powerful people.

And not-so-powerful people, Yorkton mused, thinking of Alex Bridge.

"Well, Mr. Gerenko," Yorkton said, looking at the two photographs. He copied down the address in Washington County, Maryland. "I think it's time we met."

23

FAITH SLEPT FOR OVER TWELVE HOURS, SOMETHING SHE hadn't done in nearly ten years. The strain of the last week— the hours, the travel, the emotional roller-coaster ride— finally descended on her, and she fell into bed as soon as she made it home from the airport. She'd meant to call Hendler again, and she forgot—again.

She pushed herself extra hard on the run, doing an extra mile in the daylight. Her running schedule had been erratic of late, another fact that bothered her. When she got back to the house, she started the coffee and took a shower. When she emerged, naked, her hair wrapped in a towel, the phone was ringing.

She ran to her bedroom and grabbed the phone. "Kelly."

"You want to know how Smith lured the Indian woman to Galveston?" drawled a man's voice.

Faith let the towel fall from her head. "Who are you?"

"No one very important. Just a hired hand. You can call me Jones, if you need a name."

"Smith and Jones. That's cute. You guys are very creative."

"You want what I have or not?"

Faith sat down on the bed, dripping. "How do you know me?"

"Smith's mentioned your name, and that you're sort of in- terested in all this."

"And yet, you want to talk to me? Sorry, but my bullshit alarm is starting to go off."

Jones chuckled. "Uh-huh. Well, see, it's like this: Smith stiffed me. Fifty thousand dollars he stiffed me. The deal was a hundred to do the FBI agent on the beach. I was supposed to get another fifty when it was done, and it never happened. I haven't heard from him again, and can't find him. No one stiffs me, not like that, and not for something as hot as doing a fed."

"You're saying you were the trigger on Paul Wells?"

Jones made a tsk-tsk sound. "Here, now, I would never want to say such a thing on a public telephone line. Someone might take it the wrong way. Out of context, so to speak. But look at it this way: Smith doesn't like to get his hands dirty. When he first came to me, he gave me a nice little speech about how his weapon is his brain, blah, blah, blah. If any wet work is needed, he hires a 'subcontractor.' That would be me."

Faith was silent a moment. What Jones had just said was very much in line with what she knew of Smith. He would think actual violence was beneath him. But then, would he really "stiff" a subcontractor? That would leave a loose end, and John Brown's Body wasn't the type to leave loose ends. He'd done it by allowing Alex to become pregnant. Faith didn't think he'd make two mistakes like that.

So what was the truth about Jones?

"I'm waiting," Jones said.

"Let's talk," Faith said.

"The lobby of the Hotel Marion, on Tenth just west of Broadway," Jones said. "Do you know it?"

"I'll find it."

"Midnight tonight."

"Midnight. How melodramatic."

"I need some time to get everything together. It'll be worth your while."

The phone clicked in Faith's ear.

"You bastard," she said, thinking of Smith.

The question was whether she knew Smith as well as she thought she did. Had he really stiffed his hired gun, or was it a setup? She thought of the angry e-mail she'd pounded out, the words she'd written in a white heat. Thoroughly unprofessional and probably very foolish words.

But then, maybe they would force Smith's hand. Maybe Faith's own anger put Smith on the defensive, where it was easier to make mistakes.

There's only one way to find out.

Faith dried her hair and started to get dressed.

She went to the office and immediately called Pittsburgh to check on Alex and baby Daniel. Alex was resting, but Faith talked to her father, who told her Alex was still in some pain but doing well, considering all that had happened. The baby had been started on antibiotics to fight infection, and was on one hundred percent oxygen. Dr. Nguyen still would not give them odds on little Daniel's survival.

She spent a few hours catching up on administrative work, then leaned back in the chair until her head was almost touching the window and closed her eyes. There had to be a way to resolve the Alex Bridge mess to everyone's satisfaction. She and Alex had started to trust each other, albeit warily, and Faith thought she could still get Alex to decode the strange file names she'd downloaded, then deleted, about Cross Currents Media. Yorkton and the president and whoever else in D.C. was interested in that would be happy. But, she also had to learn who was paying Isaac Smith to destroy Alex and why, the link between past and present, Jonathan Doag and Tabananika and the Blackjack Comanches. She had to give Alex her life back.

Faith doodled a bit on a legal pad, then reread the notes of her meeting with Russell Doag. It was time now to tackle the Comanche aspect of the whole thing. Faith was lost when it came to Native American culture. More Indians lived in Oklahoma—the state's name, literally, meant *red people*— than any other state, but they seemed almost invisible to

Faith, the forgotten minority. She still had trouble under-standing the concept of tribal governments and how they functioned relative to local, state, and federal government entities. Hendler had reminded her that each tribe was a sovereign nation unto itself, within the borders of the United States, with its own governing body and laws.

So she needed to find a point of contact for the Comanche Nation. Faith logged onto the Internet and did a search with those words. Hundreds of results popped up, the first being the official website of the Comanche Nation, the Lords of the Plains. She clicked over to it. The tribal headquarters was in Lawton, Oklahoma, about eighty miles southwest of Oklahoma City. Something else about Lawton rang a bell, and Faith paged through her file until she found it: Alex Bridge had been born there.

Faith wrote down the phone number for the Comanche Nation and called it.

"Comanche Nation, how may I direct your call?" said a soft, lilting female voice.

Faith cleared her throat. "My name is Faith Kelly, and I . . . well, this may sound strange. I'm looking for some information about a chief from back in the 1800s. And also I'm wondering if anyone could tell me what the phrase *Blackjack Comanches* might mean. Can you help me?"

There was a long pause. "Are you looking for artifacts?"

"Artifacts? No, just information. This chief's name is . . . well, I'm not sure how to pronounce it. It's spelled T-a-b-a-n-a-n-i-k-a. Do you know if— "

"Are you looking for burial grounds?"

Faith started to say no, then thought it might be as good a place as any to start. "Sure, why not? That might help."

"You need Hannah. Hold on, please."

She was put on hold, and after a minute another soft-spoken voice, this one male, came on the line. "Environmental Programs."

Environmental Programs? Faith wondered. "Yes . . . I was told I needed to speak to Hannah."

"Hold on."

Another minute passed. "Hannah Sovo speaking."

"Hannah, this is Faith Kelly calling from Oklahoma City. I'm told you might be able to help me with some information about a chief named Tabananika. Sorry if I mispronounced that. I'm also looking for information on the Blackjack Comanches."

There was a long silence. Faith hadn't dealt one-on-one with many Native Americans, but Hendler had told her that most of the ones he knew, especially full-bloods, were not talkative people and tended to think before they spoke.

Hannah Sovo's voice held the same lilting quality as the others, with a soft rounded drawl, but when she spoke again, the voice had a harder edge to it. "Are you on the rolls?"

"Excuse me?"

"Are you on the rolls?"

"I don't . . . rolls? I'm sorry, I don't know what you mean."

"You're not Comanche." A statement, not a question from Sovo.

"No. I have a friend who is half. . . ."

A little of the hard edge evaporated. "You need to understand. We have to be real careful. There have been a lot of cases in the last few years where non-Indians will come along and ask about burial grounds. Then they'll turn out to be archaeologists or anthropologists who go around the tribal government and straight to the U.S. government with a petition to dig up sacred sites. In the name of scientific knowledge, they'll say. Some of our most sacred places have been totally torn apart. Several of the tribes, the Comanches included, are involved in a lawsuit against the Department of the Interior."

Thank God I didn't tell her I'm with the federal government, Faith thought. "I promise you, I'm no scientist and I don't want to dig up anything. But my friend who is half Comanche is starting to look into her family history. She's in the hospital right now, she just had a baby, and I told her I'd try to help with this."

"Tell you what," Sovo said. "When your friend gets out of the hospital, she can call me. She's on the rolls?"

"What does that mean? Is that like a registry of tribal members?"

"You could say that."

"I guess she is. Her mother was full-blood Comanche."

"Then I'm sure she is. As for the Blackjack Comanches, just reread your Oklahoma history books. There's always a little section on them, even in the white histories. I better go now."

"But I'm not from Oklahoma," Faith said, before realizing the phone was dead. "Well, now, that went great, didn't it?"

She went back to the Internet. There were a number of references to Blackjack Comanches, with references to "the massacre at Sawyer's Crossing" and "heroic efforts by U.S. Cavalry troops in the vicinity," as well as a sensational trial. But the sites she saw were woefully short on details. Connecting them to Russell Doag's ancestor, and to Alex Bridge, was impossible from the online data.

By late afternoon Faith still hadn't found anything specific. She would call Alex again tomorrow and see how she was feeling. She knew the baby would be in intensive care for a long time and that it would be dangerous to think about moving him from Pittsburgh back to Oklahoma City. But perhaps Alex could at least check into the Comanche end of things, if Faith could convince her to explore that side of her heritage.

Faith began to think about the mysterious Mr. Jones and the midnight meeting. She had learned at the academy that smelling a setup meant she needed to be aware of the location before the other side got there. Contrary to Yorkton's thinking, maybe her law enforcement training could be put to use in Thirty after all. It was still eight hours until the meeting, but Faith was determined to scope out the place.

She went home and changed clothes, slipping into an all-black outfit: tank top, jeans, a light jacket. It would be hot as hell right now, but at midnight it would help her blend into the night. She tucked her hair up under a Chicago Cubs baseball cap, checked the equipment she needed, and drove back downtown.

Tenth and Broadway was actually north of downtown proper, in an area known as Automobile Alley. In the early years of Oklahoma City, many of the city's car dealerships had stretched along Broadway through the area. Faith turned the Miata off Broadway onto Tenth. On the right was a large warehouse-type building with the logo for National Pawn A Car around the front, the side facing Broadway. The front half was a glassed-in showroom, the back brick. The building was empty.

Across the street, she saw the Hotel Marion.

"Nice sense of humor," she said, thinking of Jones.

Faded glory best described the hotel. Clearly, it had not been occupied in many years. It was a three-story brick building, laid out in three sections facing Tenth Street. The center third extended slightly toward the street, with the outer thirds curving gently, turret-style, toward the back. On the east side, about halfway up, was a faded logo of the type that was now considered Americana. It read: *The Hotel Marion, The Nicest Small Hotel You'll Find!*

None of the Marion's windows was intact. Some were totally gone, a few were half-covered with plywood. Incongruous with the rest of the picture, a brand-new, blinding-white section of sidewalk had been laid in front of the building. A tall green sign with gold cursive lettering leaned against the old hotel's front door, announcing its renovation and listing the names and phone numbers of the developer, architect, and general contractor.

Faith wondered for a moment how Jones had gotten Paul Wells onto that beach in Galveston. Wells had told Hendler that Alex called him and said she was ready to come in. With what she knew now, Faith was beginning to think that both Alex and Wells had been fooled into coming to Galveston, each thinking the other had something important to tell them. She shook her head. Smith had planned it beautifully, even if certain aspects still didn't make sense.

Faith walked around to the front of the Marion, ducked behind the green sign, and pushed on the door. Not surprisingly, it opened. She knew that when a building was this far gone, and the serious renovation work had yet to begin, contractors rarely bothered to lock it.

There were a few signs of work being done, but not many. A few new beams were propped here and there, a shiny electrical outlet box affixed to one of them. A few hand tools were scattered in the entryway. Fast-food ketchup packets rested on the floor.

It was just a shell of a building, all the interior walls having been knocked out. But the entryway and lobby was wide and open, and Faith knew why Jones wanted her there. From the second floor, he would have a perfect shot at her.

"Mr. Smith, I guess we're not friends anymore," she said, and started up the stairs.

She did a thorough check of the Marion, spending half an hour scoping windows, exits, dodging broken glass, disturbing a group of pigeons and trying to avoid their droppings. They seemed to own the place. There were upended bathtubs on both the second and third floors, ornate porcelain tubs with once-beautiful fixtures.

Faith stepped back out onto the new section of sidewalk, checked the street, and emerged from behind the sign. Then she drove the Miata across the street and parked in a lot belonging to City Church, a huge nondenominational church that looked more to Faith like a government building than a place of worship. She left her car there, then took her supplies and trotted back across to the National Pawn A Car building, which sat directly across from the Hotel Marion. On the rear, brick part of the structure, most of the windows were silvered over, though some had large holes in them. A couple had what looked like bullet holes in them.

She needed a way in, a place where she could watch the hotel across the street and wait for Jones to arrive. She found a rusting fire escape clinging to the west side of the building.

It swayed a bit but held her when she started up. It led to a gray door on the second level. Again Faith wasn't worried about getting past a locked door. Someone had beaten her to this one: the lock plate had been shot away.

Faith pushed the door open. There wasn't any sign of renovation here, just dust and a few papers swirling around the floor. It was much darker in here than the Marion, with the windows painted over. Faith worked her way forward to the Tenth Street side of the building and found one of the broken windows in the southwest corner. She took off the jacket—it was also blistering hot in here—then folded and sat on it. She got as comfortable as she could, leaning against the wall and making sure she could see through the broken pane to the Marion. She had a good view of most of the hotel, including the front door.

She checked her watch: it was nearly six o'clock. It was almost like being on a Marshals Service stakeout, she thought. She knew she'd have to be here for six hours, sitting in this dusty corner, watching out the window. But unlike a stakeout, coming here this early wasn't just part of an investigation. It might save her life.

Faith took a bottle of water and some peanut butter crackers out of her bag and placed them on the jacket beside her. She also had brought a glass jar that she would urinate in when the time came. Then she pulled out her microcassette recorder. She checked and rechecked the batteries and made sure the condenser microphone was working. Her Glock was in her shoulder holster, which had been concealed by the jacket. She checked the load and made sure the safety was off.

Then Faith sat back to wait for midnight, and a man who had most likely been sent to kill her.

24

July 19, 10:40 p.m.

FAITH HUMMED A LITTLE BIT OF "SHEEBEG, SHEEMORE," trying to remember how her grandfather played it on the fiddle, and how Alex Bridge had played it on flute. She knew Alex played fiddle as well, and found herself wanting to hear Alex play the tune on fiddle so she could compare it to her grandfather's version. Thinking of such things kept her focused during the stakeout.

Oddly, she could maintain a good visual on the hotel while letting her mind wander. She'd learned the trick of compartmentalizing her senses a long time ago, in essence letting her mind and her senses be two different places at once but both fully functional. Her old friend Jen Ghezzi had told her more than once that it was a creepy quality to have. Useful, but creepy.

She'd seen the evening rush die down, the change of shifts at nearby St. Anthony Hospital, and a service begin and end at City Church. She'd seen two young men—one black, one white—consummate a drug deal on the sidewalk. A few minutes ago a black car with music blasting out the open windows had sped by and a bottle flew out the window, crashing onto the sidewalk in front of the Marion.

Now she watched as a light pickup truck, a Nissan or Toyota, pulled slowly in from the west. It parked in the lot on that side of the hotel, very near to the spot where Faith had parked hours earlier. A single man sat in the truck, though Faith couldn't tell much about him. She hoped to get a good view when he opened the door and his dome light went on.

The man busied himself with something on the seat beside him, then the door of the truck opened, but no dome light came on. Score a point in his favor, she thought, for disconnecting the light.

From what she could tell, he was of undetermined middle age, heavyset but not fat, with thinning hair. He wore dark clothes and carried a long, thin case in one hand.

"Uh-huh," she whispered, wondering what kind of assault rifle he planned to use on her.

He did exactly what she had done, squeezing behind the green sign and disappearing into the Marion. Faith almost held her breath, her eyes never leaving the window. A minute passed.

She saw a tiny light appear in a second-floor window, in the eastern third of the hotel. It moved slowly, disappearing and then reappearing at a corner window. Then it snapped off. Jones wasn't taking too big a risk with his light: no car simply driving by on Tenth Street below would have been able to see it, nor would any foot traffic.

The corner spot on the second floor was one of the places she'd judged would be a good sniper nest. From there he could look straight down into the lobby/entryway and make his shot. Faith assumed that he had some kind of nightscope on the rifle. She had no such equipment, but she wielded the element of surprise. Jones thought he had it at the moment, but Faith was going to change that.

She saw some movement in the window, Jones settling in. He thought he was prudent by arriving eighty minutes ahead of their scheduled rendezvous. Faith smiled. Even though she was cramped, sweaty, and her eyes burned from the dust, she'd beaten him by seven hours, and she'd inspected the layout of the place, which Jones didn't know.

Even though she didn't expect Jones to be looking in her direction, she ducked away from the window before putting on her jacket and loading the recorder into the pocket. The Glock went back into the shoulder holster. She sneezed once from the dust and crawled past the door where she'd come in earlier. There was another door to the outside on the north end of the building: she'd noticed it when she circled the building before. It was intact but unlocked.

Outside, she breathed in dust-free night air, straightened her jacket, and adjusted her hair. She took off the Cubs cap, twisted her hair, pulled it forward, and jammed the cap back on her head. She stepped onto the fire escape and started down. This one ended five feet above the ground, so she swung off it and dropped to the pavement, bending her knees.

She took the long way around the National Pawn A Car building, coming out on the east side, bordering Broadway. She had a few anxious moments crossing Tenth in the open, but realized that Jones would have to be hanging his head all the way out his window to see her. Logically, he would be looking the other way, keeping his eyes down and toward the Marion's front door, where he expected Faith to be.

She passed the old Habitat for Humanity offices and store and was soon a full block south of the Marion. She turned onto Ninth, walked about a quarter of the block, and found herself in the alley that ran along the west side of the Marion. She started to hug the back wall of the Habitat building. There was only a space of a few feet between the hotel and the Habitat structure, but the rear of the Habitat building had a low, flat roof, and Faith had found a way onto it earlier.

A blue metal Dumpster sat almost flush against the building. Faith climbed silently onto it. At five ten, she was just a few inches short of being at eye level with the roof. She flexed and unflexed her hands, wishing she'd spent more time at the gym working on upper body strength. Marathons were great for conditioning, but they didn't do much for developing powerful arms.

She got her hands around the lip of the roof and very slowly pulled herself up. Her fingers complained, but she got herself up and over, rolling onto the black tar roof. A little light shone through up here from the streetlights on Broadway, and she moved carefully, watching for anything that could trip her.

In a crouch, she maneuvered to the edge of the roof where it adjoined the hotel. *More pull-ups*, she thought. In an unusual architectural feature, the Marion featured a metal catwalk along the back of the third floor, which connected the two outer thirds of the building. The center section did not extend as far back, dropping down to what had probably once been a small courtyard on the ground level. A once-elegant spiral staircase led down to it from the catwalk.

Faith had to lean over the edge of the roof and extend her arms as far out as they would go to get a grip on the catwalk. She linked her fingers into the bottom of the catwalk and pulled her body forward, then swung first one foot, then the other onto it. She was on all fours, and the catwalk made a slight rattle under her. Faith held her breath and didn't move.

She heard nothing from inside the hotel. A car went by somewhere. She heard loud hip-hop blaring, then fading away.

She crawled forward and her hand came down on something sharp. Bright pain filled her.

"Shit!" she muttered, blinking back reflexive tears of pain. She felt blood on her hand. With the other hand, she felt gingerly along the catwalk until she found it: a razor-like shard of glass sticking up through the walkway. She hadn't noticed it earlier.

She put pressure on the wound, unable to tell how deep the cut was. She wrapped a handkerchief around it and tried to shake it off. It hurt like hell, but she couldn't lose focus. Very slowly, she stood up. Gripping the rail with her good hand, she started down the spiral staircase to the second floor. She pulled open the rickety wooden door and Faith walked back into the Hotel Marion.

Below and behind her, a tall, muscular man stepped onto the blue Dumpster, then pulled himself up onto the roof. Faith didn't see him.

Faith kept her eyes on her feet, trying to remember where all the obstacles were. This time she didn't try to avoid the pigeon droppings. She would worry about her shoes later. She stepped carefully and used handholds on the bare beams where walls had once stood.

Five steps into what had once been a hallway, she could see the assassin. Lights from the street filtered through the window and glinted off the rifle barrel and the man's balding head. With her good hand, she reached back and drew the Glock from the shoulder holster. She'd left it unsnapped so there would be no sound.

She took two more steps.

There was a sound from her left. Faith blinked. Jones was ahead and to the right.

She squeezed the handkerchief around her hand, the Glock tight in the other.

No, she thought. Just her mind playing tricks on her.

She took another step. The floor creaked. Three pigeons shrieked and flew out the window.

Just my luck, to get shot because of a bunch of goddamn pigeons, she thought.

She flattened herself against a beam.

Jones was a pro after all. He didn't panic and come out shooting. He kept the rifle in its firing stance and quietly said, "Hello?"

Faith breathed quietly, her injured hand throbbing. It was time to get his attention. If she could keep him off balance, let him know she was there but not exactly where, he would make mistakes.

With her bandaged hand, she pulled the Cubs cap from her head, holding it by the bill. She flicked her wrist and sailed it on a straight line toward the man with the rifle.

As soon as she let it go, she launched her body in a dive behind the upended bathtub she'd noticed earlier.

Jones caught the motion coming toward him, whipped the rifle around, and blasted into the darkness. He got to his feet, still holding the rifle, and in a moment realized he'd just blown up a hat.

"What the fuck?" Jones said.

Faith kept silent. Behind the tub, she was now at least six

feet away from where she'd been when she threw the cap. Jones hadn't been looking in that direction when she moved, so even though she'd made noise, he shouldn't be able to tell which way she'd gone.

There, across the way, the other side of the staircase . . . scrabbling, shuffling. Footsteps. She saw a silhouette.

In full voice, Jones said, "Let's not play games here. Come out and let's talk. Don't mind the gun. When you're in my business you have to protect yourself. I know you understand that."

Faith noticed he never once called her by name. He wasn't taking any chances.

Jones shuffled a couple of steps away from the window. He was looking across the staircase. He could see the shadow there as well.

As he passed the window, Faith looked over the rim of the old tub. She could see the look on Jones's bland face as he gazed toward the other side of the building. He looked confused.

So if the other guy isn't with Jones, then who the hell is he?

"I'm not quite sure what to say," Jones said. "I play fair and expect everyone else to do the same."

Keep going, Faith silently urged him. If he took a few more steps in that direction, she could come out from the cover of the tub and get behind him.

Jones took two more steps.

From the shadows, there was an unmistakable metallic sound: a gun being cocked.

"Goddammit," Jones muttered, then brought up the rifle.

The figure in the shadows moved quickly as Jones fired. Now the silhouette was almost parallel to Faith's position, on the other side of the staircase. A shot erupted out of the darkness and passed close to Jones's head.

"What the fuck?" Jones said again.

He moved quickly for a big man. He took several long steps, and Faith took the opportunity to move out from behind the tub, circling along the far wall until she was almost in the position where Jones had intended to shoot her.

Faith stared across the staircase. She could almost see the other man's face, but not quite. *Who the hell are you?* she wanted to shout.

Jones heard her moving but wasn't quite sure from which direction the sound had come. Things were happening on two different fronts in a very small area, and the confusion showed on Jones's face. He took a few smaller steps toward the back of the building, now in the hallway where Faith had entered.

Perfect, Faith thought.

She moved behind him and fired a shot over his head. The shadow man across the way fired a second later, on the other side of Jones.

Jones stumbled, throwing up both arms and losing his grip on the rifle. He spun into the outer door, which was so rickety that it splintered and pulled off the hinges under his bulk. He bounced into the night, onto the catwalk.

The fight had erupted into the open. Faith stood up straight and started after Jones. The man across the way emerged from shadows and raced down the parallel hallway toward the outer door for the western section of the building.

"Who the hell are you?" Faith shouted at him.

"Simon," he shouted back. "I work for you!"

"*What?*"

Faith heard the door on the other side splintering just as she turned the corner. Jones was on the spiral staircase, heading up toward the catwalk.

"Uh-uh, Mr. Jones," she said. "Won't work."

Simon stepped onto the catwalk, holding an automatic pistol of his own.

"What she said," he murmured.

"Fuck," Jones said.

Faith squeezed the handkerchief on her injured hand, and doing so made her think to look down, just as Jones's foot came straight down on the shard of glass protruding through the catwalk.

Jones howled in pain, trying to dislodge his foot from the glass and sprawling forward. He was on Simon's side of the spiral staircase, his body twisted. To the left of the staircase was a two-foot ledge, then a straight drop-off to the old courtyard below. Jones had hooked his fingers into the cat-walk, but his head was hanging off the side.

"This is good," Faith said. "This is really good." She holstered the Glock and lowered herself to one knee. Jones had worn thin, soft-soled shoes, and the glass was deeply embedded in his foot, blood running out the sides of the shoe.

"Well, you chose this place," Faith said. "Sorry it didn't work out."

Jones started to pull himself away from the ledge. Faith put a knee in his chest and pinned him against the staircase.

"Oh, fuck, my foot," Jones said. "And don't let me fall."

Simon squatted beside them, his automatic pointed at Jones's head.

"You work for me?" Faith said. "You want to explain that?"

"Hal Simon," the man said. "Nice to meet you."

"Pleasure. What's going on here?"

"I'm a field officer."

Faith waited a moment, periodically moving her knee around to keep her grip on Jones. "Yorkton. You're what Yorkton was before he became director."

Simon nodded. "Yorkton's concerned about you."

"Why didn't I know about you until now? And how did you . . ."

"Followed you most of the day. Yorkton's really concerned about you."

"Well, I'm starting to get concerned about him too," Faith said.

"Just doing my job. Glad I could help tonight."

"So you've been in the departmental office here in town?"

"Of course."

"What's on the wall?"

"You mean the fish?"

"What's on the back of it?"

"What is this, a test? Something about being caught in Lake Texoma and the date. Do I have to know the date? Yorkton introduced me to Dorian, not long before Dorian . . . you know."

"I know. Don't worry about the date."

"Does that mean I pass?"

Faith nodded. The idea that she had a field officer who worked for her made little sense. But then, she reminded herself, what did?

"And as for you," she said to Jones, "I guess you didn't want to talk after all."

"Fuck," Jones spat, squirming.

Simon put the muzzle of the automatic against his temple and said, "Be still."

"You've done the wrong thing, Mr. Jones," Faith said. "You've pissed off a redhead who doesn't like to fly."

"Fly?" Jones croaked. "But I don't—"

"This week I've had to fly two different places. First Galveston, then Pittsburgh. Counting plane changes, coming and going, I've been on eight different planes, and that pisses me off."

"Smith," Jones said.

"Yeah, Smith. But he's not here and you are. Tell me everything."

"Fuck you."

Faith drew the Glock and slammed it into Jones's injured foot. He screamed wordlessly into the sky. Even Simon winced.

"Tell me everything," Faith said.

"The Indian woman," Jones muttered. "Oh, shit, oh, fuck . . . the Indian woman. Smith wanted to get her to Galveston. I called her at home, then when she got to her hotel down there, I called her again. I said I was Wells, told her I could clear her name. Clear her name from what, I don't know. Smith gave me an exact script. He was all anal about how everything had to be done a certain way."

"I can see that," Faith said.

"I got my girlfriend to call Wells, to pretend to be the Indian woman, to get him to Galveston. When he was there, on the beach, I did him and called Bridge. Oh Jesus, oh, fuck, my foot hurts."

"Be nice and we'll stop the bleeding," Faith said. "Keep talking."

"That's it, I swear that's it! Smith paid me, then called yesterday and said he had another job for me. You. I've used this place before, thought it'd be the perfect setup. There's nothing else." Jones tried to prop himself up on one elbow. Simon knocked it out from under him. His head slid a little farther down from the ledge. He screamed again.

"Nothing else about Galveston?" Faith said.

"I did everything just like Smith wanted it. I'm just a hired hand. I don't fucking ask questions because I don't want to know. After I shot the fed and called the Indian, I dumped the gun exactly where Smith wanted it and got out of there. Let me up, dammit."

Faith went cold. "You did what?"

"The gun. Smith said it had to be in this fucking Dumpster down the block. I even argued with him about it. He said I had to wear latex gloves, because the woman's prints were already on it, and I had to throw it in that Dumpster. If it'd been up to me, I'd throw it in the fucking ocean. But Smith was paying the bills."

"He *told* you to put it in that Dumpster?"

"Shit, yes. Ordered me to."

Faith waited, listening to the night and Jones's labored breathing.

"What is it?" Simon asked.

"I'm not sure," Faith said.

Moments ticked by. Smith wasn't stupid. Faith knew that. Planning was his forte. Tiny details were what he did, were what he prided himself on knowing. Smith would have to know that eventually some investigator—whether it was Faith or the Galveston PD or the FBI—would have made the discovery about the location of the gun, relative to the timeline of the crime scene. He wouldn't have left that to chance.

She'd always thought the location of the murder weapon was strange, even before she figured out that there was no way Alex Bridge could have done everything on the timeline she'd constructed. Just like Jones said, it made more sense to toss the gun into the Gulf.

The world was silent around her for a moment.

Did Smith want to be caught?

Faith blinked. Her hand throbbed. She squeezed the bloody handkerchief.

Why would Smith have ordered his hired assassin to specifically put the gun in a place that didn't make sense? A place that would eventually lead to proof that Alex Bridge couldn't have murdered Paul Wells? If his job was to destroy Alex, why? *Why?*

Smith left no detail to chance, that much she knew.

Did Smith want to be caught?

Faith shook her head. "You son of a bitch," she said.

"Let me up," Jones whined. "Come on, my foot hurts like hell. You got me, goddammit. Take me in, just do something about my fucking foot."

"We can't take him in," Simon said quietly.

Jones's eyes widened.

"He's right," Faith said. "We don't have any jurisdiction to arrest you."

Jones shook his head. "Oh, fuck, no . . ."

"Oh, stop it," Faith said. She pulled out her cell phone and used the speed dial to call Hendler. When he answered, she said, "Hi, it's me."

"Faith? What time is it?"

"Late. I'm sorry. I'm back in town. But something's happened. Could you come down and arrest a murderer for me?"

"What? What did you say?"

"Scott, I have the man who pulled the trigger on Paul Wells right here beside me. Do you want him?"

"Holy shit, Faith!" Hendler suddenly sounded more awake.

"I thought so." She told him where she was. "I have a confession from him. Take him to the lockup. In addition to murder, let's hold him on some kind of terrorism some-thing-or-other, something under the Patriot Act so he can sit without being arraigned for a while."

"I'm on my way. Holy shit!"

Faith took the recorder out of her jacket and popped out the cassette. She handed it to Simon. "You're plugged into Yorkton. Take this tape. Make a copy. Get one to the director. Tell him it proves Alex Bridge was being set up. Take the other to the U.S. attorney. Owen Springs, do you know him? Tell him we have the triggerman on Paul Wells. He's running for the Senate: he'll be all over it." She scribbled on a busi-ness card. "Here's his number. Call him tonight."

"Yes, ma'am," Simon said. He vaulted across the catwalk and onto the roof next door.

Faith watched him go. Part of the puzzle had fallen into place, but several other pieces had just been scattered around, as if randomly dropped from the sky. She sat back and waited for Hendler to arrive.

Simon's car was parked on Ninth Street. He climbed in, hol-stered his automatic, and pulled out his cell phone. He called Yorkton.

"I'm bringing you something very interesting," he said.

"Regarding?" Yorkton said.

"Our colleague that you wanted photographed."

"I thought I told you to back off for now."

"I'll be on an early plane in the morning," Simon said, and clicked off.

He stared at the phone for a moment, then started the car. He did not call the U.S. attorney.

25

FAITH AWOKE IN SCOTT HENDLER'S BED. AFTER HENDLER arrived at the Hotel Marion to officially arrest Jones—whose name turned out to be Jeffrey Moreland, and who was well known in the local underworld—they woke up Leo Dorsett, the special agent in charge of the Oklahoma City FBI office and Faith gave him an abridged version of who Jones/Moreland was. The assassin's foot injury was treated at St. Anthony, and Hendler insisted that Faith have her hand checked as well. The cut wasn't deep and was bandaged with no stitches.

Jones/Moreland was put in lockup, and Faith extracted a promise from Dorsett to just let him sit for the time being, that there was more to this case than any of them knew. Dorsett didn't like it: he wanted to announce to the media that the man who'd killed one of their own had been caught, but he also understood the deeper implications of Department Thirty's involvement, so he agreed.

Even though her hand wound was minor, Hendler insisted that she stay with him. Faith didn't resist too much. The truth was, she wanted to be with him for a while. Even though she fell exhausted into bed at his house in Edmond shortly after two A.M., she liked the feeling of knowing he was right beside her.

Now, lying on her back, more or less wide-awake after barely four hours' sleep, she watched him, his face slightly stubbled, hair swirling around the growing bald spot. He had everything she needed. He was an inherently good human being, with a fine old-fashioned sense of common decency and a willingness to listen to many points of view. He wasn't terribly exciting, but then, the rest of Faith's life provided more excitement than most people could stand. She thought back to her brother's e-mail and his quotation of the Chinese curse: "May you live in interesting times."

She smiled. Maybe someday she would even tell Hendler some of these things. One day when she wasn't emotionally overwhelmed with other people's lives.

And when exactly will that day come, Faith? she wondered.

She reached out and touched the bald spot on Hendler's head. He stirred, opening his eyes.

"Sorry," she said. "Didn't mean to wake you. It's still early."

Hendler blinked at her, then glanced at the bedside clock. He propped himself on one elbow. "You do occasionally sleep more than three or four hours at a time, don't you?"

Faith remembered the night before last. "Oh, yeah."

"That's good to know. How's your hand?"

She put it in front of his face, flexing it around the bandage. "Not bad at all."

"What is it with you and broken glass anyway?" Hendler said.

"Just lucky, I guess."

She rolled out of bed, naked except for her panties. She'd been so keyed up and later exhausted last night that she hadn't thought about stopping by her own house for a change of clothes. Hendler had driven her, and in fact her car was still in the parking lot of City Church, across from the Marion.

"Ugh," she said. "I would commit felonies to get a shower."

"No felons allowed in this house. Towels are in the hall closet."

She showered, washing off the grime of last night. When

she emerged, Hendler was still in bed, lying languidly with his hands behind his head. "No wonder they call you Sleepy Scott," she said as she started to put last night's clothes back on.

He smiled and sat up. "What's the plan today?"

"Well," Faith said, "I have to figure out Department Thirty protocol for what you do on the morning after you foil an attempt on your life. You?"

"With your friend Jones in lockup, I need to see what Dorsett wants to do now. You sent a copy of the tape you made to the U.S. attorney?"

"I had Simon take it to him." She shook out her wet hair. "Simon. Add that to my list. I need to ask my boss why no one told me I had a staff."

Hendler went to shower, and Faith fumbled around in his kitchen until she found the coffee. While it was brewing, Nina Reeves called on her cell phone.

"Good morning, Faith," Reeves said. "I know you're an early riser, so I didn't think you'd mind the call."

"Hi, Nina," Faith said. "What's up?"

"Can you stop by this morning? I've completed the autopsy on your Ms. Bridge's computer."

Faith had all but forgotten about Alex's computer and the fact that there might still be information on it she could use. "Sure. Give me an hour."

"Very well. See you soon."

Within a few minutes, Hendler was dressed in his FBI-standard white shirt and dark suit. Faith and he shared coffee, then he drove her downtown to pick up her car. Faith gazed across the street at the Hotel Marion for a long moment.

Hendler followed the look. "I'm glad you got out of it with just a little cut on your hand," he said after a period of silence.

"So am I."

"Could've been a lot worse."

Faith dragged her eyes away from the hotel and looked at

him. "You're not about to tell me to be careful, are you?"

"Be careful," Hendler said. "And, Faith . . . I'm sorry for overreacting the other day."

"No apology necessary." She leaned over and kissed him gently. "You're a good man, Sleepy Scott."

"Thanks."

She poked his arm. "Don't let it go to your head."

He laughed. "Out of my car, you!"

Faith drove home and changed clothes, then drove another couple of miles to Reeves's apartment. Reeves was wearing her trademark sundress, barefoot, with a thin gold chain around one ankle.

"Come in, come in," Reeves said. "You look tired, Faith."

"It's been a busy few days."

Reeves nodded. "The Bridge case?"

"Yeah. It's a mess."

Reeves sat down in her horseshoe. "Permit me to make it a little messier, then."

"Nina—"

"My complete autopsy report on Alex Bridge's computer." Reeves tossed a stapled set of papers across the desk. "Most of that is technical jargon that does you no good whatsoever. But there is one very, very interesting item."

She beckoned to Faith, who came around the edge of the horseshoe desk and leaned over Reeves's shoulder to look at the computer monitor.

"What's this, another e-mail?" Faith said.

"Sent instead of received," Reeves said. "Again, we are quite fortunate that Ms. Bridge didn't use e-mail much. It's much easier to recover old data when that space on the hard drive hasn't been reused."

Faith read the message.

The Blackjack Comanches. Tabananika. Jonathan Doag. You stand on these people's bones. You have bathed in their blood. Everything you are, everything you have, flows outward from a few moments in time in the spring of 1893.

You are their legacy. But this deception has gone on far too long. It is past time you gave something back.

Alex Antonia Bridge

Great-great-great granddaughter of Tabananika, "Voice of the Sunrise"

"When was this—"

"March 5, a year ago," Reeves said. "Late at night: eleven forty-three P.M."

Faith's eyes trailed over the words again. "Alex . . . no. Alex couldn't have written this. The language . . . it's not . . ." Her voice faded away. "Who received it?"

"That, my dear Faith, is the very, very interesting part." Reeves tapped the monitor, showing the e-mail address to which the message had been sent.

Chief@supremecourtus.gov.

Faith felt her heart stop.

"Does this mean—"

"I think it does," Reeves said. "This message, whoever wrote it, was sent from Alex Bridge's computer to Bryden Cole. The chief justice of the Supreme Court of the United States."

26

ALEX COULDN'T IMAGINE HOW A CHILD WITH THAT MANY wires and tubes crisscrossing its tiny body could survive. An oxygen tube went in his mouth, held in place by white surgical tape. All the equipment so thoroughly covered him, Alex felt she could barely see the baby himself. But still little Daniel Alexander Bridge lived.

By far the most wrenching sight was Daniel's head. When she was wheeled into the NICU for the first time, she'd been prepared for wires and tubes, but not for an IV line running straight into his scalp. One of the nurses had explained that newborn babies' veins were better developed in the head, rather than the arm or leg, so IV lines in the NICU were frequently inserted in the scalp. Staring at the long, thin needle disappearing into her son's scalp through his wisps of brown hair, she knew she would never, ever forget the sight.

Strangely, she didn't feel weak herself. She was still sore at times, both from the surgery and the cracked ribs she'd suffered when the car hit her. She grew fatigued as the hours went by, but all in all, she felt good.

If only she could be strong enough, she thought, the baby would be strong enough too. It occurred to her that this was a very uncharacteristic way for her to think. Strength, whether of body or of character, had never been a trait she attributed to herself.

Her flute had survived the car crash relatively unscathed,

and she'd gotten permission from the NICU staff to bring it in and play when she visited Daniel. She played very, very softly, mostly slow airs and ballads, plus a few classical melodies, some Vivaldi and Mozart. She sang to him, too, in her dusky alto, folk songs like "The Lakes of Pontchartrain" and "Bonnie Jean Cameron" and "The Boatman." Alex always sang with her eyes closed, and from time to time she would open her eyes after singing and notice a group of nurses and other visiting parents gathered around the entrance to Daniel's pod.

Sitting in her wheelchair, she'd just finished singing "Wayfaring Stranger," her hand on a little patch of Daniel's arm that was free from tubes. She opened her eyes and saw Dr. Nguyen standing there.

"You sing well," Nguyen said.

Alex smiled, still looking at the baby.

"How do you feel?"

"I feel pretty good," Alex said.

Nguyen nodded. "I should tell you something. We are doing everything we can for the baby. But you should know . . ."

Alex slowly looked up at him.

"You should prepare for the worst," the doctor said. "His lungs are so immature, and he has an infection. We cannot tell what will happen."

Alex nodded.

"I will say this," Nguyen said. "If he gets through the first few days, he will most likely live. Long, long recovery, in the hospital for months, but he will live. These days are crucial. Every hour that he is here makes him stronger."

He checked Daniel's oxygen saturation—one hundred percent—and left Alex alone.

"Hey," said a voice behind her, after a few moments.

"Hey."

Danny Park came into the pod and looked at his namesake. "How you doing, little man?" He lightly touched the baby's leg, then looked at Alex. "How you doing, sister?"

"Okay."

"You in much pain?"

"Not much at all."

"You always had a high pain tolerance. Maybe it's an Indian thing."

Alex didn't smile.

"There's a phone call for you, back in your room," he said. "It's that Kelly woman again."

"Let's go."

Park wheeled her out of NICU and down the hall. "Who is she, Alex?" he asked.

"It's complicated."

"I know that, sister. I'm not stupid, I can see that it's complicated. But if she's who you came to Pittsburgh to get away from, you're sure not staying away from her."

"I know," Alex said. "It's just that . . . she knows things. She—" The sentence died in her throat.

She'd emerged from Doag Center and there was Faith Kelly, standing on the sidewalk. She turned the other way, trying just to get away from the nightmare, away from the pain. She hadn't been watching where she was going, and then the red-haired woman was yelling and running after her. There were traffic sounds, and horns, and Faith Kelly's voice.

"Alex, I think your husband is alive."

She remembered. Before, there had been nothing beyond running. Nothing until she woke up in the hospital, and there was Faith again, standing beside her.

"Alex, I think your husband is alive."

Alex blinked.

"Alex?" Park said.

"Gary," Alex whispered.

"Gary? Alex, are you okay?"

Alex nodded slowly. *Be strong. For the baby, be strong, Alex.*

"Where are Dad and Celia and Mickey?" she asked.

"They went to lunch. Why did you say Gary just now?"

"Never mind," Alex said. She picked up the phone receiver by the bed. "Hello, Faith."

"How are you?" Faith said.

"Not bad, actually."

"What about the baby?"

"He's struggling. The doctor just told me to be prepared for the worst."

"Oh, Alex. I don't—"

"Faith, I remember."

"What?"

"What you said, just before the car hit me."

Faith was silent.

"Did you hear me?" Alex said.

"Yes."

"Was that real, or were you just trying to get me to stop?"

More silence.

"Be honest with me," Alex said. "After all this, please just be honest with me."

"It's real," Faith said. "But not the way you think."

"I want to know."

"Actually, you don't. It's just more pain, Alex. It's just more hurt and more lies."

"I want to know anyway. I have to."

Faith sighed. "I know. Let me tell you why I called. I tried to get started on the Comanche end of this, following the leads from Russell Doag. I . . . let's just say I didn't get very far with the person at the Comanche Nation office." She explained her conversation with Hannah Sovo.

Alex waited a moment after Faith finished. "I guess I can understand them being suspicious." She thought for a while. "I know I'm on the rolls. One of the few things my dad ever said about my mom was that she was sure to get me registered with the Comanches right after I was born." She smiled. "Even though my mother was gone, I was still a member of the tribe, even if I never had anything to do with them."

"Alex," Faith said, "you need to talk to these people. I think . . ." Faith cleared her throat. "I think it would be best if you did it in person. Then they can be sure . . ."

"That I really am one of them," Alex finished. "I can understand that."

They both fell silent for a moment. Her first instinct was of course to stay in the hospital, never more than a few feet away from baby Daniel. *What kind of mother am I if I leave a critically ill infant to go chasing Indian ghosts?* she wondered.

But then, she didn't have much of a role model for being a mother, did she?

"I know the baby's critical," Faith said, "and I wouldn't ask you this if I didn't think it mattered. I think . . . I think it can help you get your life back. Yours and Daniel's."

"It's funny," Alex said. "You're not trying to change who I am anymore."

"No, I'm not."

"But yet here you are, still in the middle of this."

"Alex, let me ask you something. Why did you gather all that information about Cross Currents? All those financial shenanigans . . . why risk your job to do that?"

Alex waited. "It's just . . . I mean, you know this is the era of the supercorporation, and they have their fingers in everyone's pies. I didn't really plan to do anything with that stuff, but it's just . . . it's hard to explain."

"You just wanted to know if it could be done. . . ."

"Yes!"

". . . If one person, if one individual, working with their very own documents, could find proof of what the corporation was doing."

"Exactly! The whole culture there is so, so greedy. It's all about the almighty dollar. They're so huge, and they're into so many different enterprises, they didn't really even try to hide it when they cooked the numbers. They're all so arrogant, they think it's their right or something to screw everyone else. The corporate slogan is 'More than you ever imagined.' You don't know how right that is, except it really means 'More corrupt than you ever imagined!'"

"You can still do it, Alex. I think you can still expose Cross Currents, but you'll be totally safe, anonymous, and you'll have your own life. I think we can make that happen. My bosses will be happy and you can get on with raising your son."

"What do you want?"

"A couple of days. Come back to Oklahoma for a couple of days. You can stay at my house. It's probably safer than our 'safe house' now. We'll get to the Comanche side of things, I'll debrief you on the Cross Currents files, and then you fly back there to be with your baby for as long as it takes. And you can charge it all to the United States government. Your tax dollars at work."

Alex laughed a little. "I don't understand it, but . . . can I call out here to check on Daniel while I'm there?"

"As often as you want to."

"Can Dad and Celia and Danny stay here with him?"

"For as long as they want to."

"I'll do it, then. Get me on a plane. I don't think they'll want to discharge me, but I'll load up on pain meds before I go." Across the room, Park looked alarmed. "Don't worry, Danny. I know what I'm doing." She spoke back into the phone. "Faith, we'll talk about Gary, won't we?"

"Yes," Faith said. "We will. Among other things, we'll talk about Gary."

9:15 P.M.
Oklahoma City

In Faith's opinion, Alex looked terrible when she came off the plane at Will Rogers World Airport. Alex was walking very straight—*too* straight, Faith thought.

God, I hope this wasn't a mistake.

Faith was surprised when Alex took one of her hands, and placed it in both of her own. "Here we are again," Alex said, squeezing Faith's hand hard.

"How do you feel?"

"A little pain, not too much."

Alex was wearing khaki capri pants and a navy blue pocket T. "I'm glad you got some clothes."

Alex pulled at the hem of the shirt. "After I made it clear I was really leaving, Celia went and bought them for me."

"Did you have trouble with the hospital? I suspect Dr. Kaplan was cranky."

"To put it mildly."

Faith drove them across the city, the Miata's windows down to let in the warm night air. As they exited on Britton Road toward The Village, Alex asked, "Will you get in trouble?"

"For what?"

"This. Me. This isn't what you're supposed to be doing, is it?"

"Yes. No. Maybe. There aren't any simple, clear-cut answers where I live." Faith slid a glance at her. Alex looked very small in the other seat. "But I do what I have to do."

Alex noticed the bandage on her hand. "What happened to your hand?"

"A little accident with some glass. Nothing much."

"I don't believe you."

"Don't believe me, then, but that's all I'm saying."

Five minutes later they pulled into Faith's driveway. Faith quickly checked the property and found nothing out of order. For all she knew, Smith had already put another assassin on her, though it was impossible for him to know Jones had failed. Jones had been in secure lockup and under constant guard ever since Hendler arrested him.

"Let's talk about Gary," Alex said, after Faith had shown her the second bedroom and moved a pile of newspapers off the fold-out bed.

They moved back into the dining room. "Are you hungry? Thirsty?" Faith asked her.

"I could eat," Alex said. "Whatever you have."

"Bologna sandwich okay?"

"Absolutely."

Faith made her a sandwich and got her a bottle of water. They sat at the big wooden table, across from each other, both exuding weariness. Alex nibbled the sandwich and took a big drink of water.

"Gary," she said.

"Gary." Faith thought for a moment. How do you tell someone that the person they believed was their life's soul mate was only part of a plan to destroy them? That the whole relationship was an illusion?

"I have to know. I'm stronger than you think I am, Faith."

Faith smiled, then it faded quickly. "Gary St. James is . . . *was* . . . not a real person. I think . . . I think that the man who created the Gary St. James persona wanted to put himself in your path, to be your ideal man, the man you'd always wanted, and then to use whatever relationship developed to help ruin you."

Tears welled in Alex's eyes but did not fall. She nodded at Faith to go on.

"I know him as Isaac Smith. You know him as John Brown's Body. He made the phone call, he sent the e-mail. He inserted himself into your life. You didn't have a chance. He'd studied you, researched you, got to know who you were, what you wanted, how you felt. He's a master manipulator, a champion user. Then, just when you thought you were happy and had the life you wanted, he left, then made you think he'd been killed. Now you were not only alone but demoralized. The hits started coming faster and faster: the missing money from Cross Currents, Wells's investigation, the embezzlement charges, the murder."

Alex was sitting ramrod straight, the sandwich forgotten on the plate, one tiny bite taken out of it. "All of it?" she whispered. "He was all of it?"

"He was all of it." Faith took a deep breath. "And I've just discovered something else, something I can't figure out. I need to ask you a question, and I'm pretty sure I already know the answer."

Alex nodded, the tears still glistening around her eyes.

"Did you ever send an e-mail to Bryden Cole?"

"Bryden . . . who? I know the name, but . . . who is that?"

"Bryden Cole, the chief justice of the U.S. Supreme Court."

Alex blinked and a single tear spilled over. "You're kidding."

"No."

"I didn't . . . *don't* . . . even know who he is."

"You never e-mailed him about Tabananika and all the other stuff? Doag and the Blackjack Comanches?"

"No, why would I . . ."

Faith took the printout of the e-mail message out of her briefcase and handed it across to Alex. Alex read it intently, her forehead puckering. She began shaking her head.

"I didn't," she finally said.

"I didn't think so," Faith said.

"Gary?" Alex said, dropping to a whisper.

"I believe so. Reading that, it didn't sound like you. All that business about standing on bones and bathing in blood. Seems too flowery for you."

Alex pointed at the signature line. "And I didn't even know this Taba guy was my great-great-great-grandfather. I just knew he was somewhere in my mother's family tree."

Faith nodded. "To answer your question, it was all Gary."

"Why? For God's sake, why? What did I do to these people?"

"I don't think you did anything. But I'm beginning to think that maybe your ancestor, and Russell Doag's ancestor, did something, or had something done to them. And someone has a very long memory."

"But what does the Supreme Court justice have to do with it?"

"I don't know. One thing at a time. Tomorrow morning we're going to Lawton." Faith stood up. "Alex, tomorrow we're going to meet your ancestors."

27

AFTER RISING EARLY AND TAKING HER RUN, FAITH HAD quickly driven downtown to her office and completed some paperwork on one of her cases, a former CIA analyst who had succumbed to AIDS a couple of weeks earlier. She sent the data on its way to Yorkton and was back at the house before eight o'clock. She found Alex groggy but dressed.

"How'd you sleep?" Faith asked.

"Pretty well, actually. A fold-out is paradise compared to most hospital beds. I'm sore this morning, but . . . I guess I'm supposed to be sore."

"How do you feel otherwise? Any dizziness, nausea, anything like that?"

"No, Doctor, none of that. You always get up so early?"

Faith shrugged. "Can't help it. It's a character flaw."

Lawton was an easy, uneventful eighty-mile drive, southwest of Oklahoma City down the H. E. Bailey Turnpike. While the land still rolled, trees became steadily more rare by the time they passed the town of Chickasha.

Lawton itself was a city that had grown around Fort Sill, once a frontier outpost—"designed to protect your ancestors from my ancestors," Alex had wryly observed—and was now the U.S. Army's primary artillery training ground. Faith had done an Internet search and found that the Comanche Nation tribal complex was a little north of the city, just outside the gates to Fort Sill.

Faith eased the Miata off the turnpike and onto State Highway 48, passing a convenience store, a Burger King, and much construction. She missed the turnoff twice, seeing the cluster of modern buildings atop a hill, but unable to see how to get to them. Finally stopping to ask at the Burger King, a teenager told her which road to take. Five minutes later she edged the car up a curving driveway and parked.

Having never visited a tribal headquarters before, Faith hadn't really known what to expect. What she found was a group of brown office buildings that could have fit into any other kind of office complex. The major difference was the presence of the Comanche Nation's logo: a circle bordered in black with a curving section of blue and a larger curve of yellow, on which was superimposed the silhouette of a horse and rider, the rider holding a lance. On the outer circle were the words *Comanche Nation, Lords of the Plains*. Faith had read on the Internet that the Comanches had been called "lords of the plains" due to their horsemanship being far superior to that of any other plains tribe.

Alex was gazing around the complex intently. "Interesting," she finally said.

"Yeah," Faith said. "I grew up in suburban Chicago, so I never really saw any Indians . . . uh, Native Americans, I guess . . . until I moved to Oklahoma. I certainly didn't have a handle on the whole 'sovereign nation' issue. It's still confusing."

Alex nodded. "I didn't pay much attention to Oklahoma history in school. Of course there's lots of Indian stuff in there, but I wasn't interested."

"So you never even heard of the Blackjack Comanches? The woman I talked to here said they were mentioned in most history books."

Alex shook her head. "Like I said, I wasn't interested."

They passed a few buildings, including what appeared to be a busy health clinic, before spotting one labeled Administration.

"Let's try this," Faith said.

"What if she's not here?"

"We'll wait until she is."

The reception area was small but comfortable, with plaques and photos of previous leaders of the Comanche Nation. A young Comanche man, barely out of high school by the look of him, manned the desk.

"Can I help you ladies?" he asked.

"Could we please see Hannah Sovo?" Faith said. "I talked to her on the phone yesterday. My name's Faith Kelly, and this is Alex Bridge." The young man sat without saying anything for a moment, and Faith added, "She's a member of the Comanches."

"On the rolls, you mean." The young man smiled.

"Yes." Faith smiled back.

"Hannah's back there. Go through this door, turn left down the hall. Her office is the next to last door on the right."

They found Hannah Sovo on the phone in her office. She raised her eyebrows and motioned them to chairs. Sovo was a heavyset woman of around sixty, with the high cheekbones that were common to many Native Americans. Her copper-colored skin was smooth, with a few lines around the eyes. Her hair was the most dramatic feature, though: black, long, and straight, twisted into an intricate braid that was shot through with threads of silver.

"I'm not going to talk about that," Sovo said into the phone. She rolled her eyes toward Faith and Alex. "We're parties to the lawsuit and I can't talk about it." There was a pause, during which Sovo moved her head from side to side in exasperation. "Uh-huh, you tell him I said so. Look, I need to go. I've got some very important people in my office and I don't want to keep them waiting."

She hung up the phone and looked across the desk. "I don't know who you are, but you suddenly became very important people."

Faith smiled and extended a hand. "I'm Faith Kelly. I talked to you on the phone yesterday. This is the friend I told you about, Alex Bridge."

Sovo shook hands with both of them, her eyes focusing on Alex. "Don't I know you?"

"I don't think we've met before," Alex said.

"Where are you from?"

"I live in Oklahoma City, but I've lived all over. I was born here in Lawton, if that helps. But I left when I was three."

Sovo folded her hands together and looked thoughtful. The silence drew out for a long time. Sovo's eyes didn't leave Alex's for at least a minute, then they flitted down. Alex saw her staring at the tattoo on her arm.

Alex pulled up her sleeve to give Sovo a better look. "Is that what you were looking at?"

Sovo nodded. "A crown of thorns, roses, and crosses. You're JoLynda Pahocodny's daughter."

Alex drew in her breath.

"The tattoo," Sovo said. "She had it: same design, same place."

Alex nodded. "I don't really remember her, but I have one picture of her. Only one. My dad said it was taken right after I was born, and you can see the tattoo in it. I had mine done when I was in high school. Even though I spent a lot of years being angry with my mother for leaving us, I was going through an adolescent anti-dad phase then. I tried to figure out what would really get my dad. We were living in Jacksonville, Texas, at the time and I marched down to the local tattoo place with a fake consent form, gave them the picture, and told them that's what I wanted." She bowed her head. "My father cried. It really hurt him, to be reminded of the woman who left him that way. It was stupid of me. But I was sixteen: what did I care?"

"JoLynda always had her own mind," Sovo said. "She was about three years behind me in school, but we knew each other. Her father—your grandfather—and my father had been in school together too. Where did JoLynda wind up?"

"I don't know."

Sovo looked from Alex to Faith and back again. "I see. Your friend here said you just had a baby."

Alex nodded.

"Baby's with its father right now?"

"It's complicated," Alex said.

There was another long silence. "Tell me why you're here again."

"I'm doing some research," Alex said. "The names of Tabananika and the Blackjack Comanches have come up."

"You don't know about the Blackjacks?"

"I haven't had much exposure to Comanche culture or history. I just . . . no, it doesn't mean anything to me."

Sovo looked at Faith. "And what's your part in this?"

Faith started to answer, then Alex said, "She got me interested in finding my ancestors, in looking into my Comanche side."

Sovo nodded but looked doubtful. In a moment she abruptly stood up and walked to a door at the rear of the office. It opened onto a cluttered closet, and she dug through it for several minutes. When she returned, she handed Alex a photograph, about eleven by thirteen, in a black frame. The quality was grainy, with the sepia-tinted quality of the late 1800s.

"Oh my God," Alex said.

The picture showed several copper-skinned men on a wooden scaffold, each one hanging at the end of a rope. In the foreground, well-dressed white people watched the spectacle. One woman could be seen laughing.

Faith counted the hanged men. "Twenty-one," she said.

"Those," Sovo said, "were the Blackjack Comanches."

She let the silence sit for a while. Alex finally handed the photo back to her. "What . . ." Alex cleared her throat. "What happened?"

"The history of *numunuh* is a history of land," Sovo said. "That's the first thing you have to understand."

"I'm sorry," Faith said. "What was that word you just used?"

Sovo looked at Alex instead of Faith. "*Numunuh*. It means 'the people.' It's what Comanches have always called ourselves. It's a good word for you to learn as your first word in the old language."

"*Numunuh*," Alex said.

"The people," Sovo said. "After the War Between the States ended, the expansion into the west really started to come. The people's way of life was threatened. Suddenly we weren't the lords of the plains anymore. There were white settlers planting crops and building sod houses and killing our buffalo, and then the soldiers came behind them to make it all 'safe.'" She leaned heavily on the last word.

"Comanches and Kiowa and some of the other tribes—the Cheyenne, the Arapaho—were run ragged by the Army. So we met at Medicine Lodge along the Little Arkansas River in Kansas to make a treaty in 1868. The U.S. government drew a map and told us that we had a certain territory that was ours. As long as we stayed inside it, no one would bother us. No farmers, no cattlemen, no soldiers. As long as we stayed inside the boundaries, we could live however we wanted. No white person was to go inside it. That was the first time the word *reservation* was used. The leaders of the time agreed to it, including Tabananika. He was one of the signers of that treaty."

"But it didn't work," Faith said. "The more people came west, the more land was needed."

"So the Department of the Interior formed the Jerome Commission." Sovo scowled, as if she'd tasted something bad. "The land started to be carved up into little plots. All the Indians on the rolls got land allotments, 160 acres each. The rest was opened up for the white settlers. By this time the people were beaten down. Some groups were starving. We'd been hunters, following the buffalo for hundreds of years, and all of a sudden they wanted us to grow corn and wheat. So what choice was there?

"We thought they were done with us then, after Jerome. But even then, as the cattlemen moved into this country, the Bureau of Indian Affairs decided it could 'lease' Indian lands to the cattlemen for grazing. The Indian people only got a fraction of what the land was worth for grazing rights. Things were tense in March of 1893."

Sovo stood up. "Let's walk." She looked at Alex. "You look a little peaked. You okay to walk?"

"I can walk," Alex said.

They left the building and walked around the complex, Sovo pointing out the tribal clinic and police headquarters. It was nearly noon, the heat palpable in the air. Sovo seemed not to notice.

"Could I make a call?" Alex said at one point. She looked at Faith. "I just want to check . . . you know."

Faith handed Alex her cell phone. Alex moved a few steps away, out of the parking lot and into a grassy open area. Sovo watched her.

"Her baby's in intensive care," Faith finally said, to fill the silence.

"And yet, she's here and not there," Sovo said. She watched Alex's back for a moment. "She looks like she's been through a lot."

"She has."

Alex walked up and down, talking on the phone, her free hand never still, always searching for a rhythm. When she finished, she came back, handed Faith the phone, and said, "The same. He's hanging on. Dad said that Russell Doag has been there a lot."

"I called him," Faith said.

"Dad said he'd been buying their meals and got them set up in a room in an expensive hotel across from the hospital."

"He seems like a good man," Faith said. "He was concerned when I told him what happened to you."

Sovo looked at both of them, looking as if she wanted to say something, but walked on in silence for a short while before starting her story again.

"Sawyer's Crossing was south of here, right down along the Red River," she said. "You know where Grandfield is? No? Well, never mind. Sawyer's was a little south of there. It was a good crossing spot, where the Texas cattlemen liked to cross their stock when they were driving them north. A town had sprung up, and by all accounts was a thriving little place right there on the Red."

Sovo looked off into the distance. She smoothed the hem of her dress. "You girls are pretty good listeners. Not many young people now are." She glanced at Alex. "Your mom was always a smart one. She got all the good grades in school. But she had her own mind about things."

They walked the outer edge of the parking lot. A tribal police car passed them, its driver waving to Sovo, who waved back. "That's Jerry," she said. "He's probably a cousin of yours, couple of times removed. It's hard to trace the families sometimes. The chiefs, like Tabananika, all had several wives, and some of the wives were Mexican captives, so it's hard to tell who's descended from which wife, and all that. Makes it interesting. Lot of people with about two drops of Indian blood in them are trying to get on the rolls these days."

"Why?" Faith asked.

"Benefits. Health care, college scholarships. We have to have a solid family tree to put anyone on the rolls now, and the cutoff is one-fourth blood." They started back toward the administration building. "March of 1893. Sawyer's Crossing. There was a massacre. You hear that word used a lot in talking about Indian history, but this really was a massacre. Every man, woman, and child in Sawyer's Crossing was killed. Every single one. That's 118 people. Some of them were shot, some of them hacked to death with swords or lances. Buildings were burned. The oldest to die was a ninety-year-old man whose father had fought in the American Revolution. The youngest was a three-month-old baby girl."

"Dear God," Alex said.

"No, God wasn't there that day," Sovo said. "One pregnant woman was butchered and her baby cut out of her and flung on the ground like it was garbage. Today this would be called an atrocity. The town of Sawyer's Crossing pretty much ceased to exist in a single morning.

"There was a U.S. Cavalry patrol out of Fort Sill in the area. They said they hadn't intended to stop into Sawyer's that day, but someone saw smoke and they rode in that direction. They found all this, and some of the soldiers—some of them who'd been in a lot of Indian battles—were sick to their stomachs. They'd never seen anything like what happened at Sawyer's. Their captain found tracks, and they tracked along the north bank of the river for thirty miles or so until they found this little group of Comanches camped out on a ridge."

They went back into the administration building, Sovo picking up a handful of pink telephone message slips from the front desk. "People asking about this lawsuit," she muttered, shuffling the slips. "You girls want a drink? A Coke or some water?"

"I could use some water," Alex said. She was sweating, the back of her T-shirt sprinkled with perspiration. Faith thought she was a shade paler than she'd been earlier. Whether from heat, fatigue, or the gruesome story they'd been hearing, she couldn't tell.

Sovo got her a bottle of water and they went back to her office. The photo of the hanged men lay on her desk.

"This little group they found was a bunch of young guys, with Buffalo Heart being what passed for a leader. They weren't really an organized band—by then there weren't such things anymore. They were just a bunch of angry young bucks. Buffalo Heart told the cavalry captain that they heard there had been trouble in Sawyer's, and they rode over to see what was going on and found it, just like they had. Of course, the difference was, he figured that if anyone else found them there, they'd figure his group had done it. He was right, as it turned out.

"The cavalry put the men all under arrest and marched them back to Fort Sill under guard. There was a big trial, with newspapers from as far away as Kansas City covering it. One of the newspapers came up with the name *Blackjack Comanches*, since there were twenty-one defendants. Thought they were being cute, but the name stuck. They were convicted, of course, and you see what happened to them." She tapped the photo.

Faith thought for a moment. The e-mails and phone calls all talked about "knowing the truth about the Blackjack Comanches." But how could a century-old massacre and sensational trial have anything to do with the here and now?

"They lost everything," Sovo said. "Not only their lives, but their families had to give up their allotments. Their lives, their land, their dignity."

"Was there proof?" Alex said. "Or just the cavalry's word against theirs?"

"Honey, that's all they needed in those days. These were just a bunch of goddamn Indians, after all."

Faith watched closely, picking up the older woman's vehemence. It was the first time she'd cursed, the first time she'd shown much emotion, since they came to her office.

"I'm sorry," Faith said.

"All those people," Alex said.

"Most Comanches don't believe Buffalo Heart's boys did it, if that's what you're wondering," Sovo said. "Those who knew him said he had no hatred in him. His mother even said he'd been courting a white girl. It didn't make sense, but no one ever tried to figure out what happened. They had their killers, hanging on ropes. What more did they need? It's just history now, folklore, something you hear about every now and again."

"What about Tabananika?" Alex asked.

"What about him?"

"Was he involved with any of that? Was he connected to . . ."

Sovo was shaking her head. "I told you the story of the Blackjacks, but I shouldn't be the one to tell you of your own family."

"But I don't have   "

Sovo took a pad of paper and drew a detailed map. "He's buried over at Otipoby's. It's on the base, but if you go in the entrance just across the road here, you won't have to show an ID or anything. It's away from the main part of Fort Sill. Go over there. Stay awhile. The dead can talk to us, too, you know. Maybe old Tabananika could still tell you something."

Faith and Alex both looked at her.

"Think that's some old Indian wisdom?" Sovo said. She smiled suddenly. "No, I got it from TV, that *Charmed* show. You girls need to lighten up."

Hannah Sovo watched the two young women leave the building, then get in the little gold sports car and roar out of the parking lot. She watched the car until it hit the highway, then turned around and went back in her office.

She picked up the phone and called a number. "I just had a very interesting visitor," she said a moment later.

28

July 21, 12:10 P.M.

FAITH DROVE ACROSS HIGHWAY 48 AND IMMEDIATELY noticed a change in the landscape, the grounds on the Fort Sill Military Reservation being exceptionally well kept. Hannah Sovo was right: it was certainly an isolated, back-door entrance to the base. Only a tiny guardhouse, manned by a single soldier, stood at the entrance. He threw them a salute and the Miata drove right onto the fort grounds.

There was no sign of life, just the little two-lane ribbon of road cutting through rolling grassland. Alex consulted the detailed map Sovo had drawn. They topped a little rise and came to a crossroads. She pointed left, then they made another left.

Faith nodded toward a little grove of trees. She could see grave markers. "Is that—"

"I don't think so," Alex said. "It's further up the road. According to this, that's where Geronimo is buried, though."

A minute later, a little gravel trail peeled off from the road. Alex pointed and Faith turned, the gravel crunching under the Miata's tires. At the top of a hill was a sign that read OTIPOBY COMANCHE CEMETERY. The burial ground was small and surrounded by a chain-link fence.

"What are we supposed to find here?" Alex said as she got out of the car.

Faith didn't answer, looking around. The quiet was overpowering, reminding her of the country around Black Mesa, far to the northwest of here, at the tip of Oklahoma's panhandle. She'd spent some time there last year and had seen another burial ground, hidden in the rough terrain.

She took a few steps away from the car. She pulled her hair back from her face. The heat was already beginning to bother her again. Faith glanced at Alex: they wouldn't stay here long, she decided. Alex didn't need to be out in this heat.

Alex had already unlatched the cemetery gate and walked in. Faith followed a few steps behind. She had to admit that the view from the top of the little hilltop burial ground was spectacular. She could see to the turnpike and beyond, and in another direction, the Comanche Nation tribal complex looked like toys scattered on the ground. The Wichita Mountains lay in the distance, hazy and indistinct.

They walked through the rows of gray stones, reading the Indian names on headstones: Pokoro, Otipoby, Chibitty, Penateka, and a few Anglo names like Pratt and Gibson. The words *Comanche-Mexican* appeared on several stones.

"I don't know what—" Faith began in exasperation.

"Here," Alex called.

She was in the back row of the cemetery, standing before a small, nondescript gray stone.

Chief Tabananika
"Sound of the Sun"
Yamparika Comanche
Little Arkansas
Treaty Signer
April 28, 1893

"Found you," Alex said. It seemed to Faith that she wanted to say more, but she was silent, standing before the grave.

"Wait a minute," Faith said, turned and ran for the car. She dug her briefcase out of the backseat and found the notes she'd made when talking with Russell Doag in Pittsburgh. She took the pages back to Alex.

Alex never looked away from the stone. "What is it?" she said.

"The date. Tabananika's death date. April 28, 1893. It's the same day Jonathan Doag was murdered. The same day, Alex!"

Alex slowly turned to look at her.

"And the letter Doag sent to his brother, which supposedly had those affidavits in it? Those affidavits that are nowhere to be found. It was dated April 22. Six days later both he and Tabananika were dead."

"And Hannah said the whole business of the Blackjack Comanches was in March."

"The same year, just a few weeks before. Do we know how Tabananika died?"

"He was poisoned," said a voice behind them.

Faith whirled around, her hand snaking toward her holster. Alex turned as well, and they faced an old Indian man.

Faith couldn't tell his age from his features. He could be in his sixties or his eighties. He wasn't a large man; in fact, Faith was taller than he by a couple of inches. He carried some extra weight around the middle, but his arms looked muscular. His face was weathered and he was slightly hunched. Faith thought the man probably knew the meaning of manual labor.

No one spoke for a long moment.

"You're Alex," the old man finally said.

"How do you—" Alex said.

"Hannah called me. I just live a little ways down the road. You were barely walking and talking the last time I saw you."

Alex stared at him.

"I'm Lonnie," he said. "Lonnie Pahocodny. I'm your grandfather, Alex."

Alex couldn't think.

She didn't have a grandfather. She didn't have a mother. The idea that she did was totally alien, as if the old man had spoken in a foreign language. Her only family was her father, whichever current "stepmother" Bill Bridge was on, and her half-brothers . . . and now baby Daniel. That was all. There was no other.

"You'd be about thirty now, right?" Pahocodny said.

Alex nodded.

"Yeah, that's about right." The old man scuffed the ground with a booted foot.

No one spoke for a long time. Faith finally stepped forward. "Mr. Pahocodny, I'm Faith Kelly. I'm a friend of Alex's."

He nodded. "Nice to meet you."

There was another long silence.

"Tabananika was poisoned, you said?" Faith offered.

The old man shrugged. "That's what the family's always believed."

"What happened?"

The old man shuffled his feet again. "He was running to catch a train at the Rock Island station in Anadarko. He was going to Washington to testify about the latest bunch of leases and whether the Indians were getting fair pay for the grazing rights. He was late for the train and was running after it, and he fell over dead. The BIA said he died of a heart attack. His family didn't think so. His heart was strong."

Alex found her voice, though it came out barely a whisper. "Why? Why would someone poison him?"

Pahocodny shrugged again, as if he were vaguely uncomfortable with saying so much. "He was an influential chief, at least among the people themselves. He didn't have a lot of pull with the whites; Quanah was better at that, a better politician than Tabananika, and that's why he's better known today. But the people listened to Tabananika. In that time, he was the last chief actually chosen by the people. Maybe someone was upset that he was so resistant to the price offered on the land leases. Maybe they just figured he was an old troublemaker. But a lot of the people have believed for a long time that he was given some slow-acting poison to keep him from going to Washington."

He shuffled a few steps and looked down at Tabananika's

grave marker. "'Sound of the Sun.' Sometimes his name translates as 'Hears the Sun' or even 'Voice of the Sunrise.' Depends on who's doing the translating." Pahocodny looked off into the distance, across the turnpike. "You *can* hear the sunrise, you know, if you really listen. Most people don't listen."

They were all silent again. After a moment Faith cleared her throat. "I'm going to go back to the car. I need to check a few things." She trotted away, leaving Alex and the old man standing together in front of their ancestor's stone.

"You never came before," Pahocodny finally said.

"I never knew—" Alex said, then choked off the words and swallowed hard. "I was so little when she left, I really don't have any memories at all."

Pahocodny nodded but said nothing.

"I mean," Alex said, "I never felt Indian. After she left, we moved away. My dad moved us around a lot."

"How is Bill? I always liked him, you know. He was a hard worker."

"He's okay. He did the best job he could with me."

"Did he remarry?"

Alex tapped a little rhythm on her pants leg. "He always said he couldn't, because he'd never actually gotten a divorce. He's lived with several other women and has kids with them, but . . . he really never got over her leaving. Maybe I didn't, either."

The old man nodded again. It seemed to be a movement he'd practiced. "What do you do?"

"I'm a musician." Alex decided not to mention Cross Currents. It wasn't really what she *did*, anyway, just a paying job.

The old man looked at her and smiled for the first time. "Is that right? JoLynda played in the band in high school. She played flute."

Alex drew in a sharp breath.

"What?" Pahocodny said.

"I play a lot of different instruments, but my main one is flute. I can't believe . . ." She shook her head. Waves of conflicting feelings crashed through her: the desperate desire to know her mother, the anger she'd felt toward JoLynda Pahocodny Bridge for most of her life, and how it was all being tied together by the strange madness of her life. Cross Currents and Faith Kelly and Russell Doag and Blackjack Comanches and. . .

Lonnie Pahocodny smiled again. "I was a welder for nearly fifty years. Your grandma taught school."

"Where is she?"

"She passed four years ago. Cancer." He outlined one side of Tabananika's marker with the toe of his boot. "Hannah says you've got a baby."

"Yes. Daniel Alexander Bridge."

"And he's sick?"

"Very sick."

The nod again. "Hope he'll be all right. Where's his daddy?"

Alex shook her head. "My life . . . I can't explain my life. Not right now. I don't know anything." She looked up at him. "I don't know what to call you."

"When you were little, just learning to talk, you called me Gran-Lonnie. Everyone always got a kick out of that."

"Gran-Lonnie. I'll remember that." Alex shuffled her feet. "Do you know why she left?"

The old man sighed, and it seemed to come from deep within him. "She was smart, that one was. Always on the honor roll, and first chair flute in the band. But she was . . . she didn't always have her mind on where she was. Her brain, it was always going, you know, always working. Ideas, ideas, all the time. And questions. You answer one question, she'd think of twenty more." The old man blinked down at his granddaughter. "I don't know. We never heard from her, either. I talked to Bill a few times; he'd thought maybe . . . I don't know what he thought. Then we just sort of fell out of touch, like people do. The girl was restless, and always the questions. I don't know why she left. I do know she loved you, she doted on you, used to read to you every night. The Bible and fairy tales and a big book of Indian stories."

Alex felt her eyes fill.

"See there, your mama used to ask me questions I couldn't answer, and now here you are doing the same thing. Maybe it's time I asked you a question. Why'd you go looking for your roots now, Alex?"

Alex waited before speaking. "I think . . . I don't know what to think. I think he"—she pointed at the grave—"might have something to do with what's been happening to me. Did Tabananika have anything to do with the Blackjack Comanches? He died right about the same time, just after the massacre and the trial."

"It was a bad time for the people, all right. When your grandma was alive, we used to look into a lot of this history stuff. She was a history and social studies teacher, you know. It's interesting too. Old Tabananika was known for disliking whites, for being resistant to them. But right at the end of his life, he struck up a friendship with one of the assistant Indian agents. I even remember *my* grandfather telling me about this, that Tabananika and this young fellow from back east would go riding out on the plains."

"Jonathan Doag," Alex said.

"What?"

"The Indian agent from back east. His name was Jonathan Doag. I've met one of his descendants. He was killed on the same day as Tabananika."

Pahocodny looked at her. "You don't say."

"Yes." Alex felt a little touch of dizziness, some weakness in her knees. "I think this heat's getting to me, and I'm getting sore again."

"Again?"

"Very long story." She paused, then added: "Gran-Lonnie."

The old man smiled. "Sounds pretty good to hear you say that." The smile faded. "You know, I'm not sure if this would help you, but there is one old story my grandfather used to tell. I don't know if this is true or not. My granddad used to say that the old chief and this young white man he'd gotten to be friends with rode out on a spring day, not long before Tabananika died. It was a warm March, and trees were blooming early and the plains were greening up. The white man—Doag, is that right?—wanted to ride south, down toward the river, because he'd never gone that way before. So they rode and they rode. They were going to stop to water the horses and get something to eat, but Tabananika suddenly wanted to turn back. He'd seen smoke, big plumes of black smoke, in the sky, and he didn't believe in riding into smoke. Said it meant the spirits were angry."

Alex's pulse quickened.

"But the white man convinced him that they should take a look. They rode over the hill and stopped. That's where the story ends. My grandfather never said any more. You know, Indians don't make up fancy endings for stories. When it's done, we just say 'That's all.' And that's what my grandfather did, said 'That's all.' He left them sitting there on the hillside, looking down into the smoke."

"Were they—"

"So the story goes, Alex. So the story goes. Old Tabananika and young Doag were sitting and looking down at the Sawyer's Crossing massacre."

29

SMITH DIDN'T HAVE MUCH TROUBLE FINDING OUT which hospital Alex had been in. He simply started calling hospitals in the Pittsburgh area and asked each one to be connected to Alex Bridge's room. When he was told there was no patient by that name, he apologized for his mistake and hung up, crossing that one off the list. On the fourth try he found Allegheny General and was told that Ms. Bridge had checked out.

Oh, Alex, Smith thought. He could see it as clearly as if he'd scripted it himself. Alex had checked herself out of the hospital to join Faith Kelly in putting together more pieces of the puzzle. The baby would be hospitalized for a while, and there was nothing she could do for it for the moment. She would feel guilty, but she would go. It made perfect sense. It was pure Alex.

Of course, Faith Kelly was the proverbial wild card. He hadn't been able to reach Jones, and he presumed that meant Jones had failed to kill Kelly. It angered him, but mistakes happened when he trusted others. It was a part of his business, and he'd learned to deal with it. He would still have to handle Ms. Kelly eventually.

The main doors to Allegheny General were locked, so he entered through the emergency room. He consulted a building directory and took the elevator to the sixth floor, for the neonatal intensive care unit.

The unit itself was closed, with an intercom box mounted next to the locked door. Smith pressed the button on the box.

"NICU," said a scratchy female voice.

Smith cleared his throat. "Hello, yes," he said, putting on his nervous persona. "My name is Gary St. James. Uh, I think my son is here, and I wanted to visit him."

There was a long silence. "What's the baby's name, sir?"

"Well, actually, he'd have the last name of Bridge. My ex-wife took her maiden name back."

Another long pause. "Just a moment."

In a few seconds the door opened and a middle-aged nurse in multicolored scrubs came out. "I'm Cheryl Story. I'm taking care of Daniel this shift."

Smith offered his hand. "Gary St. James."

Story shook it, looking him up and down. His clothes were rumpled, he was unshaven, and his eyes looked tired. "Odd hour for a visit."

"I know. It's just that, I drove in all the way from Oklahoma. I just found out about the baby being born. Alex has . . . well, we haven't been on great terms since the divorce."

Story leaned against the wall. "Well, here it is, Mr. St. James. When Mom was admitted through the ER, she listed her husband as being deceased."

Smith tried for a crooked smile. "Deceased? Well, maybe she wishes I was dead, but you can see that I'm not. Don't I have a right to see my son?"

"Could I see some kind of identification?"

"Sure, of course." Smith opened his wallet and handed her Gary St. James's driver's license.

Story sat down in a waiting room chair and opened a chart. She placed the driver's license at the top of it, first scrutinizing Smith carefully, comparing him to the picture.

"Hmm," she said. "Well, the information checks out. Thirty-three twenty-one Northwest Fifty-second Street, Oklahoma City, Oklahoma. That's the address Mom gave."

"We've just been divorced a few months, and I haven't gotten a new license with my new address," Smith said.

"Why would she tell us you were dead?"

Smith leaned wearily against the wall, seemingly exhausted. "I don't know. The divorce . . . it was pretty painful. I mean, we never hit each other or anything. But if words were stones, well, I guess we'd both be bleeding."

Then, much to Cheryl Story's surprise, Smith began to cry, silent sobs that streaked his face and ran straight down, dripping onto his shirt. "I'm sorry," he said after a moment. "It's just been so . . ." He sank into a chair and dropped his head into his hands.

Story looked uncomfortable, as if she were struggling. She reached out and put a hand on Smith's shoulder. "Look, things are very quiet right now. I know you've come a long way and I'll let you in for a few minutes. Mom's father, stepmother, and brother are usually here during the day, since Mom had to leave so suddenly. But later today, after you've had some time to rest up, you need to get with Mom and work it out so that you're put on the official visitors' list. Okay?"

Smith nodded, wiping his face. "I'm sorry, I feel like an idiot. I just . . ."

Story patted the shoulder. "Don't apologize for letting your feelings show. Come on."

Oh, yes, Smith thought.

Smith had never been inside a neonatal intensive care unit before, but found it much the same as other critical care units in large hospitals. The only difference was the tiny bassinets and, of course, the tiny patients inside them. Story led him to the pod in the corner, where she fussed a little with one of Daniel's monitors.

"Hey, Daniel," she said, not in a whisper but not in full voice, either. The lighting in the unit was very subdued. "Your daddy's here, big guy."

"What . . . what's his full name?" Smith asked.

Story pointed to a blue card taped to the bassinet. On it was a graphic of a smiling baby holding a bunch of balloons, with the printed words *I'M A BOY!* Written in black marker underneath was *Daniel Alexander Bridge.*

"Named for her brother," Smith said. "She'd said she might want to . . ." He shook his head, as if he were about to begin weeping again.

"I'll leave you alone," Story said, and retreated to the nurses' station.

"Thank you," Smith whispered.

He walked around the bassinet, watching the sleeping child, counting the tubes and wires and IV lines.

You should never have been conceived, he thought.

He'd had the vasectomy ten years ago, and had been diligent about his follow-up appointments for the first few years afterward. *Some vasectomies don't take,* his surgeon had told him, *so we have to check every so often for those persistent swimmers.*

Smith hadn't been tested in the last three years. He'd figured he was safe, and the annual test had become an annoyance, a waste of time.

Persistent swimmers, indeed.

He looked at the child's dark hair, at the needle in his scalp, at the tiny stump where the umbilical cord had been cut.

You shouldn't exist, he thought. *You are a mistake. You are a loose end. You are a by-product of my professional life.*

Bet your client didn't pay extra for that, Faith Kelly had written.

Smith could rectify this mistake in a heartbeat. It could be done very quickly, then he could regain his focus, taking care of Faith Kelly and Alex—naïve, emotional, tortured little Alex Bridge, the perfect vehicle for this job. Aside from the naked boy in the bassinet, his work on Alex had been his most brilliant ever.

Smith had studied medical technology for a job he did five years ago. He'd assumed the persona of a respiratory therapist in a hospital, and while he hadn't actually treated any patients, he'd been able to talk the talk, to understand the equipment.

Pretending to stroke the baby's tiny cheek, he reached with his free hand and punched a button on Daniel's oxygen monitor.

The button was labeled MUTE ALARMS.

Then it was a simple matter of removing the oxygen tube from the baby's mouth. He was on one hundred percent oxygen, and without it, death would come quickly. When the baby had stopped breathing, he would reinsert the tube and leave, telling the nurses he'd visit again after he'd talked with his ex-wife.

It was actually poignant, Smith thought, and gave a certain symmetry to his life. He'd begun this journey by very carefully pulling his father off a breathing machine eleven years ago. Now he was going to do the same to this child. He couldn't think of him as his "son": that had no meaning to him. The boy simply had some of his DNA, which meant he had some of Pyotr Gerenko's DNA, which was simply another reason to do this, and to do it now.

See how much I've suffered for you, my son? It was all for you. All . . . for . . . you.

Pyotr Gerenko hadn't known suffering. He'd left Smith's mother and adored older sister behind, and never gave them a second thought. From the time they came to America, he never spoke either of their names again. It was as if they were dead. He never knew what happened to them, and the old man never cared.

He had brought Mikhail, and only Mikhail, because he thought the CIA might be able to use him, train him to infiltrate the Soviet Union. It was like he was giving them a present—not just himself, the great and powerful Russian physicist, but a bonus, his intelligent, handsome, impressionable young son, to make into whatever they wanted. Pyotr had been eager to please his new masters.

But the Soviet Union disintegrated, and neither of the Gerenkos was of any interest any longer.

It was all for you.

First his father, now this baby boy.

Smith leaned very close to the child. "You shouldn't be here," he whispered.

He stayed close. Perhaps if someone looked this way, they'd think he was kissing the boy's cheek. An attentive, emotional man, even if he was divorced from the boy's mother. The nurses would appreciate that.

He began to peel back a little bit of the white surgical tape that secured the tube around the boy's mouth. He peered at the monitor above his head. The oxygen saturation was still one hundred percent.

Smith lifted one end of the tape. He felt the tube loosen a little.

Yes, Father, he thought. He shook his head. *Don't think about Pyotr. He doesn't matter. Take care of this and get back to work. The job isn't finished: the best is yet to come.*

He blinked.

The nurse, Story, strolled into the pod.

Smith drew in a quick breath. He angled his body so that he was between the baby and the nurse's view of him.

"He's a tough little guy," Story said.

"So he is," Smith said. His right hand, the one he'd been using to peel the tape, began to shake a little. His own breathing quickened.

"Everything all right?"

Smith nodded. *Attentive, emotional, caring father, that's what I am right now. I just drove across the country, I'm concerned about this baby, that's what I am.*

"There are a lot of tubes and things," he finally said.

"I know it looks bad," Story said, "but just remember that those are what keeps him going right now. He's fighting the good fight, but we have to help him."

Smith nodded. His hand shook.

"Let me know if you need anything," Story said.

"I will. Thank you."

The nurse moved away, checking the baby in the next pod, then going farther down the row.

Smith swallowed. He flexed his hand as best he could.

Do it!

He thought of Alex. She was indeed an intriguing woman, seemingly without prejudice of any kind, never judgmental, and a superior listener. It had been difficult to get into her mind, since she would rather listen to others than talk about herself. He'd never met anyone like her, certainly not in a professional role. She was a very interesting human being, and he had made her even more interesting in his efforts to destroy her. He'd been able to watch her reactions, to see her spin and turn as her life floated further and further away from her.

Yes, she was interesting, and the last act had yet to be played.

He peeled a little more of the surgical tape, loosening the oxygen tube even further. The tube slipped a bit. He watched the monitor. The oxygen saturation number began to drop. From one hundred, it fell to ninety-one percent.

Smith's mind raced away from him. There was much to do. Since he assumed Jones had failed, there was Kelly to deal with, the hateful woman. Impressive, but hateful nonetheless: she had a temper, an unattractive feature. Plus, there were other considerations. Things only Smith knew.

The best was most certainly yet to come.

The oxygen saturation dropped to eighty-four percent.

Daniel Alexander Bridge moved a little, flexing his toes, turning his head.

Smith's hand began to shake again.

Seventy-nine percent.

He pulled the tube up from the baby's throat, edging it out an inch at a time.

The baby's eyes opened, looking straight at Smith.

Smith grunted. It was only a tiny sound of surprise, but it sounded as loud as a scream to him.

With his eyes open, the baby looked like Alex Bridge, with the dark skin tone and slate blue eyes. He knew most newborns had the same eye color, but they looked like Alex's eyes to him.

Smith squeezed his own eyes closed. *What's happening? Do it, do it, finish it!*

He heard footsteps on the tiles outside the pod.

No!

Smith felt a sensation he'd never had before: indecision. He was paralyzed for a couple of seconds, standing there with the oxygen tube in his hand.

Seventy-two percent.

The baby squirmed.

The footsteps approached.

No! No! No!

There was no more time. He reinserted the tube, working it in as if he were a licensed respiratory therapist. He tucked it back into the side of the baby's mouth and began taping it in place.

The saturation number began to go back up. Seventy-seven.

"Mr. St. James?" Cheryl Story said.

Smith couldn't see her yet, but knew she was only three or four steps away.

"Is everything all right, sir?"

He spread the tape back across the baby's mouth, tapped down the edges, and in one swift motion, pressed the MUTE ALARMS button again.

A beeping filled the pod. He glanced at the monitor: the oxygen was back up to eighty-nine.

Story, cool and professional, walked in. "Here, what's up in here?"

Smith looked panicked. "I'm sorry, I . . . I was touching his cheek. I think I bumped against this line here. I don't . . ."

"That's all right," Story said, brushing past him. She swiftly muted the alarm, not realizing it had only been un-muted seconds ago. She jiggled the tube and secured the tape.

Ninety-two percent.

"He's going to be fine," Story said. "See, his saturation's

already going back up. I tell you, he's a fighter. He keeps trying to pull out all his own lines, several times a day. Don't
worry." She patted Smith's shoulder.

"I'd better go for now," Smith said.

"See what you can do about getting on the list, all right?"

"I will."

"And you call the unit anytime to check on him. Mom's
called every couple of hours."

"All right."

Smith walked slowly, a bit unsteadily, away from the unit.
The unsteadiness wasn't entirely part of his professional role
this time. His right hand was still trembling a bit, and he finally jammed it into his pocket. He needed to get away from
here, to go home to his Maryland farmhouse for a day, to
meditate, to read, to be alone before he finished the job.

He checked his watch. Time had seemed to crawl while he
was in the NICU, but he saw that it was nearly six o'clock.
The sun would be up soon. He planned to be on the road,
heading south, before it did.

He opened the door that led out of the NICU and stepped
in front of Danny Park.

Both men froze. For a wild moment Smith thought Park
hadn't recognized him, that they were just two strangers
brushing by each other in an early-morning hospital corridor.

But then Smith saw the recognition on Park's face, looking at the man who had been his brother-in-law.

"Gary?" Park said. "You—"

Smith shoved the shorter man in the chest, turned, and ran.

30

July 22, 5:40 A.M.

SMITH RAN BLINDLY. HE DIDN'T KNOW THE LAYOUT OF Allegheny General, though if it was like most American hospitals, it would be mindlessly confusing, with wings added on here and there at various times as funds became available. He took a hard right turn coming out of the NICU waiting area and ran past the "regular" newborn nursery, healthy babies behind glass, cooing adults staring at them.

How could this have happened? How could he have run into Alex's half-brother here? He'd come here in the middle of the night with his story about having just driven cross-country, to avoid any of Alex's family. So why had Danny Park been standing outside the unit before six A.M.?

Then he remembered. Alex had told him shortly after they got married that Park was a very early riser, the only one in the entire family. Alex herself was a notoriously late sleeper. But Park had to be at work most mornings at seven, so it was nothing for him to be up at five o'clock every day.

And now Park had seen and recognized him. Gary St. James was supposed to be dead: in fact, he *was* dead, to Smith's mind.

"Gary?" Park shouted. "Hey! Hey, come back here!"

There was no elevator on this end of the sixth floor, but Smith spotted a door to the stairs and pushed through it.

"Hey!" yelled one of the nurses as he ran past. "Don't run in here!"

He pounded down the concrete steps. Smith wasn't in his

top physical condition. His most recent role, that of Gary St. James, had called for a man who was healthy but not overly concerned with physical fitness. His exercise regimen for most of a year had been limited to a fairly mild walk three times a week. Since abandoning St. James, Smith hadn't quite made it back up to his most rigorous workout routine. He wasn't winded yet, but he wouldn't last long in a foot chase with Danny Park. He knew Alex's brother worked out often, and strenuously.

He opened the door to the fifth floor. Above him, the sixth floor door flew open, banging into the wall.

"Gary? Gary, dammit, what's going on?" Park shouted.

Smith stepped onto the fifth floor. This wasn't going to work. Park was right behind him.

Think! Think!

He'd been so unsettled by the experience in the NICU, by the fact he hadn't done what he set out to do, that his mind was clouded. It was an unusual sensation for Smith. He could always plan, could always execute: This was what he did. This was who he was. But he couldn't outrun Park.

He jogged past patient rooms. The floor was still quiet, as most of the patients still were not awake. He turned a corner as he heard Park come onto the floor.

Smith passed a closed door. The brown nameplate on the wall beside the doorknob read STAFF ON-CALL ROOM. He backed up, rattled the knob, and pushed inside the room.

Danny Park slowed to a walk. Nurses had been giving him dirty looks, looks that could say *Why are you running in here?* without a word being spoken.

For a moment he'd thought he was losing his mind. Since Alex had said she had to go back to Oklahoma for a couple of days, he had promised to be near little Daniel as much as possible. He stayed close to the NICU at least until midnight and tried to be back by six A.M. Dad and Celia would be along later. They had to deal with his little half-brother Mickey, who had been agog over the whole experience from the start.

But he'd come to the NICU and was getting ready to press the intercom button when the door opened and Gary St. James walked out. Unshaven, rumpled, wild-eyed . . . but definitely his brother-in-law. His brother-in-law that Alex said was dead.

Park stopped at the fifth-floor nurses' station. "Did you see a guy coming running past here? A little taller than I am, blond hair, wearing a blue shirt."

"I didn't," said the nurse. "But I was on break and just came back."

"I saw him," said another nurse. "I told him to slow down."

"Where did he go?"

"I didn't see where he went. He probably took the elevator."

Park blew out an exasperated breath. "Could I check in some of these rooms to see if he's hiding in there?"

"Hiding?" said the first nurse.

"No, you certainly may not," said the second. "We're full, patients in every room, and you can't go poking around in them. Who are you?"

"No one," Park said. He moved away from the nurses, but was aware of them watching him.

He moved to the bank of elevators. The nurses kept watching.

He angrily stabbed the DOWN button.

Lost him. Alex's husband—Daniel's father!—was here, and I lost him.

He went into the empty elevator. He had to do something. He had to let Alex know. Her husband wasn't dead after all. He knew she was still weak, but she'd been strong enough to fly back to Oklahoma to meet that Kelly woman.

Kelly.

He pulled a slip of paper out of his pocket. Kelly had said that if the family needed anything to call her, day or night.

Park didn't carry a cell phone, couldn't stand the things.

But when the doors opened on the ground floor of Allegheny General, he immediately started looking for a pay phone.

The on-call room was small and spare: a tiny desk, a cot, a chair, a lavatory. Doctors who pulled twenty-four-hour on-call shifts would come in here for short naps, time away from the bustle and madness of the hospital floor.

Smith waited fifteen minutes, hoping that no tired physician was on his or her way in here for a break. It would be seven o'clock soon, which in most hospitals meant a shift change. He counted to one hundred, then opened the door. Metal carts filled with breakfast trays were starting to be pushed through the halls. Now was his best chance. He stepped into the hallway, walked around the corner, and moved to the elevator.

Oklahoma City

Faith slept a little later than usual and tried to be quiet as she dressed for her run. Alex had been extremely weary by the time they got back to Oklahoma City late yesterday afternoon, worn not only by physical fatigue—Faith had to remind herself that the woman had just been hit by a car and given birth—but by raging emotions. Faith had diplomatically stepped away from Alex and Lonnie Pahocodny, and she hadn't pressed Alex for details on what the old man had said, but she knew it had been an emotional moment for her.

This morning she just let Alex sleep. When she woke, they would begin to deal with some of the Cross Currents data and would try to piece together what some of the Comanche history meant.

Faith's phone was in her fanny pack as she ran through the quiet residential streets. When it chirped, she stopped immediately.

"Kelly," she said into it.

"This is Danny. Danny Park."

"Hello, Danny. How's the baby?"

"I don't know. I mean, I haven't seen him yet this morning. Look . . . Gary was here. Alex's husband. Gary . . . Alex said he was dead."

"He was there? In the hospital?"

"I ran into him coming out of the NICU. It was really early, before six o'clock. He was coming out— "

"Danny, listen to me: don't let him anywhere near the baby. Do you hear me?"

"But he already—"

"I'll get a protective detail assigned to the baby right away. Danny, go back to NICU. Stay with the baby. Where is he now?"

"You mean Gary? I lost him. He— "

"Don't try to chase him. Do you understand me? This is a dangerous man, and he's not who you think he is."

"Where's Alex?"

"She's resting. Stay with the baby!"

Faith ran the two miles back to her house at top speed. Alex was awake, sitting in the dining room. One look at Faith's face told her something was wrong.

"What is it?"

"Smith," Faith said. "He was at the hospital."

"What? Smith? I mean, Gary?" Alex stood up. "What was he—"

Faith punched Yorkton's number into her cell phone. She only had one number for him: the Department Thirty office number was set to roll over to Yorkton's home, then his cell. It rang four times.

"Good day," Yorkton said on the recording. "Please be so kind as to leave a message after the tone. Thank you."

It was the first time Faith had ever called him and not gotten through. "Shit," she muttered. "I don't have time to wait."

"What was he doing there?" Alex said. "Why would he— Do you think—"

"I don't know," Faith said. "But I don't want to take any chances."

Alex went white. "He wouldn't hurt Daniel. No matter what he may be, Daniel is still his own son."

"I don't know," Faith said again. She started to page frantically through her address book. "I can't wait for Yorkton. That baby needs protection *now*." She found the home number for Mark Raines, the chief deputy in the Oklahoma City office of the Marshals Service. Her former boss.

"Mark Raines," he said, crisp and alert.

"Chief, it's Kelly. I have an emergency."

"Talk to me." Raines was all business.

"I need a protective detail immediately."

"Where?"

"Uh . . . Pittsburgh."

"*Pittsburgh*? You mean, like in Pennsylvania?"

"Exactly. Can you call the Marshals office there and get a team mobilized?"

"I suppose I can. What is—"

"Department Thirty, A1 priority," Faith said. "There's a tiny baby in intensive care, and he may be in danger of being yanked off the machines that are keeping him alive."

"Why?"

Faith thought of the angry e-mail she'd sent to John Brown's Body. *Stupid*, she thought. *Really, really stupid*.

"I don't know," she said. "Maybe to teach me to control my temper."

Pittsburgh

Smith walked out of the elevator, smoothing some of the rumples from his shirt. He was safe, for now. Though somewhat shaken by the whole morning, he'd escaped with no real damage done. Danny Park had seen him and knew that Gary St. James was alive, but so what? What could he do with that knowledge now?

He stopped and bought a cup of coffee from a vending machine near the triage area of the emergency room. He sipped the scalding liquid, considering how close he had come to losing everything, to seeing the whole job crumble around him.

But now he had his wits about him again. Perhaps Park's appearance had been good for helping him to refocus. It gave Smith some perspective: this was only a minor setback.

He began to walk toward the outer doors of the hospital. He had a two-hundred mile drive ahead of him before he reached his own home in Maryland. Then he could rest.

Danny Park stepped out from a bank of pay phones.

"There he is!" Park shouted. "Gary!"

Smith threw the cup of coffee in Park's direction and listened to the screams as the hot liquid spattered a woman who had stepped between them at that moment.

Smith ran for the doors. Motion-sensitive, they opened with a little hissing sound that sounded like a sigh. His rental car was in the hospital parking garage, at the upper end of the ground level. It had been practically empty when he arrived nearly two hours ago.

He splashed through the decorative fountain by the hospital's main entrance, soaking his shoes and pants legs. Behind him, Park zagged around the fountain. Smith gained a few seconds.

Park had to dodge around an ambulance that had just pulled into the ER driveway. Smith's lead widened. He hit the concrete of the parking garage at a dead run, stumbling a little as he moved from one level of pavement to another. He could see the car now, a forest-green Ford Taurus.

"Who are you?" Park screamed. "What do you want with Alex and the baby? You son of a bitch—"

On the run, Smith pulled out the key on its Hertz rental ring.

Park was twenty steps behind him. Smith got into the car, his hand shaking again as he inserted the key. Park came around the back of the car. Smith saw his shadowy outline in the rearview mirror. He jammed the gearshift into reverse.

The Taurus lurched backward. Park stumbled, righted

himself, stumbled again, reached out and grabbed the driver's door handle.

"Leave it alone!" Smith shouted. "It doesn't concern you!"

He jammed on the brake and, in the same motion, threw the door open. Park, hanging from it, went over backward.

Smith capitalized on the surprise and his size advantage, charging out of the car and grabbing Park by the collar. He dragged him a few feet and slammed his head into the side of a van that was parked across the driveway. He slammed the younger man's head repeatedly, until the van was dented and blood was pouring down Park's face.

He knelt down beside Alex's bleeding brother and said, "Stay out of it."

He slammed Park's head against the van's tire and heard him moan.

"Bastard," Park whispered.

"No," Smith said. "That's one thing I'm not."

He ran back to the Taurus, dropped it into gear, and shot out of the parking garage.

Same day, 3:15 P.M.
Near Sharpsburg, Maryland

The long drive through the gorgeous hills of southwestern Pennsylvania and along Maryland's Potomac River valley settled Smith's nerves.

He'd almost been caught twice in the space of an hour. And by a half-breed auto mechanic, no less. But now he was safe. He'd changed cars twice on the route and detected no followers.

No one knew about the Maryland house. Michael Green lived here, not Isaac Smith or Gary St. James. Certainly not the infamous John Brown's Body. Michael Green, computer consultant who traveled frequently, lived here. So he would be Michael Green for a day or so. He breathed carefully, feeling relaxation come over him.

He'd lost control, but only for a short time. Now he was

Michael Green again and everything was sedate, calm—even mundane—when he was Michael Green.

Ten miles from home, his cell rang. He checked the caller ID and recognized a Texas area code.

"Yes?" he said, clicking on the phone.

The gravelly voiced man said, "You're damn hard to catch."

"Yes, I am." Smith smiled at the double meaning he took from the man's innocuous statement.

"He's concerned," said the man.

"I understand."

"No, you don't. Look, I don't know what you two are up to. I'm only the go-between, but whatever it is, you better do it." He cleared his throat. "He's running out of time."

"Of course he is," Smith said. "You should have known that."

"Now you just wait one damn minute, son—"

"Do not call me 'son.' Tell him to be patient."

"He's out of time. He doesn't have any patience left. He wants it done before they execute him. He wants to see it in the newspapers and on the prison TV before they strap him down. Got it?"

"He hired me. He should trust me. I know what I'm doing."

He clicked off the phone.

Don't I? he thought.

He drove past the entrance to the Antietam National Battlefield, and the turnoff to Chestnut Grove Road and the Kennedy Farm, where the first "Isaac Smith" had collected his arsenal and made his plans for the act of defiance that would make him immortal. He finally felt the sense of relief when he turned into the long, unmarked gravel road that led to Michael Green's property.

As farmhouses in this part of the country went, the house was of fairly recent vintage, built around 1910. It was a long, rambling clapboard structure, white with black shutters and furnished in early American, an abundance of oak and walnut. There was no garage, so he left the car in front of the house and carried his garment bag up the front steps. Now he would have quiet. Now he could empty his mind until his focus was completely clear.

He put the key in the lock, opened the door, and turned immediately to disarm the security system on the panel mounted to the right.

It was already disarmed.

Smith dropped his garment bag. He half-turned toward the living room.

A big man was sitting in his beautiful old handcrafted New England rocking chair.

"Hello, Mikhail," the man said. "My name is Richard Conway. I am the director of Department Thirty. I understand you've become familiar with us recently."

Smith backed into the doorway, finding it blocked by a tall man with a brownish-gray goatee, holding an automatic pistol.

"Sorry to block your way," the man said.

"And this is Officer Hal Simon," said the director of Department Thirty. "So, Mikhail, let me just play you a little bit of a tape I recently obtained, and then you can decide if you want me to leave." He pressed a button on a cassette machine on the coffee table.

The voices were tinny but were unmistakably Faith Kelly and Jeff Moreland, the man Smith knew as Jones.

"The Indian woman. Oh, shit, oh, fuck . . . the Indian woman. Smith wanted to get her to Galveston. I called her at home, then when she got to her hotel down there, I called her again. I said I was Wells, told her I could clear her name. Clear her name from what, I don't know. Smith gave me an exact script. He was all anal about how everything had to be done a certain way."

"I can see that."

"I got my girlfriend to call Wells, to pretend to be the Indian woman, to get him to Galveston. When he's there, on the beach, I did him and called Bridge. Oh Jesus, oh, fuck, my foot hurts."

"Be nice and we'll stop the bleeding. Keep talking."

"That's it, that's it! Smith paid me, then called yesterday and said he had another job for me. You. I've used this place before, thought it'd be the perfect setup. There's nothing else."

There were other sounds on the tape, as if someone were trying to move. Then Jones screamed, very close to the microphone. Smith even winced.

"Nothing else about Galveston?"

"I did everything just like Smith wanted it. I'm just a hired hand. I don't fucking ask questions because I don't want to know. After I shot the fed and called the Indian, I dumped the gun exactly where Smith wanted it and got out of there. Let me up, dammit."

The big man pressed STOP on the tape player.

"Mikhail Gerenko," the big man said. "Michael Green. Isaac Smith. Recently, Gary St. James. Now, the first thing you're going to do is assure me that you'll leave my Officer Kelly alone. No more hired hands going after her. Then . . . then I have an offer I'd like to discuss with you."

31

July 22, 4:35 P.M.
Oklahoma City

FAITH HAD SET UP A DRY-ERASE BOARD ON AN EASEL beside her dining room table. She'd bought it at a garage sale when she was in graduate school but had never used it. It had languished in garages and utility rooms of the various places she had lived, until today.

While Alex napped on the couch, Faith tried to organize the case. She made piles of paper that covered the big butcher-block table. With brown, green, and red markers, she made three different headings on the board. In brown she wrote: *Doag/Tabananika/Blackjacks*. In red was *Alex/Smith (Gary)/Bryden Cole?* In green: *Cross Currents Media*.

She was organizing her timeline when the phone rang. She tried to grab it quickly so it wouldn't wake Alex, but to no avail: Alex sat up on the couch.

A male voice said, "Is this Officer Kelly?"

"It is," Faith said.

"Deputy U.S. Marshal Bonds in Pittsburgh. I've been assigned to head up a protective detail here at Allegheny General Hospital. I understand this is under your . . . jurisdiction."

Faith sighed. Even other components of DOJ didn't like to mention Department Thirty aloud. "Yes, it is, Deputy. What can I do for you?"

"I understand we're here because of a particular individual's presence near this baby."

"Yes. No one, and I mean *no one*, who isn't on the official visitors' list is to get anywhere near that child."

"We'll need a thorough description of the suspect you have in mind. A picture would help."

For a moment Faith wondered if she wasn't trying to shut the barn door too late. Would Smith really try to hurt his own son? More important, would he try more than once? She wasn't willing to take that risk. "Talk to Danny Park. He's the baby's . . ." She had to think for a moment. ". . . uncle. He saw the suspect there this morning."

Bonds was silent.

"Deputy?" Faith said. "Hello?"

"Mr. Park was involved in an incident," the deputy said. "Evidently this had to do with the sighting of your suspect. Mr. Park chased him through the hospital and into the parking garage. It seems the suspect used his head for a battering ram."

"Oh, no," Faith said.

"What?" Alex said, rising from the couch. "What is it?"

Faith waved her back. "Is he all right?"

"It's early yet. He sustained a pretty serious concussion and some blood loss. He hasn't regained consciousness yet. This gentleman Mr. Bridge is the baby's grandfather and Mr. Park's father, is that right?" The deputy sounded vaguely confused.

"Yes," Faith said. "They're what you call a diverse family. Mr. Bridge should be able to give you a description of the suspect as well."

"All right, then," Bonds said. "We'll have four deputies on duty at all times, two in the NICU itself, one at each entrance. The nurses aren't happy."

"Well, I'm sorry about that, but we want the same thing they do: for that little boy to be safe."

There was a silence, as if Bonds expected Faith to say more.

"Thank you, Deputy," she finally said.

"It would be helpful if we knew some details, how the

baby is connected to your jurisdiction. That sort of thing."

"Sorry, I can't help you there. Thanks for checking in."

Faith hung up before he could say more.

"Who?" Alex said. "Is who all right? Daniel? Did something happen to Daniel? Did Gary come back?"

Faith put out both hands. "No, not the baby. Nothing about the baby." She took a deep breath. "Your brother."

"Danny? What—"

"He tried to chase Smith down, and got beaten pretty badly. Alex, I don't want you to worry—"

"Is he going to be all right?" Alex's voice went up a notch.

"He has a concussion and he's still unconscious right now. But your father's there, and—"

"Dammit!" Alex exploded. "What kind of sick world is it that you live in? Good people get attacked and get framed and innocent babies have to be protected by federal marshals!"

Faith had never seen Alex's anger before. She'd seen her emotional and in pain of all kinds, but never the anger. Faith said nothing.

"Danny never hurt anyone in his life!" Alex shouted. "He tries to help people. He's a good-hearted . . ."

Faith put out a hand to touch Alex's arm.

"Don't touch me! Don't you touch me! I don't know you, you just appeared out of nowhere. You could be working with him, with Gary! You could be partners, trying to ruin me, and now you're getting me to trust you. Was that part of the plan? Was it, *Officer* Kelly?"

Faith thrust her bandaged left hand toward Alex's face. Alex flinched.

"He tried to kill me!" Faith shouted.

Breathing hard, her body in a defensive posture, Alex didn't move.

"He tried to kill me," Faith said, more softly, lowering her hand. "The day I got back to town. He sent one of his assassins to get me. I hurt my hand going after his hired gun. The same hired gun, I might add, that actually pulled the trigger and shot Paul Wells."

Alex's posture softened. "What?"

Faith nodded. "I was going to tell you, but I didn't think you really had to know about him coming after me. I didn't want you worrying about things like that. I just hadn't come up with the right way to tell you yet." She smiled crookedly. "Okay, so I'm telling you now. We have his confession on tape. He admitted that it was all set up to frame you. The tape went to my boss, and to the U.S. attorney."

Alex was silent for a long moment.

"So, the answer to your question is no," Faith said, "we're not partners. Smith's not an assassin himself. He doesn't murder people, but he ruins their lives. This is what he does. We think he's been doing it for about ten years, all over the country." She flexed her injured hand. "And I want to nail the son of a bitch to a wall."

"I'm sorry," Alex said. "Faith, I'm so sorry. I don't know what I was—"

Faith held up a hand. "I'm not mad at you. You have every right to react that way. I'm beginning to understand that it comes with the territory. If Danny doesn't have more than a concussion, he should be okay."

Alex nodded. "I can't believe all that's happened." She looked up, meeting Faith's eyes. "But you have a confession from this assassin. So I'm in the clear, right? It's over, right?"

"Well, not quite. There are still some inconsistencies, things that don't make sense. And we still don't know *why*." She pointed at the headings she'd written on the board. "Jonathan Doag and Tabananika and the Blackjacks. Your grandfather says there's a possibility that Doag and Tabananika witnessed the massacre. What if there's more to the massacre than the history books say? All of these phone calls and e-mails have a common thread running through them: they keep talking about Doag and Tabananika knowing the truth about the Blackjack Comanches. The implication is that the truth hasn't already been told, that there's more to it than what's known."

"You're right."

Faith turned back to the board, feeling the excitement building in her. "Then jump to the present. What is it about this history that makes Smith go through all this to destroy you?" She tapped the board. "Bryden Cole, chief justice of the U.S. Supreme Court. Why does Smith, during the time he's pretending to be your husband, send an e-mail to him with this threatening tone about the historical stuff?"

Before Alex could speak, the front door opened and Scott Hendler walked in, juggling several white paper bags.

"I've got burgers and rings from Johnnie's, and I need a beer," he announced. "Let's eat."

He stopped in the middle of the living room, staring at the two women.

Faith cleared her throat. "Scott, meet my friend Alex Bridge. Alex, meet my friend, FBI Special Agent Scott Hendler."

"Alex . . ." Hendler's voice faded in his throat.

Please don't say "Holy shit," Faith thought.

"Nice to meet you, Agent Hendler," Alex said, very quietly.

"Scott," he said automatically.

Alex nodded.

"Scott knows about the tape," Faith said. "In fact, he was the one who put Mr. 'Jones' into custody."

Alex nodded again. "I'm sorry about Agent Wells."

Hendler gently set the bags of food on the table. He looked at Faith. "I guess this explains why you wanted me to pick up three burgers."

Faith and Alex both smiled.

Hendler looked at Alex. "We all thought you'd killed him. The evidence—"

"I understand," Alex said.

How incredibly eloquent, Faith thought. The way Alex Bridge said those two words conveyed the whole range of emotions that all of them had felt since the beginning of this. In her understated, minimalist sort of way, she was remarkable. Faith realized that she possessed some of the same qualities she admired in Scott Hendler. She smiled again.

"Let's eat," Faith said. "We still have a lot of work to do."

After they ate, they talked for a few minutes, the small talk of people trying to avoid bigger topics. Alex finally said, "I'd like to play a little. May I?"

Faith looked at her watch. "I don't want you to get too tired, and we do need to go over some of this tonight."

"Playing music doesn't make me tired," Alex said. "It's like breathing to me."

They had gone by her duplex earlier in the day and retrieved a fiddle. Her other fiddle was still in an evidence locker at Galveston police headquarters.

She tuned the instrument, Faith and Hendler watching with interest.

"Any requests?" she said.

"Know any Zeppelin?" Hendler said.

Faith slapped his arm.

Alex played a little riff from "Stairway to Heaven."

Hendler and Faith laughed.

"Pick something that you do when you play out somewhere," Faith said. She noticed that Alex didn't tuck the instrument under her chin the way she'd seen classical violinists do. The fiddle went into the crevice of her armpit.

Alex smiled and began to play a haunting melody, something in a minor key. Then, to Faith's surprise, she sang:

> A blacksmith courted me, nine months and better.
> He fairly won my heart, wrote me a letter.
> With his hammer in his hand, he looked quite clever.
> And if I was with my love, I would live forever.

She launched into another fiddle break, and Faith had the feeling of being in another place, another time. This music was *real*. One voice, one instrument. Faith thought of her grandfather's fiddling. She'd had the same feeling when she listened to him play.

Alex played a few more notes, then drew the bow angrily across the strings.

"What?" Faith said.

Alex started to put the fiddle into its case. "I'm sorry. It's a song about betrayal, about bitter disappointment. I can't do the rest. I can't hide from this, even in the music."

She took the fiddle down the hall and put it in the spare bedroom while Faith and Hendler stared at each other.

When she came back to the dining room, Alex had a determined look on her face. "You're right, Faith. We have work to do."

Faith looked at Hendler.

Hendler held up both hands. "Okay, okay. I'll go. Sounds like there's stuff here I'm not allowed to know." He stood up and stretched. "And I thought joining the FBI meant I got to know all the cool secrets." He started for the door.

Faith walked with him. On the small front porch she kissed him quickly. "Thanks," she said.

"For what?"

"Oh, taking care of helpless little old me."

"I'm not touching that one," Hendler said.

She raised her bandaged hand and waggled the fingers at him.

He jogged to his car and Faith went back inside. "Nice guy," Alex said. "Cute little bald spot."

Faith cracked up. "It gets bigger every week." The laughter faded. "And yes, he is a nice guy. Come on, let's get busy."

Alex sat at the dining room table. Faith stood by the board.

"Cross Currents," Faith said. "They're in green, because they're all about money. Tell me about the spreadsheet files. All those file names: Barbara Allen Cruelty, Catbird." She spread her hands apart.

"Just instincts. Impressions. 'Barbara Allen's Cruelty' is another old English folk song, about a woman who rejects the love of a dying man because of some imagined slight. He dies, then she feels miserable about how she treated him. So, in true folk song fashion, she dies the very next day."

"The point?"

"The chief financial officer of Cross Currents is a woman named Carol Joiner. She's a cold, heartless, vindictive woman. She reminds me of Barbara Allen in the song. I don't often use the word *bitch* about other women, but if the shoe fits . . ."

"What's in the file?"

"Internal correspondence with the senior accounting staff. Her explicit instructions about how to cook the books."

"Nice. What about 'Catbird'?"

"You've heard of being 'in the catbird seat,' meaning you're in control?"

Faith smiled. "Don't tell me. The CEO."

"Lawrence Effinger himself. Lots of correspondence between Joiner and him. They discuss how to prepare the annual reports to best mislead the stockholders."

"Amazing," Faith said. "Absolutely amazing." She put a check mark in the Cross Currents column. "This is the least of our worries. We can bust them after all the rest of this is over. You'll be anonymous. They'll never know."

"That's okay," Alex said. "I don't think I'd want to go back to work for them anyway."

Faith moved to the center column, the one for Alex, Smith, and Cole. "Why does Smith, or Gary, set you up? Who hired him to do it? There are things that just don't add up. I mean, we know he was behind the setup. The whole thing, your marriage—" She stopped. "I'm sorry, Alex."

Alex shook her head. Her eyes were clear. "Don't apologize. I've accepted that my marriage was a fake, that it was totally fictional. Beware of men that seem too good to be true."

Faith nodded. "He put it all together. But he also made the phone call, sent the e-mail. He wanted you to go looking into all this historical business, Tabananika and the rest. When I saw him at the lake, he said he was interested in justice. Wanted to see that you got justice." She tapped Cole's name. "And how in God's name did he get into this? Why does Smith send a message to one of the most powerful men in the country, with references to all this same historical material?"

"And the language he used," Alex said. "For one thing, it doesn't sound a thing like me. All that about standing on their bones and bathing in their blood. I didn't even know who Bryden Cole was. I don't exactly keep up with the Supreme Court. But then, who does?"

"So you've been very carefully framed for a crime you didn't commit. If he could arrange everything that led to Wells's murder, then arranging to falsify bank records would fall right in line with it. He created the case out of thin air, but then . . ." Faith shook her index finger back and forth, then placed it against her lips for a moment. "The gun."

"The gun?"

"I've thought about the gun a lot. The murder weapon. I can see where Smith could have purchased it and put the receipt in your dresser so the Bureau would find it. But your fingerprints were on it, Alex."

Alex frowned. "You don't think—"

"No, I don't, not anymore. But you have to explain to me how your fingerprints came to be on that gun."

"I told you, I've never owned a gun. I've never fired a gun in my life. I don't *like* guns. The only time I've even ever held one . . ." Her voice trailed.

Faith leaned over the table. "What?"

Alex pressed her fingertips to her forehead. "Oh God. Oh my God. I'm a fool."

"What? Tell me."

"He said it was an antique. He said his grandfather had given it to him, wanted me to see it, to hold it. It seemed important to him." She looked up at Faith. "I know zero about guns. I couldn't tell it wasn't an antique. I held it for a minute. Then he had me put it on the table instead of handing it back to him. I thought it was strange for a second or two, but then I forgot about it. About a month after that, I found out I was pregnant and he was gone."

"He had you put it on the table so his prints wouldn't be on it. He's clever, all right. That explains the gun. But there's still the issue of the Dumpster."

"Dumpster?"

Faith explained her conclusion about the times not coinciding, the placement of the gun in the Dumpster relative to the distance and Alex's condition at the time.

Alex was silent for a moment after Faith finished. "Maybe the assassin just got careless."

"No. The other night, he admitted that Smith told him—ordered him, in fact—to put the gun in exactly that place."

"But he'd have to know someone would figure that out eventually," Alex said. "Gary—I mean, Smith—is very, very smart."

"My thoughts exactly. So what does that mean? Is Smith working both sides of the same fence, or what?"

Faith began to pace.

Alex watched her for a while, then got up and went to the board. She tapped the column that started with her name at the top, followed by Smith's, then Cole's. "The picture's not complete."

Faith stopped pacing.

Under Cole's name, she drew a line with her finger across the blank white space. "Maybe another name belongs right here. I mean, we still don't know how Chief Justice Cole fits into all this. But it seems to me the foundation is missing." She picked up the brown marker and drew a line to the next column, the one with Doag, Tabananika, and the Blackjack Comanches in it. She tapped the marker against the board, leaving a series of little brown dots. "This is the foundation. Everything keeps pointing back to the past. The only thing separating these two columns is time."

Faith was nodding before she finished speaking. She came back to the board, feeling her heart start to race. "So let's say Smith knows the history and is right: that Tabananika and Doag were murdered because they knew the truth about the Blackjacks, whatever that truth is. They were murdered because they knew the truth. So someone didn't want the truth to come out. Why? Why does a person not want the truth to come out?"

Alex walked around the other side of the board. "Because

they've done something wrong. Because they've somehow benefited from what they did wrong."

Faith froze. "That's it."

Alex stared at her, blue eyes boring into green ones.

"That's it!" Faith shouted. She slapped the table. "What were the consequences of the massacre at Sawyer's Crossing? I mean, other than the Blackjacks being tried, convicted, and executed?"

They both sat back down at the table, across from each other, leaning forward. Alex shook her head. "Who could benefit from a massacre like that? No one. That's just too grotesque."

"No, Alex. Someone always benefits, even from the most hideous, heinous crimes imaginable. Someone, somewhere, gets something out of it."

"That's a pretty cynical view of things."

"I've become that way the last couple of years."

Alex looked at the board again, at the lists of names written in Faith's round script. "Look at the names," she said. "With all but one, we have a handle on what their part is in all this. All but one."

"Cole," Faith said.

"Cole," Alex said.

Faith started to go through one of the piles of paper on the table. She pulled out the copy of the e-mail that had been sent from Alex's computer to Bryden Cole.

The Blackjack Comanches. Tabananika. Jonathan Doag. You stand on these people's bones. You have bathed in their blood. Everything you are, everything you have, flows outward from a few moments in time in the spring of 1893. You are their legacy. But this deception has gone on far too long. It is past time you gave something back.

Faith drummed her fingers on the table, which made her think of Yorkton. It was strange, she thought, that she hadn't heard from the director. The silence from Virginia had been deafening since she'd had Simon send Yorkton the tape of Jones's confession.

She shook her head. *Focus! Focus!*

"So Smith knows something you don't about your history. And look at this. Look at the way it reads. It sounds as if—"

"Bryden Cole somehow benefited from what happened in 1893."

"Yes," Faith said. "That's exactly what it sounds like."

32

A LIGHT SUMMER RAIN WAS FALLING ON DOWNTOWN when Faith and Alex pulled up to the U.S. courthouse. They took the private elevator from the parking garage to the second floor, and Faith showed Alex to her office.

"What are you looking for?" Alex asked.

Faith booted up her computer. "I need the DOJ database. We're going to find out everything we can about Mr. Chief Justice Cole." She started clicking the mouse and typing in search commands. "I know he hasn't been on the court very long. In fact, he's the only justice appointed by our current president. He's tried to position himself in the center, to make the court less ideological. But that's really all I know. Like you said, who keeps up with the bios of Supreme Court justices?" She held up an index finger. "The FBI, that's who."

"What?"

Faith looked up at her. "Sit down. Pull that other chair over here. You look tired."

"I am tired. Why the FBI?"

"Before a president nominates any kind of federal judge, and especially a Supreme Court justice, they run an extensive background check. An FBI file is opened if one doesn't already exist. The president doesn't want any skeletons coming back to bite him on the ass. So the judicial nominees are researched extensively."

"But if they're vetted that well, wouldn't something show

up? I mean, we're not sure what we're looking for, but wouldn't it come out?"

"Not necessarily. What if it was deeply buried in the past? What if no one knew how far back to look?"

Alex leaned forward. "And that would give Cole all the more reason to not have it come out, since he's chief justice."

"I have to tell you," Faith said, "that I'm liking Cole more and more as a suspect."

"'Liking him'?"

"Sorry, I'm slipping back into copspeak."

"You were a cop?"

"Sort of. Let's get back to Cole." She sat back. "Why would a chief justice of the U.S. Supreme Court be afraid of you?"

Alex looked at her as if she'd lost her mind. "Afraid of *me*?"

"Sure. Why would they go to such lengths to destroy you? They're scared to death of you."

"But I don't know anything."

Faith spread her hands apart, then clapped them abruptly back together. "But they *think* you know something. Smith wants Cole to think you know something. Smith sends the e-mail that is supposed to have been from you."

Alex blew out an exasperated breath. "But if Smith works for Cole, that doesn't make sense."

"No. No, it certainly does not. Which makes you wonder . . ." Faith's voice and her thoughts trailed away, falling like leaves in November, haphazardly spiraling down.

Isaac Smith. John Brown's Body. The man who ruins people.

Bryden Cole. The pinnacle of the legal world, on the Supreme Court, unencumbered by politics. An extraordinary concentration of power.

Alex Bridge. A woman alone, wandering, struggling with her family, herself, anchored only by her music.

And . . .

Who else?

". . . wanted me to know," Alex said. "Faith? Faith, hello?"

"I'm sorry," Faith said. "What?"

"It doesn't make any sense, either, for Gary or Smith or whoever he really is to try to get me to look into all this, if his job is then to stop me from doing anything about it. It's like a circle in a circle: it never starts, it never ends."

Faith waited, her heart beating furiously. She was as pumped as if she'd just run a marathon. It was as if she'd taken adrenaline intravenously, straight into a vein. "You were right."

"About what?"

Faith placed one of her hands over one of Alex's. "Back at the house. There does need to be another name in that column with you and Smith and Cole."

"But who? And why?"

Faith turned back to the computer screen, totally absorbed. "Here's Cole's file. Bryden David Cole. Fifty-three, born in Houston. He comes from old Texas money, oil and cattle and real estate. College and law school, University of Texas at Austin, the top of his class both places. Law review, clerked for a federal judge in the Houston circuit. He was a prosecutor in Harris County, Texas, then was elected district attorney. He was a state district court judge, then was appointed to the federal bench, the Fifth Circuit Court of Appeals in New Orleans. His father was well connected politically. There's a sarcastic little note in the file to the effect that his father, Raymond Bryden Cole, 'bought' the judgeship for him. He served there eight years, and was appointed chief of the high court three years ago. The old man died before Bryden was named chief. Bryden and the president are personal friends dating back twenty years. They still play golf together every week."

Faith sat back. "Interesting, but nothing that helps us. I could get that much off the Internet or out of a newspaper."

"You said *old Texas money*," Alex said, leaning toward the computer.

Faith clicked the mouse a few times. "The classic Texas mix of oil and cattle. It says here the Coles have drilled a few wells and run a few cattle, but they really made their fortune in real estate, in selling prime land for other people to drill and ranch. This dates back more than a century. They've always been politically in step, though usually more behind the scenes. A Cole was Texas railroad commissioner during the World War II era, and then Bryden was elected DA in Houston, but mainly they've been big campaign contributors, unofficial advisors, that sort of thing." Faith slapped the side of the monitor. "Hello, this doesn't help us. It's too vague. We need specifics."

She rolled her chair back until it collided softly with the window ledge. She swiveled around and looked out across the street to the Oklahoma City National Memorial. The rain, though not heavy, had driven most of the tourists away. She saw a solitary figure, a young girl, standing before the rows of empty chairs, head bowed.

Smith.

Cole.

Bridge.

Faith played it all in her head again, everything that had happened, the chain of events that put Alex Bridge on a beach in Galveston eleven days ago, standing beside the body of a dead FBI agent. Did it really somehow lead to the top of the federal judiciary? To something as sacred and untouchable as the highest court in the land?

"Oh my God," she said.

Faith shot out of her chair so quickly that it turned over, wheels spinning in the air.

"Faith?" Alex said.

Faith spun back around to face her. "Land," she said.

Alex spread her hands apart and leaned forward.

Faith started to pace. "Land. Hannah Sovo told us that the entire history of the Comanches is about land." She stopped at the far wall, made a fist, and punched Art Dorian's fish. "How did Bryden Cole's ancestors make their fortune?"

"Real estate." Alex's voice was just above a whisper.

"But they had to start somewhere, didn't they?"

"Of course, but I don't see . . ."

Faith started pacing again. "What was it Sovo said? She was talking about the Blackjack Comanches, after they were hanged. Something about the land. What was it? I can't get it—I can't . . . she talked about how they were just a bunch of 'goddamn Indians.' And I remember thinking that it was strange to hear her talk that way—"

"They had to give up their lands," Alex said suddenly.

Faith turned. "Yes!"

"The Blackjack Comanches, all twenty-one of them, and all their family members who'd been given land allotments. They had to forfeit their lands." Alex spoke as if she were under hypnosis, slowly, deliberately.

"Yes, that's it!" Faith leaned against the desk. "So the question is—"

"What happened to those lands?"

"Amen, sister!" Faith righted her chair and sat back down, almost toppling over in the other direction. She seemed not to notice. "Where's Sovo's phone number?"

"Faith, it's nearly seven o'clock. Surely she's not still in the office."

"Shit! You're right. But didn't your grandfather know her? Would he—"

"Give me the phone."

Alex called the number Lonnie Pahocodny had given her, and he in turn found Hannah Sovo's home number for her. A man answered on the second ring. "Hello?"

"Is Hannah there, please?"

The man didn't respond, but Alex heard the phone being set down. A minute later, the familiar voice said, "This is Hannah."

"Hannah, it's Alex Bridge."

"Hello, Alex Bridge. Did the dead talk to you out at Otipoby's?"

Alex smiled. "No, but the living did. Thanks for calling my grandfather."

"You're welcome. He's a pretty good old guy, and more talkative than most men I know."

Alex smiled more, wondering about the other men Sovo knew. "I hope you don't mind me calling you at home, but I thought of another question about the Blackjacks. You said that after the execution, they and their families had to forfeit their land allotments."

"That's right."

"What happened to the land then?"

"Excuse me?"

"I mean, who got control of the land?"

Sovo was silent for a while. "Well . . . I don't know. I guess it went to the government. All our histories usually stop with the hangings and the land forfeiture. But I would assume it reverted to the Department of the Interior."

Alex mimicked writing, and Faith passed her a pad and pen. "Would they have held on to it, or allotted it to other Indians, or what?"

Another long silence followed. When Sovo spoke again, she sounded exasperated, as if she were unaccustomed to not being able to answer questions. "I don't know, Alex. I'm sorry. I've never had any reason to look into it. I suppose you could ask the BLM."

Alex wrote it down. "The BLM?"

"Bureau of Land Management. They'd have all the records of the land grants and the history of plots of federal land. Why are you asking me this? It doesn't really have anything to do with your ancestors."

Alex scribbled *Voice of the Sunrise* on the pad. "Maybe it does," she said.

"Alex . . . if you find out what happened with those lands . . ."

"Yes?"

"Let me know."

The local Bureau of Land Management office, located in the suburb of Moore, was closed for the night. Using her federal government directory, Faith was able to find out the name of the office's director. Three calls later she caught the man on his cell phone at his son's Little League baseball game.

"You want what?" the man bellowed into the phone.

Faith told him.

"And who are you again?"

"Faith Kelly. I'm with the Justice Department."

"What part of Justice?"

"The part that wants this information from you, right now."

"But I'm at my—"

"I know. Have your wife videotape the rest of the game. Fax the information to this number." She gave him the fax number of the Marshals Service office down the hall.

"Dammit, I'm—"

"And I'm waiting."

"Tough girl," Alex said after Faith hung up. "I think I'd like to call and check on the baby."

She called the NICU and spoke to Daniel's nurse, who confirmed that the baby was stable. In other words, no change, better or worse. She then asked to be transferred to Danny Park's room.

Her father answered the phone. "Dad, it's me," Alex said. "How's Danny?"

"He's going to be okay, they say," Bill Bridge said. "Jesus, Alex, what's all this about?"

"Is he awake?"

"Sort of. They did X-rays and they don't think there's any brain damage. He's gonna have a hell of a headache for a while, though."

Alex flinched. "I'm sorry, Dad. Tell him I'm sorry."

"Alex, Alex, listen here, I'm in a city I've never been to before, with this rich guy Doag putting us up in a fancy hotel. I've got a son and a grandson both in intensive care and you off doing God knows what. Can't you explain any of this?"

Alex glanced at Faith. "Not yet." She hung up and looked

at Faith. "I want to finish this. I want to finish it, and I want to go to my son."

"I know," Faith said.

Same day, 10:10 P.M.

Faith answered the phone on the first ring. "Kelly," she said.

It was the BLM office director. "I just sent your damned fax. Your supervisor will hear from me." The phone clicked in her ear.

"I just bet he will," Faith said.

Alex had been overpowered by exhaustion and nagging pain by about eight thirty. Faith scavenged a mat and a pillow from the Marshals office and set her up in a corner of her own office, right under the fish.

She ran to the Marshals office, passing Paige Carson, who was on night desk duty. She retrieved a multipage fax from the machine and gave Carson her best sardonic smile as she went back out the door.

Back in her own office, Faith switched on the little desk lamp and started to read. Her eyes quickly glazed as she read charts of land grants to individual Comanches in 1893. It was nearly midnight, twenty-seven pages later, when she saw a name that made her sit up straight in her chair.

"Holy shit," she whispered.

A full page was devoted to a commendation of sorts. It spoke of "meritorious service in extreme circumstances" and "extraordinary valor under fire."

In deepest appreciation for service to the United States of America on the Western Frontier, to wit, with regard to the recent and horrific events at Sawyer's Crossing, Oklahoma Territory, the following sections of land are granted, in perpetuity, in lieu of military pension.

A list of longitudes and latitudes followed, with section numbers in the southwestern reaches of Oklahoma Territory, as well as some plots in far north Texas.

There were over one hundred plots of land in all. Faith

compared the section numbers to those earlier in the fax that detailed which lands were forfeited "in the case of the notorious and so-called Blackjack Comanches." Twenty-one plots from the defendants themselves, the rest from their family members who had individual allotments. The land grant was dated September 1, 1893.

"Alex!" Faith shouted. "Alex, wake up!"

Alex stirred on the mat. "What?" she said, sitting up.

"I found it. I found the land!"

"What do you mean, you found it?"

"What happened to it. All the lands forfeited by the Blackjacks were granted to one person. Captain Jonas H. Cole, cavalry officer, United States Army."

33

FOR AT LEAST A FEW MINUTES, CHIEF JUSTICE BRYDEN Cole tried to do what he'd told his colleagues he was planning to do over the summer: write. He sat at the computer in his spacious, oak-paneled study and dawdled over a couple of paragraphs. But he had no interest in the social ramifications of the Nineteenth Amendment to the Constitution, the subject of the article he was supposed to be working on.

He was wearing a pair of jeans and an old polo shirt and the infamous scuffed boots that all of official Washington loved to hate. He wore the boots under his robes on the bench, he wore them when having meetings with the other justices. More than once, he'd thumped his boot heels on the floor to get them to stop bickering.

While most of the world had no idea who he was—a recent survey showed that seventy-one percent of Americans could not name the chief justice of the Supreme Court—he wielded more power than anyone in the world. Certainly more than the president. The Congress could pass all the laws it wanted and the president could sign them, but Bryden Cole could strike them down, or send them back to Congress with orders as to how they should have been written. With a thump of those run-down boot heels on the floor, he had absolute and almost totally anonymous power. He never had to run for office. He was in office for life, and at fifty-three, he planned to be there a very long time. He never had to bother with campaign fund-raising, was above all the nonsense that passed for political discourse in American society. He was untainted by such things.

Only one thing could taint Bryden Cole.

He hadn't heard from Isaac Smith for days. He had no idea what was happening in Oklahoma. Since the last Harpers Ferry meeting, where Cole had given him the information on DOJ's curious little Department Thirty, the man had dropped off the face of the earth.

It put Cole in a position to which he was unaccustomed: he was not in control.

When the woman's e-mail had come, sixteen months ago, he'd spent a few days in absolute terror before he regained control. He'd begun to make discreet inquiries: it was amazing the resources the chief justice had, even those that fell outside the law itself.

He had been pointed toward the man who used the name of Isaac Smith and was sometimes known as John Brown's Body. After his first meeting with the man, he'd known Smith was what he needed. After all, Cole didn't want Alex Bridge killed. He had no thirst for blood. He just wanted her credibility ruined, so that if she tried to talk, no one would believe her.

He hadn't known Smith would have an FBI agent killed. That hadn't been part of the plan. Smith counseled patience, assuring Cole that he knew what he was doing, and Cole—a man who personified power—began to wonder who had the upper hand here. Smith seemed to enjoy what he did a bit too much.

Out of control, Cole thought. *It's all out of control.*

When the phone rang, it was almost a relief, although Cole generally disliked talking on the phone. "Good morning, Mr. Chief Justice." It was Aaron Boone, his chief aide at the court, who called him every other day when court wasn't in session and Cole was away.

"Good morning, Aaron. Anything interesting happening?"

Boone briefed him on routine business at the court, various administrative and procedural matters that were pending. One of the associate justices—in fact, the oldest member of the current court—had had knee replacement surgery the week before. Boone reported that he seemed to be fine, and irascible as ever.

"Cases?" Cole said, rubbing the bridge of his nose.

Boone updated him on the status of cases working through the lower courts, which were projected to reach the high court at some point in the future.

When he'd finished, Cole let the silence linger for a moment too long, then said, "What about that damn Rojas case?"

"Oh, the Texas bar-fight killer?" Boone said. "The Texas courts have set an execution date of September 15. The appeal should reach us by the first of September. Justice Jameson is still insisting that the court should hear it. Of course, he believes we should hear every death penalty appeal, no matter how frivolous. Justice Kamerer is against it, but then he doesn't think the court should bother with death penalty cases at all."

Cole tapped his temples. "So everything's status quo. Hard being in the middle sometimes, isn't it, Aaron?"

"Yes, sir." Boone sounded properly sympathetic.

"Well, we shouldn't hear this. From the briefs I've read, there's no issue of proper warrants, no problems with the trial jury, no problems with his counsel, evidence was all handled properly. There are no real legal issues involved at all. The DA just didn't offer him a plea bargain his counsel liked. I'm not going to grant Cert for this foolishness." Cole shook his head. "And we wonder why people hate lawyers, with frivolous crap like this coming to the high court."

"Yes, sir."

Careful, Cole thought. He didn't want Boone to think he had a more than passing interest in the case of Eduardo Rojas, and then have Boone go off gossiping with the other clerks at happy hour.

"Anything else, Aaron?"

Boone's tone changed. "One unusual phone call, sir. It sounds like a personal matter."

"A personal matter?"

"Of sorts. There was a call first thing this morning from a Faith Kelly with the Justice Department. She wanted to pass on a message. Normally, sir, you know that I wouldn't trouble you with this, that I'd just leave it in your office for when you came back."

Cole's pulse quickened. "Get on with it, Aaron."

"She said she needed to speak with you in regard to Captain Jonas H. Cole and Sawyer's Crossing."

The phone slipped from Cole's fingers and crashed to the floor.

It was the same feeling he'd had when the message from Alex Bridge first came across his computer screen over a year ago: moments of pure paralytic terror, the feeling of freefall, of not being able to breathe.

Cole placed both his hands flat on the surface of the beautiful antique desk, fingers splayed apart. He closed his eyes. He breathed deeply. His heart rate began to calm.

I'm the chief justice of the United States Supreme Court, dammit! he thought. *They can't touch me with this.*

But it wasn't 1893 he was worried about.

He'd known the truth of his family's fortune for a long time. Appalled when his father first told him, and later resigned to the fact that he couldn't change the past, he accepted that it was a family secret to be protected, and that was that.

What worried him was where the path would lead Alex Bridge, and now this Kelly woman from Justice. If they really knew the truth about what happened in 1893, they could find other things. More recent things. That was why he'd hired John Brown's Body. That was why Eduardo Rojas had to die on schedule on September 15.

Otherwise, it could destroy him.

After a moment he realized Boone was still talking.

Cole slowly reached down for the phone and put it back to his ear.

". . . and did some checking," Boone said. "Sir?"

"I'm here, Aaron. Sorry, I dropped the phone."

"I understand, sir. Anyway, I did a follow-up call to human resources at Justice, and they did confirm that there is a Faith Kelly on their payroll. She's stationed in Oklahoma, but they didn't specify which component of Justice—"

"All right." Cole rocked back in his chair. "Thank you, Aaron. Did she leave a number?"

"Yes, I have it right here. Is this a family matter, sir?"

"I guess you could say that."

"Very well, sir."

Even though Boone was from New Jersey, his clipped speaking style and manners made Cole think of the stereotypical English butler. He gave Cole the Kelly woman's number, promised to call in two days, and hung up.

Cole stared at the legal pad where he'd written the woman's name and number.

"Now who is Faith Kelly?" he said aloud.

In a moment he had it. He unlocked a desk drawer, and slid out the papers he'd obtained from the attorney general, the information on the mysterious Department Thirty. He'd made copies for himself before giving the originals to Smith. Sure enough, there she was, Faith Kelly, Department Thirty case officer, Oklahoma City regional office.

"Damn you, Smith," he muttered, snatched up the phone, and called John Brown's Body.

"Yes?" Smith said on answering.

"I thought you were taking care of this Department Thirty business," Cole said.

"Excuse me?"

"The Kelly woman. She called me. She called the court, for God's sake! She knows about 1893."

Smith was quiet for a moment. "This is not unexpected," he finally said.

"Damn you, Smith, don't you get it? You were supposed

to keep it from going this far! That was the whole point, or have you forgotten? Bridge was supposed to be so far gone that no one would believe anything she said, but somehow she's convinced Kelly."

"There's no need to shout, sir."

"Don't patronize me!"

"Not at all. We're getting very close to closing the deal. It'll be over soon. Call Ms. Kelly back. If she wants to talk, you talk to her. If she wants to meet you, agree to it."

"Are you out of your mind?"

Smith's voice rose slightly. "I told you there would be some slight risks when you hired me. Now, Mr. Chief Justice Cole, you either see this through or see everything you've worked for crash down around you. You've achieved ultimate power. Use that power: face them down. I guarantee you, they don't know as much as they want you to think. You're not going to give in to a musician and a bureaucrat. Just one thing: if they want to meet, tell me where and when. I'll be there, and I'll make sure it stops there."

Cole gripped the phone so hard his knuckles ached. On the one hand, he was angry with Smith. No one talked that way to the chief justice. On the other, he knew Smith was right. Bridge and Kelly were nothing, and the only way they could hurt him was if he let them.

"Take care in your tone," Cole said.

"Of course," Smith said. "It's been a stressful few days. My apologies."

"I'll get back to you."

"One thing before you go. Are you familiar with the name of Lafayette Baker?"

Cole loosened his grip on the receiver. "Vaguely. Should I be?"

"Oh, yes. You definitely should be."

Smith broke the connection.

More games. Head games. That was what Smith did. That was why Cole hired him. He remembered an old Texas saying: *You mess around with snakes, and sooner or later you get bitten.* Cole had so far been very careful not to let Smith play the games with him.

Still . . .

Somehow, Cole felt a shift had just occurred in his relationship with John Brown's Body.

His old boot heels thumping on the floor, he went to the far wall, which was entirely covered with floor-to-ceiling bookcases. He selected a Civil War volume, and started to look for Lafayette Baker.

July 23, 9:18 A.M.
Near Sharpsburg, Maryland

Smith allowed himself to be pleased for a moment. Alex Bridge and the ever-persistent Faith Kelly had done as he expected them to do. Now it was only a matter of place and time, and whether he understood Bryden Cole the way he thought he did.

Only a few seconds after hanging up on the chief justice, Smith picked up the phone and called a Texas number. The craggy-voiced Texan answered.

"Tell him he'll see it in the newspapers very, very soon," Smith said. "Chief Justice Cole's destruction is very nearly complete and will soon be public."

He hung up quickly. Smith had much on his mind. He'd been presented with a set of choices, and he believed he'd made the right one. In fact, there was great irony in it. He thought Faith Kelly would appreciate it. In hindsight, it was just as well that Jones hadn't succeeded in doing away with Kelly.

Smith smiled and went back to his packing.

34

"ARE YOU SURE THAT WAS A GOOD IDEA?" ALEX SAID.

They were in Faith's office, the blinds up, brilliant sunlight bathing the room.

"Hmm?" Faith said without looking up from her computer.

"Calling up the chief justice of the Supreme Court like that," Alex said.

"Oh, I didn't talk to him," Faith said. "I didn't really expect to. But I talked to his aide, and I think the message got his attention, so he'll pass it to Justice Cole, I hope. I didn't accuse him of anything. What really matters is whether he calls back."

They were quiet for a while. "I can't believe it," Alex said, walking to the window behind Faith's desk.

"What part?"

"Any of it, but especially that someone like this chief justice could be involved in ruining me because my ancestor might have witnessed something his ancestor did over a hundred years ago."

Faith swiveled around in her chair. "Let me tell you something I learned last year about the very wealthy and very powerful. They hate scandal, and many of them will go to great lengths to avoid it. Holding on to their name, holding on to whatever power they've accumulated—that's critical. I knew a man who called them 'the American aristocracy.'" She folded her hands together. "But you're right too. It seems extreme that he would hire Smith and go through all this because of what happened 112 years ago. Then there's Smith. Who is he, really? Whose side is he really on? He did all these things to you, to turn your life inside out, but he's also done things like sending the e-mail to Cole, having Jones hide the gun in a spot that was just a bit off, and that any good investigator would eventually figure out."

Alex waited a moment, looking out the window. An ice cream truck went by on Robert S. Kerr Avenue. She finally turned back to Faith. "I can see why you're cynical."

Faith shrugged. "What did the doctor say about the baby?"

"You change the subject every time I bring up something about you."

"This isn't about me. What did he say?"

Alex sighed. "The same. That's all I hear: the same, the same, the same. But he's still alive, Faith, and every hour he lives makes him stronger. Danny's conscious and mad. Dad's getting crankier by the minute, but he'll stay as long as it takes."

"I have a feeling you'll be getting back to Daniel pretty soon."

"Oh?"

"Just a feeling." Faith stood up and stretched. "I've e-mailed The Basement, and—"

"Whoa, wait, back up. You've e-mailed the *what*?"

"The Basement. When someone comes into our department's protection and we assign them a new identity, we have to create the paper trail, the database trail. We have to *make* that new person. The Basement does that."

"Why do you call it The Basement?"

"The departmental folklore is that it's in the actual basement of one of the main buildings in D.C., just a little corner room with a few people and a few computers. There's no telephone line to it: everything is done by computer. I have no idea about any of the people who work there, just what they can do."

"Why did you e-mail them about this?"

Faith smiled. "I think they can work both sides of the same street. Maybe they can build a new identity, but maybe they can also research and build a history for a real, existing person."

Alex leaned across the desk. "Cole's family tree."

"Yep. But I also want to cover our bases in the present. It doesn't make sense that all of this is because of what happened in 1893, but maybe 1893 led to something else, something closer to home with the chief justice."

"Okay, but what?"

"If I knew that, you'd have your life back, you'd be with your son instead of here, Cross Currents would be feeling some heat, and I'd be working on something else." Faith started toward the door. "I had an idea. If Cole is behind all this, he has to have met with Smith. I'm going to request the logs from his security detail, and see if we can pin that down. I don't think a meeting between Chief Justice Cole and John Brown's Body is going to be coincidence. Not that I believe in coincidence anyway."

Faith locked the office and they walked down the hall to the Marshals Service office. Faith waved to her friends Mayfield and Leneski, who did a classic double take on seeing Alex Bridge. By now they all knew about Jones/Moreland, but they also knew the case was ongoing, and the sight of the original suspect walking casually beside Faith was a surprise.

Deputy Paige Carson, who had worked Alex's protective detail and lost her during Alex's fake labor, pointedly got up and left the room as they came into view.

"Touchy," Faith muttered.

Alex smiled, remembering that she'd nicknamed Carson "the bitchy one." Faith rapped on the open door to Chief Deputy Mark Raines's office. Raines was in his forties, a neat, small, and trim man. He wore glasses and Faith had never seen him wear anything but dark suits, much in contrast to the Marshals Service image, and that of his predecessor in the Oklahoma City office. Faith respected him enormously for his intellect and his scrupulous honesty.

"Hello, Chief," Faith said.

Raines was behind his desk, glasses slipping down his face, staring at his computer monitor. He looked at them and pushed up his glasses. "Faith. Did you get your Pittsburgh detail?"

"Sure did. That baby's as safe as we can make him now. Thanks for handling that request for me."

"Glad to do it. I always like to stay friendly with"—he glanced toward Alex, who stood just behind and to one side of Faith—"former employees." He stood up, smoothing out his suit pants, and extended a hand. "I'm sorry, I don't believe we've met. I'm Mark Raines."

Alex came forward and shook his hand. "Alex Bridge."

Raines looked at Faith. Faith looked at Alex.

"Mark is the chief deputy marshal for the Oklahoma City office," Faith said. "The U.S. marshal is a political appointee. The chief deputy is a real person, who runs the place. He got the protection for Daniel."

"Thank you," Alex said. "That's my son in that hospital."

Raines turned his head at a slight angle, which he often did when hearing new information. In the months after Raines came to Oklahoma, and before Faith left to join Department Thirty, it had become a regular practice to parody Raines's little head motion. Always a good sport, the chief had once judged a contest among the staff to see who did the best parody of him. Faith smiled at the memory.

"Well," Raines said, "I have two boys of my own. I understand."

Alex nodded.

"I'm here to ask another favor," Faith said.

"Aha," Raines said, sitting down again and motioning the other two to chairs.

"Since the Marshals Service provides security to the federal judiciary," Faith said, "that means there's probably a personal protective detail for, say, the justices of the Supreme Court. Right?"

Raines looked over his glasses. "The Supreme Court?"

"Right."

"That's what I thought you said. Yes, there are protective details, but it varies from one justice to the next. Most of them drive themselves to work and don't have security at home. The judiciary is so anonymous to most of the American public that it's one of the easiest jobs the Marshals have."

"You seem to be familiar with it," Alex said.

Raines looked at her for a moment, then smiled. "Two years on protective detail to Justice Kamerer. There was a particular group, left-wing radicals, making specific threats against him. This was a good ten years ago, when I was in D.C. He's kind of a paranoid sort anyway, so he demanded extra security. We stood behind him when he was on the bench, drove him everywhere, followed him to the bathroom, took his wife shopping."

"Yikes," Faith said.

"Uh-huh. Worst assignment I ever had. Why are you asking?"

"You keep logs on each shift, right? I mean, of where the justice would go, that sort of thing."

"Sure. You know we like our paperwork, Faith."

Faith made a pained face. "I do know that. Could I somehow get a look at the logs from Chief Justice Cole's protective detail for, oh, the last year or so?"

Raines stared in silence for a moment, then slowly took off his glasses and tossed them onto his desk.

"I wouldn't ask if it weren't important," Faith said.

"I know, I know." Raines shook his head. "Last year the executive branch, this year the judicial. You going after Congress next?"

Raines was so dry that Faith could never be sure if he was serious or joking. "Wait and see," she finally said. "It would be a big help, Chief. The same case, if you know what I mean."

Raines knew what she meant: the murder of Paul Wells. He nodded. "I can make a couple of phone calls. No promises, though."

"I wouldn't expect any promises." She stood up, Alex following. "You can just have them fax over the logs."

"A year's worth?"

"Good point." Faith waited, thinking.

Alex cleared her throat. "Maybe you could narrow it down by having them see if he's been to any Civil War monuments or museums or anything. Didn't you say that Gary—I mean, Smith . . ."

Faith put a hand on Alex's arm. "You're brilliant, Alex. Chief?"

"You want to know if the chief justice of the U.S. Supreme Court has been to any places connected to the Civil War in the last year?"

"That covers it."

"I'll say."

Faith and Alex returned to the Department Thirty office, then Faith suggested they get some lunch.

Faith drove them north out of downtown, and Alex directed her to the Asian district on Classen Boulevard. They lunched at a little storefront place with the creative name of Vietnamese Noodle Soup Restaurant.

"Who says Oklahoma's not diverse?" Alex said, eating soup.

"What do you mean?"

"Vietnamese soup and good old Oklahoma iced tea on a summer day."

"Good point." Faith had never been fond of soups in general but enjoyed the texture and spice of the meal. When she was finished, she leaned back, sipped her tea, and said, "I've been thinking."

Alex was still eating. She nodded at Faith to continue.

"We still can't prove anything, you know. Everything we have is circumstantial at best, speculation at worst. I mean, your grandfather said that it's folklore that Tabananika and the white man—who we're assuming is Doag—saw what happened at Sawyer's Crossing. We're assuming that somehow Bryden Cole's ancestor played some part in the massacre instead of the official history, which says he came to the rescue. We assume the Blackjacks were framed."

"But we're not assuming that Jonas Cole was granted all that land, which was the foundation for a huge fortune. That's fact."

Faith tapped her spoon against her tea glass, watching rivulets of condensation run down the sides. "Yes, but do you go after someone as powerful as Bryden Cole with only that?" She let the spoon clatter back to the table. "Smith said that he knew things, but couldn't prove them, that you were supposed to find the proof. I think that means the proof exists, and we just haven't found it."

"But that was before you knew Smith was Gary, and that he was playing two parts in all this."

Faith nodded. "That's true. But he—I don't know how to explain it. He takes all this very seriously. Regardless of his motivation, I think that if we're supposed to find proof, then there's proof to be found. He's too smart for it to be otherwise."

Alex stopped with a spoonful of soup halfway to her mouth. "The affidavits," she said. "The ones Jonathan Doag sent to his brother and that Russell Doag's grandfather said he didn't have anymore. Where did they go?"

"We find them, and that's enough to at least prove what happened in 1893. But it's not enough. We have to know how 1893 relates to the here and now."

Alex closed her eyes.

"You look really tired," Faith said. "Any pain?"

"A little."

Faith stood up, throwing money on the table. "Come on."

"Where?"

"I'm taking you back to my house. Take your meds and rest. Let them knock you out. I'll continue the legwork and we'll talk tonight."

"But—"

Faith took her by the hand and led her out of the restaurant. At the Miata, Alex pulled her hand gently away. "You don't have to lead me. I'm not that far gone."

Faith dropped Alex in The Village, made sure she took some pain medication, and left her to sleep. When Faith returned to her office, she tried calling Yorkton.

"Good day," the voice mail greeting began.

Faith hung up.

What the hell is going on?

This was the first time she hadn't been able to reach Yorkton since she'd joined the department.

Am I being cut loose? Faith wondered.

Yorkton had heard the Jones tape by now. He may have been interested in scoring political points, but he wasn't corrupt. Now that there was conclusive evidence that Alex Bridge hadn't killed Paul Wells, he had to understand. Maybe the case had turned into an embarrassment, and Yorkton was going to let Faith take the heat.

Her e-mail inbox had a message from The Basement, with a very large attached file. The message read:

> *Officer Kelly,*
> *Requested information attached. Assuming your interest is in Cole, Bryden David. Additional information included on this subject.*
> *The Basement*

"Friendly," Faith muttered.

She opened the file attachment. It was several hundred pages and nearly a thousand kilobytes of data. "Amazing," she said. It began with Jonas Hiram Cole, born in Kentucky in 1862. He joined the Army in 1882 as a junior cavalry officer and was posted to the frontier. He fought in engagements with the Comanche, Kiowa, Cheyenne, Arapaho, and Apache. He was posted in Fort Sill late in 1891 and promoted to captain.

"Hello," Faith whispered.

On three separate occasions, Captain Cole had been reprimanded by superior officers for displaying unnecessary cruelty toward Indian captives, including women and children.

In one instance, Cole was accused of taking a Bowie knife and slicing the nipple off a Kiowa woman's breast because the woman was nursing her child within view of a group of whites. However, not a single witness would corroborate the incident, and subsequently the charges were dropped.

"My God," Faith said.

A few months after Sawyer's Crossing and the execution of the Blackjacks, Captain Cole was granted an extraordinary pension, the lands the Comanches had forfeited. He retired from the Army and began leasing lands to cattlemen. A few years later, oil was discovered in north Texas, some of it on Cole's land.

Faith shook her head. Jonas Cole's son, James, quadrupled the family's land holdings and oil leases. Within thirty years the Coles owned much of west Texas and the new state of Oklahoma.

Faith scrolled down. She was reminded of the Old Testament of the Bible, all the *begats*, the generations of the people of Israel. She read how one Kenneth Cole moved the family seat to Houston after World War II, to take advantage of the real estate boom along the Gulf. Kenneth's grandson was Bryden David Cole, born not long thereafter.

Bryden Cole grew up as a scion of privilege. By all accounts, during his childhood his father was the wealthiest man in Texas, and one of the ten wealthiest in the nation. They had a mansion in the most exclusive section of Houston, a beachfront home a few miles away in Galveston, and a villa in Spain, where young Coles went every summer.

Still, much to his father's chagrin, Bryden Cole wasn't interested in business, but in the law. Of course, in true Cole fashion, he'd now reached the pinnacle of the profession, the zenith of power.

And it all started with Jonas Hiram Cole, the cavalry officer who hated Indians.

Faith began to wonder. Did Jonas Cole hatch a plan to get rich, to make a land grab at the expense of anyone who came near him? After all, in the post–Civil War west, land was everything. Did he orchestrate a heinous massacre of 118 people, then see twenty-one innocent men die for his crime, so he could be a hero and claim their lands?

Prove it, she heard Smith's voice say.

"I can't," she said, frustrated. She pushed back from the computer and lightly kicked the underside of her desk.

Had Jonas murdered Tabananika and Jonathan Doag because they somehow stumbled on the truth of what he had done at Sawyer's Crossing? Did Doag's "conspiracy of silence" stretch 112 years into the future, to a Supreme Court justice and a young woman who only wanted to make music?

What if Alex had known the truth? Regardless of what she'd told Alex, she didn't think this kind of scandal would bring down a man like Bryden Cole. It happened long before he was born. People can't control the actions of their ancestors. There would be a furor, then it would go away. The American public, Faith knew, has a short attention span, and generally doesn't care about history.

She imagined a network newsroom: *So what? His great-great-great-grandfather butchered a bunch of people, blamed the Indians, and got some land. So did thousands of others. What do you have for me right now, today, this minute?*

Faith went back to the file from The Basement. Bryden Cole had been married for twenty-four years. He had one son, now in law school at Yale. Faith viewed a copy of his marriage license and his son's birth certificate. He was known as a pragmatist, a centrist, on the court. Faith read an overview of some of his opinions from the last three years of Supreme Court sessions, and his appeals court opinions from the eight years before that.

She rubbed her eyes. She was getting nowhere.

Bryden Cole, in true Texan fashion, liked steaks. But he also liked French wines that cost hundreds of dollars a bottle. He liked to answer his own phone and composed his own correspondence. While pragmatic, he was also known to have a temper, and there were times he had exploded at his fellow justices, subordinates, and even friends. He had little patience with dissent. He wasn't especially interested in the outer trappings of power, but in the exercise of power itself. He didn't usually travel with a security contingent, just a driver. And of course there were the boots: the scuffed old boots that he always wore. The boots were the stuff of legend in Washington.

Faith saw that The Basement had even put together Bryden Cole's financial records. "Overkill?" she said aloud, then thought: *What the hell—I'm not getting anywhere anyway.*

She looked through financial statements. Cole's net worth was in the tens of billions, numbers Faith could scarcely imagine. Much more family money was in various trusts.

Halfway down a page, she started to notice a pattern, a certain number that kept reappearing.

"Hmm," Faith said, leaning forward.

She was scrolling through Cole's bank records from the 1980s. *How does The Basement get this stuff?* she wondered, then immediately decided she didn't want to know. February 1, 1982—a wire transfer in the amount of nine thousand dollars. March 1, 1982—another transfer, the same exact amount, but into a different account. April 1—another nine thousand was sent from Cole to yet another account.

Faith's pulse quickened.

She scrolled back up the page. An hour later she found the earliest nine-thousand-dollar transfer, in February of 1978. In another two hours she found the last one. October of 2000. There were four different accounts to which the monthly funds went. Two went to accounts with banks in the Houston area, one to a bank in Louisiana, and one to an offshore account.

For twenty-two and a half years, Bryden Cole had paid nine thousand dollars a month to . . . someone. Someone who had at least one offshore account.

Faith did some quick calculations. It came to more than two million dollars.

She sent an e-mail back to The Basement, asking if they

could identify the owner of the bank accounts. They wrote back within five minutes with a stiff reply that they did not have jurisdiction to discover the owner of an account that was held outside the borders of the United States.

"Fine, fine," Faith said. "Just get me the ones stateside." She wrote the message back to them.

Faith got up and stretched. It was nearly four o'clock. She'd lost more than four hours wandering around in the Cole family's history.

Before five o'clock she had the name. All three stateside accounts were in the name of Anna Trevino, with an address in Friendswood, Texas. Faith checked an Internet map site: Friendswood was a southern suburb of Houston, between Houston and Galveston.

Galveston again, she thought.

A terse note in The Basement's e-mail said that Anna Trevino's phone was unlisted but had been obtained. Faith wrote it on her legal pad.

Her mind raced. The past and the present—she had to find a way to merge the two, to make what Jonas Cole might have done in 1893 relevant to Bryden Cole now and would make him go after Alex Bridge.

History, history . . . Doag and Tabananika. They lived only in history now. Oklahoma history. But Faith knew nothing of Oklahoma history. She knew someone who did, however.

"Hendler," he said on the second ring.

"My favorite Oklahoma-born and -bred FBI agent," Faith said.

"My favorite redhead from Illinois," Hendler said.

"What are you doing?"

"Paper on your pal Moreland. The SAC's wondering when we're going to do something with him."

"Soon, I promise. Can you get the SAC to give you to me for a while?"

Hendler waited a moment, then laughed.

"You know what I mean," Faith said. "To reassign you for today."

"Oh, such disappointment. I don't know. Why?"

"The same case, Scott. Jones, Smith, Alex Bridge, Paul Wells. It's all tied together. I need some research, and I need an Okie to do it."

"Okay, now I'm suspicious."

"Where would you go to look for documents, original source material, related to Oklahoma history? Journals, land records, all that sort of thing."

Hendler waited a moment. "The state historical society over by the capitol has a lot of that kind of stuff."

Faith slapped her desk. "There you go! That's why I need you. Write this down. Got a pen? Come on, hurry up!"

"Impatient."

"Damn right. Ready? Jonathan Doag. Tabananika. Blackjack Comanches. Buffalo Heart. Jonas Cole." She spelled Tabananika's name for Hendler.

"What do you need on them?"

"Anything. Cross-reference them, mix and match. I'm making this case, and I don't have what I need to make it."

"And you think what you need is in the historical society."

"Could be. Maybe they worked their way back to Oklahoma from the Doag family. Maybe—"

"What are you going to be doing?"

"I think—" Faith said. She looked at the name of Anna Trevino again. "I think I may be going to Texas."

35

July 24, 8:20 A.M.
Houston, Texas

ALEX HAD SLEPT MOST OF THE PREVIOUS AFTERNOON, got up for a while in the evening, and then slept through the night. Saying she felt much more rested and less sore in the morning, she and Faith took the earliest available Southwest flight to Houston's Hobby Airport.

The latest report on baby Daniel was mixed. He'd had a bad episode in the night, adding an irregular heartbeat to his list of problems. But Dr. Nguyen assured Alex that the fact that he'd come through it and was stable again was a very positive sign.

"This baby does not give up," Nguyen had said.

While they were standing at the airport car rental counter, Faith's cell phone rang. "Where are you?" Mark Raines said.

"I'm sort of out of the office," Faith said.

"I figured that out. Do you want these security logs or not?"

"I do. Anything interesting?"

"Chief Justice Cole made a speech at Gettysburg last July. Other than that, he's visited Harpers Ferry National Historical Park a total of five times."

"Harpers Ferry," Faith said. "Of course."

"He never stays more than fifteen minutes. His driver is the only deputy who goes with him. The deputy stays in the car. The chief justice meets with a 'slender man, blond hair, approximately midthirties' and then they drive back to D.C. Is this what you wanted?"

"Jackpot," Faith said, nudging Alex. "Yes, Chief, that's exactly what I wanted. Slide the pages under my door, if you would."

"Anything for Thirty," Raines said.

They rented a car and drove south. Friendswood was a pleasant, upper-middle-class bedroom community that straddled the line between Harris and Galveston counties. They drove through the center of town, passing a beautiful old stone Quaker church before heading into a subdivision of lush green lawns and large homes.

Faith followed the directions she'd pulled off MapQuest, and they stopped in front of a brick split-level.

"Don't you believe in calling ahead?" Alex said as they got out of the car.

"Element of surprise," Faith said. "I go where the answers are. You generally don't get the answers you want on the phone. It's harder to lie or evade if you're looking right at someone." She stopped in the driveway. "Nice house, but not a mansion. Certainly not what you'd expect from someone who's received two million dollars from Bryden Cole."

Before they reached the front door, it opened and a woman stepped onto the small porch.

"Go away," she said. "I'm not doing any interviews."

"Interviews?" Faith said. "Ms. Trevino, I'm Faith Kelly. I'm—"

"I don't care who you are. Go away."

Anna Trevino was in her early fifties, Faith guessed. She had an elegant air about her, even though she was dressed simply, in creased blue jeans and a long button-down shirt with sleeves rolled to the elbow. Her hair was carefully styled and pulled away from her face, her makeup conservative and carefully applied. She had what Faith thought of as a very "put-together" look.

"I'm sorry," Faith said, "but you seem to have misunderstood. I'm with the U.S. Department of Justice. I'm not a reporter. Why are you concerned about reporters?"

Trevino looked surprised. "You don't know?"

"No. Should I?"

The woman smiled slightly. "Maybe not. What do you want, then?"

"I'd like to talk to you about Bryden Cole."

Trevino's smooth brow wrinkled. "I don't understand."

"Chief Justice Bryden Cole of the—"

"I know who the chief justice of the Supreme Court is. Why do you from the Justice Department want to talk to me about him?"

Faith noticed the way she accented all the pronouns—*you, me, him*—very strongly. "Could we come in? It's hot and it's humid out here."

"Well, that's Houston in July. What do you want with me?"

So much for niceties, Faith thought. "Okay, Ms. Trevino, I want to ask you about payments into four bank accounts that you received from Bryden Cole between 1978 and 2000."

Trevino flinched. "Maybe you should come inside."

They entered the cool house, and Trevino directed them into a sitting room. Glass and crystal and highly polished wood abounded. "The accounts," Faith said when they were seated.

Trevino waited a moment. Her eyes, large and the color of charcoal, studied both of them. "I do *not* know anything about Bryden Cole."

"What about all that money?" Alex said, speaking for the first time. "More than two million dollars?"

"What's the point of this?"

"Maybe you can tell us," Faith said. "We have the chief justice's bank records. We traced ownership of the accounts to you. Why did he pay you nine thousand dollars a month for twenty-two years?"

"Now, of all times," Trevino said. She sagged against the chair. "It all happens now. You know, we lived pretty well for a long time. We bought this house and our girls got to go to good schools. They're both in college now." She shook her head. "Now, of all times."

"Why? Why did he pay you? And why nine thousand a month?"

Trevino sniffed. "It was set up for nine thousand because of the bank regulations. You know, if ten thousand dollars is transferred, it kind of sets off alarms, makes the banks look closer at it."

Faith nodded. "Of course. Keeping it under ten thousand meant less scrutiny of the transactions. But what is Cole to you, or you to him?"

"I told you, I know nothing about Bryden Cole."

"But you said—"

"I never knew who the money was coming from. I just set up the accounts and one of them got a deposit on the first of every month. We thought it was better that way, if I didn't know too much." Trevino crossed her legs, very demure, very proper. "The chief justice of the Supreme Court, Bryden Cole. Isn't that something? Don't you think that's something? It's funny how these things go."

"Funny?" Alex said.

"See, I never knew why we were getting the money. Eddie just said that it would take care of us for the rest of our lives, and I believed him. We put the accounts in my maiden name so no one would ask questions. But here you are, asking questions, all these years later."

Faith stared. "I don't understand."

Trevino looked from Faith to Alex and back again. "You really don't know?" She started to laugh, and Anna Trevino laughed until tears streamed down her cheeks. Then the laughter devolved into crying, sobs that shook her body.

When she could speak again, she said, "Trevino is my maiden name. I'm really Anna Rojas and have been for nearly thirty years. My husband is Eduardo Rojas."

July 24, 11:47 A.M.

FAITH FOUND THEM A MOTEL ROOM NEAR INTERSTATE 45, then began working her cell phone and laptop. Ninety minutes after they left Anna Trevino Rojas, Faith had downloaded several pages of information on Eduardo Rojas.

Alex was lying on her back on one of the beds. Faith sat cross-legged on the other, computer in front of her. "Eduardo Felix Rojas," she said. "Fifty-one years old. Born in Houston, son of a bricklayer who migrated from Mexico ten years before Eduardo was born. He had minor scrapes with the law in high school, did handyman work, construction, was a caretaker for some of the vacation homes on Galveston Island for a few years. Then he went into the brick business with his father, but was always rumored to be plugged into the Houston underworld: a little drugs, a little prostitution, a little protection here and there. Nothing major. In 1998 he was arrested and charged with killing two men in a Houston bar. Rojas told the cops he'd done some brickwork for the men, but they refused to pay him. He went to the bar to try to get his money. He had a knife, they fought, and the guys wound up stabbed. Rojas was convicted and sentenced to death. It was a fairly ordinary Texas death penalty case until he started making noise about this silly appeal he's filed."

"But no connection to Cole," Alex said.

"None that I see. Wait a minute: Rojas was a caretaker for some homes on the island. Cole's family has a big beach-front house there."

"Long shot."

"True, but what's not a long shot?" Faith uncrossed her legs and stretched them out on the bed. "Hmm. Rojas's attorney is a guy named Sam Jarvis, from here in Houston."

"Why do you need him?"

"The Texas State Penitentiary isn't far from here, in Huntsville. I think I need to pay a visit to death row."

Faith reached Sam Jarvis at his office, and the craggy-voiced Texas lawyer didn't seem too surprised that a representative of the U.S. Department of Justice wanted to visit his client immediately. He gave her excruciatingly detailed directions to the prison and offered to meet her there in two hours.

Alex decided to stay in the room. She'd told Faith that she was strongly against the death penalty, and the idea of visiting a death row made her skin crawl. Faith didn't argue: Alex needed to rest anyway.

Maneuvering alone through the traffic heading north out of Houston, Faith's phone rang. She glanced at the caller ID and saw a number in area code 703.

"Oh, yes," she said, and answered the call.

"Ms. Kelly, it's Bryden Cole."

Gotcha, she thought. "Thank you for calling me, Mr. Chief Justice. I hoped your aide would give you the message."

"What's this concerning, Ms. Kelly?"

"I've just met with Anna Trevino Rojas this morning. As we speak, I'm in my car on the way to the Texas State Penitentiary to meet with Eduardo Rojas. I can place you at Harpers Ferry five times over the past year, meeting with a man known as John Brown's Body, or Isaac Smith, or Gary St. James, if you prefer."

"That's all very interesting, but do you have a point?"

Faith nudged the rental car up to eighty. "You're a very powerful man, sir. I'd like to know what happened in 1893, and I'd like to know why you hired Smith to destroy Alex Bridge's life. Alex is with me: you can tell her at the same time."

There was a long silence.

"Hello? Mr. Chief Justice Cole? Sorry to catch you off guard, sir. Why don't you fly down here and meet us? Say, tonight?"

"What are you talking about?"

"I have an idea. We can meet on the beach at Galveston, on the same spot where Special Agent Paul Wells was murdered. In case Smith didn't tell you, it's along the Seawall, just before Thirty-ninth Street. The last beach umbrella before you reach the jetty there."

"I don't like your tone, young lady. And I don't like your insinuations, either."

Faith gripped the phone harder. "And *I* don't like people who grab power for its own sake, and who use others to protect their own power. Smith was right about one thing: there has been injustice done here."

"How dare you!"

"No, how dare *you*, sir. You're the chief justice of the Supreme Court, so you should be able to find a flight that'll get to Galveston by about nine o'clock tonight. Ask Smith where Wells was killed. If we don't see you tonight, I release everything I have straight to the news media."

Cole's tone was low. "Don't threaten me, Ms. Kelly."

"Or what? You'll have Smith send someone to kill me? Sorry, he already tried that. Didn't work." Faith cut across two lanes of traffic, drawing the finger from a truck driver. "Court's not in session, so you're flexible. See you tonight, Mr. Chief Justice."

She clicked the phone off. Faith was trembling with anger. Most of it was directed at Smith, at the man who carefully plotted how to ruin people's lives. A bullet to the head would have been much more merciful than what he did, but then Smith wasn't interested in mercy. He was interested in watching people dance at the end of their own rope, just the way the Blackjack Comanches had done 112 years ago. But she also had a healthy dose of anger at the arrogance of power, of people like Cole, who used others at their pleasure.

She just hoped Bryden Cole didn't call her bluff. She still

had no conclusive proof, nothing she could release to the media if Cole didn't show. At least not yet.

Same day, 3:15 P.M.
Huntsville, Texas

Two hours after entering the Texas State Penitentiary, Faith drove out again. After collecting her belongings, she sat in the Miata for a moment with her hands on the wheel, feeling the heat reflecting from it.

Sam Jarvis, Rojas's attorney, was a stoop-shouldered, chain-smoking man in his sixties, who wore a brown suit and a cowboy hat. "Just a country lawyer," he'd told Faith, though he practiced in Houston, one of the five largest cities in the nation.

The two of them had sat and listened to Eddie Rojas tell the story he'd been waiting to tell for twenty-seven years.

There were still some holes. Rojas himself didn't know all the details of 1893, and said he didn't care. He only knew what Bryden Cole had done on a January night in 1978 in Galveston.

And now Faith knew.

She drove in a trance. The arrogance of power, indeed. But now she also understood Smith's role, and his brilliance. A circle inside another circle, with no way in or out, just as Alex had said.

Faith actually jumped when her phone rang, swerving in traffic.

"Hey," Hendler said. "Where have you been?"

"In prison."

"What?"

"They wouldn't let me take my phone onto death row."

"What?"

Faith sighed. "Just talk to me, Scott."

"I've been at the historical society all day. I cross-referenced all these things. The only real hit I got was cross-referencing

Tabananika—did I pronounce that right?—and Jonathan Doag. Who are these people, anyway?"

"Never mind. What's the hit?"

"Well, the news is good and bad. The two names turned up in some papers that belonged to a man named Frank Wayne Cleaton."

"Who's he?"

Faith heard papers shuffling. "He was a contractor. Built bridges and such in Oklahoma for a long time. He died in 1961 at the age of ninety-eight. He was an Oklahoma history buff and willed all his papers to the historical society. Mr. Cleaton said that when he was a young man, he worked for the Army on the frontier, at Fort Sill, in the last years of the nineteenth century. He knew a lot of the Indian leaders and learned the languages of several of the tribes. The Army employed him as a translator."

"This is all really interesting, but what does it—"

"Evidently Cleaton mentioned both Tabananika and Doag in a deathbed statement he wrote."

"A deathbed statement."

"Yes."

"And it said . . . what?"

"Out of answers there, Faith. The document is missing."

Faith pounded the steering wheel. "Missing?"

"As in *gone*. I looked for it, based on where the computer said it would be, but it wasn't there. I got one of the librarians and we looked everywhere. It's not in the historical society anymore."

"Then where is it?"

"No one knows. All we know is that the last person to look at it never returned it. Those things are not supposed to leave the building, but they keep a log of who looks at them."

Hendler read her the name, stumbling over it a little bit. Faith swerved again, this time nearly running onto the shoulder of the highway.

"Sweet Jesus in heaven," she said, and pressed the accelerator to the floor.

37

FOR A WHILE COLE FELT NOTHING AT ALL, JUST A WEARY emptiness, as if everything inside him had been scooped out and left hollow.

Anna Trevino Rojas.

Connections had been made, connections he had worked very hard to avoid. He didn't know how, but the Kelly woman had found the money, the payments.

And now she could ruin him.

He began to feel angry. He'd paid Isaac Smith a great deal of money to make sure this didn't happen, to keep it away from Cole's doorstep. Yet, here it was.

He made the call on his private phone line.

"You bastard," he said when Smith came on the phone. "Kelly knows."

"Of course she knows," Smith said calmly. "But can she prove it? Tell me, Your Honor, will it stand in a court of law?"

"Don't get flip with me! I mean, she knows—she knows things that you don't even know."

"Does she, now?"

The silence drew out, long and electric.

"Where and when?" Smith finally said.

"Galveston, nine o'clock tonight. Something about being on the beach where the FBI agent was killed." Cole looked at his watch. "That doesn't leave much time."

Smith sounded thoughtful. "How artful of Officer Kelly.

You have access to a private jet, don't you, sir? I suggest you get it ready to go. I'll meet you."

"I don't want you near me!" Cole shouted.

"Oh, yes, you do," Smith said. "You certainly do. I'll be bringing some friends."

"What?" Cole said, but Smith had already hung up.

Cole sat behind the huge desk for a moment, unmoving. He couldn't think, couldn't feel. He had made decisions that affected the lives of millions of people. He had the power to decide life and death: where life began, how it should end. But he was paralyzed with the thought of dealing with this, of dealing with himself, of facing what his family and he had done. People like Smith were supposed to deal with that.

He lifted the phone very slowly and called his pilot, told him to service the jet for immediate takeoff from the private airfield at Tysons Corner. He packed a small overnight bag: whatever this was, it wouldn't take long, he thought. He would either come back from Texas a ruined man or more powerful than ever.

Cole had no idea which it would be.

Near Sharpsburg, Maryland

Smith had already packed everything he needed. He knew he would never be coming back to Michael Green's farmhouse.

He had a few clothes and personal items, plus a few of his favorite books. Into one satchel went some of his professional papers. Names, addresses, amounts, services rendered, dates, times, all recorded in great detail. These were his bargaining chips. Somewhere in his subconscious, he'd known he would need such things. So Isaac Smith had been very scrupulous in his record keeping.

He made one phone call of his own, relaying the time and place of the meeting. Then he walked into the utility room of the house. Above the washer and dryer, along with laundry soap and spare lightbulbs and a few hand tools, was a SIG Sauer nine-millimeter automatic pistol and a box of ammunition.

Smith did not like weapons. His general feeling was that weapons were for those who had run out of ideas, who had no aptitude for creativity. But he was also a realist. In his business, he knew about necessity, and also that there would not always be the possibility of hiring a subcontractor.

He tucked the gun and ammunition carefully into the satchel with his papers, zipped it shut, and picked up his other bag, slinging it over his shoulder. He turned off the lights, took a last look around, and walked out onto the large porch. The beautiful, lush Maryland hills rolled before him, painted in broad strokes of green. They were stunning in high summer. He would miss this place.

"I'm ready," Smith said.

The tall man with the goatee rose from the porch swing and picked up a small bag of his own. "Let's go, then," said Officer Hal Simon.

Same day, 7:10 P.M.
Between Houston and Galveston

Faith was strangely silent as she steered the rental car through the southern suburbs and into Galveston County. She kept both hands on the wheel, her jaw set, a muscle working on one side of her face.

"You really think he'll come?" Alex said.

Faith nodded.

"You like to talk, Faith," Alex said. "So why aren't you?"

"A lot on my mind."

"Oh, well, that explains everything. Why won't you tell me more about what Eddie Rojas said?"

"You'll find out."

"You don't trust me anymore?"

"Goddammit, Alex, leave me alone!" Faith shouted, her voice straining like a dog against a leash. "There's a lot going on here and I'm trying to work it out in my head." She glanced sideways. Alex was staring at her, coolly, evenly.

They were silent for a good five minutes. The land flattened as it approached the Gulf. Faith pressed buttons on the radio until she found a smooth jazz station. "I'm sorry I yelled," she finally said.

"Don't be sorry," Alex said. She looked out the window. She could see Faith's reflection in the glass, and it looked painfully distorted.

Galveston Island

Most of the families who had spent the day on the beach were beginning to pack up their beach toys and picnic baskets by the time Faith coasted to a stop, parking within sight of the traffic light at Thirty-ninth Street. After she turned off the engine, she looked at Alex. The other woman had her arms wrapped tightly around herself.

"This is it," Alex said. "This is where it happened. Wells—"

"I know. That's the idea. Smith had a reason for putting you and Wells here on this beach. And I have a reason for us being here now."

Alex unwrapped her arms and breathed out very slowly. "You think the chief justice will just drop everything and come?"

"I don't think he has a choice," Faith said. She drew the Glock and checked its loads.

Same day, 8:15 P.M.

The Learjet touched down at Scholes International Airport at Galveston, and within ten minutes, Bryden Cole and three other men had deplaned. Cole stood impatiently on the tarmac, taking care to keep some distance between himself and Smith. When the pilot came down the steps, Cole snapped, "Get me a car."

"Two would be better," Smith called. "I think we should ride separately."

Cole waved a hand. "Two, then!"

The pilot was a deputy U.S. marshal on Cole's protective detail. "Mr. Chief Justice," he said, "shouldn't we get in touch with the local Marshals Service office and arrange for additional security?"

"No, dammit!" Cole shouted. "This is my hometown, I don't need additional security. Get me two cars and stay with the airplane. We won't be long."

The pilot walked away muttering. Isaac Smith smiled.

Faith and Alex walked down the steep steps from the Seawall and onto the beach. With twilight setting in, the Gulf was beautiful, the sun dying over it, shards of pink and orange against the far western horizon. Faith stopped and listened for a moment to the constant crash of the waves against the shore. The one offshore oil rig in view was just starting to turn on its lights. A shrimp boat cruised by, far off to their left, heading into the bay.

"Amazing, isn't it?" Alex said.

"It is," Faith said. "Come on."

They walked across the beach to the last umbrella. Alex's steps slowed, but she didn't stop. The last time she'd been here, she had touched Paul Wells's body, felt his blood. She shuddered.

"Can you do this?" Faith said.

"Do I have a choice?"

"Alex—"

"I can do it." She ducked under the umbrella and sat in the chair, in the same spot where Paul Wells had sat. "I can do it," she repeated.

Cole's car, a Lincoln, glided into a parking spot on the Seawall. Cole's knuckles were white on the wheel. While he'd certainly been back to Galveston many times, he'd stayed away from the Seawall, from this stretch of beach.

He stepped slowly from the car. The other car, smaller and dark, with the three other men inside it, drove silently past. It turned left onto Thirty-ninth, away from the beach.

His boot heels thumping on the sidewalk, Cole started toward the nearest set of steps.

Faith stood at the very edge of the water, her feet just inches away from where the waves made landfall. The last family had packed up and left. Faith remembered the man with the three boys that she'd seen here a few days ago. She wondered if the family was still in Galveston.

She saw the figure coming toward her in the fading light. Bryden Cole was tall and lean, with a bearing that bespoke wealth.

You're standing on their bones.

You bathed in their blood.

Smith had written those words, attributing them to Alex. But maybe they were true, after all. Perhaps in the middle of all of Smith's shifting realities, that had been a truth.

Faith looked at the man's feet. There were the boots, scuffed and scraped and completely out of place.

"They're not very good on the sand," she called.

"Excuse me?" Cole said.

"The boots. They're not made for walking on sand."

Cole affected a shrug. "Kelly?"

Faith nodded. "Mr. Chief Justice. I'm pleased you made the decision to come."

She watched him. He was trying to project an air of nonchalance, but she saw his body was tight as a spring.

"What exactly is it that you want?" Cole said, moving a little closer to her.

Faith shuffled a few steps along the beach, closer to the umbrella and the chairs under it.

"The truth," Faith said. "Sounds hokey, but that's it."

"Pardon me, young lady, but it seems interesting that someone affiliated with Department Thirty would be interested in truth."

Alex stepped out from under the umbrella. "Don't tell her, then. Tell me."

38

July 24, 9:00 P.M.

COLE STOOD ABSOLUTELY STILL.

"This is Alex Bridge," Faith said. "The woman you hired Smith to destroy."

Neither Cole nor Alex moved.

"She has a son," Faith added. "Daniel Alexander Bridge. He's in a hospital in Pittsburgh, fighting for his life. He was born eleven weeks early, in severe trauma. Alex was in Pittsburgh meeting with Russell Doag, by the way. He's a wonderful man, and very interested in his family history. You should meet him, Mr. Chief Justice."

"What happened?" Alex said. "What did Jonas Cole do?"

Cole shifted his feet. "So you don't know. You really don't know. What a fine bluff, Ms. Kelly. Good-bye to you both. I'm going back home."

Faith took a couple of steps. "You forget yourself, sir. I've spoken to Eddie Rojas. I know what happened here in Galveston, not eleven days ago but twenty-seven years ago."

Alex looked at her strangely.

Cole froze. "This is pointless. We're dancing around each other, that's all we're doing. You have nothing. You don't have the affidavits or anything else. You're fishing. That's all you've ever been doing."

"Then why would Alex e-mail you saying she knew the truth about Tabananika and Doag? Why take that risk?"

"Fishing, I said. That's all."

"Pretty big risk," Faith said. "I mean, to contact a man like you, arguably the most powerful man in the United States, without having real knowledge of what had happened. Doesn't make sense, does it?" Faith moved up the beach toward Alex. "But then, you probably panicked, didn't you? You were probably terrified that all your dirty secrets were about to come out."

Cole was silent for a moment. "This is pointless," he said again. "What do you want?"

"I've already told you," Faith said.

"The truth? Oh, stop it! I work in the law, Ms. Kelly, and there is no truth. There is only what you can prove. You want me to say that Jonas Cole oversaw the butchery at Sawyer's Crossing? Fine, he did. By today's standards, Jonas would be considered a sociopath. He was a bitter, evil man. He wanted more than he had, so he concocted a wild scheme. He whipped his troops into a frenzy, convinced them that Sawyer's Crossing was filled with people who were collaborating with Indians and easterners to take land rights away from whites in the west. He played to racism, he played to paranoia, he played to fear. And they butchered them all."

Alex held her breath.

"But that's not all he did," Faith said. "The Blackjacks."

"Oh, yes," Cole said. "He knew Buffalo Heart and his group of young bucks were in the area. He'd planned all along to blame the Indians. After all, no one would believe that a company of United States Cavalry would massacre a whole town. So the Comanches were hanged, their lands forfeited, and here was Jonas, a bona fide hero. Instead of a pension, he got the land. It was worth more anyway." Cole spread his hands apart. "There's the truth. Does it set you free?"

Faith noticed that Cole refused to look at Alex. "That's not all of it, though. Tabananika. Doag. Remember them?"

Cole clasped his hands behind his back. "What can you possibly hope to gain from this?"

"My life," Alex said, staring at him.

Cole looked at her for a long moment, then dropped his eyes and shook his head. "As the story came down to me, they'd been riding in the area that day and came across the massacre. They saw what Jonas had done. Jonas caught up to them but didn't want to kill them outright. After all, Doag was an Indian agent and Tabananika a chief. People would miss them. People would ask questions if *they* were dead at Sawyer's Crossing. Jonas supposedly bought them off with promises of land, but they didn't stay bought. Doag and the old Comanche rode back to Fort Sill, where Doag wrote out a statement of what they'd witnessed. He had Tabananika dictate one, translating into English. Then Doag asked for a leave from the territory to return to Washington. He got on the train and made plans for Tabananika to follow him by a few days, so no one would be suspicious. He gave out the cover story that the chief was going to testify before Congress about the latest round of land leases. Since he was a BIA agent, he was in a position to arrange such things.

"Jonas felt betrayed, of course. He left for Washington the day after Doag. After all the heroics he'd exhibited, the Army generously granted him a leave. He murdered Doag himself, smothered the poor little man to death with his own pillow, making it look like a robbery."

"And Tabananika?" Alex whispered.

They were all silent for a few moments, listening to the waves. A car went by, up on the Seawall. A horn honked. A door slammed.

"The main translator at Fort Sill was a man named Cleaton. So the story goes, Jonas paid him to poison Tabananika. It was supposed to look like natural causes, so no one would be suspicious. Cleaton had come from the Appalachians, and his mother was what was known in those days as a 'wise woman,' who knew all about herbs and plants and such. Apparently some of it had rubbed off on him. At that time, wild pokeweed grew on the plains. The unripe berries are a deadly poison. Cleaton ground them up and put them in Tabananika's coffee. The poison was slow-acting. I was told that Cleaton was worried that Tabananika wouldn't die, that he hadn't used enough berries. It had been two days since he put them in the coffee. But the old man died while running to catch the train, the perfect excuse for a heart attack."

"And you—" Alex said, then choked off the words.

"You've known all this for years," Faith finished for her.

"Every Cole male has known it for generations," Cole said. "It's sort of a rite of passage. When you turn eighteen, your father tells you how your family's wealth came to be. That's the way it's always been. Yes, what Jonas Cole did was horrific, and it's sad that those Comanches were blamed for it. But it was 112 years ago. I didn't do it and my father didn't do it and *his* father didn't do it."

"If it's such past history," Faith said, "why go after Alex when you thought she knew something about it?"

Cole cleared his throat. "I thought maybe the affidavits had finally come to light after all these years."

"Really?" Faith said. "Is that all? The most powerful man in America is worried about a few old documents?"

"Faith?" Alex said.

Faith took a few steps toward Cole. "Isn't there something else closer to home? Of course there is, Mr. Chief Justice. Eddie Rojas. Remember Eddie? Remember January 3, 1978?"

"Faith, what are you talking about?" Alex said, her voice rising.

"Alex, would you come over here, please?" Faith said. "I'd like the chief justice to get a better look at you."

"I don't understand," Alex said, but she walked to Faith's side. They faced Cole, six steps apart.

"Remember, Alex," Faith said, "how we didn't think it made sense for this man to hire Smith to ruin you, just because it was possible you knew what had happened in 1893? It just didn't add up. It seemed too extreme. I think we've just proven that. He came right out and told us everything he knew about it, without much concern. He doesn't think we can prove it, so why not tell us? But see, that's not all that happened."

"That's enough," Cole said. "You don't have anything."

"Don't we?" Faith said. "We know what happened in 1978, on another stretch of beach, not far away from here. Smith had a reason for having Paul Wells murdered in Galveston, didn't he? Mr. Chief Justice?"

"What?" Alex said. She alternated her glance between Cole and Faith. "What happened?"

"Mr. Cole committed murder," said another voice. "That's what happened."

Smith stepped between them.

Alex let a small, breathy sound escape her.

"Smith?" Cole said. "Smith, you were supposed to take care of all this. All of it!"

"Be quiet, Mr. Chief Justice." Smith turned to Alex.

"Gary," she whispered. "Oh my God, Gary . . . you . . ."

Smith smiled at her. "Alex, my dear. You were always so intriguing, so fine. Such humanity and creativity, in one small package."

Alex's eyes flashed.

"Don't you see?" Smith said to her. "Don't you know what I've done for you? You hate me, and you should. But I've given you a great gift, Alex. You're strong now. A year ago you would have fallen apart by this point. But look at you: not a tear. You're even showing anger. You're not so needful and dependent anymore. A great gift."

"You—" Alex said. "You son of a *bitch!*"

Smith's expression didn't change.

"It was all a lie," Alex said. "I know that now. Every bit of it. Nothing I knew of you was true. But our baby, that boy, he's the only bit of truth I got from you."

"A mistake."

"I don't think so," Alex said.

Cole had backed away a few steps. "Oh, no," Faith said. "You're not leaving."

"This is—" Cole seemed at a total loss.

"The word was *murder*," Faith said. "January 3, 1978. Am I right, Mr. Smith?"

"You're right, Officer Kelly."

Cole was shaking his head. "This is all wrong. You want to bring me down? There's more in play here than just 1893, and just one death in 1978. If you destroy me this way, it brings the United States down as well. I am the chief justice of the highest court in this land. It will destroy our country."

"Oh, bullshit," Faith said.

Cole stared at her. "How can you be so . . . so cavalier?"

"And how can you be so arrogant?" Faith shot back. "The United States is bigger than one person or one office or one branch of government. I don't like scandals any more than you do. You're a man of the law: you should understand that if the United States is anything, it's a nation of laws. And no one is above those laws, not even the chief interpreter of them."

"Don't you presume to talk to me about the law!" Cole shouted. "How dare you . . ."

"Indeed, Mr. Chief Justice," Smith said. "I think Officer Kelly has summarized it perfectly. That's the reason I came into this: to bring about justice."

"More bullshit," Faith said.

Smith flinched. Faith smiled at him.

Very slowly, Smith turned back to Cole. "Tell her," he said, pointing at Alex.

Cole was silent.

"Tell her or one of us will," Faith said.

"What is this?" Alex said. "Faith?"

"Look at her, Cole," Faith said. She gently pulled on the sleeve of Alex's T-shirt, tugging it up until the tattoo—thorns, roses, and crosses—was exposed, circling her upper arm. "Recognize this?"

Cole took a step back as if he'd been slapped. He bowed his head, then raised it slowly and nodded.

39

January 3, 1978, 5:05 P.M.
Galveston Island, Texas

JoLYNDA PAHOCODNY BRIDGE DROVE HER TEN-YEAR-
old Volkswagen Beetle into the parking lot of the main post
office on Twenty-fifth Street in Galveston. Her hands were
shaking as she pulled to a stop.

She sat with her hands on the wheel, and for a long moment she contemplated turning the car around and driving
back across the causeway to the mainland. Then she would
keep going north. She could be back home in Lawton, with
Bill and little Alex, in eight hours or so.

As it was, her husband didn't know where she had gone
or what she was doing. It pained her, not being able to tell
him, but there were things Bill just didn't—*couldn't*—
understand. Things about being Comanche, about being *numunuh*. She couldn't explain it to him, either. Some things
just *were*: there could be no explanation. Like music or art or
poetry, they disappeared with the telling.

Boy, that sounds really Indian, she thought with a mixture
of amusement and pride. Plus, it was just for a couple of
days. She could explain it all when she got back.

She finished addressing the big manila envelope, and let
out a little smile when she did. They would have no idea
what this was, even when they opened it, but she was glad
she'd made the copies. They were her insurance, her protection, if this didn't go well.

She bought stamps from a vending machine and dropped

the thick envelope in the mailbox. She climbed back into the VW and started it up again, leaving the window down. Early January and sixty-five degrees at nearly sunset. She wondered how people could live here, with no real seasons. The world needed its season of cold, its season of rest.

JoLynda consulted the directions she'd written when she talked to the man on the phone yesterday. He'd sounded at times both dismissive and concerned, and in the end had said he'd meet with her if she would come to him. She headed toward the Seawall, checking her mirror every now and again. She saw only herself: her face with its high cheekbones, strong chin, full lips, just a tiny touch of makeup. She wore her arrow-straight black hair in a single long braid that hung past the middle of her back. She'd worn glasses for the last few years: Bill liked them, said they made her look like an intellectual.

There was very little traffic on a winter evening along the Seawall. Summer was the beach and tourist season in Galveston. Winter tourism consisted mainly of retired people from the north: "winter Texans," they were called. By the time she reached the west side of the island and began to wind her way through the increasingly grand vacation homes, there was almost no traffic at all.

The address he'd given her was for a huge Mediterranean-style mansion at the end of a beachfront lane. A sleek black Jaguar sat in front of the four-car garage.

Clutching the envelope, she walked to the door past a beautifully sculpted winter garden and rang the bell. At first she heard nothing, then a shuffling, and finally a hollow thump of footsteps coming toward her. She kept her eyes on the ground.

The first thing she saw was a pair of boots. Brand-new, stylish gray cowboy boots. The next sensation was the overpowering smell of alcohol.

He didn't even take this seriously enough to be sober? JoLynda wondered.

"I guess you're the Indian," Bryden Cole said.

JoLynda drew herself up, but to no avail: the man was almost a foot taller than she. He was about her age, midtwenties, but seemed like he was bigger in dimension, somehow *more*. She'd never really been intimidated by rich people, but she had to wonder at the old saying about the very wealthy truly being different.

He threw the door open further. "Come on in." He showed her his back and walked away from her. The house was a strange combination of unimaginable wealth—French paintings, crystal, life-size sculptures—and a frat house, with empty beer and whiskey bottles, dirty plates, stale food, and cigarette butts everywhere.

"Had a little party here for New Year's Eve," Cole said, still walking away from her.

"Little party"? JoLynda wondered as they went through six rooms, all equally opulent and equally littered.

They finally came to a sitting room that faced a wooden deck with a set of stairs that led to the beach. Beyond that was the Gulf.

"Tell me," Cole said, sitting down in a leather swivel chair. He had a drawl, but not a deep one, and his words were dimmed by alcohol.

JoLynda cleared her throat. The fingers of one hand fluttered at her side. The other hand held the envelope tightly.

"You said on the phone that you'd meet me," JoLynda said, in her soft, lilting voice. "I guess that means that you already know about Tabananika and Sawyer's Crossing."

"I don't know shit about shit," Cole said, and laughed. "Tell me what *you* know, Indian."

"My name is JoLynda. I'd appreciate it if you—"

Cole flapped a hand. "Yeah, whatever. Talk."

She cleared her throat again. "I did volunteer work for the Oklahoma Historical Society. I used to go up to Oklahoma City once a month and help them catalog things that were donated to them."

"Why do I care about that? Get to the point, will you? I've got better things to do."

"I was going through a big bunch of papers that a man had willed to the society, and something caught my eye. It was a statement that a man named Frank Wayne Cleaton made on his deathbed a few years ago."

At the mention of Cleaton's name, Cole went still.

"I'm glad I got your attention," JoLynda said. "I took time to read that. It mentioned my ancestor, Tabananika, 'Voice of the Sunrise.' It talked about how this man Cleaton was paid by a man named Jonas Cole to murder Tabananika, and how Jonas Cole also planned to kill a man named Jonathan Doag, because they knew the truth of what had happened at a place called Sawyer's Crossing a few weeks before. Should I go on?"

"I already know all this." Cole was more composed now, less the drunken frat boy and more third-year law student.

JoLynda nodded. "I guess you do. I cataloged that paper but I couldn't get it out of my mind. I'd heard family stories about how the people believed Tabananika had been poisoned, but I never knew what to think. Maybe it was myth, maybe it was legend . . . who knew? It sure didn't have anything to do with me. But I went back and got that paper, Cleaton's deathbed statement. I checked it out and never took it back. I started trying to find everything I could about Tabananika and this man Doag."

Cole thumped his boots on the floor and swiveled the chair to face the big window. "Ever seen the Gulf before?"

JoLynda shook her head.

Cole stood up. "Come on. Sun's setting. Quite a sight if you've never seen it." There was a slight taunt to his voice.

JoLynda tightened. She'd agreed to meet him at the house, not on a secluded stretch of beach. She knew nothing could happen to her here, in this rich house. She knew it intuitively, the way she knew what kind of mood her husband was in by one look at his face, the way she'd known the difference in each cry her daughter made when she was a baby. Right now, right here, JoLynda was safe.

"What, are you afraid of me?" Cole said. "Give it a rest."

JoLynda was silent.

Cole shrugged. "You wanted to do this, not me. I'm going down to the beach. You do what you want. Find your way out." He slid open the glass door and thumped out onto the deck in the fading light. He cast one look back at her and started down the steps.

JoLynda stood motionless.

She'd driven all day, she'd used every ounce of courage she had to do this, to try to find some justice, some peace, for the descendants of the Blackjacks, for the descendants of Tabananika—for herself, for her daughter, for *numunuh*.

What harm could there be in stepping onto this man's private beach? He might be obnoxious, but Bryden Cole certainly wasn't dangerous. He was well-bred, a product of prep schools and summers in Europe.

What harm? she thought, and stepped onto the deck.

When she reached the bottom, she walked onto the sand, smelling the Gulf air, January warm, wet and thick. Cole was near the surf, a few yards away from a stone jetty that extended out into the water. She'd seen many just like it as she'd driven along the Seawall earlier.

Cole shuffled his feet in the sand. He pointed to the west, to a brilliant sunset across the water. They watched it in silence for a few moments, then he turned to JoLynda. The voice of the casual host was gone. "All that shit you said in there? It's nothing to me. It doesn't mean anything."

JoLynda swallowed hard. "Maybe, maybe not. I even went all the way to Pittsburgh, Pennsylvania, and visited Doag's great-grandson. I told my husband I was going to visit a cousin who'd just had a baby. Doag is a rich man, just like you. He's a banker. When I told him my story, he showed me some papers he'd come across, some papers Jonathan Doag mailed to his brother before he left to go back to Washington. Sworn affidavits from Doag and Tabananika, telling what they saw at Sawyer's Crossing.

Telling the truth, that Jonas Cole killed all those people, that the Blackjack Comanches were nowhere near there that day.

"And you, Mr. Bryden Cole, you're the one who benefited from your ancestor's actions. He built an empire on the land the people forfeited. That's why you can go to your fancy law school, and drive your fancy car, and play on your private beach."

"What the hell do you want from me, girl? You want money, is that it?"

JoLynda smiled a little. "I'm not blackmailing you, if that's what you're thinking. I just think . . . I think there needs to be an accounting, that the truth needs to be told. Those families, the families of the Blackjack Comanches . . . they've lived with this a long time. This is just about getting the truth out. That's all."

"My, that's noble. And you don't want any money for yourself?"

"I don't want any more or any less than I should have. If some kind of settlement could be made for the families that had to forfeit lands, that would be the right thing to do. I have a little girl who's three years old, and I'd like her to go to college someday. But no, I'm not threatening you. I'm not going to call up Walter Cronkite and tell him to put it on the news. I just want to see it all set right."

Cole shuffled past JoLynda, closer to the surf. He prodded sand with the toe of his boot.

"You know," he said, "the only reason I'm here is because my father's in Spain for the holidays. Spring term at school starts next week. I've just been down here partying, taking a break, thinking about things."

JoLynda said nothing.

"No comment?" Cole said. "I guess it's right what they say. You goddamn Indians don't talk much. But wait, no, that can't be right. You already talked quite a bit, didn't you?"

JoLynda stood silent, unmoving.

"You expect me to buy all this?" Cole said. When he spoke again, it was a shout. "Don't you know who my father is, girl? He's the richest man in Texas! My father's got U.S. senators in his pocket. He hangs out with kings and queens of other countries. I could buy and sell the likes of you a thousand—no, make that a million—times over."

"You can't buy what's not for sale," JoLynda said, "and you can't sell what's not yours."

"Fuck you, you stupid little bitch!" Cole shouted. He stumbled and rolled into the sand.

Get off the beach! JoLynda thought.

"I guess this was a mistake," she said, trying to sound calm. She edged away from the line of surf, toward the rock jetty and the steps back up to the house.

Cole struggled to his feet, swaying a bit. "*Hey, bitch!* You don't fucking talk to me that way. I'm a Cole. Get it? I'm a Cole, and it doesn't matter how my family started making its money. What matters is, I've got it and you don't. And I'm not about to piss on my family name by trying to make a bunch of goddamn Indians feel better!"

JoLynda looked back at him. When he fell, he'd rolled partially into the water and now was dripping. She started to move more quickly away. "I'd say you've already disgraced your family name," she said, and kept walking.

"Hey!" Cole shouted.

JoLynda kept walking, now almost at a fast trot.

"Stop! Hey, goddammit . . ."

JoLynda smelled him before she heard him, the liquor odor preceding him by a few feet. He moved surprisingly fast on the sand wearing those stiff new boots, and he grabbed her by the arm and spun her around.

JoLynda tried to pull away from him. "Let go of me."

"You want to talk about my family some more?" Cole glanced down at the spot where he had hold of JoLynda's arm. "Here, here, now what do we have here?" He pushed up her sleeve and looked at the tattoo. "Oooh, look at that. A girl with a tattoo. An *Indian* girl with a tattoo. I thought only slut girls got tattoos. Is that what you are? Would your grand-father, Chief Tabby-whatever, approve of you getting a tat-too? Are you a bad, bad girl?" He bent close to her face, mocking her, his liquor breath hard in her face.

JoLynda slapped him.

It wasn't a hard slap, but it rocked Cole back in surprise for a moment. Then he bellowed wordlessly and crashed his fist into JoLynda's face.

She screamed and went down, the envelope flying out of her hand. Her glasses tilted but stayed on.

"Don't you touch me!" Cole bellowed at her. JoLynda was crawling across the sand toward the spot where the envelope had landed, five or six feet away. "What's that? Is that your proof? Your precious statements that you think—"

Cole ran toward the envelope.

"No," JoLynda whispered. She lunged and got an arm ex-tended toward the envelope. She snatched it and rolled over. The pain was coursing through her, like the sharpened teeth of a saw raking across her cheek. Her eye was beginning to swell. She shambled to her feet.

"Give me those fucking papers," Cole growled.

JoLynda took a step. She was almost to the jetty.

Cole launched himself at her and grabbed one of her legs. They both went down, tumbling over and over toward the Gulf.

JoLynda felt her back scrape against something hard, stopping the roll. Through her good eye, she saw that they'd run into the rock jetty that extended out from the beach into the Gulf.

Cole's momentum kept him going and he landed a few feet away from her. JoLynda heard him grunt. She flipped onto her stomach and began to claw up the rocks, still clutching the envelope.

"No you don't," she heard Cole say.

He grabbed her leg again and pulled her down. They were both in the water now, up against the edge of the jetty.

Finally, JoLynda began to scream for help.

Cole slapped her. "No one's coming, don't you know that? This is my own private beach, and no one's in the houses on either side. There's no one here but you and me."

"Even if you get these papers," she breathed, "I made copies. The truth doesn't die."

She struggled under him, fighting him. But he was a big man and powerful, and she was barely five feet tall. She screamed into the night again.

"Goddamn, I hate that noise!" Cole said. He slapped her again, then his hand landed on her neck. "Stop that noise!" The other hand came down next to it.

Cole began to squeeze.

Light exploded in JoLynda's head. She heard the waves, and their roar seemed to be getting louder. She tried to move her arm, to dig her nails into his back. She did, but he didn't seem to notice. He squeezed harder.

JoLynda's tongue rolled back in her mouth. All she could see was Cole's face, filling her vision, that well-bred, handsome face, that was killing her.

Killing her.

She thought of Bill. He would never know. He would think she'd left him. She knew she'd been acting distracted and out of sorts for the last few weeks, ever since she'd been on this crusade, and now he would simply think she was gone.

And little Alex, the truest blessing of JoLynda's life. Little Alex, with her mother's dark skin and her father's blue eyes, the way she was beginning to put sentences together and ask more and more questions, the way she always paid attention when they played music on the record player. Any music: Mozart or Miles Davis or Waylon Jennings or Leadbelly. Bill even had a record by a group from Ireland called The Chieftains. JoLynda had never heard of them, but they played energetic, soulful music.

Little Alex. *I'm sorry, baby. I didn't mean to leave you alone. I'm sorry.*

JoLynda's vision was filled not with Cole's wild-eyed face

but with a reddish mist, gray at the edges. Then the gray crept slowly inward. She heard one more wave crash onto the jetty, and she thought again of her daughter. She wished Alex had been able to see the ocean.

JoLynda's body relaxed and her hand opened, the envelope dropping onto the jetty.

Bryden Cole wasn't sure how long he lay beside her body. It might have been five minutes or five hours. He couldn't tell. Time had no more meaning. There were only the waves and the jetty and the water sloshing in his shoes.

And a dead woman beside him.

She was on her back, arms flung to either side, one leg bent at the knee, crumpled against the rock jetty. The envelope with all the papers—the papers the woman had died for—was on the sand, right at the edge of the surf. He finally crawled around the corpse, collapsing beside the envelope. He opened it and sifted through the papers. The woman was right: the statements laid out in clear terms what had happened at Sawyer's Crossing, the story his own father had told him six years ago. Such a story could have crucified his family.

He looked back toward JoLynda Pahocodny Bridge.

What have I done?

Cole turned and vomited onto the sand.

He heard an engine.

It sounded badly tuned, like some of the old pickup trucks that rattled around the Texas back roads. He lifted his head toward the house, then looked back. The woman's body had slid downward from the jetty and was fully in the water, washing up against the shore in the surf. Incapable of walking, he crawled back to her. To his horror, he saw that her mouth was open, and each wave had been washing more water into it. The corpse had begun to bloat.

"Oh Jesus," he muttered.

Cole looked up. A figure was coming toward him, down the stairs, across the sand. He tried to struggle to his feet, to run, but he slid down again.

"Oh, shit, look at this," said the man in the shadows.

Cole blinked hard, willing the man to take shape in the darkness.

"Eddie?" he whispered. "Eddie, is that you?"

Eddie Rojas was about his age, and worked as a caretaker for some of the beachfront homes on the island. His father had hired him a year ago on the recommendation of a neighbor. He was a nobody, just a handyman and a drifter, but Cole had discovered that he liked to party and drink beer. When none of his real friends were around and Cole was in Galveston, Rojas was good company, and they'd spent some nights trolling the bars, drinking and picking up women. They'd planned to drive up to Houston to drink and party a little more tonight, and Cole had gotten an early start. That seemed like a very, very long time ago now.

"Look at this, Bry," Rojas said. "Look at this. Guess we're not going to the city tonight, huh?"

"What time . . ."

"Nearly nine. Man, you are in deep shit."

Cole struggled to his knees. "Eddie, help me. I can't—" He sank back down.

"What happened, man?"

Cole shook his head.

"I guess it don't take a genius to see, huh?" Rojas said. "You fucking killed that girl."

"Oh Jesus, Eddie, help me."

Rojas knelt beside him. "What's in the envelope?"

"Papers. Have to destroy them. Burn them."

"Okay, pal, first things first," Rojas said, helping Cole to his feet. He glanced back at the body. "Man, you stepped in it, Bry. What, she wouldn't put out?"

"Papers," Cole said again. He blinked rapidly, several times.

"Yeah, papers." Rojas rubbed a finger across his wispy mustache. "Man, this is one hell of a situation we got here."

Cole nodded. He felt completely sober now and could smell the liquor on Rojas's breath.

"What's your old man gonna think when he gets back?"

"Eddie—"

"Guy like you, third year of law school. Something like this pretty much flushes your career right down the crapper."

"Eddie, help me. It was a—" He glanced back at the body.

"Don't tell me it was an accident. I saw the marks on her neck, Bry. No fucking way that was no accident."

"No, I just— Please, Eddie. You've got to help me."

Rojas sighed. "Yeah, I guess I do. But here's the deal, Bry. See, I don't have a rich daddy and I don't have a trust fund. My old man works laying brick for twelve or fourteen hours a day, and he gets paid shit wages. So, see, no trust fund for me. My old man's too worried about feeding my seven brothers and sisters to think about a trust fund. I'm out of the house now, he thinks that's good. One less mouth to feed."

"What are you saying?"

"I'm saying I'll help you in your little situation you got yourself into here. But you're gonna take care of me. For the rest of my life, I mean. You can think of it as a trust fund for a guy who was never gonna have one. You're gonna pay me, every month for the rest of my life. We'll work out the details later."

"Eddie, you're kidding. I thought—I mean, we're friends, aren't we?"

Rojas laughed. "You don't have friends like me, Bry. When none of your prep school or law school buddies are around, you go slumming with me and think it's a public service. Deal or no deal? You decide, right now."

Cole thought it was a cruel insult, a strange twist. The woman he thought was going to blackmail him really didn't want to after all, at least not in the conventional sense. A man he knew and trusted did want to blackmail him. It was as if someone had taken a hammer to a jigsaw puzzle and scattered the pieces all around.

He finally nodded. "Deal." Cole shuddered.

"Come on, then," Rojas said. "We've got work to do."

40

CHIEF JUSTICE BRYDEN COLE STARED AT THE GROUND, as if he were contemplating the old, scuffed boots.

No one spoke for a long time.

"What did you do with her?" Faith finally said.

Cole didn't raise his head. "Rojas borrowed a boat from a friend of his. We took it about five miles offshore. We wrapped her in sheets, tied the arms and legs with ropes, and he weighted her down with bricks. We threw her into the Gulf. Later Rojas drove her car into the garage that was behind the little shack where he lived. I never saw it again."

"And the papers?" Smith said. "What did you do with the papers, the affidavits from Tabananika and Doag, and Cleaton's statement?"

Cole slowly looked up. "I burned them in the sink of the boat's little galley. Rojas watched me do it. He even gave me the matches."

"So you started paying him," Faith said. "And you transferred money every month into the accounts he'd set up in Anna Trevino's name."

Cole nodded. "She was just his girlfriend at the time. They got married a year or so later. Rojas liked to joke that if anyone went snooping through my bank records, they'd just think I was paying off a mistress or supporting an illegitimate child or something."

"Yet, you stopped paying him in 2000," Faith said. "Why then?"

Cole drew himself up. "He'd already killed those two men, the idiot. Gotten himself into trouble. A guaranteed lifetime income, and he goes and kills two men in a bar." He shook his head. "I paid through his trial, his conviction. . . . No doubt *my* money paid many of his legal fees. I'm quite sure it paid for his appeals." He waited a long moment, looking toward the lights of the oil rig offshore. "I was on the Fifth Circuit Court of Appeals in 2000. The president was just a candidate then, but I knew if he won that I'd have a good chance for a seat on the high court. Two of the justices at the time were already talking retirement. The president and I had been friends for years. He asked me if there was anything I needed to tell him before he nominated me for a seat on the court. I said no. It was then I stopped the payments. Rojas had lost one appeal after another. He was going to be executed: it was just a matter of time. I'd already paid him two million dollars. Why pay more money to a walking dead man?" Cole bowed his head again.

They were all silent.

Alex took a step toward Cole. Cole tensed.

Alex came to within two steps of him but didn't speak.

"I was young," Cole said. "I was young and stupid and arrogant, and I was drunk that night."

Alex said nothing.

"I make no excuses and I make no apologies," the chief justice said. "It happened. It shouldn't have happened, but it did. Now you know. Does that give you satisfaction, knowing that Chief Justice Bryden Cole killed your mother? Is that what you wanted to hear?"

Alex was still silent, watching the man's eyes.

"Say something," Cole whispered.

The two stared at each other.

Cole dropped his eyes.

"You have no power over me," Alex said. "And the most important thing you said is what you didn't say."

"What does that mean?"

"My mother didn't abandon my father and me. She wanted to come back to us. She didn't just leave and never come back. She was coming back."

Cole looked from one face to another. "Are you insane? I've just admitted to killing your mother, and this is all you say?"

Alex looked him in the eye again, then turned away and walked back to stand beside Faith. "Yes," she said.

"Bravo, Alex," Smith said. "You are finally the person I always thought you could be."

Alex didn't look at Smith.

"The unfinished part of the story is mine," Smith said. He looked at Cole. "Did you find who Lafayette Baker was?"

"First head of the National Detective Police, forerunner of the FBI and the Secret Service," Cole said. "Stanton, the secretary of war, hired him during the Civil War."

"Ah, yes," Smith said. "But he was what you would call a loose cannon. He really worked only for himself. He was later found to have bugged Stanton's own telegraph wires." He spread his hands apart. "Do you see certain parallels?"

"What the hell are you trying to say?"

"Rojas hired Smith," Faith said.

"Yes," Smith said.

"*I* hired you," Cole said. "What are you talking about?"

Smith smiled even more widely.

"Your deal with Rojas was to take care of him for the rest of his life," Faith said. "In return he helped you with your situation and never told a soul. In his mind, he kept his end of the bargain and you didn't. Sort of an 'honor among thieves' kind of thing."

"He killed two men!" Cole shouted. "He's on death row, and he's going to die in a few weeks. I think that makes any agreement null and void."

"You're thinking like a lawyer," Faith said. "Rojas doesn't see it that way."

Cole looked at Smith. "What the hell is this?"

"You see, Mr. Chief Justice," Smith said, "it was never about Alex and her ancestors, or the Blackjack Comanches. It was all about you."

"Quite a little game you played," Faith said to Smith. "Let me see if I know the rules. Rojas, through his connections to Houston's underworld, is given your name. The two of you meet at the prison. You jump at the chance. What a challenge, to ruin the chief justice of the Supreme Court!"

"You're right," Smith said. "I couldn't turn it down if I wanted to."

"Rojas gave you all the details, and you researched the rest," Faith said. "You discovered Alex and decided to make her your way of ruining Cole."

"I don't understand," Alex said. "I'm his way of ruining Cole?"

"There were two scenarios playing out at once," Smith said. "My way of destroying the chief justice and fulfilling the contract with Rojas was to have Cole destroy Alex."

"Dear God," Cole said.

"That's why there were tiny little subtleties in what you did to Alex," Faith said. "Leaving the incriminating evidence about the embezzlement right on her hard drive, not even deleted. Having Jones dump the gun he used to kill Wells in that Dumpster." She pointed up and away from the beach. "Our little episode at Lake Hefner. For a long time you had me wondering what side you were on."

"Neither," Smith said. "Both."

"But these little things added up, and any good investigator was going to eventually find them. Whether it was the FBI or the Galveston PD or whatever, someone would eventually see that the case was a little too pat, a little too good to be true. They would start to ask questions, and would work backwards."

"And they would see that Alex couldn't have committed these crimes," Smith said. "They would work their way to Gary St. James, Alex's poor dead husband, and they would find evidence that he had been hired to destroy the young woman's reputation. That he'd been hired by Chief Justice Cole to protect his family name from scandal, and to keep the fact that he'd murdered JoLynda Bridge in cold blood from becoming public. Oh, yes, it was set up and planned perfectly. Alex's life was in tatters, and Cole was crumbling. I watched him, watched that famous composure of his slip, watched him losing control. It was a remarkable transformation." He looked at Alex. "Not as remarkable as yours, my love, but quite interesting."

"Don't you use the word *love* with me," Alex said.

"A poor choice of words. My apologies."

"But the e-mail—" Cole said.

"Smith sent the e-mail," Faith said. "When I saw it, I knew Alex hadn't written it. The words weren't right for her."

"Correct, Officer Kelly," Smith said. "It was one of the earliest things I did, before I'd even met Alex face-to-face. I didn't know her quite as well as I would later."

"But the e-mail to the Chief Justice came from my computer at work," Alex said. "How did you—"

"Really, Alex, you should already know the answer to that," Smith said. "Cross Currents Media, in their pursuit of profit margins, cut many, many corners."

Alex thought for a moment. "Computer network security."

Smith nodded. "Any teenage computer hacker could have broken through their pitiful little firewalls. It took me all of fifteen minutes to get onto the Cross Currents server, find your e-mail account, write the message to Cole, send it, and log out again."

"Then you started calling Alex and e-mailing her, trying to get her to work at digging up what had happened to her ancestor," Faith said. "But she wasn't interested."

"So I had to put myself even more deeply into her life," Smith said. "Everything was working quite well—"

"Until I showed up," Faith said.

Smith's voice hardened. "Your little department made

things more difficult. But then, it increased the challenge at the same time. And there have been certain . . . unexpected additions to the mix."

Cole started to edge away from the others. "You have no proof. All this was for nothing, because you still cannot prove any of it. I burned the affidavits, and the copies JoLynda Bridge said she made have never surfaced. I think she was bluffing, trying to scare me. All of this is smoke and mirrors. You think you're bringing me down?" He looked at Faith. "You. Don't insult me by claiming you've recorded this conversation. Even if you have, it would never stand in court."

"No," Faith said. "No recording, Mr. Chief Justice. Not this time."

Cole turned toward Smith. "I want my money back. Every dime, you bastard! You were working for Rojas, and none of this had to happen. Do you hear me? *None of it had to happen!*"

"Nothing changes," Smith said. "The facts are: Your ancestor did wipe out that town, and did blame it on the Comanches, and did build a land empire on their bones. When presented with the proof of that in 1978, you committed murder. All of that stands. You will be ruined, Mr. Chief Justice. This will destroy you. Perhaps not in the way I originally envisioned, but you will fall." He looked at Alex. "I'm sorry, dear Alex. I manipulated everything about you. But you were such a willing vehicle."

"Not anymore," Alex said. "What about Daniel?"

A shadow crossed Smith's face.

"Don't want me to talk about him, do you?"

"That will do, Alex."

"Why did you go to the hospital in Pittsburgh, Gary? *Why?*"

"I don't want to discuss your child."

Alex took a step toward him, fists clenched at her sides. "You were going to kill him, weren't you? Tie up some loose ends, is that right?"

Smith said nothing.

"But you couldn't do it, could you?" Alex said, coming closer.

"The child is of no consequence."

"Then why did you go there?"

"That will do!" Smith shouted. One hand snaked around his back and pulled out the SIG Sauer.

"Oh, I'm so disappointed," Faith said. "I thought you didn't do weapons."

Smith took a step back and swung around so that Cole, Faith, and Alex were all in front of him. "Extreme circumstances call for extreme measures."

"Oh, that's such a crock of shit," Faith said. "You just couldn't think of another way to deal with us, could you?"

"You are a hateful woman, Officer Kelly. And, unfortunately, you have made some connections that I would rather you hadn't. As for the child, he's of no consequence. In a few minutes it won't matter whether he lives or dies."

"What?" Alex said.

Smith smiled. He raised the automatic.

Faith had left her own holster unsnapped, and in less than a second the Glock was in her hand. Smith swung the SIG toward Alex.

"No!" Alex screamed.

Smith fired the SIG. Faith lunged toward Alex, arms extended, pushing to get Alex out of the line of fire.

Faith felt the bullet as it tugged at her sleeve, felt a hot wind of pain as it barely creased the skin of her upper arm. She and Alex tumbled to the sand, rolling in opposite directions.

Faith came up firing, but her aim was off from the awkward position. Then Smith's SIG roared again. She heard Alex make a sound, then Alex was rolling again, farther away from her.

"What—" Faith said, and for a moment froze in confusion. Then she saw the dark stain spreading across Alex's torso and crawled across the sand to her.

When she looked up again, Cole was backing across the sand.

Smith was gone.

Hal Simon was across the street, in the shadows of the corner convenience store. He'd bought a cup of coffee and smoked two cigarettes.

He'd thought it was a bad idea to let Smith come here. He was afraid he would do something stupid, something that could jeopardize the whole case.

But the director hadn't seen it that way. He wanted Smith to have "closure." The director also seemed to think this kind of final resolution would bring in Kelly's case.

Screw closure, Simon thought. *I think the director's losing his mind, is what I think.*

Then he heard the three gunshots, very close together.

Simon dropped his cup of coffee, splattering the concrete. He unholstered his own weapon and ran for the beach.

"Did you know?" Alex whispered.

Faith was cradling her head. "What?"

"That he killed my mother. Did you know?"

"Not until this afternoon. Rojas didn't know the woman's identity. It was only after Scott called me and said that JoLynda Pahocodny Bridge was the last person to check out Cleaton's documents from the historical society that I put it together."

"Ah, Faith Joan," Alex said, her voice fading. "You think of everything."

Faith looked up in desperation. The beach in front of her was empty except for Bryden Cole.

"Stay with her!" she shouted at him.

Cole shook his head. "I won't get involved in this."

"Goddammit, can a man like you really be that stupid? *You are involved!* Stay with her!"

Cole froze.

"Now," Faith said. "Come on, she's bleeding. Do you have

a belt? Good, you can use it to stem the bleeding. Come on, move!"

Cole began to walk back across the sand, then started to jog. When he reached them and knelt beside Alex, he said, "I can't believe—"

"Believe it," Faith snapped, then her voice softened as she looked down at Alex. "I'll be right back, Alex."

She started into the darkness.

Planning was everything, Smith had always believed. With the proper plans, there could be no failure. He'd staked eleven years of his life on the premise.

He hadn't had time to properly plan this confrontation. He'd planned to kill Alex, and kill Kelly, and be done. It was like tidying up after a storm: it was difficult to slog through all the muck, but it had to be done to set things right again.

He ran into the night, pounding on the sand, reaching the far side of the umbrella. He was almost to the jetty.

"We're not finished here, Smith," Faith called into the night. "Your little reign of destroying lives is over. You know that, don't you? I'm putting an end to it . . . right now."

She fired a round into the air.

She saw movement ahead, in the shadows from the street-lights above. She veered to the left, closer to the water, closer to the rock jetty.

"Don't be ridiculous, Officer Kelly," Smith's voice drifted out to her. "People like you and I, our work never ends, does it?"

Faith put both hands on the butt of the Glock in the classic firing stance. She swept the darkness ahead of her. "Don't lump me in with you, you son of a bitch. I'm not even thinking about what Cole did. But what you did to Alex—that's absolute evil."

Rocks fell. Faith ran for the jetty. She scrambled onto the top of it. She could see Smith twenty steps ahead.

"Stop now and I'll let you live!" she screamed.

"Are we so different, then?" he yelled back. "You think

you can decide whether I live or die. Is that less evil than what I do?"

More loose rocks went over the side. The jetty was only about three feet wide with sloping sides, and it extended at least a hundred feet into the Gulf. Faith was already halfway to the end.

"Where do you think you're going?" she shouted. "Unless you can fly, you're not getting off this thing."

"Am I not?"

More rocks fell, and for a wild moment Faith thought the sound came from *behind* her. She shook her head. Just the circumstances and the sound of the waves playing tricks on her.

She took another step. Ahead, Smith stumbled and fell. He shouted wordlessly into the night.

Faith ran, oblivious to the footholds. The farther out she went, the closer the waves came, crashing against the rocks that formed the long, narrow strip.

She heard a metallic sound, metal on rock. Smith's gun clattered into the Gulf.

"No," she heard him say.

"I'm coming, Smith!" she shouted. "I'm coming for you, you sorry bastard!" She slipped, but there was nothing in Faith but rage. And for a moment she felt what she'd felt as she started to create Alex Bridge's new identity: a surge of power. Smith was unarmed, alone, with nowhere to go out here.

Another wave smashed the jetty and Faith slipped. One long leg went out from under her. She braced her fall with the hand that she'd injured at the Hotel Marion, scraping it across the rocks. Bright new pain bloomed behind her eyes.

But she held on to the Glock. Smith, prone on the rocks, was less than ten steps away. She regained her feet. Two more steps.

Another wave, this one close enough to soak her. But still she held her weapon.

She could see his face now, hard and soaked in spray. He'd cut himself when he went down, and a trickle of blood dribbled from his forehead.

She raised the Glock, rock steady. The next wave came and tore both feet from under her. She pitched forward but held on to the gun.

She landed at Smith's feet. She pulled herself up along his body.

Rocks tumbled.

"What is that?" Smith said. Faith saw him smile. There was blood in his mouth. "Did you hear that, Officer?"

Faith jammed the Glock against Smith's temple. "You see," she panted, "I'm in Department Thirty now. Unlike the FBI or the Marshals Service or the ATF or even the Galveston Police Department, I'm authorized to use deadly force to protect my department's security. I won't have to fill out incident reports, and I won't have to go on suspension pending an investigation. And, see, you just tried to kill me, wounding a civilian in the process. So it's also self-defense. Pick your scenario. You're good at that, aren't you?"

Smith wriggled. He lifted an arm. "As you said, we're not finished."

"What?"

Rocks tumbled behind them. Faith looked up. Simon towered over both of them, his own weapon pointed at her.

"Simon?" Faith shouted into the waves. "What the hell are you doing here?"

"Back off, Kelly. Very carefully, get off him."

"What?"

"So that none of us gets hurt," Simon said, "I'm telling you to lower your weapon and move away from him."

"I thought you worked for me!" Faith shouted.

"I do! Now back off!"

"Listen to him, Officer," Smith said. "Don't you think he has your best interests at heart?"

A large shadow stepped out from behind Simon. "He does," Yorkton said. "As do I, Officer Kelly. I'm ordering you to stand down."

Faith felt as if the earth had shifted under her. Then another wave broke and she felt like she was drowning. For several long moments she didn't even realize that the Glock had been torn from her hand and rolled into the sea.

She was soaked to the skin, her hair hanging in strings around her face. She looked up at Yorkton.

"Why?" she said.

"I told you," Yorkton said, "that John Brown's Body might be quite a catch for the department. You were quite angry with me at the time. I don't blame you for not taking the meaning."

"But you—"

"He can give us a great deal of information," Yorkton said. "And it will be used in the right ways." He shifted his glance to Smith. "I made a small mistake in allowing this meeting tonight. I asked you to stay away from my officer, and you assured me you would."

Smith said nothing.

Yorkton waved a hand. "Be assured, both of you, that you'll never see each other again. Mr. Gerenko's protection begins now. In fact, at this moment, he has no name. All his other identities have ceased to exist, and The Basement isn't quite finished with his new documents. Of course, we have much debriefing to do." He looked around. "I'd like to get off this rock as soon as possible."

"Goddammit!" Faith shouted, wiping water from her face. "But Alex—"

"Ms. Bridge will receive proper medical attention. The ambulance is on its way as we speak. Assuming she recovers, she'll be taken back to Pittsburgh to be with her son. You're relieved of any jurisdiction in this case, Officer. In fact, there is no case. We've taken the information on Cross Currents that she gathered, and that you helped to decipher, and forwarded it to the FBI. Ms. Bridge's Department Thirty file has been closed and sealed."

A wave broke. Yorkton's pants were soaked. "May we leave? I'm losing my patience out here."

"Cole," Faith said.

"Don't worry about the chief justice. He's on his way back to his private airplane."

"I don't believe this," Faith said. "I don't believe *you.*"

"This is sometimes the way things work," Yorkton said. "I'm sorry your first recruitment didn't work out. But there will be more opportunities." He gestured at Simon, then turned and started picking his way along the rocks, back toward the beach.

Simon helped Smith up. Smith looked at Faith.

"So now you just disappear into Department Thirty," Faith said. She couldn't keep the bitterness out of her voice.

"Thanks to you," Smith said. "By eliciting that confession from Jones, you gave your boss an idea."

"It was just meant to prove Alex's innocence."

"And so it did," Smith said.

He walked behind Simon and started toward shore.

Simon looked back once. "Coming?" he said.

The waves crashed. Faith stood immobile for several minutes, then she started to work her way along the rocks.

41

July 29, 1:50 P.M.
Oklahoma City

FAITH WAS STILL A LITTLE SORE, AND HER LEFT HAND hurt like hell from being reinjured on the rocks of the jetty. She'd slept for nearly twenty hours and woke up to find Scott Hendler sitting by her bed. She'd never seen a more welcome sight.

Alex was still in the hospital in Galveston. The bullet hadn't pierced any major organs, though it created a bit of a mess as it tore through her. She'd had twelve hours of surgery, with more to come, but was expected to make a full recovery within a couple of months.

Baby Daniel was still in Pittsburgh, still fighting. Danny Park was as well, recovering rapidly from his head wounds.

All because of Smith.

And Smith was nowhere. Smith didn't exist. Yorkton told her that he would be assigned to one of the other regional officers, so that he and Faith would never cross paths again.

As a precaution, of course.

Faith smiled. *Of course.*

But what Yorkton didn't know was that Faith wasn't quite finished. She couldn't get Smith, but there were other things yet to be done.

She got out of the Miata and walked up the gravel driveway to the small frame house. It was in the Capitol Hill section of south Oklahoma City, a lower-middle-class neighborhood with many Latino immigrants.

Bill Bridge had told her on the phone this morning about the spare key under the flowerpot. She found it and let herself in. The floors were wood, the furniture cheap, but there were many books, ranging from bestsellers to quantum physics to Mexican folktales.

Alex's father finally understood Faith's role in his daughter's life when Faith asked him the question. He'd hesitated for a long, long time on the phone. By that time she'd already told him about what happened to his wife in 1978. Faith assured him that as soon as Alex was in better shape, they'd need to talk to each other. A lot.

He finally answered the question. He sounded vaguely ashamed, but Faith didn't judge him. After all, at the time he'd thought his wife had abandoned him and their daughter. His own pain had been too great.

"I thought maybe it was a letter," Bridge had said, and, to Faith's surprise, the man had wept on the phone. "But it was just all those papers, those Indian things. There was nothing personal in it at all."

He'd told Faith where to find it. The back bedroom was an office of sorts, with overflowing file cabinets filled with credit card receipts as far back as 1981. There was a computer desk on one wall, but no computer on it. An old-fashioned rolltop desk sat against the other wall.

Faith found the key to the desk drawer right where Bill Bridge had said it would be, under yet another flowerpot. She unlocked it and found the manila envelope under some old issues of *Time* magazine.

Faith turned the envelope over and over in her hands. It was taped shut, but Faith could see that it had been opened at one point and retaped. The tape was now curled a bit at the edges. She read the address and smiled.

Miss Alex Bridge.

The address was a post office box in Lawton, Oklahoma.

It was postmarked Galveston, Texas, January 3, 1978.

In the spot for the return address was simply written: *Mom.*

Faith peeled up the edges of the tape and pulled out the papers JoLynda Pahocodny Bridge had copied, the papers for which she had died.

Faith leafed through Jonathan Doag's eyewitness account of the massacre at Sawyer's Crossing and his naming of Captain Jonas Cole as the leader of the men who "perpetrated the deed." Tabananika's statement was in less formal language, translated from the Comanche to English. Faith wondered if Cleaton, the man who killed Tabananika, had translated the statement for him.

She found the statement of Frank Wayne Cleaton, who on his deathbed confessed to a murder he'd committed some sixty-eight years earlier. This statement, in a pile of mostly insignificant papers willed to the Oklahoma Historical Society, had started JoLynda Bridge on the road to Galveston.

Final justice, Faith thought.

Smith had kept telling Alex that the final justice lay in Galveston. But he was wrong. For once, John Brown's Body didn't have it planned perfectly after all. The final justice was right here in an envelope that had sat in a desk drawer for twenty-seven years.

Faith slid the papers back into the envelope, looking again at the name on the front.

Miss Alex Bridge.

JoLynda had sent the proof to her three-year-old daughter. Something about it made a sort of sense. But Bill Bridge, angry and hurt, had never shown her the last communication he would ever have from his wife, her mother.

What if he had? Faith wondered.

Faith left the house, relocking it and replacing the spare key.

In the Miata, she pulled out her cell phone and the card she'd been given by the president of the United States.

If you ever need anything, let me know, the president had said.

"Here goes," she said, and called the number on the card.

She spoke to the president's chief of staff for fifteen minutes. The president was in Florida today for a speech on health care. Faith waited patiently, then explained again who she was and that she only needed the president to call her. She would take less than five minutes of his time.

Two and a half hours later Faith was in her office, catching up on some administrative work, when her phone rang.

"Hello, Faith," said the president. "I didn't expect to hear from you again so soon."

"Well, sir, I certainly didn't expect to be calling. How's Florida?"

"Beautiful, of course. Great people here, and I love the ocean. You ever spend much time by the sea, Faith?"

Faith waited a moment. "Just recently, as a matter of fact." She cleared her throat. "Sir, I'm going to be sending you some documents that will be disturbing to you."

The president's voice went down a notch. "What's this about?"

Deep breath. "Your friend the chief justice."

"Bry? What about him?"

"You won't like it, sir. I'm sending you some historical documents relating to Mr. Chief Justice Cole's family history, plus a statement from Eduardo Rojas."

"Who? Wait a minute. Rojas, that killer in Texas?"

"Yes, sir. He has a connection to Mr. Cole that should concern you."

"All right, Faith. My radar's gone up."

"My own statement is attached as well, Mr. President."

"Department Thirty's not involved unless it's damn serious. What's this about?"

"Sir, I'm sending you the documents. I think that after you read them, you'll do the right thing with regard to Mr. Chief Justice Cole. You and I can consider ourselves even."

After a few moments of small talk, Faith hung up.

"There," she said. "Now it's done."

EPILOGUE

November 2, 8:45 P.M.
Oklahoma City

HENDLER PARKED IN FRONT OF DIFFERENT ROADS, A small storefront bar and grill on Classen Boulevard. Alex had described it as "a little folkie place." Light spilled out the small door. They could see people milling around inside.

"I don't usually go to places like this," Hendler said.

"Neither do I. But it's a folk music bar. What could happen?"

Hendler smiled. "I guess everyone got what they wanted, when all was said and done."

"What do you mean?"

"You know, the whole Alex business."

Faith looked out the window. "I guess."

"I mean, Cole resigned. He's no longer in a position of power, and for him, that's probably as bad as death. Cross Currents got busted and the president scored lots of political capital with it. Alex got her life back. She doesn't have any lingering problems from all the injuries. The baby's doing great, finally out of the hospital."

"Mmm," Faith said.

"And the Comanches. How's the settlement fund work again?"

Faith sighed. "Anyone who can document that they're descended from Tabananika or one of the Blackjacks gets a cash settlement."

"But Cole's still said nothing publicly. He made vague

noises about a serious family crisis when he resigned from the court. So how does that work?"

"You don't really need to know, Special Agent Hendler."

"But I *want* to know, Officer Kelly. And this part isn't classified."

"Gray area," Faith reminded him. "After the president sort of convinced Cole that it was in everyone's best interest for him to step down, Cole's attorneys met with the president's counsel and the attorney general and they hammered out a compromise. The fact that Bryden Cole is a descendant of Captain Jonas Cole, who we now know as the butcher of Sawyer's Crossing, is kept secret. The Comanches receive the documentation of the Blackjacks having been innocent and Tabananika having been murdered. Cole pays money out of his family trust into an anonymous fund; that's filtered through a couple of different accounts before coming to the Comanche Nation, who administer the funds to the descendants."

"Oh, what a tangled web," Hendler said. He was quiet a little longer. "And Eddie Rojas got the needle after all."

Faith shrugged. "When all was said and done, he was still guilty of killing those two guys in the bar. But at least the court heard his appeal."

"What if they'd had a tie vote, with only eight justices on the court?"

"The vote was seven to one. Not an issue. I guess in a way Rojas got what he wanted. Even though all of it didn't come out, he saw Cole's career ruined. All of that—what Alex went through, everything—was because Rojas wanted Cole ruined. And he actually succeeded. That's the crazy thing: he succeeded."

"But he was still executed."

"Not until after Cole resigned from the court, though."

Faith kept looking out the window. Hendler didn't know about Smith, didn't know that he'd been offered protection by Department Thirty. He didn't know all of what happened on the beach and the jetty. He didn't know of Yorkton's threat to her.

"Let's go in," she said.

Different Roads was a small place, with two dozen small round tables. Beautiful photography covered the walls: portraits, nature shots, urban scenes. Faith saw instantly what had given the place its name: a large photo hung behind the stage, a picture of a rural highway and a gravel road as they diverged from each other. Different roads.

They squeezed into a table. The main food item on the menu was Barry's Chili, offered in mild, medium, and "Watch out." Faith and Hendler both ordered bowls of medium with homemade corn bread and two beers.

Alex was already on stage. Her instruments were arrayed around her: fiddle, guitar, mandolin, and two flutes. Behind her, a tall woman with black hair sat at a keyboard.

To the side of the small stage, Faith saw Danny Park at a table. Bill Bridge sat beside him. A baby carrier rested on the table between the two men.

Alex was at the microphone. She was a little thinner, a little paler, but she was all right. Her eyes still burned with the bright intensity and humanity Faith had noticed at the safe house the first time she'd met her. They talked on the phone almost every week, and Alex was putting her life back together.

Alex leaned into the microphone. "Those of you who know me remember that I'm half Comanche, and you also know that I've never really cared about that side of my heritage."

Faith smiled.

"I've kind of changed that lately," Alex continued. "A lot of things happened over this past summer, and I've learned quite a bit about Comanche history and culture." She held up her wooden flute. "Now, this is your basic Irish flute." She turned it around and around.

"This is not—I repeat, not—a Native American flute. But I've found that you can get some sounds from it that are quite a bit like the Native flute." She raised the instrument to her lips and blew a couple of notes. "This is a new piece I wrote in the last few weeks. It's called 'Numunuh.'"

The crowd made interrogative noises.

"It means 'The People.'"

She played, and the music was slow and eerie and evocative. Alex played unaccompanied, and Faith thought her playing had a lilt to it, the same way that Hannah Sovo and Lonnie Pahocodny and even Alex sounded when they spoke.

The modest crowd applauded. A woman in the back yelled, "You go, Alex," and others laughed.

Alex smiled, lowering the flute. "I'd like to do the next one for a friend of mine, and it's kind of nice to put it after the Comanche piece. You know about the great Irish bard, Turlough O'Carolan. The first time I met this friend, she asked me to play Carolan's 'Sheebeg, Sheemore.' I played it for her on the flute and told her the story of the big fairy hill and the little fairy hill. She told me her good Irish grandfather used to play this tune on fiddle. Later on, after we'd been through some stuff together, I swore that if she ever came to hear me play, I'd do it for her on fiddle. This is for my friend Faith Siobhan Kelly."

She did a little bow in Faith's direction, then Alex closed her eyes and played the lilting notes that opened the tune. The piano joined in a few measures later. Faith remembered her grandfather playing it as a dance. Alex took it much more slowly, a ballad, a lullaby. She imagined the two groups of fairies and the truce that put an end to the fighting between the two hills.

Faith closed her eyes as well and slipped her hand into Hendler's. For a little while she didn't have to live in any strange gray areas. This music was truth, and Scott Hendler's hand in hers was truth, and while it didn't exactly set her free, it was at least good to know that there were places where the truth still existed. It wasn't much, but for Faith, at this moment, in this place, it would have to do.

She squeezed Hendler's hand. He squeezed back. They listened to the music.

AUTHOR'S NOTE

WRITING FICTION WITH SOME BASIS IN HISTORICAL FACT is a dicey business, and I feel compelled to tell you which is which.

Tabananika was real, and my children are his direct descendants. There are many different English spellings of his name, though the spelling used in this story is the one that appears on his grave marker. There seem to be just as many English variations of what his name meant in the Comanche language. He was born sometime around 1835 to 1840, and he died on April 28, 1893, the date referenced in the book. The physical circumstances of his death are as accurate as I can make them, at a remove of 112 years: he died in Anadarko while running to catch a train that was to have taken him to Washington, D.C. Also true is the fact that his family, and other Comanches, believed he had been given a slow-acting poison to prevent him from going to Washington.

References to Medicine Lodge, the Treaty of the Little Arkansas, and the Jerome Commission are all factual. The treatment of the plains tribes at the hands of the U.S. government is true, I'm sorry to say. In the story, "Isaac Smith" read William T. Hagan's book *U.S.–Comanche Relations: The Reservation Years*. Published by University of Oklahoma Press, it is an excellent resource for this era.

And now the fiction: I invented the Blackjack Comanches and the Sawyer's Crossing massacre. The community of Sawyer's Crossing never existed.

A final note: I do not speak the Comanche language and do not have the skills to create character names in totally unfamiliar languages. For this book's modern-day Comanche characters, I used the surnames of real Comanche families. The characters should not be taken to have any resemblance to the real people whose names I borrowed.

D.K.